RAGE IS A WOLF

An uncorrected proof is the place where the author and publisher hope to find all of the book's last errors (grammar, punctuation, spelling, formatting...) before going to the final print. Because of the cost of printing books, they often double as an ARC (advanced reader copy) that publishers send out ahead of the book's launch to try to create some buzz.

Because this book is being published by a very small publisher, we weren't planning to do many print ARCs. But then a lovely twist of pandemic-work-from-home-transition fate occurred and we suddenly had many uncorrected proofs on our hands. It occurred to me that I had a great opportunity to send these books out into the world for free which is a truly great joy for me as a debut author in this time of weirdness..

I hope you like the book. I hope it makes you laugh and maybe cry. I hope it makes you think and feel and hope and love. If you do like it, please spread the word in whatever way feels comfortable and meaningful to you. I am partial to Instagram pics featuring the book with plants and animals, but I'm open to mostly whatever.

Below are the epigraphs that didn't make it into the ARC!

No one teaches a flower to grow.
M.A. Kiteheart

O Raphael, lead us towards those we are waiting for, those who are waiting for us! Raphael, Angel of Happy Meetings, lead us by the hand towards those we are looking for!
Prayer to St. Raphael

There are these two, young fish swimming along and they happen to meet an older fish swimming the other way, who nods at them and says, "Morning, [kids]. How's the water?" And the two young fish swim on for a bit, and then eventually one of them looks over at the other and goes, "What the hell is water?"
David Foster Wallace, Kenyon Commencement Address, 2005

RAGE IS A WOLF

KT MATHER

w

WHISK(E)Y TIT

VT & NYC

Published in the United States by Whisk(e)y Tit: www.whiskeytit.com. If you wish to use or reproduce all or part of this book for any means, please let the author and publisher know. You're pretty much required to, legally.

ISBN 978-1-7329596-7-5

Cover design by Jennifer Pockers.

First Whisk(e)y Tit paperback edition.

For James and Lucy Kate.
For kids and friends.
For love and hope for the future.

SEPTEMBER

NOT LOOKING GOOD FOR YOUR PROGENY

It was the sea turtle.

You know the one.

I wasn't even supposed to be on the phone. That was one of Mama Jane's rules, In the presence of humans, interface with humans, not device.

But Jenn and I had been texting before I got in the car, so, I was like, I just need to check this one thing. Mama Helen, who was driving me to school and was kinda distracted, didn't say anything.

Suddenly, there was the sea turtle. The one with the straw shoved so far up its face, you couldn't believe it was actually a straw.

Next thing I knew, it was 2nd period physics and I couldn't stop seeing them holding the writhing turtle down, trying to get ahold of the straw with pliers, and the turtle's confused eyes, like, What the fuck, dudes?

I'd passed 1st period in a trance. All I could do in 2nd was try to write it out...

So, between the straws and bags and water bottles and microfibers from stretch jeans and ohmygod the k-cups, we're filling the entire ocean with plastic.

On top of that, we're poisoning the whole planet with carbon emissions while also cutting down all the trees that might help to clean the air we're polluting.

Plus, rising temperatures and sea levels.

And corporations that don't pay taxes.

And we're killing the orangutans so we don't have to stir our peanut butter.

And you know as well as I do that we're not doing anything to fix it.

Oh, Christ.

We really might die.

So, no insult to my physics teacher, Mr. Banerjee, who is a tall, Indian, pocket-protected, mustachioed mega-nerd whom students literally, physically fight for a front row seat in his class, no insult, Mr. Banerjee, but just then in late September, 2nd period, I couldn't have given a rat's ass how quickly a falling object reaches terminal velocity. All I could think was, The glaciers are melting and nobody gives a fuck.

Maybe you're like, Well, why didn't *you* do something about it? I know! Why didn't I? I'll tell you why. There was nothing I could do.

I was never gonna be one of those kids from the internet who builds a spacelab under her bed or figures out how to quintuple barley yields using a common household bacteria. I wouldn't invent a contraption to get all the plastic out of the giant plastic vortices in the ocean. I wasn't going to chain myself to or live in a tree (that's real—one of Mama Helen's cousins did it in Oregon).

One time I fantasized about getting bumper stickers made that said, "I'm the reason we're at war," and going to the outlets in Rosemont and slapping them on SUVs and Hummers and other gas-guzzlers, but...

What I'm saying is, I had no idea how to be the change I wanted to see.

So, what? Keep learning Civil War battle dates (spoiler alert: no one cares), so I could go to a "good" college and get into $100,000 debt and still not be able to do anything to help the world?

Like seriously? What's the point of school if it's not teaching us to fix any of these messes?

There I was, just a 16-year-old white girl, daughter of two moms, who felt like I was crawling out of my skin and going to lose my mind if I had to sit in that stupid desk a second longer. "School isn't helping." I wrote in my notebook. "School is making it worse!"

"Elaine. Are you alright?" Mr. Banerjee asked. Or I'm guessing that's what he *had* asked. Cause the first thing I heard was, "Elaine. Elaine. Earth to Elaine..."

"What? Sorry? What?" I asked.

"You are obviously distracted," he said, gesturing to my notes. And then, "Are you alright?"

"Not really," I said and closed the notebook.

Pin-drop-silence from the rest of the class.

Mr. Banerjee held his palms out. "Would you like to say more?" he asked. "Now? Privately? Or to someone not in this room?"

I appreciated the thoroughness of his options, but I was not in a polite head space and I blurted, "I mean, aren't you a little distracted by catastrophic climate change? Even if *you're* dead by the time the shit hits the fan, aren't you worried? Do you have progeny?"

Mr. Banerjee gave me a look that said, I'm not sure where to begin.

"If you have progeny, they're just as fucked as we are," I said, indicating my fellow classmates. Said classmates leaned collectively backward—they were not going down with me. "And that's just the Earth stuff. That's not even counting any of the horrible shit humans are doing to each other."

I attribute Mr. Banerjee's next move to his summers at NASA. I find that teachers who have interests outside the sphere of Daniel Burnham High are much more chill about things. Like if he got fired, he could just go work at NASA some more. Whatever it was, something made it so Mr. Banerjee said, in the same tone of voice he uses for talking about objects sliding down frictionless planes: "1) I do have progeny, 2) I am concerned with, if not distracted by, climate change, and 3) I am hopeful that the life spans of both myself and the Earth are going to be quite a bit longer than you think."

"Vf^2-Vi^2 ain't gonna solve it," I said.

Banerjee cracked a smirk at that and said, "Not directly, perhaps. But an educated populace is the most important part of our democracy. I believe that."

I attribute my response to my affection for Mr. Banerjee. What I wanted to say was, How many of these test-cramming, test-cheating, and test-flunking assholes are going to remember a goddam thing you teach them? What I said instead was, Shrug, "I guess so."

Mr. Banerjee narrowed his eyes at me, perhaps skeptical of my reply. But the bell rang. Notebooks slammed. The room emptied. We were on to the next thing.

PERSONAL PHILOSOPHY

When I was 9, I tried to get the moms to stop calling me Elaine, and start calling me Ripley. From the movie *Aliens*. Yes, it's probably weird that I'd seen *Aliens* at 9. Mama Jane was like, It's fine. Mama Helen was like, She's too young. And of course, I was like, I'm not too young! My reccurring *Aliens* nightmares might prove that Mama Helen was right, but that's not the point. The point is, I think *Aliens* might be my Bible—the thing that tells me what the world is and what it should be. The point is, Holy shit, I love Ripley.

In one of the greatest movie scenes of all time, she's on the mission to a space colony with a group of Marines and the prick, Carter Burke, from corporate HQ. Ripley's been telling him and telling him that when she was on the planet 50 years before (cryo-sleep plot stuff), an alien killed the shit out of her whole crew. Everyone except her and her cat. But Corporate Prick Burke is like, We're colonizing it. It's cool. But, incidentally, we've lost contact with them, you wanna come down there with me and a bunch of Marines as, like, a consultant? At first she's like, Fuck no. But PTSD, so...

Guess what happens as soon as they get there? The Marines get out of the little armored vehicle. They go into the compound. They get killed to shit by aliens.

Ripley takes over. Hasty escape. She drives the armored car through some walls and flames and shit...They clear the compound. It's like chaos, chaos, chaos, all the ranking officers are dead or concussed, everyone is freaking, Marines are burned by the aliens' acid blood, the crybaby Marine, Hudson, is like, "What the fuck are we gonna do now, man? We're fucked!" and Ripley is totally chill and like, Listen, we have one choice here. We get back into the ship, clear the atmosphere, and nuke the whole planet from space.

Crybaby Hudson is like, Fucken A.

Corporate Prick Burke is like, Whoa, whoa, whoa. This installation has a substantial dollar value attached to it...

And without missing a beat, Ripley says, "They can bill me."
Fucken A.

I didn't know it at 9, not in my brain, but that was the emotion I was feeling. Am feeling. All the time. Hey corporate assholes, I am *not* going to sacrifice myself, my friends, and the whole fucking Earth so you can make a profit. And if you don't like it, You can bill me. Only Ripley could do something about it. She had a planet she could nuke. There was nothing I could do.

There's also a character named Corporal Hicks who is sexy AF...

WHAT'S CORRELATION?

I arrived to 4th period Algebra II.

Don't ask what happened in 3rd.

"Mr. Washington?" I asked after he'd taken roll, assigned the night's homework, and wrestled a few functions out of us. "Can I ask you a question?" Mr. Washington is a nice enough guy. He's a tall, Black guy who has that oldster body that looks like he was probably a good athlete back in the day—like strong arms, big belly. He's not inspiring any fights for proximity, but he doesn't have dragon breath, or play favorites, or give unfair tests.

"Hit me, Elaine," he said. See, nice enough.

"What's the point of Algebra II?" I asked.

"The point?" he asked.

"Like seriously. Are we *ever* gonna use this?"

He sighed. A midwinter sigh. Not an early fall sigh. A winter-break-is-over-spring-break-is-no where-in-sight sigh. "Probably not," he said.

The over-achieving sophomores in class came to shocked attention.

"I fucking knew it," I muttered.

"Mr. Wash..." one of the sophomores started.

"Then why do we have to take it?" I asked. The sophomore could hold that thought.

Mr. Washington sighed again. "Well, evidently, the former Secretary of Education came across a fun fact... Evidently, students who finish Algebra II are more likely to finish college. Ergo, the Secretary of Education decided that Algebra II should be a public high school requirement..."

I furrowed. "Wait..."

"That's not logically sound," the sophomore said.

"Nope," Mr. Washington said.

"What's 'logically sound'?" one of the under-achieving seniors asked.

Unable to control herself, the sophomore blurted, "Correlation doesn't equal causation!" Her braces flashed as she spoke.

Mr. Washington nodded sadly.

"What's that supposed to mean?" the senior asked.

The sophomore knew better than to answer.

"It means the former Secretary of Education failed Logic 101," Mr. Washington said. "It means he's an idiot. It means I have to teach Algebra II to a bunch of kids with no interest in or need for Algebra II."

Perhaps made brave by Mr. Washington's sarcasm, the sophomore said, "Just because students who take Algebra II are more likely to graduate college, doesn't mean Algebra II *caused* them to graduate."

"Wait..." the senior said, thinking it through.

"*That's* why I have to take this class?" I asked.

"Pretty much," Mr. Washington said.

"That doesn't make any sense," I said.

It was clear that Mr. Washington was going through something because he said, "To be honest, I don't think *school* makes sense. If I were you, I'd be outta here."

The sophomore and the two other precocious sophomores gasp. The seniors rose from their slumps. And I became interested in Algeb for the first time in my life. "Seriously?" I asked.

"Seriously," he said. "First of all, if you're over 16 you aren't required to attend school. And second of all, you could homeschool or unschool."

My heart pounded. I could already feel my last day of A retreating behind me and my days of Calculus vanishing into

of dumb shit I was never going to do. Like bungee jumping. "What's unschool?"

Honestly, I can't believe Mr. Washington kept going. The sophomores were beyond tense. They were in some sort of collective, terror-stricken, I-can't-hear-you-I-can't-hear-you trance. But Mr. Washington was on a roll. "Unschooling is when you don't follow a set curriculum, you just learn whatever you want to learn. The student decides."

"Do you still come here?" I asked. "And just do your assignments how you want?" Maybe Algebra II and Calculus would have me yet.

"No," Mr. Washington said. "You stay home. Or go to pottery class. Or a library. Or an auto-body shop. Or anywhere. You just find a way to learn anything you want to learn. If you want to knit sweaters for your whole family by next week, you get someone to teach you. Anything you want to learn, you find a way to learn."

"You're blowing my mind," the senior said. He wasn't taking a single word in.

When the bell rang a moment later, the other kids leapt from their seats and I knew they'd already forgotten what we were talking about. They'd go home. Some of them would do the homework, some of them wouldn't. But it wouldn't be because of anything that Mr. Washington had said today.

I stayed after. "Mr. Washington?" I asked.

He was back at his desk, shuffling through papers. He sighed and the thrill of the unschooling lecture fell off him like chalk dust from the ass of his pants. "Yes, Elaine?" he asked.

"I think I want to do that," I began. "Unschool."

"It'd be nice," he said. All his zest for the subject was gone and he was back to being Mr. Washington, nice enough guy.

"How would I go about doing it?" I asked.

He didn't hear me. He was grading quizzes, far away.

AGAINST SCHOOL

I bumbled through the rest of the day and then went home and did what you do—I asked the internet. I googled "homeschooling" and "unschooling" and "homeschooling & unschooling & college" and everything else I could think of. By dinner, I'd made up my mind.

Here's what you should know about the moms. The moms are great. Mama Helen is the dark haired one (straight, shoulder length, with bangs) and Mama Jane is the blonde one (long and curly and crazy and usually jammed in a bun). Mama Helen is the sweet, but serious, one and Mama Jane is the funny one. Mama Helen is slender and Mama Jane is athletic. They're both tall (I'm not). They're both jeans and t-shirts (I'm jeans and t-shirts). But Mama Helen is sweaters and Mama Jane is sweatshirts (I'm either). They work on houses. Like sometimes they help someone with a refurb and sometimes they do a start to finish build. Mama Helen is finance and Mama Jane is construction.

"Moms," I said after initial dinnertime pleasantries, "I wanna quit school." I probably could have put it more gently, but I was nervous.

"Bad day?" Mama Helen asked. She put her fork down. She's a *listener*.

"I'm being serious," I said. "I want to homeschool." I was at least smart enough not to open with "unschool."

"Are you pregnant?" Mama Jane asked. She kept eating.

"No, I'm not pregnant," I said.

"So, 'I wanna quit school' isn't some bluff to soften the 'I'm pregnant' blow?"

"I haven't even done it," I said.

"Really?" Mama Jane said.

"For heaven's sake, Jane," Mama Helen said.

"But that would be smart," I said.

"You're smart," Mama Jane said.

I grinned and shrugged.

Mama Helen put her hands on the table so she didn't start picking her

9

manicure. She's a real polish-picker when she gets agitated. "Can we get back on track here?" she asked.

"I just don't want to do it anymore," I said. I told them about the turtle and the ice caps and oil and plastics and corporate greed and the Earth is dying. I told them about Mr. Banerjee and Mr. Washington, about my homeschool research, and "lots of homeschooled kids go to college...I'm being serious," I said and laid my supporting documents on the table.

The moms stopped laughing, but still showed no real concern. "What are these?" Mama Jane asked.

I lifted the first. "This is an essay by educational theorist (and winner of the both New York City and New York State Teacher of the Year several times) John Taylor Gatto." Yeah, I'd rehearsed. "It's about how the current model of education (separate by age, sit in a desk, accept random rules from random authority figures...) is based on the Prussian military model." I emphasized the "Prrrrr," so they didn't think I was just accidentally flubbing 'Russian.'"

Mama Helen took the sheaf of papers. *Against School*, she read the title.

"His point is that school is designed to create a society of good little worker bees who are are trained to accept rules and boredom. Then they never revolt," I said.

"Against school or against the government?" Mama Jane asked.

"The revolting?" I asked.

Mama Jane nodded.

Mama Helen skimmed the article.

"Both, ultimately," I said.

"Ultimately?" Mama Jane asked.

I went on. "I spend all this time taking these classes that don't mean anything to me. All just so *maybe* I can do something with them in the future? For what? To make money? All these adults say, 'Just wait until you're in the *real world*...' I used to want to tell those people to shove it up their asses..."

"Elaine!" Mama Helen said.

I knew I was pushing it, but I couldn't stop myself. "But then I read that essay, and I think they should *definitely* shove it up their asses," I said.

"Whoa," Mama Jane said.

I kept going. "As far as I can tell, most grown-ups live just the same way we do. They do a bunch of shit they don't like, for a boss they don't respect, and talk about how this boredom and drudgery is going to affect 'the future.' But here's a goddam spoiler alert..."

"Too far," Mama Helen said.

Mama Jane nodded.

"Fine," I said. "Spoiler alert...there is no future. What is today, but yesterday's tomorrow?"

"I want to make fun of that line..." Mama Jane said, "...but I see now is not the time."

"Good call," I said.

"Sweetie," Mama Helen said. "We had no idea you were so unhappy. Why didn't you tell us?"

"That's the thing," I said. "I didn't think I was unhappy. I mean, every kid talks about how boring and sucky school is. And every adult agrees. So, I mean, it felt normal."

"For heaven's sake," Mama Jane said.

"Right?! Meanwhile, the world is literally falling apart!" I said. "And school isn't teaching me a single thing that's going to help...Every single kid is in school, only we're not teaching them how to do anything that might help... That should be ALL we're doing."

"I need to process this," Mama Helen said.

"I should probably process it, too. I wasn't taking you seriously at all," Mama Jane said.

"You're taking it seriously now?" I asked.

The moms looked at each other and shrugged. "We're going to need a few days with this," Mama Helen said.

I nodded. That made sense. I mean, Mama Jane can be a little impulsive, but there's no way Mama Helen would pull the trigger on something this big without serious mulling. Like mulling.

We finished dinner in silence. Not a bad, you're-in-trouble, silence. Just silence. The moms went to their room. I did the dishes.

MEMORIZE, DON'T RATIONALIZE

I don't know how you cope with freaking, but I do research. After I finished the dishes and got my good night loves, I went back to my room and kept googling. I came across this article in *The Atlantic* (magazine for oldsters) by a dude named, Karl Taro Greenfield, entitled, *My Daughter's Homework Is Killing Me*. Under the title, it says, "What happens when a father, alarmed by his 13-year-old daughter's nightly workload, tries to do her homework for a week?"

When I read that, I was like, Yes. This is going to be awesome. This is going to be the article where the guy is like "that's enough" and pulls his daughter out of school. I mean, the whole thing opens with his daughter's motto, "Memorize, Don't Rationalize." You know, memorize it, don't try to understand it. I was all set to print the thing out and take it to the moms like, Okay, here it is. Here's the parent who did what you need to do. Don't be scared. It happens.

Well, it didn't happen.

What happens is that the dad sees how much homework the daughter has, sees that she's not really learning anything (other than how to fake learn—I mean, she has a mnemonic device to remember how to not learn), sees that she's tired and miserable and doesn't even have time to watch *Pretty Little Liars* without feeling guilty, and he doesn't do anything about it.

He's just like, When I was in 8th grade, I didn't do shit... "After school, I often went to friends' houses, where I sometimes smoked marijuana..." Did he say, "Smoked marijuana?" What an asshole. Then he talks about how sometimes, when he and his wife are out on the town, and his daughter's at home doing all that homework, he bumps into a pal who, "... is smoking a joint, and he hands it over. I haven't smoked in a few months...so I take a few tokes,"—just like when he was a teenager. Please note where he's like, "I haven't smoked in a few months," which is his way of saying, Hey *Atlantic* readers, I still sometimes smoke marijuana...I'm still a cool kid...just like in the 70s...The article is just a dude who wants you to think he's cool.

At one point, he writes about how his daughter got a C on her math homework cause even though she had all the right answers, she didn't have an answer column. His response to her not being pissed? "School is training her well for the inanities of adult life." What?! John Taylor Gatto is rolling in his grave. This is *exactly* what he was talking about. And this dad knows it and doesn't do anything!

I'd never publicly commented on the internet. We'd had like 40 billion lectures since 6th grade about how, "You can never erase your cyber-footprint...it's like an elephant walking in cement," so I never say anything that's not private times a million.

But I couldn't stop myself and I commented, "So, this guy's action plan is: observe, complain, and do nothing? He's too busy still being the pot-smoking teen to bother being a parent. Well, at least he got that sweet *Atlantic* article out of it. What a douche."

To which someone replied, "I hear you. But it could be that his daughter is committed to it. She sounded pretty hardcore, and sometimes that's a tough call—whether to remove your kid from something that seems harmful to you, but they're really enjoying."

To which I wrote, "I go to a school like hers. I agree that the inmates are pretty well brainwashed by the time we hit middle school. But his whole, Well, whaddya gonna do? (Did I mention that sometimes I smoke weed?), sucks. Can he at least ask the daughter a single question about her, Memorize, Don't Rationalize, motto? Instead of just saying that she'll sure be set for dealing with how much adult life sucks."

Then this other rando chimed in. She was like, "I was always secretly pleased when my boys made it clear on day one that they weren't going after a 4-point GPA. They did homework when they felt it mattered, ignored assignments that were stupid (they were pretty bang-on), graduated with honors and went on to competitive programs at high-ranked universities. There's a huge element of learning how to game the system in all this."

Don't get me started on all the things I *wanted* to say to this woman like, You were "secretly" pleased? Why weren't you openly pleased? And, They didn't do all their homework, and still graduated with honors? That's not right. I mean, if something is assigned and you don't do it, how are you an honors student? And, Well, thank god they got into "competitive programs at high-ranked universities" cause that's the important part, right?

What I said to her instead was, "Spending most of your time 'learning how to game the system' makes me sad for students and sad for teachers."

To which she said, "I know what you mean, and I'm sure you're a very dedicated student. But my boys also did music and sports and theater...They argued about how to solve the world's problems around a backyard campfire...They read books—a LOT of books—because they loved them (and their mother put them in their hands)...They did stuff they weren't supposed to do and dealt with the consequences...If they were doing 3-5 hours of homework a night, none of those things would have happened..."

I cut out like 4/5 of her bragging. You're welcome.

I wanted to say, We're saying the same goddam thing. Did you even read my previous comments? I wanted to say, Imagine how much more of that amazing shit (shit you could brag about) they could've been doing if they weren't spending 8 hours a day, "gaming the system." Presumably, if this woman had boys who got into "competitive programs at high-ranked schools," then she was an adult who ought to have slightly better reading comprehension than she was exhibiting in the comments section of the stupid article. Maybe she and Mr. Greenfield were both too busy getting high.

Instead, I wrote, "Yeah, exactly. So, instead of teachers assigning what they know most kids will memorize, not rationalize, how about they don't assign homework? It's a mutual lie—the teacher's assigning it knowing it's pointless and the student's either doing it knowing it's pointless or not doing it, but pretending they did... How about just don't assign the homework?" FFS.

She didn't respond.

I tried to sleep. I didn't sleep.

I kept thinking about school. How am I gonna go back there and keep doing all that? I mean, the truth was, I was exactly like Stoner Dad's daughter. I mocked, Memorize, Don't Rationalize, but, yeah, that was pretty much me, because somewhere back there, I got the idea that you have to have straight As.

MOMS' ROOM, 5AM

I arrived at their bedside at 5AM.

Mama Helen, the catastrophe mom, sat up immediately, "Elaine," she said. She had her glasses off her nightstand and on her face before I sat down on the bed.

"What's happening?" Mama Jane moaned.

"I need you to read something." I said and thrust Mr. I-Still-Smoke-Weed's opus at them. "Now."

"Oh god," Mama Jane said and pulled the covers over her head.

It's wasn't the first time I'd showed up in their room at 5AM *needing* to talk about something. But I *needed* to talk to them.

"Sweetie," Mama Helen said, looking at me through her old cat-eye glasses. I'd tried to get her to buy some cooler ones, but she was like, These are my glasses.

"I can't go back there," I said and tapped the sheaf of papers.

"More documentation?" Mama Helen asked and took it from me.

Mama Jane pulled the covers down slightly. "What's this one about?"

"It's the worst," I said. "I thought it was going to be the best. I was so excited to show it to you, but then I read it and it's the worst and now you have to read it and I can't go back to school. Ever."

Mama Jane sat up. She pushed her hand through her tangled hair and looked at Mama Helen who held the article up for her to see. "What time is it?" Mama Jane asked.

"It's 5 in the morning," Mama Helen said, then she looked at me and squinted. "How much sleep did you get?"

"You wouldn't have slept either if you'd read what I read," I said.

"For heaven's sake, what's it about?" Mama Jane asked.

"You didn't sleep at all?" Mama Helen asked, handing the papers over to Mama Jane, and waving me toward her.

Mama Jane put the article on her nightstand and got up.

"You're not going to read it?" I asked. I crawled over to Mama Helen and let her take my face between her hands. She turned me this way and that. I don't know what she was looking for. Finally, I pulled away. "You're not going to read it?" I repeated.

"Honey," Mama Helen began.

Here we go.

She went on. "It's Friday. Your mom and I will read that article..."

"It's everything that's wrong with school," I said.

"... Your mom and I will read all the things you've given us. We'll talk. We'll ask you some more questions. And we'll have a decision for you by Sunday evening."

I have to hand it to Mama Helen. I mean, I've been known to present cockamamie ideas and demand instant satisfaction on those ideas. And while Mama Jane was avoiding me in the bathroom under the guise of brushing her teeth, Mama Helen had given me a very specific timeline that succeeded in shutting me up. She's clever, that mom.

"Can I be sick today?" I whined. The thought of being back in that school building was nauseating.

"You cannot," Mama Helen said.

I already knew that.

I leaned forward to receive her kiss.

JUST LIKE RATS

Walking through the doors and metal detectors of Daniel Burnham High, all I could think was, Fuck this. What if they say no and this is life from now?

It's like in *Aliens*. Before Ripley ends up on the mission back to the alien-infested space colony, she gets her pilot's license revoked (because of blowing up the previous alien-infested spaceship) and has to work on the docks driving a loader. Let's be honest, she doesn't want to be working on the docks driving loaders. But when Corporate Prick Burke is like, Ew, you're working on the docks? She's like, Yeah, I'm working on the fucking docks...Because she just found out that she's been asleep in space for 57 years after she'd promised her daughter she'd be home in time for her birthday (ps, the daughter is dead). I mean, let's think about that. You go to sleep one night, after you've just had The. Most. Harrowing. Experience. Ever. Where everyone on your crew is stalked and killed by an alien, and you wake up 57 years later. And your kid is 67 and dead. Leaving no kids of her own. We're talking about being 100% alone. And with PTSD. So yes, working on the docks is fine. That's life now.

DB High. That's life now...

All right, well, when I put it that way, I don't feel that bad. Jesus.

But being at school sucked.

I slogged down to mine and Jenn's locker. She was already there, unloading and reloading her backpack. On paper, Jenn and I didn't make sense. She should've been a "popular kid." She's rich, pretty, and likes going to parties...And yet, there we were...

"Where were you last night?" she asked. "I texted you a billion times."

She'd texted twice.

"You started these extra credit essays?" Jenn went on.

"No," I said. "Not even thinking about it."

"Since when are you not even thinking about it, Miss I-Write-for-Fun?"

At that moment, Casey Woods passed Jenn extremely closely. Like, closely. He trailed down the hall leaving a wake of body spray. He didn't look back. Jenn didn't look at him. But something was going on there. "What was that?" I asked.

"What was what?" she said.

"That," I said, tilting my head after him. "Casey."

"What do you think's on this test?" she asked.

Shrug. Dammit. I was supposed to read something other than the internet last night. "Who cares," I said.

Jenn looked at me, like, Um, what?

"Doesn't school just seem pointless to you?" I asked.

"Are you on downers?" she asked.

"Yes. Twelve years of downers," I said. "Plus preschool." Actually, preschool was pretty great.

Jenn looked around. "What is happening?" she asked. "Are we being filmed? We need to get to class. How am I the one reminding us of that?"

"Class..." I said, gazing away. Memorize, Don't Rationalize. That doesn't even make any sense. That's not what "rationalize" means.

The five-minute bell rang. "Sister, we got to go," Jenn said, grabbing my notebook and slamming our locker.

"My god," I said. "Look at us. Jumping at the sound of a bell. Like rats."

"You *are* on downers," Jenn said, pulling my arm.

THE MILLIONAIRES' CLUB

Have you ever seen a list of recommended reading for AP English Literature and Composition? I'll spare you the details, but in general, it's not filled with humor. Or lightness. It's a list of books about terrible things happening to people. We buy fresh copies of the texts, so we can make fresh notes on the pages. We talk about very deep topics like going against your entire society to be your true self. We talk about the injustices that one people visits on another for the sake of profit. We read books and ask, "Does god exist?" and "What does it mean to be human?" and "Is it true that, 'Whosoever would be a man would be a nonconformist...?'" (p.s., AP books are almost always only about white dudes, so that's cool).

Then the bell rings.

Memorize, Don't Rationalize.

We read all those books and have all those conversations so that we can take the AP and the SAT and write admissions essays and blahblahblah. It turns out the point of all those conversations isn't to make us better humans. It's to make us better *applicants*.

During last night's online research, I found this one school in Houston, Texas that has a thing called the "Millionaires' Club" where the school gives its students a free ticket to their team's opening football game if they read five books off the AP recommended reading list over the summer. To which I ask, 1) Why the hell is it called "The Millionaires' Club"? There's not one thing in it to do with millions. Is it just because people love money? Why not call it "The Blow Job Club" to get those reluctant dude readers interested? 2) You win a ticket to the school's football game? Is that really going to motivate me to read? I mean, I know Texas is crazy about football, but really? 3) Football? Really? If I'm choosing to read *Jude the Obscure* for funsies over the summer, what're the chances I'm a football fan? Oooh, I wasn't going to read *Nausea*, but there's a football ticket in it if I do.

SEE YOU NEXT TUESDAY

Everyone always likes their English teacher the best. Usually I liked my English teacher the best. My 9th grade American Lit. teacher, Ms. Crosse? Amazing. But Mrs. Sternin can suck it. She's so unbelievably full of herself. She spends at least 35 of every 50-minute class regaling us with all the awesome shit she's done. It's like the only reason she became a teacher is so she could have a captive audience for her spoken memoirs. There's probably thousands of AP English teachers like her all across the land.

Maybe I sound like some kind of woman-hater because I'm like, Mr. Banerjee = rad, and Mr. Washington = nice enough, and now I'm like, Mrs. Lady Teacher = insufferable self-promoter, but the truth is the truth.

Remember when I said that Mr. Washington is a nice enough guy and I was like, Doesn't play favorites or give unfair tests? Mrs. Sternin is the opposite.

Her preference in girls runs to fluffy (almost exclusively white girls, though a Black or Latina cheerleader slips in there every now and again). Her preference in boys (race inconsequential) runs to those who would consider her a MILF (if she had kids). Basically, she likes girls who are like her and boys who want to bang her.

Jenn and I skidded into our seats just after the bell rang. Our seats. Not through the door of the classroom. Our seats. "Nice of you girls to grace us," Mrs. Sternin said from behind her desk.

Her back was to us and she was clicking her bright red nails through the files in her tall cabinet. She's that kind of a teacher—she gets off on calling you out when her back is turned like she has super powers. She also has this whole "Mrs. Sternin's Rules of Success" thing that includes this, "On time means ready to begin" garbage. It's not part of the school handbook— she just made up her own rules. Rules that were almost physically impossible to achieve—like being physically in your desk, ready to go, when the bell rings. There were locations in the school that made it so you could not get from there to your desk, with your notebook open, unless you ran. Which *is* in the handbook as against the school rules. That's the stuff that drives me and J.T. Gatto crazy.

It was like we were in a movie about being in school. Mrs. Sternin made her snarky remark, the fluffy girls and the MILFers scoffed, the outliers (like Jenn and myself) silently moaned, and Mrs. Sternin spun on her black high heel, with a file in her hand. "Here it is, Scholars," she announced holding the manila folder in the air. "I'm sure that you have been looking forward to dazzling me with your deep knowledge of Ibsen's *The Doll House*." Cue the fluffy laugh-track. "When I was in college, I played the role of Norah..."

Of course, you did. Spoiler alert: If the audience has no choice about being there, you're not a celebrity.

And then Jeremy Hoosier burst through the door. "Sorry. Sorry. Sorry," he said as he ducked toward his desk in the far back corner. Jeremy is Black and lives on the South Side and I really believe Mrs. Sternin gave him that seat because she knew he had to take 47 busses and trains to get to school and is therefore most statistically likely to be late.

Mrs. Sternin closed her eyes, sighed (teachers sigh a lot), drew the folder to her chest, and shook her head. "Mr. Hoosier," she said and let the accusation hang in the air.

"I'm sorry, Mrs. Sternin," Jeremy said. He had somehow managed to get out of his jacket and get all of his materials ready in under 15 seconds.

"It is not I to whom you should be apologizing. It is your fellow classmates. They are the ones from whom you are stealing valuable class time," she said.

Jeremy crumpled in his seat.

Jesus Christ. If anyone is "stealing" our time, it's you and your "role of Norah." I clenched my fists, "Bitch," I muttered, loud enough for her (and everyone) to hear, but not loud enough for her to know who it was.

The fluff, the MILFers, and the outliers all gasped. Mrs. Sternin's kohl-lined eyes squinted and her red mouth pinched.

Jenn went rigid.

"Pardon me," Mrs. Sternin said, scanning the room, trying to draw the culprit out.

I stayed silent, but looked around just enough to seem like one of the other kids looking around. My heart was flipping in my chest, but I refused to be busted. Don't barf.

This is a critical kind of moment for a teacher. I mean, a line had clearly been crossed. At least a line in the student-teacher relationship (in the human-human relationship, she had been a bitch and that fact had been made clear) and it was up to her to decide if she wanted to ferret the mutterer out.

Hard to know exactly what went on in that dye-job head of hers, but she held the file out to one of her fluffy minions who leapt to grab it and began passing out its contents. Mrs. Sternin scanned the room again and said, "You will have the remainder of the period to finish the test."

I would like to say that I nailed the test and really stuck it to her. But I hadn't done any of my homework. So, yeah...

"What in the hell is going on?" Jenn asked after we'd cleared the classroom.

But before I could answer, I felt a tap on my shoulder. I turned and there was Jeremy Hoosier. "Hi," I said.

"I don't need you talking for me," he said.

"Um. What? I..." I stammered.

"I don't need some little girl trying to handle my business," he said.

We were in the middle of the hall and though the students flowed around us, people were staring. I didn't know if they'd already heard about Mrs. Sternin's class or if they could tell that this was a confrontation and not a chat.

"She was being a huge bitch," I said.

He shook his head. "How do you think she's gonna treat me for the rest of the year?" he asked, crossing his arms over his chest.

Oh no. Now my heart felt like barfing. I hadn't thought of that. I had thought of the fact that I didn't want to be there. That I might not have to be there. That Mrs. Sternin sucked. "I'm sorry," I said.

Jeremy Hoosier shook his head again and walked away.

THIS IS OUR YOUTH I

Jenn's parents had season tickets to the Steppenwolf Theater even though neither one of them liked plays—or anything, really. It was just what the Cartwright family did—had always done.

The good thing about Paul and Marcie not using their tickets is that Jenn and I got to use them whenever we wanted. We love plays.

The first thing we ever went to when we were twelve made me realize, there is no rating system in the theater. Because if that shit had been a movie, it would've been NC-17.

Last year we were sitting in a play and this dude pranced onto the stage naked AF and Jenn smacked my arm and was like, "That's number five!"

The woman next to Jenn said, "Shhhhhhh."

Jenn said to me, "In my whole life, I never expected to see so many limp dicks!"

I choked back a laugh. It was true, in our four years going to plays together, we had seen a lot of flaccid penises.

"Five..." Jenn not at all quietly whispered to me.

The woman hissed at us again.

Jenn turned right to her and said, "Are you getting a load of this?" indicating the stage.

I ducked my head and smirked into my chest.

The woman scowled and shifted in her seat so she could at least be partially turned away from us.

"I guess she wants to concentrate on the penis," Jenn said. "Must be married."

That was when *I* smacked *Jenn's* arm.

Jenn grinned and sat back in her seat, satisfied. That's a thing about her, she does not get embarrassed by embarrassing people. She's like, Oh, you're judging me? Prepare to be made *super* uncomfortable.

Last summer we went to see the first play that I've ever been actively excited about. I almost always enjoy them, there's something so amazing and transfixing about watching people act on a stage. It's so obviously fake. But I watch and watch to see what little kinds of things they do that make me think, Yes. That looks like real life. Some gesture, or smile, or touch, that makes me think, That person isn't *acting* like that character. That person *is* that character. It doesn't happen very often, as far as I can tell.

The play last summer was called *This Is Our Youth*. For some reason, I was like, This play is going to change my life. It's going to tell me a truth about the world I've never known, and everything will change. It's about two rich, hipster white dudes who are trying to make a drug deal and a hipster white girl who gets roped in. And there's a love story between one of the dudes and the girl.

Unfortunately, the play was only just fine. It didn't change anything.

There was this one part, though, where one of the dude's dads says to him over the phone, All the shit you and your friends do (he's talking about the drug deals...) the only way it will make any impact is if somebody dies. Look at all the other kids doing what you're doing, going to jail, killing each other. The only difference between you and them is money...

... And being white. That's another difference... Only the dad didn't say that.

All of which is to say, I got Jeremy Hoosier's point.

THE RED-HEADED ANGEL

I was in the 3rd grade the first time someone called my moms "dykes" and I knew what he meant. I was swinging at recess and wouldn't give my swing up to an older kid named Walt Peck, so he said something about my "two dyke moms." I got off the swing. I cried.

And then an angel appeared. She had a burning red halo and she appeared out of nowhere and punched Walt Peck in the face. He covered up and fell down and red rivulets streamed between his fingers. The blood hit the ground and I ran.

That night when I went to bed, I prayed to the angel and thanked her for punching Walt Peck. I didn't know the word "smote" yet, but that's what had happened.

About two weeks later, I saw a girl with a poufy red bob in the lunch line and I knew she was the angel. It was Jenn. She was in the other 3rd grade class.

When I saw her, I remembered that Walt had laughed while I stood by the swing and cried. As I watched her from across the cafeteria, gripping my *Alice in Wonderland* lunchbox, I felt both excited and disappointed that it was a real person, not an angel, who smote Walt Peck.

When Jenn strode over to our locker at lunch after the Sternin Debacle, she looked just as she had the day Walt Peck called my moms "dykes."

"Mrs. Sternin is a cunt," I said before she could say anything.

"Yeah. Duh. As usual," she said.

"I don't think she should be able to treat us like that," I said.

"I don't think drugs should be illegal," Jenn said, making a face that said, But they're illegal.

"Goddamit," I said and pulled both our lunch bags from the locker. Neither one of us ever stepped foot in the cafeteria.

The weather was still nice enough for us to be outside, so we went to the bench in the small courtyard between the art wing and the gym. As we sat, I had a sudden feeling like deja vu. What if this was the last time I ever sat here? "This has been our bench since the first day," I said.

"Do you have a brain tumor?" Jenn asked.

"I'm acting weird." I opened my lunch sack and pulled out my little metal sandwich box. Over the summer, I read an article that said that whatever thing they now put in plastic instead of the cancer-causing shit they used to put in plastic is worse than what they took out...so no more sandwich bags for me. I waited for the ration of shit Jenn had been giving me about the box for the last two weeks, but it didn't come.

"Beyond weird," Jenn said. Her bag sat, unopened, on the bench next to her. "What is going on?"

I told her I had asked the moms to let me leave school.

You know when you're watching a movie and there's a non-main character and you're rooting like crazy for her, and you're not sure if she's going to live because she seems like she's *might* be expendable? But she *does* live (it's always a she or a kid). In fact, the movie ends with the hero popping up in her scooter shop on some Grecian island and being like, Hey, remember me? I'm the dude who made it so you can never see any of your loved ones again...let's kiss. And you're so stoked that he finds her and it ends that way. Cause, love.

Then what happens in the first 15 minutes of the sequel? She gets shot in the head.

That's how it felt to tell Jenn I wanted to quit school. Like I was writing her out of the script. We'd been best friends since I realized she was the red-headed angel, and I was writing her out.

Her face told me she felt the same—I was making myself the hero. "Why didn't you tell me last night?" she asked.

"It's not that big a deal," I said.

Why hadn't I? "You should quit, too," I said. But I had to force the excitement into my voice. There was no way in hell she was going to quit school. Jenn is obsessed with getting into University of Chicago. She must go there. Every male member of her family (including her two older brothers Geoff and Philip) going back to the founding of the school has gone to U. Chicago. There was one aunt in the 1940s? who got in, but she didn't finish. It was Jenn's only goal in life to go to the University of Chicago. It's really goddam hard to get in there. Even when you're a legacy.

Jenn gave me a look that said, What are you even saying?

I shrugged.

The bell rang. Neither one of us had eaten. I didn't make a snide comment about us being rats. And I didn't answer her question, "Why didn't you tell me?"

TAKE IT EASY ON THOSE GIRLS

I spent the rest of the school day debating if I should say something to Jeremy Hoosier about being an asshole, something to Jenn about quitting school, and/or something to the moms about Mrs. Motherfucking Sternin.

The moms got home late. They were working on a big new project that was super different for them. A family had hired them to find a small house in our neighborhood, tear it down, and build a new house on the wreckage. Our neighborhood is a mix of small, crappy, old houses; really cool, well-kept, old houses; and big new houses built on torn-down crappy ones.

We moved when I was about five. Before Old Irving Park, we lived in a condo in a part of the city called Wicker Park. It was a cute condo. I had a room on the first floor with the laundry room. The moms had a room on the 3rd floor with the office that had been the nursery. There was a kitchen and a living room in between. It was perfect. We could have stayed there forever. When we moved, I was totally like, "I don't want to go! I hate the new house," with like, nightmares and bedwetting to prove my point. I was 13 when they told me why we left.

One night, the moms heard a woman screaming out the window. She screamed, "Help me!" And Mama Helen called out the window, "Do you need us to call the police?" And the woman said, "Yes." Mama Helen said the woman's voice was like a whimper and a whisper and a croak and she's not sure if she *really* heard the woman or just imagined it.

The police car came. One officer stayed and the other drove away again. From their bedroom window, the moms saw a young woman being interviewed by an officer under the bright porch light of the apartment building across the street. Together the moms watched the officer look down and take a note. Together they watched the young woman...

"...Just a girl..." Mama Jane said when they told me the story.

They saw her very discreetly, surreptitiously even, zip up her jeans. The moms held hands.

A moment later, the other officer returned and he stood on the porch and he made the girl stand and he positioned her "just so" under the porch light and took pictures. First he took pictures of her hands (backs, palms, fingers). Then he took pictures of her face. He positioned her under the porch light with her chin angled just so. The moms could see that she'd been beaten.

"Her eyes were swelling shut," Mama Helen said.

"Like a Halloween mask," Mama Jane said. "I hate to put it that way, but it's true. It's the worst *actual* thing I've ever seen."

"Her entire face from her chin to her eyebrows was purple and swelling and..."

The moms put the condo on the market the next week.

"It's not like rapes don't happen in cities," Mama Helen said. "But we saw that girl's face."

They got an offer on the place really fast even though several other women were attacked in the neighborhood over the summer.

That's how we ended up living in Old Irving Park.

We live in one of the nice, old houses. It's not too big and it's not too small. It's perfect for the three of us.

After the moms got home and we sat down for dinner, I just said it, "I fucked up pretty bad today." I figured if there was even a *tiny* chance of Mrs. Sternin figuring out who said it, it was best the moms hear it from me...

Mama Helen plopped her pizza on her plate. Very not like her..."What is *with* this language?"

I was cussing a lot in front of them the last couple days. "Sorry," I said.

"What'd you do?" Mama Jane asked.

"Mrs. Sternin's class," I began.

The moms looked at each other like, Here we go. They'd gotten an earful about her.

"She was being super mean (obvs I meant "bitchy") to this kid Jeremy Hoosier who lives on the South Side and has to take about 100 busses to get to school. He was like, half a minute late, and she was running her mouth as usual, so it's not like he was missing anything..."

"Oh boy," Mama Jane said.

"What did you say?" Mama Helen asked.

"I called her a bitch," I said. "But I said it quietly, so she didn't know it was me."

"I was expecting something way worse," Mama Jane said.

"Jane!" Mama Helen said.

In that case, "I wanted to call her a 'cunt,'" I said.

"Elaine!" Mama Helen said.

"Then after class Jeremy Hoosier told me to mind my own business cause how did I think Mrs. Sternin was going to treat him for the rest of the year," I said.

"Kid's got a point," Mama Jane said.

"Yeah, I know," I said. "But she was just such a...so mean...and we all sat there and took it. And I'm not only saying this to talk you into something, but it's another thing that makes me feel like, What am I doing there? Sure, most of the teachers are really nice...even if the shit...I mean stuff...that we're learning is pretty pointless...but the ones who aren't nice. They just get to be as mean as they want and there's nothing we can do. She was trying to *humiliate* him. It wasn't just her telling him not to be late. She told him that he was *stealing* class time from the rest of us. It was awful."

"There are always going to be people like that in the world, sweetie," Mama Helen said.

Mama Jane went to the refrigerator. She got herself a second beer. She shook her head. Then she shook it again.

"She was so mean!" I said, defending myself against whatever Mama Jane was thinking. "She said he was, 'stealing' from us. It was so goddam nasty."

"Elaine," Mama Helen said. "Enough with the language."

"But she did say it," I said. The bitch.

Sitting back at the table, Mama Jane continued to shake her head.

"I swear!" I swore.

"Jane," Mama Helen said and laid her hand across Mama Jane's forearm. Mama Helen has long, graceful fingers. I wish I had her fingers. Mine aren't Mama Jane's, either. I think they must be the donor's. There's lots of things I think must be the donor's. I wonder sometimes if my anger is his anger.

"Fuck that teacher," Mama Jane finally said.

"Right?!" I said, grinning, but also like, Whoa.

"Jane. Honestly?" Mama Helen said.

"She's done," Mama Jane said.

"What?" both Mama Helen and I asked.

"We're letting her quit," Mama Jane said.

"Yes!" I said, and threw my arms in the air.

"Sweetie," Mama Helen said.

Mama Jane didn't hear her. "That Sternin is just like Mr. Selfridge," she said.

"Who's Mr. Selfridge?" I asked.

"Oh, sweetie," Mama Helen said and made to hug Mama Jane. Now Mama Helen is a hugger, so it's not like it's weird for her to hug mid-conversation, but add to that the, "Oh sweetie..."

"What's going on?" I asked.

Mama Jane swatted the hug away. Not violently. Not dismissively. Just a wave of her strong hand that said, I understand your desire to hug me, but I need to say what I'm saying.

"Who's Mr. Selfridge?" I asked again.

"He was my high school gym teacher," Mama Jane said. She looked away—into the past—into a dusty gymnasium in semi-rural, semi-strip mall, Eastern Washington. She shook her head again. "What an asshole," she said. She didn't glance at Mama Helen to see her response to "asshole." I did. Mama Helen was sad. Not angry. But also not scared.

"What did he do?" I asked, though I wasn't sure I really wanted to know.

Mama Jane heard the fear in my voice, because she looked at me and smiled just enough. "He was just an asshole, Elaine," she said. "He used to make jokes. He called me 'boy.' We'd be lined up for role and he'd yell, 'Boys! You're one short! Who's missing?' He'd look around and look around. I'd just sink and wait for it. We all waited for it. The girls standing next to me would look at me. 'Oh, Fossey comma Jane,' he'd say and slap his forehead. He'd look at me lined up between Carrie Carver and Kim Lawton and laugh. Oh, god, that laugh," she said and shuddered.

"What did you do?" I pictured Jeremy Hoosier ducking in his seat.

"Nothing," Mama Jane said. "Laughed with him. Laughed with the other kids."

Mama Helen closed her eyes and folded in a bit.

"He'd say things like, 'Take it easy on those girls, Fossey.' You know, when we were playing basketball or field hockey. Sometimes he'd actually switch me over to play against the boys..."

I thought about how the boys in my class would take to being beaten by a girl (because I'm sure Mama Jane *did* beat them) and I shook *my* head.

"I mean, I mostly liked playing with the guys better," Mama Jane said. "Not that it wasn't awkward. But at least I didn't have to worry about crushing anyone."

"Were the guys jerks about it?" I asked, not sure I wanted to know that either.

"Some yes. Some no."

"Did you ever say anything to Mr. Selfridge?" I asked.

"No. I just took it," Mama Jane said. "I was too embarrassed not to. And too worried that if I didn't play along, he'd call me something worse than, 'boy.'"

Things Walt Peck had called her. Things her own mom had. "Ew," I said.

"Sweetie," Mama Helen said. "Elaine's situation isn't quite the same..."

Oh crap! I poised to defend myself, though she was kinda right. Jeremy Hoosier's situation was pretty the same. But I was Elaine Archer. Even with two dyke moms, I'm not a Black guy from the South Side. And I'm not queer. Shit.

"But the school's the same," Mama Jane said. "The environment. The nerve of some of the teachers."

"They're not all like that," Mama Helen said.

It's true. Most weren't Mrs. Sternins and Mr. Selfridges. Most were Mr. Washingtons, nice enough guy. A few were Mr. Banerjees. Just a few.

Mama Jane nodded like she agreed and then said, "Can you imagine what your life would've been like if you hadn't had to 'Watch your mouth' and 'Do what you're told' and 'Look at this. Read that. Memorize this. No time for that.' Can you imagine?"

Internal fist pump. Mama Jane had obviously been reading my propaganda.

"It's just such a risk," Mama Helen said.

I kept my mouth shut.

"Is it?" Mama Jane asked. "I mean, what's the worst that can happen?"

"College," Mama Helen threw out, but there was a hesitation.

Tell her it's no riskier than a gap year! Tell her lots of homeschooled kids go to college. Like lots. Colleges love homeschoolers!

"If it doesn't work," Mama Jane said, "She repeats junior year and it's fine."

Wait. "What?!" I blurted.

Mama Helen nodded.

I didn't nod. Repeat?!

Mama Helen took a deep breath.

I held mine. Repeat?! That's not cool. That had *never* occurred to me. I was like, Once I'm out, I'm out! Now it was, I might have to go back and I might not be in my own grade (Jenn's grade) anymore.

"I can live with that," Mama Helen said.

Oh, Christ.

IS THERE ANYTHING YOU CAN DO?

Of course, Mama Helen's, "I can live with that," was the beginning of the story, not the end.

Good to their word, the moms spent the weekend reading the documents I'd presented. When we convened in the kitchen on Sunday night to discuss, Mama Helen opened with, "So, I'm seeing this word 'unschooling' a lot more than I'm seeing the word 'homeschooling.'"

I had figured they might notice that. "To me is seems like 'homeschooling' with like, a curriculum (research word) and whatever, is more for little kids who don't know how to read or add or tie their shoes or anything..." I said.

Mama Helen was nodding. But it was that nod that said, I hear you...and I question you.

"What are you going to do all day?" Mama Jane said, cutting right to it. She leaned back in her chair and smiled, clearly fascinated to hear what I was going to come up with.

There's a scene in *Aliens* where they're on the ship that's taking them (Ripley, the Marines, and Corporate Prick Burke) to the colony. At one point, Ripley is down in the cargo bay and she's like, "You know, I kinda feel like a fifth wheel around here. Is there anything I can do?"

Sergeant Apone (bald, muscled, Black guy) and Corporal Hicks (muscled, sexy, white guy) are standing there and Apone is chomping on a cigar and he's sassy and says, "I don't know. Is there anything you can do?"

Ripley (who's daughter is dead and who's had her pilot's license revoked and basically has nothing) is pretty psyched to have someone to sass with. She says, "I can drive that loader" and points to a bulldozer-yellow machine that you strap into like exoskeleton-forklift-overalls.

Apone chomps his cigar and glances at Hicks. Hicks is like, shrug, If she says so...but with his eyes only. He has very expressive eyes.

Ripley says, "I've got a Class 2 rating."

Apone says, "Be my guest."

Ripley puts it on and is like...I mean, I don't know how to write the sounds of the machine, cause it's really the sounds that render the scene, but let's just say she's has a Class BAMF rating and does all the things the exo-forklift can do and lifts this giant crate of Marine-alien-colony gear and is all sexy voice, "Where do you want it?"

Apone laughs a big laugh and says, "Bay 12." Pause. "Please."

She machine-stomps away. Apone and Hicks bust out laughing. But it's not *at* her. And not even at themselves. It's just at how badass she is for driving that loader. They have this interaction all together and they laugh. Simple.

Plus Hicks, as I said, is sexy.

My point is, I didn't have that. I didn't have any skills. Thanks, school. I didn't have a Class Anything rating at anything. Not a single thing where I could show up some place and say, "I can drive that loader." I wanted to be able to *do something*.

I looked at the moms, waiting for my answer. "I've been thinking about it all weekend," I said. Which I had. That and how there was no way in hell I was going back to school. No way. "I want to write a book," I said.

"What?" Mama Helen said.

"Yes!" Mama Jane said and held her hand out "Five bucks," she said to Mama Helen.

"You told her," Mama Helen said to Mama Jane.

"Pay up, poor sport," Mama Jane said.

"You bet on what I was going to say?" I asked.

Mama Jane was glowing. "Absolutely," she said.

"How did you know?" Mama Helen and I asked at the same time. It's funny how you think someone isn't paying attention (because, in Mama Jane's case, half the time she isn't paying attention) and then all the sudden they just get it.

"I knew," Mama Jane said, so satisfied. "You're always scribbling some damn thing or another."

It was true. I *was* always scribbling. Only it was stuff I wrote down cause I knew I shouldn't say it. Like, by week three of school I had almost a whole notebook of the different ways I would've liked to tell Mrs. Sternin to shut the hell up. But I'd never thought that I might try to be a *real* writer.

It had taken me *all* weekend to come up with it. I was like, I'll do an Outward Bound. I'll read all the Nobel Prize winning novels. I'll watch 5 TED talks a day. I'll become a baker. I'll learn to urban farm. I'll knit. I'll podcast.

And then at like 11PM on Saturday night, I remembered something.

Saturday morning is donut morning. Once, when I was about six, I got up before the moms and went downstairs—I was used to the new house by then, but still pissed about it and I proved this to myself by refusing to sit on the comfortable couch in the front room which is where I would have liked to eat my breakfast.

Instead, I stood in the kitchen, licking the icing, and staring out the window into the backyard. Out of nowhere, this mama raccoon and her four little fat bandit babies appeared over the side of the fence—Mama first and the babies one by one behind her. They waddled along the top of the fence and disappeared on the side of the house. I ran to the front window, and yes, they'd climbed down the fence and scuttled along the driveway in their wobbly line. Mama led them down into the gutter filled with dried leaves (one of the goddam babies sneezed!), over to a tree, up one side, down the other, back into the gutter (her little babies following right along on their urban obstacle course) across the street, alongside the Grubman's house, and out of sight.

First of all, I think that was the day that I accepted the new house. I don't remember any more screaming, or bed wetting, or withholding from the couch when I ate my chocolate glazed.

Second of all, I made up this little song called, *I Wish I Was an Animal*. I don't remember a single word—no, that's not true, there was something where I rhymed, "bandit trees" with "leafy sneeze."

I remember thinking it must be so cool to be a writer, but that it obviously wasn't me. It was too special to be me. It had to be something you were born with and if you were born with it, you would know. I didn't know. So, then it couldn't be me.

So, when I scribbled songs or ideas or whatever, I never thought of those as writing.

But ten years later, at 11PM on Saturday night, right after I realized I had no interest in learning to compost, it occurred to me that even if you're born a writer, you might not know it.

Mama Jane said she always knew she was queer—even before she knew what sex or sexual orientation or sexual attraction were. Like in 1st grade, they'd be playing boys chase girls and most of the girls would get caught and dragged to the dungeon and kissed by the boys. Mama Jane would spend all her time rescuing the captured girls. "It was *so* easy not to get caught. I couldn't figure out how it kept happening..." It wasn't until way later that she was like, "Ohhh...they *wanted* to get caught and kissed."

Mama Helen, on the other hand, had no idea until college. She had boyfriends and everything. "I just thought I hadn't met the right guy yet," she said.

So maybe I was like Mama Helen. Maybe I *was* born a writer and I hadn't realized it.

Then again, maybe it wasn't at all like being queer. Maybe you're not born a writer. Maybe you just decide to be one. Like Ripley wasn't born with a Class 2 rating on that loader—she just decided to learn to do it. And those science fair kids who make prosthetic limbs out of legos and 3D printers, it's not like they were born inventing that shit.

So what do Ripley and those science nerds have in common? What *are* they born with? Curiosity? Imagination? Determination?

I've totally got all that. I'm totally imaginative and totally determined and I'm totally writing a book. By then it was, like, 1AM on Sunday.

"What's it gonna be about?" Mama Jane asked, bringing me back to Sunday evening.

"I have no idea," I said.

"I'm going to get so old, so fast," Mama Helen said.

OCTOBER

LIFE WITHOUT SCHOOL

Day One:
Yes! Freedom! Endless summer! I drank coffee and watched from the window as all the kids who hadn't dropped-out headed off to school. Losers.

Internet

Mama Helen asked me what I did all day and Mama Jane said, "We made a deal—weekly check ins..." Mama Helen said, "I wasn't checking-in, I was making chit-chat." Mama Jane and I made faces like, Yeah, right. And then we had stir-fry.

Short facetime with Jenn. She didn't seem pissed that I wasn't at school, but I also didn't mention anything about it.

Day Two:
Epic sleep-in
Internet
Moms at meeting with new client. Dinner in front of tv.

Day Three:
Desire for epic sleep-in. Tossing and turning all night.
Internet
Meaningful glances passed between the moms at dinner.

Went to Jenn's house. She was supposed to be doing math. I was supposed to be writing. We talked about boys and argued about her music.

Day Four:
Another bad night's sleep
The dream where I show up to school with only a long t-shirt (like

just past my butt-cheeks) and no underwear, plus a belief that if I just don't lift my arms up, no one will notice.

Mama Jane put her hand on Mama Helen's shoulder when Mama Helen said, "...so..."

Skipped talking with Jenn.

Realized I have no idea how to write a book.

Discovered a million useless answers to "How to Write a Book" on the internet. Some that said, "You have a less than 1% chance of publishing a book." Some that said, "If you pay me $19.95, you can have access to my website giving you ALL the secrets of how to write and publish a hit." And some that said, "You just need to write."

Day Five:
Bookstore
Thank god.

Motherlode people. Here's what I don't like about the library—you can't find anything. Bookstore, you're like, "Where's the books about writing books?" The dude with the lanyard says, "Second floor. Back." You go there, and, Yep. Suck it, Dewey Decimal. In retrospect, I suppose I felt a little sorry for Mrs. Sukers, our grade school librarian, who tried to teach us about using pluses and parentheses and whatever to look things up, with Jenn and me saying, "Boolean. Boolean. Booooooolean."

I texted Jenn.

Elaine: Boolean.
Jenn: Filthy.

My phone vibrated. "Boolean," Jenn said when I answered.

"Boolean," I said. She wasn't supposed to be on the phone at DB High, but that kind of thing never stopped her.

"What are you doing?" Jenn asked.

"Bookstore," I said and nodded to the shelf in front of me even though she wasn't there to see.

"Get me this month's Nylon, would you?" Jenn asked.

"Don't you subscribe?" I asked. I usually borrowed her copy.

"My mom cancelled when she saw there was an article about safe blow jobs," she said.

"Makes sense," I said.

"Ruled by logic, that's our Marcie Cartwright."

"Did you know you can get syphilis from blow jobs?" I'd watched a movie about it (based on a true story of a massive oral syphilis outbreak in a suburban high school—ewww) when I was having non-clinical insomnia.

"Is that what they're teaching you at that new school? You're supposed to be writing a book," Jenn said.

"Um. I have no idea how to write a book," I admitted.

"Yes," Jenn said. "The moms know you don't know?"

"I'm beginning to suspect they suspect."

"Awesome," Jenn said, gleefully.

"Get together tonight?" I asked.

"Can't. Going out."

"What? Who?" How do I not know?

"Whom," Jenn said. "You're getting stupider so fast."

"With whom are you going out?" I asked.

"Shh! Some of us have to worry about our speaking environment."

"Well, what about tomorrow," I said.

"SAT prep in the AM. After that?" she asked.

"Hopefully by then I'll know how to write a book." 😄

THAT'S HOW I KNOW

"Marcie says I'm going out too much," Jenn said on Saturday morning, so I went to her house after she finished SAT prep.

Jenn lives in a mansion that happens to be a one-floor apartment in the Gold Coast right by the lake. Her mom redecorates it like every 6 weeks. Including Jenn's room. Last time it was this red-white-black-cherry-blossom Japanese theme, but then Jenn's mom got into 80s decor and now it's all cabbage flowers a nd a b lue-green c arpet. J enn h as one bulletin board over her desk where she's allowed to put "personal" items.

My room is plastered floor to ceiling with magazine pictures, photos, ticket stubs, a giant button that says, "The More You Complain the Longer God Lets You Live," a row of shoe boxes stapled to the wall holding my stuffed animals, my custom-made, "What Would Bill Murray Do?" bumper sticker, a Beatles poster, a Tegan and Sara poster, a Rushmore poster, tickets from my first concert (Death Cab for Cutie— who are Mama Jane's favorite band from her free-wheeling life in Seattle in the 90s) a whole section of panda greeting cards, shelves crammed with books, an original movie poster from *Aliens*, pictures of me and Jenn, pictures of me and the moms, pictures of me and Uncle Alex, etc, etc...

"So who were you out with last night?" I asked as I flopped down on her bed. She has a queen sized bed, which is *a lot* of bed.

She was leaning over her vanity, about four inches from the mirror, putting on eyeliner. "O'Connell," she said.

"*Blake* O'Connell?" I asked. We'd known him since 7th grade and although they'd "gone together" for two days in 8th grade, they had hardly looked at each other (I thought) in high school. Here's the thing about Blake O'Connell, I guess he seems like someone girls might want to go out with. He takes hard classes. He plays ice hockey. He's good looking. But there had always been something kinda wankery about him. Like he's the kind of dude who will ask you what grade you got on something and then only tell you what grade he got if it's *better* than yours. "What's up with that?" I asked.

Jenn shrugged, "I started talking to him the other day and decided to go out with him," she said.

"I thought you thought he's a wanker," I said.

"He laughs at my jokes," she said. She finished with one eye, stood back, looked at her work, then leaned in to do the other eye. She uses this liquid liner and can draw the most perfectly straight lines I've ever seen. Like computer-generated-straight. I tried wearing makeup once in middle school and felt like everyone was staring at me all day. Not worth it. "I like a guy who laughs at my jokes."

Fair enough. "Did you make out?" I asked.

"Obviously," Jenn said, looking herself in the eyes.

"Ohmygod. Was it fun?" I asked.

"Yeah. He's a good kisser," she said. She finished the second eye, examined her work, and recapped the liner.

"Like how so?" It's not weird to ask for specifics.

She turned around and leaned against the vanity. "You know. Into it," she said. "And...it's like I could tell he wasn't spending the whole time thinking about how he was gonna feel me up or finger me or whatever..."

"Eww. I hate that," I said.

Jenn had about 40,000 times the sexual experience that I did. Like she had a high school boyfriend, Dane, when we were in middle school and they did it. I'd done some making out or whatever. Once we were playing a drinking game at a party and there was a cute guy from another school there and we ended up in a bedroom together. He tried to go down my pants, but I wouldn't let him. He was like, I could make this feel way better for you. I was like, No way, dude. I just don't understand the point of it. I mean, kissing obviously feels good. But otherwise I'm always wondering if the dude is just trying to get me to do stuff so he can call me a slut later.

Jenn doesn't worry about that.

"So, are you gonna go out with him again?" I asked.

"Sure," she said.

"What about Casey?" I asked.

"What about him?" She turned back to the mirror and started brushing her hair.

"Sister, I *know* I saw something the other day." His close-walking was *not* a coincidence.

"We'll see," she said, and I could hear that she wasn't gonna spill any more. "So what's your book gonna be about?"

I let the subject change. "Ugh. I have no idea. There's like a whole section in the bookstore about how to come up with ideas and I can't come up with one," I said. I sat up and leaned back against the wall of pillows at the head of Jenn's bed. The scent of strong, chemical detergent flooded me.

"Write about Lucca," Jenn said. "You were obsessed with him."

I froze. I tried not to think about Lucca. And I thought Jenn and I had an unwritten rule not to talk about him. Maybe she was more pissed at me than I thought.

"I wasn't obsessed," I said. I was so obsessed.

"If you tell me you don't still have his schedule memorized, I'll call you a liar," Jenn hoisted herself onto her vanity and let her legs dangle.

"I did not have his schedule memorized." I totally had his schedule memorized. And maybe sometimes when I'd been at school, I'd still walked the route.

"He was cute," she said.

"You hated him," I said.

"Cute for you," she said. "So cute for you. All that talking. All that thinking. All those books and movies." She shivered in disgust.

"I don't know what the hell to write about. I've been thinking about it for days," I said, hoping she'd be willing to change the subject.

"Can you make my character Black?" Jenn asked. She pulled her hair back, then let it down, and talked to me through the mirror.

"Who says you're gonna be in it?"

"With natural hair. Big," she said and showed how big she wanted it.

I flopped down on my belly toward the foot of the bed. I had to get away from the pillows. How much detergent do they use? "I'm not making you Black," I said.

"So I AM in your book," she said.

I leaned over and sniffed the duvet. Not as strong. "I have no book," I said. There are *so many* books about writing books, but unless you have an idea, you're kinda fucked.

"Why can't I be?" she asked.

"First of all, the Black one can't be the slutty one," I said.

"I'm the slutty one?!" She made mock-offended face.

I raised an eyebrow.

"Okay, but that doesn't answer my question."

I had never even considered writing non-white characters. That sounded like even more dangerous territory than the plastic vortices in the oceans. "Listen, I'm gonna have a hard enough time writing characters of color without getting accused of being racist. Or worse..."

"What's worse than being racist?" she asked.

Exactly. "So I'm not making the slut non-white."

"Make us ALL non-white. Sluts. Non-sluts. Lucca," she looked at me pointedly. "We can ALL have natural hair," Jenn said. She'd always been good at telling me what I should do. The number of times she told me to just tell Lucca that I loved him...

I shook my head. "I'm sixteen. I do not have the chops to write whole cultures and ethnicities not my own." And I have no book idea.

"Coward."

"Anyway." I said.

Jenn pulled her hair back into a ponytail. "So remember those book reports for Sternin's class?" she asked.

"I've been gone a week," I said. Dramatic.

"I'm gonna need you to write my first one," she said and twisted the ponytail into a high bun.

"What the hell are you talking about?" No way.

She suddenly swung down from the vanity, walked over to her desk, grabbed a book, and brought it to me.

I was shaking my head. "No way. I quit school," I said and refused to take it.

"That's how I know you have time," she said and plopped the book down on the bed next to me. "It's perfect."

"Jenn, seriously. I have my own work to do." No, I don't.

"You said you don't even have an idea, yet. This'll inspire you. It's about sex." She said.

I rolled my eyes and glanced at the book. *Sex at Dawn: The Prehistoric Origins of Modern Sexuality.* "Yeah, this looks incredibly inspiring."

"It's due next Friday. Five-paragraph," she said and walked back toward the mirror.

"You're a bitch," I said, but I tossed the book over toward my bag. "So, is O'Connell your boyfriend?" I asked by way of revenge.

NERVOUS BANANAS

The moms and I agreed to have weekly progress-reports on Sundays.

"How's it going," Mama Jane asked after we'd settled into our spots in the kitchen.

I decided not to lie. "I don't really know how to write a book," I said. I also decided not to tell them I was writing Jenn's essay, instead.

Mama Helen clasped her hands and laid them in her lap. That's one of her signs that she's trying really hard not to freak out.

"Honestly, not being in school is kinda hard," I said. Even if it's bullshit. "Having someone tell you what to do all the time is way easier," I said.

"Having you not in school isn't that easy for us, either," Mama Helen said.

"We're freaking out a little," Mama Jane said, but she gestured over to Mama Helen, like, Mostly, she's freaking out.

"Since you're feeling a little unmoored and we're feeling a little..." Mama Helen started.

"...Bananas..." Mama Jane said.

"...Nervous..." I said at the same time.

They laughed. "We're feeling like nervous bananas," Mama Jane said.

"So, I did some research," Mama Helen said and pulled out her computer.

Of course, she did research. Keep calm and do some research. That, I inherited that from her.

"Professional organizations can be very helpful. This one looks reputable," Mama Helen said and turned the screen toward me.

I read the screen, "The Association of Writers for Young People."

"They're having a conference next weekend," Mama Jane added.

"We'll pay for it," Mama Helen said.

They must be nervous bananas.

WHAT'S A WIP?

I went back to my room and checked the site out. It actually did look helpful. There were links like, *Getting Started in Publishing* and *How to Make Your Manuscript Great*.

I registered to become an Associate Member (someone who hasn't published yet).

Then I tried to register for the regional conference, called *First Things First*. But it said I had to be 18 to attend. Per the moms and per my Uncle

Alex who are always like, You should ask for what you want...I emailed the regional coordinator, Cynthia Swann-Griffin.

From: Elaine Archer <LV426er@gmail.com>
Date: October
To: Cynthia Swann-Griffin <c.swann_griffin@awyp.org>
Subject: First Things First Conference

Dear Ms. Swann-Griffin,

My name is Elaine Archer. I am writing to ask if I might get special permission to attend the regional conference on October 11th. The speakers and workshops look so interesting. I am currently at work on a novel, but I'm only 16. Please let me know if I can attend the conference. I think it would be very helpful.

Sincerely,

Elaine Archer

She g-chatted me immediately.

Ms. Swann-Griffin: Hi Elaine, this is Cynthia Swann-Griffin, the AWYP regional coordinator.

That was quick.

Me: Hi Ms. Swann-Griffin. Thank you for writing.
Ms. Swann-Griffin: You can call me, Cynthia. We're very casual at AWYP.
Me: Okay. Thanks.
Cynthia: Regarding the conference, do you have a WIP?

Oh geez, quick google "WIP." Hmm, I'm guessing it's not a Philadelphia Sports Radio station, or a stock that doesn't seem to be doing very well, or a piece of Carhartt clothing. Dammit.

Me: WIP?

Cynthia: Work-in-Progress.
Me: Oh. Yes. I have a WIP.
Cynthia: Is it complete?

It's not even started...which is to say, I don't actually have a WIP.

Me: Not complete yet, no.
Cynthia: Do you have an agent?
Me: Like an actor?
Cynthia: Yes, like that.
Me: No. I don't.
Cynthia: Have you sold or self-published anything?
Me: No.

Jesus. Is she gonna ask for my PSAT scores?

Cynthia: And you've signed up to be an AWYP member?
Me: Yes, just now.
Cynthia: Alright, have your parent or guardian send me an
email giving you permission to attend the conference. We've
make exceptions.
Me: Yes, definitely. I'll have one of my moms send an email.
Cynthia: Will you be staying at the hotel?
Me: Hmm, I don't know. We haven't talked about it.
Cynthia: It really is preferable. There are events after
dinner...honestly, it's the chance to connect with other writers
that really make the conferences special.
Me: Okay. I'll ask. Is there anything else I should know?
Cynthia: Not really. I'll look for you at registration so you can
put a face with my name.
Me: Great! Thank you so much!
Cynthia: No problem. Looking forward to meeting you, Elaine.

Of course, at first there was *no way* the moms were going to let me stay at a hotel by myself. They were going to stay with me. But then Mama Helen remembered that they had to fly somewhere to look at some special stone their new client wanted in their bathrooms or some nightmare like that. "They're proving to be a little difficult," Mama Helen said. That was her way of saying, A pain in the goddam ass. I was supposed to stay the weekend at Jenn's. So in a twist that none of us saw coming, the moms said that as long as I called them from my room 20 minutes after the last event, it was okay for me to stay in the hotel alone. Let me just say what you are probably thinking, "What's with these moms? They let her quit school, they're paying for this conference, and now they're letting her stay at a hotel by herself (and presumably paying for that, too...)?" All I can say is, I know. It's crazy. But here's the thing about the moms—when they do something, they *do* it.

UNDER THE RADAR

It was lunchtime and there was no food in the house, so I rode my bike to Zero Drop, the coffeeshop on Irving Park. It's a huge, old warehouse (according to the moms, it used to be a sewing machine factory) that was empty forever and with boarded up windows and rumors of drugs and murder inside...But about three years ago, some hipster couple bought it and now they roast coffee, brew beer, and the moms say they're trying to get permits to make whiskey. Mama Jane thinks they have a "snowball's chance in hell" of getting the permits because I guess people are worried that if you have a liquor factory down the street, the whole place is gonna explode in crime...But like, wasn't it already?

Anyway, it's cool. It's big in there, super high ceilings, lots of mixes of small tables, and long wood tables, and a tall bar that always has 15 people with laptops standing at it, their cords behind them like tails plugged into the wall.

I was about to start reading Jenn's dumb book in the nook to the right of the door when these two, white, super tattooed, 20-something guys, one with sunglasses and a mega-beard, one with short hair and a tank-top, (it was way too cold for a tank-top) came over and scoped it out. They didn't appear to see me.

Bearded guy was like, "Yo, let's sit outside."

Tank-top guy was like, "Dude, too cold."

Bearded guy looked out the window and said, "Cold and wet." He took off his glasses. He looked tired.

Tank-top guy said, "No rain, dude." They sat at the table in front of me.

I tried to get back to work, but then in walked this white, 20-something girl, with dark hair in a low spiky mohawk, like meringue. She was wearing very short, very high waisted shorts with opaque gray tights. Starting just under her butt-cheeks and running to the middle of her thighs, she had these huge, colorful, amazing tattoos of giant flowers. She sat down and was like, "I can't believe how terrible I feel."

Bearded guy was like, "I feel terrible, too. I feel like one dollar." He had tats scattered here and there all over both arms, down to his wrists. Is that how full sleeve tattoos start?

"I feel like one nickel," Mohawk girl said. She set her forehead on the table.

Tank-top guy said to Bearded guy, "I don't think your friend liked me. She didn't like any of my jokes." Even though he was talking about some other girl, his body language told me he liked Mohawk girl.

Bearded guy shook his head. "She liked your jokes," he said, "She's just not that good at laughing. Why do I feel like such shit?"

"I feel awesome," Tank-top guy said. As far as I could tell, none of his tattoos had any color.

"Because you snorted ritalin like an 8th grader," Mohawk girl said to Bearded guy.

"That's right!" he said. So pleased. Then he said to Tank-top guy, "Why don't you feel bad?"

"Under the radar," he said and made a flat hand gesture to go with.

"You always do that!" the other two said.

Bearded guy picked up his sunglasses, considered putting them on, laid them back on the table. "One dollar," he muttered.

The blonde waitress (also in a tank-top. What's with the tank-tops in October?) walked up with a tray of juices.

"Here comes life!" Bearded guy yelled.

The waitress handed the juices around and Mohawk girl said, "Rina, this is Tony (Bearded guy) and Isaac (Tank-top guy)..."

"Hi," Rina said holding her tray under her arm.

Tony (Bearded guy) pointed to himself, Isaac, and Mohawk girl,

"We're all friends," he said. "And you and Audra are friends..." he pointed to Rina and Mohawk girl.

"So, we're friends now, too," Rina said and looked around the table.

Mohawk girl (Audra) raised her juice to Rina, as did the two dudes.

Rina smiled and bowed her head just a bit.

"Tony's the mayor of the world," Isaac said after Rina went back to the bar.

Tony shrugged, like, It's true...Then he pointed his juice at Isaac, "Yo, whaddya mean 'Under the radar'? I thought you drank all that whiskey."

"That was Mason," Audra said.

The way their conversation flew around reminded me of me and Jenn.

Tony picked up his cell phone, "I've been calling Mark all morning," he said.

"He sleeps forever," Audra said.

Tony still had the phone to his ear when he said, "When cats stay in bed, they stay in *bed*."

"And if you try to wake him up he's like, Blaaaaag, I'm sleeping!" Isaac said.

Tony rolled his eyes and set his phone on the table. "And then when he wakes up, he's like, 'What's up?' like he wasn't just a wasteoid for hours," he said.

Isaac nodded while he sipped his juice. Then he said, "Did I tell you about the time I went to his parents' house and it was like 9:45AM and his mom was making pancakes and then she went up to his room like 8 times in 3 hours? She was just like, He's not ready to get up yet."

Tony and Audra were both like, No wonder.

"When I was a kid, not getting up was not an option. Like my dad would throw a bucket of cold water on me," Tony said.

"Totally," Isaac said.

"Actually, that's not true." Tony said. "He'd put our baseball uniforms in the dryer so they were nice and toasty when we got them on."

"That's nothing like cold water," Audra said.

Tony smiled, "Yeah, he's a total sweetheart." Then picked up his phone again and pushed some buttons.

Texting his dad?

Audra got up from the table and rushed to the bathroom.

"Is she puking?" Tony asked Isaac.

He shook his head. "She once had this stomach virus and I kept making her all these nice dinners and then she just kept puking them up and I was like, Goddamit. That was for a week."

So maybe they were dating. Or used to. Or something.

I think the thing I liked about the group, and I did like them, immediately, was the fact that they had a girl as a full member of their crew. Like whether she was or is or will be a girlfriend to either of those guys was beside the point, she was obviously a full-fledged member. And the thing I really liked about her was that she clearly liked Rina. When she raised her glass, it was definitely cool, but it was also sweet. There was no sarcasm. None of that, I'm pretending to like you, but girl-to-girl we know I hate you and these are MY boys and find your own.

Tony got off the phone.

"What was that?" Isaac asked.

"Some kind of craigslist weirdo," Tony said and he stared into the middle distance, calculating.

Audra came back from the bathroom, sat down, and finished her juice in one drink.

"I wanna get a new tat," Isaac said. "I saw this cool drawing of two glass bottles and one said 'seltz' and one said, 'zer'. I think it was Mason's."

Audra looked at him like he was crazy. "That's mine," she said.

"I love seltzer," Tony said. "I feel like I'm one seltz away from total revivification."

"Other people than you like seltzer," Isaac said to Audra. He sounded annoyed. Maybe he was still mad at her for barfing all those dinners.

She yanked her phone from her bag and started tapping away.

Texting Mason?

"I love seltzer, too," Isaac said and he was looking at Audra who was not looking at him. Sorry, Isaac.

"I just want to ride around with a tank on my back and give people seltzer on the street," Tony said.

"Free the seltzer," Isaac said.

"Was it this?" Audra asked and held the phone in Isaac's face.

"Yes!" Isaac said.

She pointed to herself. "Mine," she said and put her phone back in her bag.

"She did bottles and cans," Tony said.

Why didn't he say so before?

"I though Mason did it," Isaac said.

Audra pointed to herself again.

"I want those bottles or Wall-E for my next tattoo," Tony said.

"I want those bottles, too," Isaac said.

Of course, you do.

"I can do it tomorrow," Audra said.

She's a tattoo artist?

Both Isaac and Tony nodded.

She grabbed her bag and stood up. "I gotta start work," she said.

"You're working today?!" Isaac said.

She pushed her chair in. "Why do you think I suggested we come to where I work?" she asked.

"Sucks," Tony said. "You coming thrifting?" he asked Isaac.

Isaac shrugged.

"What did I tell you?" Audra asked.

"That I need to get out and go thrifting," he said.

Tony finished his juice. "I'm borrowing Mark's truck to get this P.A. this cragislist dude is selling," he said.

Audra was standing with her back to me and I couldn't stop staring at her flower tattoos. She didn't have very athletic legs and normally I'd have been like, It's too bad you don't have nicer legs...but there was something about her that I couldn't even get a thought like that to make sense. "Tell him to go with you," she told Tony.

"Come with me," Tony said to Isaac.

"I can't," Isaac said. "I'm seeing that movie with my brother."

"Not 'til 4, dude," Tony said.

"That's true," Audra said. "If you hit that one shop first..."

Tony stood up, shoved his phone into his front pocket, and grabbed his backpack off the floor. "I need to stop by my house and do a hit of weed," he said.

Isaac also stood up and grabbed his backpack off the floor. But he was shaking his head.

"Daddy needs a recharge," Tony said. "And I want to stop at Illuminati and get an americano. No offense," he said to Audra.

She shrugged. "I don't give a shit whose americanos you drink."

Isaac was still shaking his head. "That's all day."

"Five minutes, dude, I can drink an americano in five minutes...Okay, I'll make the americano at home and get a hit of weed," Tony said.

Audra pulled a lip balm out of her bag, then dropped it. She and Isaac bent down to pick it up and almost hit heads. She is not in love with him.

Isaac stood back up and tried to act like he wasn't awkward. "Or you can get an americano at the shop by my house and get a hit of my hash," he said.

"*That* offends me," Audra said. "That place is disgusting."

Tony put his sunglasses on. "No and no," he said. "Not drinking that coffee. Not doing your drugs." He pulled his phone out of his pocket and considered the front screen.

Isaac smirked.

"Hash?" Tony said, like that was the craziest thing he'd ever heard. "*That* would be all day." He put his phone back.

"You can't drive Mark's truck on hash," Audra said. Once again, she wasn't looking at Isaac, but he was looking at her.

They left the side nook.

Whoa. Is that what people are like? When I was in school, I never would have seen a scene like that—I would have been in class. Maybe the real reason that they put us in school was to keep us separated from 20-somethings. I mean, the longer I was out of school, the more I was willing to believe that the reason for school could be anything other than educating us.

GODDAM FARMING

Here's a tip—if you're setting out to do something you've never done before and you're freaking because you have no idea how to do it, just go back and do something you already know how to do.

Let's say you quit school after 12+ years and are like, I'll write a novel. No biggie. Then you realize there's a reason not everyone writes novels. It's because, Holy shit, it's goddam hard. How does *anyone* write novels? So, instead of bailing out and going back to school after a week, just do someone else's homework.

I may have called Jenn a bitch for unloading her essay on me, but after Audra, Tony, and Isaac left, I cracked open *Sex at Dawn: The Prehistoric Origins of Modern Sexuality*, pen in hand, ready to write some notes in the margins...It was the first time I relaxed all week. Also, why would I even try to start a book before the *First Things First* conference? That makes no sense.

Jenn tried to sell the book to me as "about sex" and I guess it kind of was, but as far as I could tell, it wasn't about sex in the way someone like Jenn would enjoy.

I was only through the intro, but I was pretty sure the point the authors (Christopher Ryan and Cacilda Jetha) were going to make was that everything our culture *seems* to value in sex (monogamy; hot, young, fertile chicks; wealthy, powerful dudes) is not what we humans *actually* evolved to value. Or, to put it another way: The world is fucked up. And it's farming's fault.

First of all, the authors are like, Consider the whole of human existence on Earth which started like, 200,000 years ago. That's out of the Earth's 4.543 billion years... Did you know that? I didn't know that.

Of that 200,000 years we were hunter-gatherers for about 190,000 years. Then we became agrarian (farmers) like 10,000 years ago.

The authors, Ryan and Jetha, say that if you look at current hunter-gatherer societies (or ones that anthropologists studied before some military or corporation came and killed them all or moved them to reservations or whatever conquerers were doing to indigenous people at the time) and if you look at our closest ape cousins—the chimps and bonobos (who behave kinda like traditional hunter-gatherers) and if you look at the way all those cultures have sex, what you find is that they're all banging each other all the time. No such thing as monogamy.

According to Ryan and Jetha, monogamy was invented at the same time as farming. Ten thousand years ago. So, we evolved one way for 190,000 years and then did a big, fat swicheroo 10,000 years ago. The reason is because that's when property ownership got invented. Suddenly, unlike hunter-gatherer societies which only survived if everyone shared everything (including who they had sex with), farms were owned by single groups. In order to be sure that dads were passing land on to their own sons, they had to make sure their sons *were* their sons. The only was to do that 10,000 years ago was to make sure your woman was only banging you. The best way to do that was invent monogamy. Which would be fine,

I guess, except, they were also like, Just in case, we should probably make women the property of men.

Here's a real fucking zinger:

...before the advent of agriculture a hundred centuries ago, women typically had as much access to food, protection, and social support as men...upheavals in human societies resulting in the shift to settled living in agricultural communities brought radical changes to women's ability to survive. *Suddenly women lived in a world where they had to barter their reproductive capacity for access to the resources and protection they needed in order to survive.* But these conditions are very different from those in which our species had been evolving previously. (Ryan and Jetha, 8)

Yeah. You read that right. Women have to trade baby-making for food and not getting raped and killed.

Motherfuckers.

Are you kidding me?

I'm not claiming, even now, that I've connected *all* the dots...but I have a sneaking, goddam suspicion that women having to trade our ability to make babies in order to eat and not be raped or killed by dudes is intimately connected to the way we've been eating, raping, and killing the Earth for centuries.

And even if 10,000 years is *nothing* in the scheme of human existence, it's still 10,000 years! How am I supposed to unravel that bullshit?

I thought about that sea turtle.

I thought about catastrophic climate change.

Maybe everybody dying is a good thing.

Maybe what the Earth needs is a plague and a do-over.

Although I guess there was no telling *who* would be the ones doing-over. Or if they would do anything differently the second time around.

Of course, I couldn't write Jenn's essay about how the world needs 99.9% depopulation (including you, Mrs. Sternin—Banerjee can stay). It was gonna have to be something stupid like, Farming affected the way we make families...Goddam school.

Goddam farming.

Goddam humans.

Goddam men.

THE FINAL COUNTDOWN

It was on that note that I headed to the *First Things First* conference.

The moms both came to drop me off. The way they carried on (the kissing, the hugging, the patting) you'd think I was going to war. I was just waiting for one of them to remind me to always wear clean underwear, "Just in case..." I could've easily taken the L down there, but they were like, No way, we're driving you.

"It's a two-day conference, you weirdos," I said as I got my bag from the car.

"Be friendly," Mama Helen said.

"Be smart," Mama Jane said. Not like, Make good choices...but like, Go ahead and show off...

"I stay at Jenn's for 10 times longer all the time," I said.

The moms actually held hands and waved as I walked into the hotel with my *small* backpack.

The lobby was packed. Who knew so many people wanted to write books for kids? And by "people," I mean middle-aged white women. Oh no, take that back. There was one younger white dude and one younger Black dude. There were two middle-aged white dudes. And there was one Black woman. At least in the foyer.

My room was standard hotel. I was on the 16th floor—which seemed like good luck cause I was 16. There were semi-fancy soaps and shampoos in the bathroom that I would take home, put in a drawer, and throw away in two years after they'd begun to mysteriously ooze.

I unpacked my backpack: two pairs of *clean* underwear, two pairs of socks, two extra t-shirts, and a sweater for the evening stuff. Daytime attire—jeans, t-shirt, sweatshirt. The standard, I'm-keeping-it-casual-not-trying-to-prove-anything-to-anybody-I-don't-care-etc-etc uniform.

That was a totally unexpected perk of leaving school.

When I was there, it wasn't possible that I was going to compete style-wise. I mean, I wasn't disgusting. But I was no Jenn. She has that magical ability to take things that are just so damn ugly, *should be* so damn ugly, and make them seem like some Hollywood stylist hand-created the look. If there was a *Project Runway* where you shopped at TJMaxx and Goodwill, Jenn would win the shit out of that. Not me.

I could wear jeans.

Sometimes I wore black jeans, but never to school, cause I didn't want anyone to be like, Oh, Elaine's wearing black jeans like she's cool or something.

Not being in school, not being trapped in there with 2,000 kids who were looking for any and all ways to create a social hierarchy, I felt so damn free. I mean, I pretty much wore what I wore then, but at least I wasn't looking over my shoulder anymore.

Meanwhile, the dress code of the conference appeared to be as follows:

Three-quarters of the white middle-aged women were wearing skinny jeans, tunic sweaters, and knee-boots.

The other one-quarter of them were wearing these flowery overall dresses with turtlenecks under.

The knee-boot contingent all dyed their hair.

The turtleneck contingent appeared to have forgotten they had hair.

Look, I never said I was any better than those judgmental assholes at school.

The dudes—seemingly regardless of age or race were weaing fashion jeans. Oh, except that dude in mom-khakis. 😑

I signed in and Cynthia Swann-Griffin waved at me, but didn't come over. She was brokering something with an angry Knee-boot. I got my folder and followed the crowd with matching lanyards to the beige conference room.

Do you ever do that thing where you expect something to be one way and then it turns out another and you're like, That sucks.

What I'd expected, was spectacle.

The lights go black. The room goes black. The audience gasps. Laser lights slowly skim the crowd. A sound like a spaceship being powered-up comes blasting out of the speakers. The lights become frantic. Stripes of light like the blades of swords sweep the audience. First the people whisper to each other. Then the music starts. "Dah dah dah dahhhhh. Dah dah dah dah dahhhhh." *The Final Countdown.* The people can only stare. The music gets louder. The lights move faster. The frenzy builds and builds and builds. STOP! Darkness. A single column of light at the center of the stage. A voice comes over the speaker, "Ladies and gentlemen. Artists! Geniuses! Prepare your souls for greatness!" A dude all in black, shrouded, with his arms outstretched, descends down through the column of light (obviously he's suspended by wires, but even when you squint, you can't see them).

What I got was a glorified school assembly.

- a lanyard
- a meal plan
- a digital copy of the schedule, scanned to your device upon entry and confirmation of payment
- Knee-boots vs. Turtlenecks

Though there was a good buffet. With danishes. I goddam love danishes. I took three (cause no one else was at that end of the table) and found a seat toward the back.

There was a crash from coffee station—again, in a moment unlike school, no one laughed or clapped—there was just an, "Oh my goodness," and two Knee-boots helping a Turtleneck sop up her spill.

I started in on danish #2, feeling pretty confident. Look at these people. These women look like teachers, not rock stars. I got to work on the 3rd danish, like, I totally got this.

And then a rock star sauntered to the front of the room. Well, a rock star escorted by a Cynthia Swann-Griffin—a Knee-boot.

The two of them walked to the podium. Cynthia S-G made the "settle down" gesture to the room and a few of the women started clapping which brought the rest of the chit-chatters to attention and they started clapping, too. Then everyone stopped clapping and CSG said, "I know you all find it charming when I ramble on about upcoming events..."

"We're faking it," someone called from the audience and all the women laughed. The rock star smiled and tucked his chin.

CSG laughed, "I've always suspected," she said. "Well, in that case. Without further ado...it is my great honor, great great honor, to kick off this weekend's *First Things First* conference by introducing Printz Award winning, Edgar Award winning, New York Times bestselling author, and all-around great guy, Brenden Carter..."

The applause deafened.

Brenden Carter smiled with some kind of adorable shyness. He was a white guy, late 20s(?), messy brown hair, a little stubble, and what looked like light eyes. He had on (not douchey) fashion jeans and a blue t-shirt that looked old, but not thrashed.

I could hear Jenn saying, Yes, please.

This conference just got a whole lot better.

Then he started talking and it got terrifying.

NEVER QUIT

When CSG vacated the podium and Brenden Carter stepped up, the crowd was out of control. It was a little embarrassing, honestly. Hold it together, ladies.

"Can you hear me?" Brenden Carter asked into the microphone.

The crowd whooped. Then slowly, slowly, with a few re-erruptions, the mania quieted down.

Brenden Carter smiled into the microphone and then out to the crowd. "When the organizing committee for this *First Things First* conference called me..."

"Called his agent!" a Knee-boot yelled.

Again, the crowd laughed. Oldsters evidently love it when they publicly interrupt each other. Another difference from school. I can just see Sternin's pinched face if the peanut gallery dared joke at her expense.

Brenden Carter also laughed. "Called my agent..." he said "...and asked if I would speak about my first book, I had to ask them to specify. Were they talking about the first book I wrote?" He held up one finger. "The first book I let anyone read?" He held up a second finger. "The first book I shopped to agents and editors?" He held up a third finger. "The first book an agent wanted?" He held up a fourth finger. "Or the first book that sold?" He held up his thumb. "Because those were all different books." He looked over at his hand, made a startled and terrified face, snatched the hand back down, and hid it under the podium.

The crown laughed and clapped.

I laughed, too.

Brenden Carter smiled at the room full of women laughing and clapping at his jokes. He took a sip of water and had a little side smile like a kid laughing at his own joke.

The crown quieted down more quickly.

"So yeah," he said. "I wrote five full books before I sold one. Five. Full. Books."

The crowd murmured to itself, like, Five books?

"You're all writers," he said and gestured to us. "You know what that means..."

The Knee-boots and Turtlenecks nodded like, Yes, we do.

But let's be honest. We didn't know. More than half of us were probably like me and didn't have the first clue what it was like to write one book, let alone five books. Let alone one that sold. I doubted any of those ladies (and token dudes) had sold a book. Otherwise, why were they at a *First Things First* conference? The nervous muttering in the crowd lead me to believe most of them had shifted from, Yes! We're just like that extremely successful (and handsome) writer up there, to, WTF? I'm 45. I'm wearing really expensive boots. Oh, Christ.

Brenden Carter went on, "When I won the Printz for *Moonlight Moonlight, Iguana Iguana*, interviewers asked me all the time how it felt to win for my 'first book.' I tried to explain what I just explained to you. But of course, most people, especially most non-book writers (critics are a different breed) didn't want to hear that story."

The crowd laughed again, brought back from failure and self-doubt by a jab at fake writers. Critics, ew.

"Most people didn't want to hear a five-book story. It's not sexy." He combed his fingers through his hair in a little self-deprecating nod to "sexy."

I love him.

"What's sexy is the story of a person who writes one book, sells it, receives critical praise, does a lot of readings, and wins a really lovely and flattering award. People love that story." Then slowly, almost growling, he said, "That is a bullshit story."

"Oooh," the crowd liked his rakishness.

I did, too.

"That's the story of a person who didn't have to work to achieve his dream. Who didn't have to take low-paying and thankless jobs so he'd have the mental space to write. It's the story of a person who didn't experience rejection after rejection after devastating to-hell-with-it-I'm-just-going-to-drink-all-the-gin-in-Pittsburgh-and-be-too-drunk-and-surly-to-even-get-laid rejection..."

The women in the crowd loved this so much. I loved it so much.

He wasn't smiling anymore. He wasn't sipping water. He was looking out at us wondering if his words were sinking in.

"Look," he said.

We looked.

"I'm not trying to say I suffered. Not in the global sense. But I am saying I struggled. I'm saying I worked hard for what I achieved. That's the story I wish someone had wanted to tell about me. Because that's the story that I wish someone had told me. Maybe then I wouldn't have felt so..."

He paused. Looked down at his notes. Sort of shook his head. Looked back up. "Lonely," he said.

We sighed. We wished we could go back in time and hold his hand. Reassure him.

"You're not alone!" a Knee-boot yelled. I mean, I didn't see her, but it had to have been a Knee-boot. The crowd laughed. Relieved. You're not that lonely guy anymore, Brenden Carter.

He held up his hands, smiling. Then put his hands to his heart. "I'm not," he said. "And neither are you."

We looked around at each other. Our competition. Our compatriots.

"That's why I decided to tell this story—since no one else seems to want to cover it. So you will know you're not alone. There will be times you want to quit," he said. "There will be rejections...Then there will be more rejections...Don't quit," he said and shook his head at the notion.

The clapping started.

He raised his voice. "There will be the feeling that all your ideas are garbage," he said. "But don't quit."

The clapping got louder.

He got louder. "There will be well-meaning friends who ask if you're 'still writing.' There will be times you would like to tell those friends, 'Nope, I've finally come to my senses and quit.'"

The cheering started.

He started yelling. "I'm telling you this story to tell you not to quit..."

The cheering was screaming.

"Don't quit!" He raised his fist in the air. "Never quit," he yelled.

Screaming.

"First thing first!" he yelled. "Never quit!"

We were cheering and clapping and whistling and breathless and we will never quit.

I will never quit.

He brought his fist to his mouth and smiled behind it. Embarrassed that he'd gotten so carried away? He gave the smallest bow and left the stage.

There's a chance he's sexier than Hicks.

LONELINESS IS A CANARY

I'll be honest, I didn't hear much of the speech or panel that came after Brenden Carter's talk.

I was buzzing.

I wanted to move and think and write and already be not quitting. I was like, I don't know what I'm supposed to write about. Where am I supposed to put all this energy? I'm going to have to run or scream or something.

I heard Jenn's voice, "Write about Lucca. You were obsessed with him..."

I remembered him and how talking with him gave me that same buzzing energy surging through me and I wanted to talk and think and laugh for hours.

I felt like it would be rude to start psychotically writing while people were giving talks—like some kind of deranged teen-girl-journaler cliche. But I couldn't stop running idea after idea, image, gesture, snippet of conversation, over in my mind.

Lucca was in 10th grade when we were in 9th. But he'd moved from Japan (his dad was in the military) and he hadn't had American History yet, so he was in my class.

The very first week of school, we got assigned a project together on state capitals where we drew a map of the U.S. and made little flags on tooth picks with the capital's name on one side and the state flag on the other. And it was just a...click...

I'm going to say something that is going to make me sound like a huge, arrogant, asshole, but so be it...

Lucca is the only person I've met who I didn't have to slow myself down for. If anything, talking with him sped everything up. We just talked and talked in an endless overlap of, What about this? And, what about this? He startled me all the time. When I talked with him, I startled me all the time.

He wore the same green, khaki pants everyday and sometimes when he leaned across the table, his t-shirt would lift up and I could see the edge of his plaid boxers and I had to recite the state capitals in my brain to keep from going crazy. He was white and had light brown eyes and there was a little, tiny broken blood vessel in the skin under his right eye that never went away and I wanted to touch it and ask, What happened?

Of course, he had a girlfriend within forty seconds of getting to school. And of course, she was pretty and stylish and arty (photographer) and I wanted him to love me instead.

But he didn't love me. He loved Veronica Sawyer.

One afternoon we were in the library working on the project. All day, I'd been bursting with anticipation and energy about where our conversation was going to go. But he was, like, flat. He was never, ever, flat.

We talked a lot about *stuff*, but we'd never really talked about ourselves, so I had to close my eyes and just blurt, "Is something wrong?"

He didn't even pause before he said, "My girlfriend says I'm not emotional enough."

"Oh..." I said. I didn't want to talk about his girlfriend. But I did want to talk about his emotions. So I said, "Do you think you're emotional enough?"

He thought about it for a second, twirling the tiny, tooth-picked Alaska state flag between his fingers. He shrugged, "I don't know. I guess I have a hard time being able to think about them and talk about them. Or...like I have a hard time telling the difference between them."

Don't ask me how I came up with this idea, but suddenly I just said, "What if you anthropomorphized your emotions. Like the Greeks did with the gods and goddesses."

He shook his head. "Remind me."

"Well...like in *The Odyssey*, when it says things like '...then Athena helped Odysseus kill the Cyclops...' what if they don't mean *actual* Athena? What if it's just like the spirit or emotion of what she represents (war and wisdom) that filled him? But the only way that the Greeks could write a story about being filled with the spirit of war and wisdom was to turn that emotion into a person. A goddess. Athena." Again, don't ask me where that came from. I was filled with the spirit of unrequited love. Who's the goddess of that?

Lucca looked at me sideways. "Did you make that up?"

I shrugged. "I guess I did."

He stabbed the flag into the foam board. "That's genius!"

And yes, I ate that up. Of course, I did. But at the same time, I thought, So why isn't that enough to make you want to kiss me? I mean, I know we were talking about his girlfriend, but why didn't he want to kiss me if I was a genius?

I smiled, shrugged, and said, "Maybe you could do that with your emotions."

He shook his head, "I'm not sure I could think of my emotions as gods." So humble.

I thought for a second. "What about animals?"

"Animals!" he exclaimed. He was a real exclaimer. "I love that."

He said love. "Rage is a wolf," I said.

"Happiness is a monkey," Lucca said.

"Loneliness is a canary," I said.

He laughed. "Loneliness is a canary?" he asked.

I nodded. "Yeah. It's a canary."

"You're the angel on my shoulder from now on," he said.

I don't want to be the angel on your shoulder. I want to kiss you and build an encyclopedia of inside jokes with you. I pointed at the flag in his hand and said, "Is Juneau the capital of Alaska?"

Then one day in Spanish I had this *vivid* waking dream of Lucca on a bus, sitting there, having a conversation with his imagined me, the angel on his shoulder.

What about that? What if *that's* my book?

OLD ENOUGH TO KNOW

Then it was lunch-time at *First Things First* and I was tired and overwhelmed and I needed to get the hell out of hotel conference rooms. I went down the street to the Starbucks and made I'm-going-to-order-as-soon-as-I'm-out-of-the-bathroom face to the barista. The door was locked, so I sat down on the steps outside and waited.

My heart was still pounding, my thoughts still racing. For the first time since I thought, I'll write a book, it seemed like I really might write a book. I had an idea. I had gotten an idea. I sat there, outside the bathroom, waiting, grinning like a freak, repeating to myself, "This is so much better than school. This is so much better than school."

Then a group of women—all white—probably in their 40s or 50s (definitely older than the moms, but not like older, older), all wearing the same AWYP lanyard and name tag that I had, sidled over talking loudly, effusively, and gesturing to one another (how Jenn and I probably do). Unlike how we do, *they* took cuts on me. They walked right past me, one of them knocked on the bathroom door, and when the person inside was like, "Just a second..." they stood right in front of the door, blocking me out.

I looked around to see if it was even remotely possible that they didn't see me sitting on the stairs, so obviously waiting for the bathroom. Not goddam possible.

My heart pounded and the blood flooded to my face. That's what always happens when I know that I'm going to say something to someone (instead of just writing it down) about some bullshit they're trying. I know that I might seem like the kind of person who's just says whatever, but I actually don't. Jenn says whatever. Jenn yells "penis" in the middle of the Steppenwolf theater. I get red and short of breath and want to barf. "Excuse me," I said.

They gaggled on.

"Um. Excuse me," I shoved the breath out of my lungs trying to raise my voice.

They turned their eyes on me.

"I'm in line," I said. They were cutting and they were turning my excitement to rage and...

And then they laughed. Together. As if scripted. They were probably playing hooky from their lives as housewives and mothers and thought it was extra fun to be mean to a kid.

I came *that close* to saying, "You took cuts!" but somehow, I managed to stop myself. I could just see those bitches running with it. Instead, I said, "This is the line."

"Oh, honey, you can wait," a short one with a blonde (dyed) pixie cut said and they all cackled again.

"I've *been* waiting," I said, still at least trying to give them an opportunity to be fair. The bitches were giving Mrs. Sternin a run for her money.

The tall one separated herself slightly from the group. She was wearing that expensive, pastel, flowy-knit clothing that manages to stay flowy, and not wrinkled or stretched out, even after all those hours. She smelled like roses and she could go to hell. "How old are you?" she asked.

Fuck you, how old am I? Honestly, I don't know what I would *normally* do in a situation like that. Normally, a whole group of moms doesn't act like teenage bitches. But goddamit, I finally had a book idea and these oldsters were stealing my excitement. Suddenly, Athena was with me. I looked that flowy-oldster in the eye and said, "Old enough to know where the goddam line is."

The coterie gasped. One of her group leaned around her and said, "Not old enough to remember her manners."

"I guess we're all tied for last in that department," I said, breaking eye contact with the alpha so I could step around the group and resume waiting. Athena immediately deserted me. I wanted to run away and burst out hysterically laughing or crying. Or call Jenn and freak-out, "I just told off a whole pack of moms." But I obviously couldn't run away—we call that losing. Instead, I stood there in front of them, heart pounding, stomach and legs queasy with adrenaline. Snatches of, "Kids today," and "If it was my daughter," and "The conference director," burbled behind me.

Weren't we all in this conference together? Hadn't we all just listened and cheered and screamed as Brenden Carter demanded that we never quit? It was both comforting and disheartening to know that the packs of high school bitches would likely follow their trajectory straight into being packs of oldster bitches.

WINNING

I got back from my Starbucks lunch, but all the excited energy was gone. Those oldsters stole it. How would I summon it back up?

We took our seats and Cynthia Swann-Griffin once again approached the podium. "Everyone," she said and shushed us. "I have some really exciting news."

We all looked at each other like, What's more exciting than what's already happened? Pretty easy-to-please audience, actually.

"If you'll all look in the back of your name tag pouch, you'll see a little ticket. Like a raffle ticket," CSG said.

We all looked in our name tag pouches.

We all looked back at the CSG, like, Now what?

"Go ahead and grab your ticket," she said.

We grabbed our tickets like rabbit's feet even though we didn't know what was coming.

"There's a number on the edge," she said.

CSG smiled. "Brenden Carter has very generously offered to have private meetings with a select group of you," she said

What? My failed excitement surged.

"If you have a winning ticket," she said, you can choose to meet for 10 minutes with Brenden this afternoon and pitch your current project."

We gasped. Meet with Brenden Carter?

"We've built the time into the afternoon schedule," she said.

"Enough with the suspense!" someone yelled.

I nodded my agreement. Seriously.

"Which numbers?" someone else yelled.

Seriously.

CSG smiled again. "If you have ticket with a number ending between

001 and 025," she said. "You have the opportunity for a private audience with Brenden Carter."

We all pulled the tickets to our faces and searched for our numbers. I was 017. Yes! Suck on that, line-cutting bitches. I'm in.

THIS IS GONNA BE COOL

Two hours later, I stood in line and very nonchalantly returned my ticket to my back-pocket for the millionth time. Five seconds later, I chalantly felt my back-pocket to make sure the ticket was still there. I knew it was still there. I kept checking to see if it was still there.

I felt like I was going to barf. Please don't let me be the girl who barfs. It was bad enough being the girl who was almost barfing. I bet Ripley never almost barfed. I wished the spirit of Ripley, not the spirit of sweaty-barf, was filling me. I can drive that loader...I can drive that loader...

"What are you pitching?" a guy in line behind me asked. He had short black hair, looked like he was maybe Latino, and needed to stop talking to me.

"What?" I asked, in a distracted, can-you-please-stop-talking-to-me-so-that-I-can-stress-out, way.

The guy didn't take the hint. "To Brenden Carter. Pitching?"

"What am I pitching?" I asked. And a little bit I couldn't remember. I'm gonna barf in there if I don't calm down. Inhale. Exhale. "It's a love story," I said. "Unrequited love story..." I didn't want to talk about it. Obviously.

"Hmm. Cool. Why's it unrequited?" The guy asked.

I couldn't even. "Look, I'm really nervous and I'm sorry...What's your name?"

He smiled. It was a nice smile. One of his front teeth slightly overlapped the other. Just a tiny. "Javier," he said. "What's yours?"

"Javier, can you please go back to reading..." I looked down to see the cover of his gigantic hardback book (who carries a hardback around with them?) "...*The Singularity*."

"Oh, do you know it?" he asked.

"What?" I shook my head. "No," I said.

"Oh, you said the title like you knew it," he said.

"I said the title like I can read," I said, rolling my eyes with my voice.

Javier raised his eyebrows.

"Yeah. See. That was obviously super rude of me. That's what I'm telling you. I am super nervous," I said. I pointed down at his book.

"I'm just gonna read," he said and held up his book.

I mean, not that I normally like talking to strangers, but at least I usually know how to not be a total jerk. But this was not normally. "Thank you," I said, trying to make up for it.

"You're welcome..." He left that last bit dangling.

I thought we had resolved not to talk anymore... "Oh," I said. "Elaine."

He smiled and went back to his book.

Eight and a half minutes later, the door to the pitch room opened. I expected a shining light, like in movies when the door to heaven swings open. But it was just a blushing Knee-boot.

"Thank you so much, Brenden," the Knee-boot gushed.

"Thank *you*," he said and gently guided her out the door and kept his whole attention on her and didn't seem to hurry her or even look-up to make eye-contact with the next in line—me—until the Knee-boot had cleared the zone.

He smiled and nodded at me once she was gone. "You ready?" he asked.

Oh, god. Please don't let me barf. I hoisted my bag off the floor and onto my shoulder.

"Good luck," the kid from the line said.

"Mm-hmm," I mumbled, never taking my eyes of Brenden Carter. If I break eye-contact with his shoulders, I'm gonna trip on my face.

"Come on in," Brenden Carter said as I passed by him and walked into the pitch room. He smelled glorious. Like trees and woods and non-chemical cleaners. I could imagine sitting at a campfire, his arm around me, a universe of stars filling the darkness over our heads.

Oh, god, please don't let me smell gross.

He led me to two arm chairs facing each other at a tasteful, but friendly distance. Where was the other furniture? What a weird, small, lamp-lit room for a hotel to have.

Brenden Carter glanced at the list on the table next to him. "So," he began. "Elaine Archer. What's your story?"

Don't blow it. I scratched my eye. "Um. It's the story of a 16-year-old boy, Lucca, who discovers one day that a girl in his history class is also his imaginary friend," I said.

Brenden Carter stared at me. Like in a way that made me think that maybe I hadn't actually spoken out loud. Had my nervousness made me mute? Was I hallucinating? Oh, god.

"Say that again," Brenden Carter said, and leaned a little closer.

The fear that I'd gone catatonic had dried my mouth and I had to swallow a couple times which wasn't easy with him sitting there in his t-shirt and messy hair. I took a breath. "It's about Lucca. A teenager, like a high schooler, who realizes that the girl in his history class is also his imaginary friend," I said.

"So, he's *imagining* the girl in his class?" Brenden Carter asked.

"No," I said. Oh god, this idea sucks. "It's like there are two of her. The one who really exists (they're doing a project together) and the one who shows up as his imaginary friend." I tried not to sound like I hated my own idea.

"Hmm," Brenden Carter said. "Does the girl know? The real girl?"

I shook my head. "No. In fact," I hesitated—it was embarrassing...

"In fact?" he said, leaning forward.

You smell amazing. "In fact, she has a crush on him, but he has a girlfriend," I said.

He tilted his head. "Does he know she has a crush on him?"

Something in his tone made my heart race even faster than his stardom and smell already were. I shook my head.

He sat back and took a deep breath. "And I'm guessing she doesn't know she's his imaginary friend?" Brenden Carter said.

When he said it, it sounded so far-fetched and convoluted and stupid.

"Nope," I said.

Brenden Carter looked at me. For, like, a minute. "How far along is it?" he asked.

"Not very," I said.

"Half way?" he asked.

Oh, god. Should I lie? Will he know? Does being a best-selling author make you psychic? "Actually, I haven't started it. The idea is pretty new."

"Really?" he said. "Elaine. This sounds promising"

Oh, god. "It does?"

"What are you calling it?" he asked.

I blurted before I could even think, *Loneliness Is a Canary.*

"Yes," he said. "I love it."

I remembered Lucca in his green pants and he'd loved my idea, too.

"Yes. Yep," Brenden Carter said and leaned forward again, "I don't say this to people, but Elaine..."

Say my name again.

"...Elaine, done right, this is a home-run."

"It is?" Does a home-run mean what I think it means?

"You'll have to be careful it doesn't get cutesy," he said. He was sort of looking off—imagining. Imagining my story. Brenden Carter was imagining *my* story. "You don't want it to end up an episode of *Three's Company.*

"Of what?" I asked. Why don't I know what that is?!

"Ha. Bit before your time. Bit before my time, too..." he said and raked his hand through this hair like he had on stage. "It was a show where two women and a man, Jack Tripper, all live together, but Jack has to pretend he's gay so the landlord will let him live there."

"So the *advantage* is to be gay?" I asked. Based on experiences the moms have had, that did sound far-fetched.

"Yeah. They spend most of the show running in and out of doors so that Jack doesn't get revealed. Lots of dumb jokes," Brenden Carter said.

"I don't want to write dumb jokes," I said. I want to write the story of how it felt to love Lucca and know he didn't love me.

Brenden Carter gazed off again. He started talking, almost to himself. "What's the angle? Romantic. Surreal." He nodded. "Yeah, this could work."

I sat quietly trying to a) memorize his words, b) memorize the sound of his voice, and c) not barf.

I jolted at the sound of his phone. Who was calling him?

He looked down. Annoyed? "Damn," he said. Then he looked at me, but like it took him a second to come back from wherever he'd been. "That's our time."

How had it already been ten minutes? I picked my bag back up and stood.

"Listen Elaine. I don't ever do this, but I want to help you with this book…"

Am I still hallucinating? "You do?" I asked.

"Trust me," he said, walking me back to the door. "It'll sell."

"Whoa. Sell?" I just wanted it to be a good idea. I just wanted to make sure I didn't have to go back to school. But sell?

"It obviously needs fleshing out." He looked at his phone again.

I took my cue and reached for the door's handle. "That's really helpful…" WTF is fleshing out? What am I supposed to actually do now?

Brenden Carter put his hand on my wrist. "Are you staying in the hotel?" he asked.

I looked down at his hand touching me and he must have felt my heart pounding through my pulse. I took a breath, but didn't look at him. "Yeah," I said, trying to sound like I could breathe.

His hand lingered firmly on mine, "You remind me of myself when I was starting out. I could've used a mentor."

A mentor?

"Why don't we meet tonight after the mixer and brainstorm some more?" Brenden Carter said.

I nodded. Mute.

He put his hands in his pockets. "Let me think about a good place and I'll send a note to your room. Archer, right?"

"Elaine," I whispered. "Elaine Archer."

"Nice to meet you Elaine Archer," he said, and looked at me and smiled and the edges of his blue eyes crinkled. "This is gonna be cool."

MOTHERLESS MOTHERS

You know that thing where you're in class or in the cafeteria or at a party and you're trying not to spend the whole time thinking about and looking for a particular person? You're acting all *lalala* and talking to people, but you can't stop your body from trying to sense that one person. So, you spend the whole conversation with whatever other person like, "Wait? What about your dog?"

That's what I was like at the mixer, but without anyone to talk to.

I did see that pack of oldster bitches right after the short one with the pixie saw me and pointed me out to the alpha. The alpha had changed into a different flowy, knit outfit—pale gray with a fuchsia scarf. She was wearing some kind of pale pink beaded moccasin that could never set foot on a city street. The rest of her knee-booted clique circled her and stared over at me. They flanked her like she was the Queen Alien and they her acid-spewing offspring.

We gazed at each other. They nuke the whole planet from space, bitches.

"Hi," a voice said.

I broke eye contact with the group.

"Hi," I said and squinted at the dude, trying to place him.

"Javier," he said and pointed to himself. "We met this afternoon. In the line."

Oh, right. The dude who made me yell at him. "Hi," I said again, disappointed and wondering with my back where Brenden Carter was. Was he talking to a Knee-boot? A Turtleneck? Then I heard Mama Helen say, "Be nice." I couldn't remember if I'd told this guy my name in the pitch line or not. Given how nervous I'd been, it didn't seem likely. "I'm Elaine," I finally said.

Javier held his hand out and I took it. It was warm and slightly rough. He had a firm, but not finger-busting grip. I'm always surprised by dudes who really crush me in handshakes—I thought they reserved that for dominating other dudes.

"How was your pitch?" Javier asked.

Just mentioning it made me half scan the room for Brenden Carter, but I managed to suppress the full scan. "Um. It was pretty good," I said both distracted and not wanting to jinx things by discussing them.

"I liked his speech," Javier said.

I wished we could stop talking about him because it was making my eye twitch. "Yeah," I said. "Good story."

"Have you been to this conference before?" Javier asked. He was wearing a very soft-looking navy blue sweater with the tiniest hole in the collar.

"Nope. This is my first *First Things First* conference," I said. I couldn't tell if I was being sarcastic mean or sarcastic funny. I kinda wanted the kid to get lost so I could keep stalking Brenden Carter, but I was also kinda glad to have someone to talk to. Shockingly, neither the Knee-boots nor Turtlenecks were rushing to chat us up. "Do you ever wonder why grown-ups are so afraid of teenagers?" I asked.

Javier tilted his head and I tried not to think of Brenden Carter. "What do you mean?" he asked.

"Has any one of these adults talked to you?" I asked.

He started to reply.

I pointed at him, like, hold your horses. "Cynthia Swann-Griffin doesn't count."

He laughed. "Yeah. So, no."

"Right?" I said. "I mean, these are supposed to be writers for *young people*. We are young people. You think we'd be a valuable resource."

"People clamoring to ask us questions," Javier said.

"Middle-aged white, women clamoring," I said.

"Ha. They *are* almost all middle-aged white, women," he said, glancing around.

"Sure, it's not like I've introduced myself either, but there are clearly middle-aged women here who have been to these things before. Many times before. Didn't their mothers teach them it's polite to make the new-comers feel welcome?" I asked.

"Maybe they don't have mothers," Javier said. For one-tenth of a second I thought he might be serious. Then he smirked and his eyes crinkled.

I clutched my heart in mock concern. "A whole conference of motherless daughters," I said.

"Writing for young people," he said. And shook his head like it was a shame.

"For their own lost, motherless childhoods," I said. "Well, when you put that way, it's no wonder."

"I'm going to go get another non-alcholic beverage," Javier said and nodded back toward the bar like, You wanna come?

Just as I looked over, Brenden Carter looked up from the conversation he was having at the bar and we made eye contact. My whole being clenched in fear and longing. Brenden Carter smiled the tiniest. "Actually," I said. "I should go back to my room, I think."

"Oh, okay," Javier said. "I'll see if I can get any answers out of these motherless daughters."

"Good idea," I said and lurched off.

IT'S JUST TIME MANAGEMENT

It was almost 10PM and time for the chat with the moms. I thought for 1/100th of a second about mentioning Brenden Carter, but a) I was worried to jinx it, b) I was worried that something in my voice would fly them back to town to camp out in the queen bed next to mine, and c) there was something about it that I just wanted for myself. To have a *real* author, an inspiring and successful author, tell me, "It's a home run" and "It'll sell." There was something small and secret that I wanted to keep.

So, I didn't tell them. I mentioned the Knee-boots vs. the Turtlenecks, the spilled coffee, the panel on querying agents (that I didn't really hear because I was in fantasy land coming up with a "really interesting premise"), how no one talked to me at the mixer, and how you have to write a "shitty first draft." Then I said, "Don't blame me for saying 'shitty.' Blame that woman who gave the talk entitled, 'Every First Draft Is a Shitty Draft.'"

When I'd gotten back to my room before dinner, there was already a note under my door that said, "Meet at the rooftop bar at 10:30? -BC," So I was talking to the moms and trying not to be all, OMG, I have to get off the phone because I'm supposed to be meeting best-selling author, Brenden Carter, in eight minutes at the roof bar and I still have to brush my teeth.

Lying to your parents is funny. I think most parents, the moms included, would consider it a moral failing. A breech. A disappointment. But honestly, in this case, it was a simple scheduling issue. I had to meet Brenden Carter in seven minutes. And what could I say? "It's not like *that*, moms. He's going to talk to me about my book because we didn't have time to talk during the pitch and he's super busy the rest of the conference and then going on tour (yes, like a rock-star, but it's not like *that*). And yes, okay, he touched my wrist and I found it thrilling in ways that are obviously sexual, but it was a tangent and nothing I could control or that he intended. It's just so not the point of why I'm going out after our agreed upon curfew (to a bar 😶). I'm going out for my *writing*." There was no good way to cover all that ground (especially not with Mama Helen and her gift of 1,000 questions) in the four minutes before I had to meet him.

Instead, efficiency demanded that I say, "Night. I love you. Yes, I'll call you in the morning before I go downstairs."

I hung up the phone guilt free because it wasn't a betrayal, I just didn't have all the time in the world to argue with those people. It was my career we were talking about. It was never having to set foot in D.B. High ever again, except maybe to give a public reading as a famous, honorary alum.

THE LEAST LONELY PEOPLE

I didn't change my clothes, because obviously. I did brush my teeth because who wants to talk books with someone who has dragon breath? I double-checked to make sure I had my key. I checked my phone (10:29). I tried not to sprint to the elevator.

When it opened on my floor, he was in there. Alone. And remember how it felt when he touched my wrist? Oh god, times a million.

Can I pretend I didn't see him? Can I duck?

Then the smell again—wood and fire and health and spicy. "Elaine," he said and stepped to the side to make room—there was plenty of room.

Still. I wanted to run away. Or barf. Always with the barf. Get it together.

How does the body decide to do things when the mind is screaming the opposite? My legs moved me forward. I never told them to do that.

He was wearing a sweater (thick gray cable knit with a zipper) that he wasn't wearing at the mixer. I love that sweater.

We got to the bar and Brenden Carter led us over to some patio couches away from the elevator, but within sight of the bartender. He waved at her—20-something, attractive, hip, white, nose-stud. She came over and Brenden Carter said, "You still have Stella on?"

"We do," the bartender said. She didn't look at me. She stood with her hand on her hip in a way that thrust her boobs out just enough. Does she decide this posture on a case by case basis or is it just natural at this point? Like her brain doesn't have to be involved, her body just does it. And does her body take a different stance when the guy doesn't have blue eyes, dimples, ruffled brown hair, and a cable knit sweater?

"Two Stellas, then," Brenden Carter said.

The girl glanced at me. I tried to smile in a way that said, A Stella sounds delicious. Not, I'm obviously no where near 21. She sauntered away. I watched her. Brenden Carter did not. Seriously, how do some girls learn to walk like that? Do they practice? Is it just a natural consequence or byproduct of a confident relationship with your sexuality? Jenn walks like that. Is it an indication you're willing to trade offspring for food?

"You enjoying the conference?" Brenden Carter asked.

What? "The conference. Yeah. It's awesome." Don't say "awesome." "It's a lot to take in. Lots of info."

"Is this your first one?" he asked.

"Yep. First things first, right?" Dork. I stopped myself, somehow, blessedly, from blathering the whole story of how I came to be there...

"You seem young to be a novelist. How old are you?" Brenden Carter leaned back and spread his arms over the back of his chair. A fresh wave of his scent cascaded over me. Can a person's smell make you high?

"I'm sixteen," I said. "But I'll be seventeen in January." I had a sudden flash of his hand on my wrist.

The bartender sauntered toward us with our beers. "We won't tell her," Brenden Carter whispered and winked.

My heart pulsed in my chest. No, we won't tell her.

She set coasters and beers in front of us. "Anything else?" she asked.

"This is perfect," Brenden Carter said.

"Open a tab?" she asked.

"Put it on my room?" he asked.

She nodded.

I felt like they were flirting or saying something other than they were saying, but I didn't know what it was.

Brenden Carter held up his beer. I held up mine. "Cheers, Elaine," he said and we lightly touched glasses. "To the idea," he added. It was warm on the patio, but I shivered.

We both took sips. He looked into my eyes as we drank. Yep, there's the heart in the chest. There's the desire to run away. There's the heat on my wrist. I set my glass on the coaster. It had a picture of one of those voluptuous women they painted on the side of WWII bombers. Mine was a redhead, her hand on her hip, just like the bartender.

Brenden Carter took another, longer drink and set his glass down. His was a brunette. I'm a brunette. "Let's talk," he said. "Tell me again, how far into it are you?"

I think I need to tell him the truth. How can he help me if I lie to him?

"I'm kind of embarrassed," I said. "But I just go the idea today." I didn't add, Because your talk was so inspirational that I fell into a memory wormhole straight to the moment of my idea.

"Really?" he said and took another drink.

I took another drink, too. It wasn't that disgusting.

"Have you talked with anyone else about it? Here? At home?" he asked.

"No. God. I haven't had time," I said.

He reached out and covered my hand with his. "Don't," he said and squeezed.

My heart pulsed in my temples. "Okay," I said.

"You have to keep a new idea close," he said, his hand still gripping mine.

"Close," I repeated, barely able to speak, barely able to breathe.

He looked into my eyes again. "This is the most delicate moment with a new idea—when you're just starting to glimpse its outline, its potential. If you talk too much about it, to too many people, you ruin it. Understand?" He pulled his hand away and took another drink.

I was relieved and devastated. I took another drink, too.

"Have you written any of it? Notes? An email to yourself? A writing buddy?"

A writing buddy, funny. I shook my head. "No," I said. "I've just been, like, thinking about it. Kind of, I don't know how to describe it..." When I used to sit next to Lucca in class, (trying to see him from the corner of my eye), I imagined him on a bus, sitting next to his imaginary me, asking for advice. "I guess it's just like imagining it. Like I can almost see it?" I said. It was hard to explain.

"You're living in the story," Brenden Carter said. His voice was so confident, so nonchalant. Like "living in the story" is a real thing that real people do. That I am doing.

"Yeah," I said. "That's how it feels. Like I'm living in it. Or dreaming it. Only it's almost someone..."

"...Someone else's dream," Brenden Carter finished my sentence. He smiled. His eyes changed from bright to dark blue.

"Yes," I said. "Like that." It was so weird and wonderful to talk to someone about whatever you call the thing we were talking about. Someone who knew what I meant. Who didn't think it was crazy.

"Talking with another writer feels pretty great, doesn't it?" He drank his beer.

I drank mine. Somehow it was almost gone. "It's amazing," I said. "I don't know any other writers..." Wait, he said, "Other writers." Does that mean I'm a writer?

"Being a writer day-to-day can be pretty lonely. But when you meet someone who knows what you're talking about and how it feels—in those moments," he said. "I think writers are the least lonely people."

The least lonely people.

Then he waved at the bartender and I was like, Oh no. Are we done? But she took down two more glasses and started to fill them. Oh shit. I hurried to finish. I took a deep breath and looked up into the sky. Of course, it was that perfect dark blue that it turns right before it turns black. Of course, it was the same color as Brenden Carter's eyes. Remember the whole night, I told myself.

"Okay," Brenden Carter said, his voice all business, like a teacher. "Let's talk specifics."

"Okay," I said and nodded.

The bartender brought the beers, but Brenden Carter didn't even look up.

"Thanks," I said as she took my empty glass and replaced it with a full one. I was definitely feeling buzzed. It was warm and fuzzy and wonderful. I am a writer.

Brenden Carter picked up his glass. I assumed we were going to toast again, but he took a big drink, set it back down, and said, "Walk me through it. Where'd the idea come from? Tell me every detail."

I remembered standing in the library with Lucca. How badly I wished that he would love me. I'd never met anyone like him. Never talked to anyone like him. Never met anyone who understood exactly what I was saying. A tiny part of me didn't want to share that story, wanted to keep it a secret moment, a memory that lived in me. But there on the roof, the air smelled crisp and fresh. The city was miles away. Lucca and the library were miles and years away. I could still feel Brenden Carter's hand on my hand and on my wrist, and *he* knew exactly what I was saying. *He* wanted me to say more. Lucca was gone. Moved away. "The guy in the story," I began. "That was a real guy." I hesitated.

"And the girl in the story is you," Brenden Carter said, gently.

I looked up at him. "The girl is me," I said. I told him the story. The project. The library. The Greek gods. The way Lucca used staples to sew his pants and there were forty-two of them. I told him rage is a wolf. Loneliness is a canary.

"I love that so much," Brenden Carter said.

I tried to smile. I couldn't smile. My face was frozen. I couldn't look away. "He had a girlfriend," I said.

Brenden Carter nodded.

"And when he said to me, 'You're the angel on my shoulder from now on,' I just started having these daydreams...you know, like he was talking to me, asking me for advice..."

"Like an imaginary friend?" Brenden Carter asked.

"Exactly. It sounds crazy," I said. Describing it sounded crazy.

He held his chalice of beer in his hands and slowly turned it? "Your friends think it was crazy?" he asked.

"Oh god. I never told *anyone* about that." Jenn would've thought it was *crazy*.

He finished his beer in one long drink. I took another sip of mine. He leaned forward. He put his hand on my knee and every edge of my body dissolved. "Listen to me," he said, leaning in. His eyes were almost navy. The sky was almost navy. "This isn't crazy. This is being a writer."

"Oh," I whispered. "Okay." The first star appeared in the sky.

He leaned in farther. His eyes were just so blue. His breath was warm and sweet and beery and my heart was everywhere and I had no edges and he kissed me. My whole body felt it. His mouth opened. My mouth opened. His hand squeezed my thigh. I gasped. I wanted to grab him. I wanted him closer. Oh my god, closer.

He broke away from the kiss and slid his hand up my leg to my hip. "You're amazing, Elaine."

I could only stare.

"I could kiss you forever," he said.

Yes.

Instead, he sat back.

My edges returned.

He laughed and shook his head. "But kissing you is not helpful to you or your story."

Fuck that story. "That's true," I said.

"You want another beer?" he asked.

My glass was still about half full. I shook my head. "No," I said. "No, thank you."

He nodded, looked over at the bartender, and raised one finger. She nodded. Oh god, the bartender. She had to see the kiss. My face burned.

She brought his beer. She leaned down to take his empty glass. I swear her v-neck was lower than it had been. "Enjoy," she said to him. He couldn't help but look.

"All right, one thing," he said. "We have to get rid of that 'rage is a wolf' and 'loneliness is a canary' bit?"

Wait? What? "We do?" I asked.

He obviously heard the worry in my voice. "Listen," he said. "I *love* that. But it's too out there for most people. They won't get it. We can't sell that."

"Oh. Yeah. I guess I see what you're saying," I said. I guess there's a difference between what a person wants to write and what will get published.

"We can think of another way for her to become his imaginary friend. One that's a little easier for a reader to follow."

I nodded.

"And you're going to want to publish using your initials. You know, so boys will read you," he said.

Ew. "That's weird," I said. Not only do women have to trade our fertility so men won't kill us, but we can't use our own names if we want dudes to read our books? The lights of the city glowed in the distance. What a fucking world.

He shrugged, "It's just business," he said.

I guess.

"So where do you do your writing?" Brenden asked.

There was no way I was telling him that all I'd written was one essay for my friend, "There's a pretty cool coffeeshop in my neighborhood... "

"I write in a coffeeshop, too!" he said.

We are the same. "Which one?" My heart was only minimally pounding. I still felt his lips and hands and god...kiss me again. But he was right. That was not the important thing. The book is the important thing.

"Almost exclusively at the Jabberwocky in Wicker Park. You know it?"

I shook my head.

"That coffeeshop with the DeLorean..." he said.

I shook my head again.

"You don't know the coffeeshop or you don't know what a DeLorean is?"

"Both?" I said.

"You've never seen *Back to the Future?*" he asked.

"Umm..." I said and shook my head.

"You kids these days," he said and laughed.

Don't think I'm a kid. Don't think I'm a kid.

He laughed. "It's fine. When I get back from my trip, we'll watch it."

"Together?" Don't sound so desperate.

"Of course, together," he said. "You didn't think this was the last you were going to see of me, did you?"

And then his phone rang.

"Sorry," he said, "Hold on..." He looked at it and said, "Sorry. Sorry. I gotta take this..."

"Yeah, totally," I said. I mean, seriously, who was I to have all of his attention for that long?

"Larry," he said. "Yeah. I know. Listen. I've got something," he stood up, "I'll have a proposal next week," he said and walked to the edge of the patio. He looked out onto the city.

I looked out onto the city. The city where I was born. Where I had spent all my 16 years. And just then, looking at Brenden Carter's back, still feeling his kiss on my mouth, thinking about the dream that is someone else's dream, I thought, I goddam did it. Girls like me don't drop out of school, but I did. How did I get so badass? I mean, the moms are cool, but we won't call them badass. Maybe that's the donor, too. I'm gonna write this book. I'm gonna sell it. And best-selling author Brenden Carter is gonna help me. Suck on that, too, oldster bitches.

Brenden Carter hung up his phone and walked back to the table.

We're totally making out again.

"It's getting late," he said.

I looked at my phone. It was almost midnight. Whoa. "Yeah. I should go."

He walked me to the elevator and pressed the down arrow. "I'm just going to settle up the tab," he said.

He's gonna go talk to that hot bartender...

Then Brenden Carter leaned forward, took a piece of my hair, and ran his fingers down to the end. "You're very pretty, Elaine," he said.

I looked at him. Standing in front of me. Please kiss me again.

The door opened.

KEEPING IT CLOSE

Normally, I would've texted Jenn the moment the elevator doors closed to tell her Every. Single. Thing. about Brenden Carter. But I kept hearing him say that I needed to keep my ideas close.

Plus, she'd been sorta pissed when I told her I was going to a conference and not staying at her house for the weekend.

"It's fine," she'd said. "I'll find something to do."

"Or someone," I'd said, trying to make her laugh.

"Well, text me or whatever when you're home."

"I will," I'd said.

What's funny is I hadn't thought about her being pissed at me even once all weekend.

So instead of calling her before I went to sleep, I got into bed and lay there. I am very pretty. I am a writer. I am going to sell this book.

LOOK AT ME!

I managed to convince the moms to let me take the L home from the conference. As I walked passed the park down the street from our house, I remembered these two girls I'd seen there over the summer.

The first was little Black girl, maybe six, hair in braids with small, plastic, multi-colored flower barrettes at the end of each braid. She ran over to the equipment, scampered to the top, looked down at the Latina woman digging in the dirt with her baby and screamed, "Look at me! I have to do it right!" At which point she did one of those backward knee-drops where you hook the monkey-bar behind your knees, flop backward, dangle, reach up and grab the bar with your hands, flip your legs off, hang by your hands, and drop. She executed it perfectly. When she landed, she looked right at the digging mom like, Well?

The mom said, "Did you do it right?"

The girl flung her arms in the air, screamed, "YES!" and ran away.

A few weeks later, I saw a white, tween girl with shoulder length, light brown hair, wearing black leggings, uggs, a sweater with a kitten in sunglasses, and a denim jacket walking her goldendoodle. She wandered around the edge of the park, looking at people, but not really looking at them. She talked to her dog a little. Sat down on a bench to pat the dog. Got back up. Walked around. Looked at people. Sat down on the swings.

I was watching her and I was like, Who do you remind me of? And then, duh, the Look-at-Me girl. Kitten-Sweater so obviously wanted to be looked at, too.

I remembered those two and I thought, We must all come into the world wanting people to notice us. Wanting to notice other people. Little kids who just stare and stare at people. Who scream, "Look at me!" Shameless.

That's what it is.

Shamelessness.

See me. I see you. Look at me. I want to look at you.

But then you're a tween in a kitten sweater and uggs and somehow it's gone. That's what that girl felt like to me—ashamed. She wanted to look and be looked at, but she couldn't. How did that happen?

I felt like that.

I wanted to look and be looked at. But I was like, Who am I? Where does that come from?

I wanted to go back and tell Kitten-Sweater, It's okay. Just say, Look at me.

I wanted to talk and be listened to.

I wanted to write and be read.

Brenden Carter said I'm a writer.

I *am* going to write this book. And it's okay to want people to hear my story.

THE BITCH ANNETTE

I smelled her before I saw her. Grandma Annette was in the house. The moms didn't tell me she was coming. Why didn't they tell me?

I texted Mama Helen from the foyer. "Is Annette here?"

They must have heard me come in because I got an immediate reply, "She is. We didn't tell you before you left because we didn't want to overshadow your weekend."

"How long?"

"Ten days."

"Did she get here Friday?" Please say, Yes. Please say, Yes.

"This afternoon," Mama Helen replied.

Ugh. "I'm gonna put my stuff away first," I said. What I wanted to say was, Can I please get a pass? There's nothing worse than coming home from something awesome and finding The Bitch Annette. I went to my room, flopped my bag on the bed, and texted Jenn.

Elaine: Code Bitch.

It was Sunday night, so Jenn was home. Marcie puts her foot down about Sunday nights.

> Jenn: TBA?
> Elaine: WTF?
> Jenn: Worst part is you're blood related to her.
> Elaine: I hate you.
> Jenn: 😾

I had to go into the kitchen. I was sure The Bitch Annette would say something about how long it took me to get in there no matter what. But the longer I took, the more she would go on about it. I read somewhere that after you break up with someone, it takes 3 months for every year you were together to stop thinking about them. With TBA, she gives you 5 minutes of shit for every imagined slight.

I know there's a whole, "respect your elders" thing that people like to splash around like holy water, but there's a reason I call Mama Jane's mom, The Bitch Annette. You'll see.

I slogged to the kitchen. They were sitting at the island. The Bitch Annette has that older woman spike haircut that she dyes frosty blonde. She is very thin. Like indignantly thin. It's obvious she's doing it to prove a point. "Hi, Grandma," I said as I walked in.

"Glad you could finally join us," The Bitch Annette said.

"Yeah, I just got home," I said.

I hugged the moms.

And then I hugged The Bitch Annette. She smells like powdered flowers. I could feel her feeling my body to see if I'd gained any weight. When I stepped away from the hug, she looked me up and down. I waited for it her to say it, So, those are the pants you kids are wearing. Or, Gaining a little. Or, Your mother didn't tell me she let you pierce your ears—so young. Or. Or. Or...

Mama Helen took my hand. "Glad you're home, sweetie," she said.

Mama Jane smiled weakly. Having TBA around always throws Mama Jane off her game. In addition to all the other terrible things The Bitch Annette does, her favorite terrible thing is to talk shit on the moms for their "aberrant lifestyle." Which 1st of all, obviously makes me "aberrant" in her eyes and 2nd of all, It's not a goddam lifestyle. We don't live on a golf resort. We're not vegans.

"Tell us everything," Mama Helen said.

I didn't want to tell them *anything* in front of TBA, but I was excited remembering it. Remembering Brenden Carter saying, "Trust me. It'll sell."

"It was really cool," I said.

The moms broke into huge smiles. "Tell us," they said.

"I can't believe you're not in school," The Bitch Annette said.

And that's The Bitch Annette. In a nutshell. She could've said that any time in the last 5 minutes. I'm sure she *had* said it at least 20 times to the moms since they told her (I can't believe they told her, though I don't know what else they would've done...), but she waited until I was saying something that obviously made me feel good.

"Mom, I know it's not what you..." Mama Jane began, no longer smiling.

The Bitch Annette held up her hands, "You always make your own choices," she said. The Bitch Annette is Mama Jane's mom. We knew she wasn't talking about school or my pants or ear piercing. She was talking about my moms, *choosing* to be queer.

"Go on sweetie," Mama Jane said. Mama Helen squeezed my hand.

"It was all just really interesting," I said. But I couldn't feel how it was interesting anymore. All I could feel was that I wanted to punch The Bitch Annette in her face and then I wanted to cry.

The moms knew. "Did you meet anyone nice?" Mama Helen asked.

"Yeah, there were some really nice people there," I said. I thought about Cynthia Swann-Griffin. I thought about that dude in the pitch line and the mixer—what was his name? And I thought about Brenden Carter. "Trust me. It'll sell." I couldn't help myself. "There was this one guy...This author...One of the presenters...He said my idea is really good."

They smiled again, but before they could ask any questions, The Bitch Annette broke in, "Well what else is he going to say? You were paying to be there, right?"

Mama Helen gripped my hand.

"Mom," Mama Jane said.

I gripped Mama Helen's hand back. I don't care what she says. I don't care what she says. I don't want to care what she says.

The Bitch Annette held up her hands again.

"How about some pizza?" Mama Helen said.

I OBVIOUSLY GOT AN A

Obviously, I wasn't going to start writing my book before Brenden Carter got back. Obviously, Mrs. Sternin loved the paper I wrote. Obviously, Jenn texted me to write her another.

> Jenn: So, Mrs. Sternin really liked that essay.
> Elaine: Nothing like praise from satan to warm the heart.
> Jenn: Yeah, well. She says that I should do another non-fiction.

I pretended that I didn't see where this was going.

> Elaine: So, what do you think you'll read?
> Jenn: 😶
> Elaine: Jenn...
> Jenn: Do not even tell me you need the whole day, everyday, to write a book.

I had to pretend a little.

> Elaine: Fine. Jesus. When's it due?
> Jenn: Well, anytime in the next month...but the sooner I get it in, the sooner I get a grade...
> Elaine: I'm guessing that means you got an A?
> Jenn: B+. You can lay-off the formatting errors next time.
> Elaine: What am I reading?
> Jenn: Do you still have Sternin's list of suggestions?

She can't even pick the fucking book?

> Elaine: It's fine. The moms and I listened to a pretty good one last summer.

Jenn: Moms approved. Like it. What's it called.
Elaine: Do you actually care?
Jenn: Nope. When you thinking?
Elaine: What's today?
Jenn: The 12th.
Elaine: No. What day of the week?
Jenn: Wednesday. Freak.
Elaine: Days of the week. So cute. So Industrial Revolution.
Jenn: Spare me.
Elaine: End of next week?

THE WORLD WITHOUT US

The reason the moms and I had listened to a book last summer is not just because we're huge nerds. Though we are. It was because of The Bitch Annette.

Last July, we drove from Chicago to Pasco, WA to move TBA from her gigantic, rambling, falling-down house in semi-rural Eastern Washington State to an assisted living community near Seattle.

Mama Jane and her sister (my Aunt Lydia who is kind of a snob, but not at all in a "your aberrant lifestyle" way) decided that since TBA would be living near Aunt Lydia (and thus Aunt Lydia would be doing the inevitable more regular visiting in which she, Lydia, would absorb her own ration of shit about *her* life) they decided that because of this, it was only fair that Mama Jane help TBA close the house and actually, physically leave.

That was all firmly decided in January of last year—like *six months* prior to our visit. Mama Jane tried to convince TBA to get packers and movers, but The Bitch Annette said she would do the packing herself because "none of those psychopaths are stepping foot into my house." Where movers = psychopaths...

And so while we were driving across country, we listened to this book

Mama Helen got from the library called *The World Without Us*. It's about what would happen to the Earth (like houses, buildings, roads, zoos, etc) if humans suddenly disappeared. Not like nuclear attack or plague or aliens. Just POOF! Gone.

For instance, because NYC was built on a swamp (a lot of major cities are...um, okay) and since tens of thousands of gallons of water are pumped out of the NYC subway system everyday, if humans were gone, the pumps would eventually break and the city would flood. Broadway would be a river again in a few years. On a positive note—aside from the barrels of radioactive waste buried deep in mountain cores (who's idea was that?) and the tiny plastic pellets they used to put in their exfoliating scrubs and antibacterial soaps that are now being found in the fatty tissues of the ocean creatures great and small and are potentially making them sterile (something to do with the effects of plastic on hormones...) other than those couple of things, the news is that if humans disappeared tomorrow, the Earth would be pretty okay. Nature would begin shredding everything human-made immediately. Dams would burst, freeways would crumble, McMansions would burn, and domesticated dogs would go feral (eventually they'd be killed out by wolves and mountain lions).

We listened to it the whole time we drove from IL to WA, taking the *long way*, "making a vacation of it," hitting the Grand Canyon (big), Bryce Canyon (pink), and Yosemite (cluster-fuck of cars and tourists) and cruising through all these landscapes. At one point I asked the moms, "Is this book plus this drive tripping either of you out?"

Not surprisingly, "Yes." Both of them.

Then, we were at this place called Fogarty Creek State Park where you can have a picnic in the woods on one side of the Oregon Coast Highway, walk along the creek under the highway, and come out on this cool little cove at the ocean. Under the bridge, in the middle of the creek, was a huge huge huge fallen tree. Like bigger than a semi. I pointed it out to the moms, "Don't you wish you could know the story of how that tree got here?"

"My goodness, it's so old," Mama Helen said.

"What if you could hook a tree up to a computer and see its memories," I said.

"Weirdo," Mama Jane said and gave me a smile and a nudge.

We walked out onto the beach and sifted through the sand for about two hours. I couldn't stop thinking about that tree. Where had it lived?

What had it seen? How did it get *here?* What if it had memories stored in it, we just didn't know how to access them?

What *would* the world be like without us?

Then we got to The Bitch Annette's. Not one thing was packed. She told Mama Jane that she was waiting to make sure Mama Jane didn't want any of the stuff that she was planning to throw away.

I have rarely seen Mama Jane furious. I have *never* seen her working at her full physical capacity. I saw *plenty* of both in the two days it took us (let's be real, mostly Mama Jane) to sort, pack, and load the truck that she also had to emergency rent because it turned out the movers = psychopaths applies not just to movers who come into your home and touch your naked belongings, but also those who just load your boxed belongings, drive them from A—> B, and unload them. Though The Bitch Annette failed to "ever make this goddam detail clear," as Mama Jane said.

That kind of thing was also *classic* The Bitch Annette.

Honestly, I think TBA made that shit up about movers being psychopaths and therefore not getting anywhere near her prized possessions. I also think she made up giving a shit if there was anything amongst those possessions that Mama Jane wanted. I think she left all that to do because she *wanted* to make Mama Jane do it. She *wanted* to make Mama Jane's life miserable. I'm sure of it.

My *only* question is whether or not she was *aware* she was doing it. Like some mean old grandmothers might consciously believe movers = psychopaths while subconsciously they want to punish their queer daughter who has refused, her whole life, to "act like a lady" by making that daughter be the mover. But those mean grandmothers aren't aware they're doing it. Whereas there are other mean old grandmothers who might know very well what they're doing and take great, sadistic joy in watching their strapping daughter do all that man's work—serving the dyke right.

So, I hadn't really thought about *The World Without Us* since the trip because the drive home wasn't very fun. Poor Mama Jane.

HOW DO YOU NOT CARE?

Since Brenden Carter and I were the same and I needed to work on Jenn's essay, I went back to Zero Drop where I'd seen those tattooed hipsters.

That girl with the Mohawk and the giant flowers, Audra, was working. I wanted to say something like, Hey, I heard you and your crew of dudes talking and you seem cool and did you give them those seltzer tattoos? But more than wanting to say anything, I didn't want to sound like an idiot.

"I'll have a coffee and a fennel bagel with cream cheese," I said.

"What kind of cream cheese?" she asked. She was wearing a short sleeve khaki shirt with tiny cacti on it.

"Just plain," I said. But I always got plain. "Actually what are my options?"

"Plain, veggie, garlic herb, honey pecan..." she made a face at the mention of that last one.

"Doesn't go with fennel," I said.

"Totally doesn't," she said.

Why is she so cool? "Garlic herb," I said.

"Cool," she said. "You want fresh tomato with that? It's good with tomato." She tapped my order into her iPad as we talked.

"No thanks," I said.

"Maybe next time," she said.

"I don't eat any of the nightshades," I said. I don't think I'd ever said that out-loud before.

"I don't eat avocado," she said, looking up from the screen. "Try that working here."

"It's an avocado heavy menu," I said.

She made a face, like, That's an understatement. But just like she'd been so obviously not sarcastic when she raised her juice to Rina, she wasn't sarcastic with me.

I was at my table about to crack into the destruction of all that humans have created, when a group of dudes walked in. And by "dudes,"

I mean "bros." You know what I mean. Fit. Preppy good looks. No acne. No braces. No sign of too many or too few nutritious meals.

My gut clenched as I awaited the clash of cultures over the register as one dude after another ordered his slice or wrap or smoothie. They mostly ignored Audra's existence as anything other than the thing that ran the ipad. She mostly ignored their existence as anything more than a preference for no sprouts.

I breathed a sigh of relief as the last bro approached the register, certain that they would *not* succeed in humiliating her. And yes, *that* was my gut-clench—somehow that group of mainstream, chiseled dudes would find a way to shame Audra in her khaki men's short-sleeve-button-up-novelty shirt with its tiny cacti and their tiny red blossoms. I knew that said more about me, or as much about me, that *that* was my worry, that I assumed the power was on the bros' side, but it wasn't an assumption from the void. It was the assumption of a former attendee of a public high school with a robust boy's athletic program. Evidently, it was also an assumption from 10,000 years of trading fertility for not getting raped.

The last bro approached, "Beautiful day," he said. "How's it treating you?" He wasn't wearing a baseball hat, but if he had been, it would've been backward.

Oh shit, *that's* the tone. The tone that says, I find you unattractive, but I'm going to speak to you like I find you attractive, but you will know I'm bullshitting and my sarcasm will shame you. I thought about the way Issac looked at her.

"I'm hitting winners. How're you?" Audra replied in a tone that said, I know what you're doing and I invite you to try it.

Back and forth they went. Back and forth. It occurred to me that Audra was taking just about the same exact tone as the bro. What would Ryan and Jetha say about that? Is mimicking her way to a tie the best that women can hope for?

Finally, he was done ordering. She was done asking for specs on his order. He was done paying. She was done giving him change and apologizing for the "abundance of dimes."

"It'll be up in no time," she said to their whole pack.

I held my breath.

He flashed her a thumbs up and she replied with the ok sign. I wished one of them had offered the hang loose because no one ever offers the hang loose. But it was life, not a book. So, I had to live with it. If I were to write the scene, *he* would lead with an ok and *she* would follow with a hang loose, complete with the wrist waggle and everything. And that would make him laugh so non-sarcastically, so appreciatively, that *she* would be immediately won over to him and his willingness to drop his guise. She would smile authentically at him revealing teeth that never wore braces, but were strong and lovely nonetheless. In my book, of course, they would fall in love.

In real life, she delivered their food and I watched them all watch her ass as she returned to the kitchen. Of course, they'd all caught the spirit of the last bro to order and they first tittered, then laughed.

She didn't flinch. She appeared not to hear them.

If I were her, I would've heard them. When I've been her, I *have* heard them. I have flinched and felt their judgements (not pretty enough, not thin enough, not girl enough) and I've agreed with them and I've hated myself.

I was capable of *acting* like I didn't care, but I always cared. And most of the shit that I did that looked like not caring, was just an attempt to seem like I didn't care. But what if you really didn't care?

I thought about all the times that The Bitch Annette had said terrible things to me. Not in the exact tone as the bros, but the Bitch Grandma version of it. Little things that added and added and added. And I gnashed my teeth because I wanted to tell her to go fuck herself. Why couldn't I? Instead, I lied to her. I created a persona that *almost* made it impossible for her to criticize me. But there's a difference between being so vigilant about a million things that you can't easily be criticized and not giving a shit if people try to judge you.

Imagine that? Imagine a short mohawk, a cactus shirt, and giant flower tattoos on the backs of unathletic legs, that are not a middle-finger to magazine examples of beauty, but just something you're interested in trying. Imagine being so *not* affected by what people see when they look at you, you don't even have to give it the finger. Imagine feeling like you don't have to trade your body and fertility for anything?

By that point, the bros were finishing up. There'd been several rounds of high fives. Drinks were spilled. Forks clattered to the ground and were left, unretrieved.

Audra walked past their table to deliver other food and the last dude to order called out, "That was just spectacular!"

And she, still walking, said, "I'll give your compliments to the chef."

He called after her, "Thanks! You're the best!" And then, slightly quieter, perhaps meant to be heard, perhaps meant to be heard only by the bros, he added, "I love you."

That brought the table down. They couldn't believe it. They burst into laughter. Were still laughing when she passed the table again and one of the bros said, "Classic. Classic."

Still, Audra did not respond.

I was like, Fuck these guys. I don't give a rat's ass if she truly doesn't care what they think. I wanted to put a chair across that bro's back.

The bros began noisily and smirkily rising from the table. They knew they'd won.

Oh god. There she went again to deliver another order and she had to pass them and shimmy to get by.

I wanted to barf. And I wanted to do or say or even think *one thing* that might have deflated these guys even a little.

They were three steps from the table and three steps from the door when she appeared in front of them and said, "I'm gonna have you boys bus your table." She pointed to the tub in the corner with the arm holding two plates.

And they stopped. Automatically. At the absolute you-will-fucking-do-this-ness of her voice. Their shoulders dropped. They turned and did their chores.

The bros left and I wanted to leap from my table and run to her, standing back at the register, rolling silverware into paper napkins, not giving a shit what they thought. I wanted to grab her khaki lapels and ask, "Jesus Christ! How did you do that? How did you not care what they think?" Her feathered earrings fluttered in the hot wind of the café's ovens and I wanted to ask her if she had been roiling inside or if she was as calm as she seemed. I'd been roiling. Was still roiling. I wanted to say, "My god! When they laughed? But then you caught them, 'I'm gonna have you have you bus your table.'" How?

THE AUTHORITY HERE

The *other* best thing about Ripley's "They can bill me" scene is that it's not just an argument between her and Corporate Prick Burke where she nails a sweet zinger.

After the aliens have shredded half of everybody, all the surviving Marines, plus CPB, plus Ripley, are trying to decide what to do. Vasquez wants to nerve gas the nest. Hicks likes Vasquez' idea, but isn't sure it'll work. Hudson just wants to go home. Then Ripley says, "I say we take off and nuke the entire site from orbit...It's the only way to be sure."

And CPB chimes in and is like, "Hold on...This installation has a substantial dollar value attached to it."

What's awesome isn't just "...they can bill me." It's that CPB is arguing with her as someone he has to convince. She's the consultant and CPB has totally been in-charge of her the whole time. He's the one who told her she'd been asleep and adrift for 57 years. He's the one who told her her daughter was dead. Remember, he's the one who shamed her for working on the docks since her pilot's license got revoked. He's all, Look at my sweatervest, your job sux. Then he's like, If you go down to the planet with us, I'll get your old job back. So, he'd totally been the boss of her. But now he's like, "There's a substantial dollar value attached..." And she's like, I work on the docks, DGAF.

CPB tries to be like, I cannot authorize that kind of action. I'm sorry...

And cold as ice, Ripley says, "Well I believe Corporal Hicks has authority here...This operation is under military jurisdiction...Am I right, Corporal?"

Hicks looks down and makes a face, like, Oh, Christ, she's right. I *am* in charge.

CPB goes *back* to arguing with Ripley. He's like, *That* dude can't decide. *That dude's* just a grunt. But it's too late. Ripley wins. She's the boss now.

Hicks gets on his little headset, calls for evacuation, and says, "I say we take off, nuke the site from orbit. It's the only way to be sure."

And he and Ripley look at each other like, I feel you.

THE CARPETBAGGER'S HOUSE

Jenn's parents...well, the Cartwright family...well, the Cartwright males...(sorry Jenn/congrats Geoff and Philip) have a house on Torch Lake in northern Michigan. Actually, they have three houses. So, like a mini Cartwright compound. There's the 1st house that has a downstairs (kitchen, bathroom, couches, fireplace, books, small bedroom off the kitchen) and a lofted upstairs with dorm-style beds. It's wood and stone and was built by the first Cartwright to come to the Midwest from New York.

You know that term "carpetbagger" that they use for the shit-birds who went from the North to the South after the Civil War and did pretty much whatever the fuck they wanted down there to both the Blacks and the whites? Well, the first Cartwright was an East to Midwest Carpetbagger. Or so Jenn says.

The little house is the Carpetbagger's House (as Jenn and I call it) and that's where she and I prefer to stay when we visit.

Jenn's parents and brothers stay in the 3rd house. Jenn's dad and his brother, Dick (seriously, how is the name Richard not extinct?) built it. I mean, they had it built. Those dudes can't build.

The main hall is covered with big, sepia portraits of Native Americans. You know the ones—proud, stoic, wrinkled faces. Giant feather headdresses and bone chest shields. Women with long braids and necklaces...

At the end of the hallway is the great room. It's like a giant log cabin made with trees as big as the one from Fogarty Creek. Like hundreds of years old. I don't even know where Paul and Dick got them. Probably hired some dude to secretly chop Redwoods.

Bridging the gap between the main hall and the great room is, I kid you not, a buffalo head. It's like, Here, you have the dead Indians. And here you have the dead livelihood of the Indians. And if you'll follow me through these doors, you'll see dead First Trees.

The great room itself is packed from baseboard to primordial roof-beam with dead animals. Probably arranged counterclockwise around the room from most to least endangered.

Again, I am not kidding, there's an entire, beautiful rhino next to the wall of windows that overlooks the lake. He gazes wistfully into the room, his back turned from the water, as if to say, That shit ain't my habitat.

When I look at the black bear, brown bear, cougar, cougar, coyote, ptarmigan, raccoon, beaver, regular deer, some deer with funky horns, and owl after owl after owl, plus a fucking lion, I'm like, This place ain't it either, dude.

The house is a metaphor for the rape of the land.

The house is a metaphor for what happened when agriculture was invented and everything changed.

Jenn and I avoid the 3rd house as much as possible, except that's where the food is and the Cartwrights expect us for dinner every night.

The 2nd house was built in the 20s and it's where the grandparents stay. It smells like grandparents. We never go in there.

Maybe I'm a hypocrite for even going to Torch at all. But it was fun to be with Jenn. I went because Jenn went.

So, when she asked if I was still going to Torch over fall weekend, I was like, "Hell yes. Let us view the atrocities anew."

Plus, Brenden Carter was still on tour.

We were back in the Carpetbagger's House after dinner. I was getting the fire in the bedroom going (the house has no electric heat), and Jenn was on the bed, loading the bowl.

"Where's the rocks?" I asked, after the fire was blazing.

Jenn took a hit, held it in, and nodded to the cupboard near the window.

I pulled four big, brick-like stones from the bottom shelf and put them in the fire. Then I climbed under the covers with Jenn and she handed me the pipe. I took a big, fat, earthy hit. We pretty much only smoke weed when we were at Torch. No safe place to do it at home.

"God I love hot-rocking," Jenn said as she exhaled. She was wearing a dark brown sweater that looked like a buffalo hide.

I nodded, holding my breath.

Don't worry, hot-rocking isn't smoking pot laced with PCP. It's where you heat rocks in a fire, wrap them in flannel when they're scalding hot, and then stick them in bed down by your feet to keep toasty.

If you're smart, you put four in the fire and when those get hot, you put two in bed, and leave the other two where they are. When the first two get cold, you trade them for the ones from the fire and put the cold ones back. Hot rock rotation.

"You miss school yet?" Jenn asked after she exhaled another hit?

I shook my head. "Cached," I said, handing the pipe back and holding the smoke in my lungs.

Once, last year, when Jenn's parents were out of town and we were smoking in her room, I tried to see if I could hold my breath so long I passed out. At first, it was really hard and I felt like my chest was going to rip open and I was, like, on the verge of panic. But I just said to myself, Keep holding. Keep holding. Yes, I'm pretty sure I was already high. And then I felt totally calm. It felt like some force was actually *helping* me hold my breath—like my lungs felt like they were made of wood and didn't even want to breathe, but just wanted to keep being my solid core, holding me up from inside. I sat and sat while Jenn texted with who knows.

Suddenly, on the very far periphery of my vision, on both sides, was like, a line of total darkness. The edges of curtains of nothing. I kept holding and holding and the edges started to quiver and then rushed toward each other from both sides, mirrored waves, crashing toward each other. Just before they collided in front of me (and I'm sure, just before I passed out) I gulped in a giant pulse of air. Zoom! The black tide raced away.

Maybe I could use that as a scene in my book. The book that Brenden Carter thinks is a home run.

"Not at all?" Jenn asked.

"Huh?" I asked, still dreaming of that black tide. The curtains of nothing.

Jenn patted the bed, "Come back to the boat, sister."

"What was your question?" I asked. She handed the pipe back to me, but I shook my head. I'd had plenty.

"Do you really not miss school at all?"

Hmm, how to put this, "Fuck no."

"Wow. Sure about that?"

"You know, it's like we've only been given two options," I said and sat cross-legged on the boat. "On the one hand," I said and held out my right hand, "We do all the shit we're supposed to do. We go to a good college. We're a success. In all the normal ways. And even if, like, you and I aren't Sternin zombies, we're still doing a version of what we're supposed to be doing. And it's like, a version that's not going to change a single thing about the world..."

"Pot makes you super philosophical," Jenn said. She wasn't wrong.

"Then there's the 'be the change' option," I said and held out my left hand. "And you know I'm not going to sew teddy bears for the homeless or invent a robot that eats carbon and shits honeybees."

Jenn snorted at that. It was a pretty good line, I'll admit. Probably cause of being a writer.

I shrugged and went on, "I'm mean Jesus Christ, can't there be a third option?" I held my two hands in front of me and then dropped them dramatically. "I mean, *something* for girls who *aren't* interested in STEM?"

"I'm so goddam sick of STEM," Jenn said.

"I'm so sick of STEM," I said. "And I'm not saying I think I'm going to change the world by leaving school..." I told her that I just wanted to be like Ripley—I just want to be able to show up somewhere and say, "I can drive that loader..." I *almost* told her about Brenden Carter. Sometimes pot makes me blab things.

But then Jenn said, "Well, here's hoping you don't have to repeat next year, cause for sure nothing Sternin has to say is gonna change anything." She took another hit and handed me the pipe.

"Seriously," I said. But what I was thinking was, I am pretty. I am a writer. And Brenden Carter is going to show me how to write my novel and I am going to sell it. And whether or not *that* changes anything, I will not be back at DB High next year.

ECO-TERRORISM

Later that night, after we'd docked the boat and were raiding the kitchen of the Carpetbagger's House, Jenn said, "Just don't mention you're not in school."

I pulled some chicken out of the fridge and was like, "What am I supposed to say I do all day?"

"No one's even going to ask," Jenn said. She was having leftover lasagna.

Jenn had these Torch Lake "friends" from when she was growing up and she wanted us to go to a party while we were there. I don't like going to parties, but Jenn was like, I *never* see them. Please just come.

I sat down with her at the twenty-person table that sat in front of a huge wall of windows. "What am I supposed to talk about?"

She shrugged. "What do you usually talk about?"

Here's what I hate parties. Chit-chat. I have no idea what to talk about. And I *especially* hate the whole will-we-or-won't-we hook-up vibe. "Well, I usually mention what I do all goddam day," I said. Which may or not be true, but still, what the fuck?

"Don't get testy," Jenn said. "You sound judgmental when you say you don't go to school."

What?! "How do I sound judgmental?"

You're just like, "Yeah, I don't go to school. That's for brainwashed, conformist, world-destroying, eco-terrorists..."

"Eco-terrorists?" I asked.

"That's what you think, right?" Jenn asked.

I was like, Are we still talking about the party? "I've never said anything like that." Was that her takeaway from our conversation on the boat?

"But that's what you think," she said and ate a bite of her lasagna.

What I thought was, I'd never think "eco-terrorist" because eco-terrorists are the ones who blow up whale ships and free animals from cosmetics testing labs to call attention to the atrocities done to the environment. They're not the ones injecting chemicals into the Earth that set tap-water on fire. Those aren't eco-terrorists. Those are just people. Okay, so maybe that was what I thought. What was I supposed to think instead of thinking that? "Whatever, I'll just talk about the books I read for your homework."

"See. So easy," Jenn said and went for a second helping.

I ate my chicken, but I didn't taste it. Yeah, I was judgmental. Cause why wouldn't I be? I didn't say it to Jenn, but I was thinking, The world is fucking dying and I love the moms, but what have our parents, our grandparents, our great-great grandparents given us? A dying world. And you know where it starts? School. (Well, it probably starts at home before that...) But as I said on the boat, school gives you the idea that your life will be a success if you just follow the milestones. You get on the conveyor belt and glide into the future. Do all the things you're supposed to do and then you can have all the money, status, boyfriends, girlfriends, outfits, television channels, cars, houses and smartphones that make life great. But that's bullshit. *That's* what's killing the Earth. No one talks about that, though. And no one talks about an alternative. No one talks about jumping off the conveyor belt and finding a way to live your life that doesn't require you to sell your fertility and kill everything.

DO SOMETHING. FUCK!

The part in *Aliens* that leads to Ripley being like, We gotta nuke this place from orbit, is when they go looking for all the colonists. They drive this flat, rectangular, armored tank / mobile command center to where the colonists are, discover them all "cocooned" in this brown-black resin structure up against the walls, like walls made of cockroach material.

Ripley immediately understands what it is. Alien nest. She's like, Get your people out of there!

Gorman (the stupid Lieutenant who's supposedly in charge) is like, Zip it, to Ripley and, Keep going, to the Marines.

Then Ripley is like, Um, am I mistaken or are they under a giant nuclear reactor?

Gorman is like, So what? He didn't finish physics, either.

Corporate Prick Burke is like, Oh, shit, yeah, if they shoot in there, it's going to cause a nuclear explosion...

Gorman's like, Stow your weapons, Marines.

Hudson, who's always whining, says, "What are we supposed to use? Harsh language?"

Apone says, "You heard the man. Stow your weapons." Good Marine. Follows orders. Too bad he's about to die.

Ripley's like, Get them out of there.

Gorman, Zip it.

Then, BAM! Aliens attack. New POV every 3 seconds. Fire. Screaming. Alien acid blood. Guns. Gorman wanting to know, "Who's firing?!" Apone's dead. Everybody's shooting and cursing and accidentally setting each other on fire.

And here's my favorite part—Ripley's yelling and yelling at Gorman who, at this point, is like a stuttering mess and finally Ripley's like, "Do something!" Only, she's obviously talking to both him and herself cause at the moment she says it, she turns away toward the cockpit, to "Do something." But just as she's half turned, she goes, "Fuck!"

"Do something! Fuck!"

It's the "Fuck!" that makes me watch and rewatch the scene. It's so convincing that it can't be acting. Like I can't believe it's in the actual script. She's legit furious.

The thing that I hadn't thought about before is that's the moment where Ripley actually takes control. It's even before, "They can bill me," or "I believe Corporal Hicks is in charge."

Gorman doesn't do something. Ripley does. She takes over the armored car, slams it all the way to the heart of the alien nest and rescues the Marines. Then she drives it out of there. And right after she saves all their asses, CPB tries to argue her into not blowing the place to bits. It's after *she* does something that she promotes Hicks to being in charge.

But it's the "Fuck!" that's interesting. It's like Ripley doesn't want to have to do something, but she knows no one else is going to.

That was the other thing I didn't tell Jenn. Not only did I not miss school, but for the first time, I was starting to feel like maybe I was really going to do this. I had an idea. I was going to learn how to write. I was going to fucking do something. For once. I was the one in charge. Not Gorman, not CBP, not Mrs. Sternin, not even Mr. Banerjee.

KILL MARIUS

I went to the party. Within three minutes, Jenn was off with some dude. I decided to take her advice and, "Have two vodka drinks really fast and then nurse a 3rd, (but never leave it unattended!) for the rest of the night." I reminded myself not to tell anyone I didn't go to school.

It turned out that two vodka drinks (really fast), coupled with the will-we-or-won't-we thing, coupled with Brenden Carter's assurance that my book would sell, made me a little argumentative.

About 45 minutes into the party, I found myself sitting with a group of kids who were basically Sternin's Dream Team. Or rather, it was like a young Mrs. Sternin—Sternin-in-Training (only blonde, not brunette) holding court to a bunch of rapt dudes.

I have no recollection of how I'd gotten out of the previous conversation with a dude I was *never* making out with and that was veering precipitously close to an I-don't-go-to-school reveal. I have no recollection of how I'd stumbled into Sternin-in-Training's group. I was just suddenly there.

Sternin-in-Training was going *off* about this giraffe, Marius, that the Copenhagen zoo had killed. I happened to have read about that giraffe (there was a lot of time to internet while I waited for Brenden Carter).

Sternin-in-Training, literally, tossed her hair, and said, "I mean, the director of that zoo should be shot or sued or whatever. I tweeted about it. It's disgusting."

There were three white dudes sitting with her. A blonde one and two brown-haired ones.

Blonde dude said, "What happened?"

Sternin-in-Training said, "They *shot* this poor 18-month-old giraffe. In the *head*. Then they dissected him. In front of *children*. Then they *fed* him to the *lions*."

Brown-haired dude said, "Damn. Harsh."

Blonde dude said, "Why'd they do that?"

SiT said, "Because they're heartless."

Both the dudes were wearing fake sports jerseys.

Brown-haired dude, "Was Copenhagen Nazi?"

Brenden Carter's certainty, the 2.5 vodka drinks, and I interrupted. "Marius was part of an international breeding program," Brenden Carter, the vodka, and I said. "The zoo found out that he wasn't genetically novel enough to keep in the program." All their eyes on me. How did I get here? Don't set your drink down. Don't mention no school.

"Meaning?" The second brown-haired dude asked.

SiT said, "Meaning they're heartless." Obviously.

Brenden Carter, the vodka, and I said, "Meaning if any of the giraffes had been bred with him it would've weakened the stock. So they had to kill him."

First brown-haired dude said, "Sounds Nazi to me."

It did sound a little Nazi.

SiT, "But other zoos wanted him."

The dudes nodded. Other zoos wanted Marius. I couldn't figure out if SiT and I were arguing against each other or to convince the dudes.

BC, the vodka, and I said, "I read that the Copenhagen zoo couldn't find another place for him that could offer their standard of care."

SiT said, "They could've just kept him and not let him breed."

The dudes were finally skeptical. We're talking about sex, right?

"I don't think the zoo could afford to keep him," I said.

SiT thought about that for a second. The dudes looked at her. She looked at them looking at her and blurted, "Then they shouldn't have let his parents mate." Either her anger or whatever was in her red cup was making her cheeks very rosy. "They should've chosen the mates. Or they never should've let Marius be born."

The dudes were pretty sure she was right. She was pretty sure, too.

BC, the vodka, and I said, "Well then you're advocating giraffe rape? Or giraffe forced abortion?"

The way they looked at me, I guessed none of them followed the vodka's and my logic. Fair enough. But it made sense to me. If you choose the mate for someone and then *make* them mate, isn't that the same as rape? If you find out that a mother is pregnant with a baby giraffe that won't fit the breeding program, and you terminate the pregnancy, isn't that forced abortion?

SiT looked at me like I was absolutely disgusting.

"You're disgusting," one of the dudes said.

I nodded. Yeah. "See you guys later," I said.

But seriously, why was killing Marius so bad? I really wanted to know. Why was publicly dissecting him so bad? It wasn't like they did it without warning. All the kids who were there wanted to be there. It's called science. And why *not* feed him to the lions? What did they usually feed to the lions? Not tofu. Why is meat different if it used to have a name? I was 100% sure SiT and her pack of dudes were not vegans. I should get bumper stickers that say, Kill Marius, Save the Giraffe.

That's why I hate parties.

ANGEL OF UNREQUITE

I got back from Torch Lake, finished Jenn's essay (with a thesis like: turns out nature is always trying to take the Earth back from humans...), and was "immersing" myself in the publishing world. That was what they told us to do at *First Things First*, find blogs, follow agents & publishers on twitter, read about what kind of things are being sold (to whom and by whom)... "Immerse yourself and it won't feel so intimidating," Cynthia Swann-Griffin had said. So that's what I was doing while I was waiting for Brenden Carter to get home from his book tour and call me and become my boyfriend—I mean, mentor.

I clicked on my Publisher's Weekly bookmark and there on the "Right's Report" was a picture of Brenden Carter and the news that YA sensation, Brenden Carter sold a new book tentatively titled, *Angel of Unrequite*.

Wow, that was fast. Ten days ago he didn't even have an idea and now he's sold a book? I guess that's how it works when you're a famous writer. I kept reading.

"The author of several realistic teen fiction novels will try his hand at the speculative with his story of unrequited love."

That's weird. He didn't mention he was *also* writing an unrequited love story.

"The story, Carter said, will focus on 17-year-old Eleanor and her imaginary friend Luke (whose real-life counterpart is her science partner). Eleanor doesn't realize that Luke has a crush on her. And Luke doesn't realize he's become Eleanor's voice of reason."

Wait a minute.

Of the inspiration for the story, Carter said, "You know, I've been in a couple of situations where I've had really strong, well, romantic, feelings for a woman and she obviously didn't see me that way. I started thinking about that—how different people see you, and know you...somehow my brain just made the leap to—maybe Eleanor doesn't love Luke, but what if there *is* a connection...so much so that he, or rather, the imagined he, becomes her conscience. So, she's not talking intimately to the "real" Luke, but to her imagined version of him. I mean, the agony and the ecstasy, right? Also, fingers crossed, but there's some interest in making it into a movie..."

I slammed my computer closed. Fingers crossed they make a movie?!

That motherfucker. He stole my fucking story. That motherfucker stole my story. He stole my story. MY STORY. And sold it. In less than two weeks. He stole my story.

I paced the kitchen, trying to figure out how to find a that-guy-stole-my-fucking-story lawyer when it hit me...I had no way to prove it. He knew I had no way to prove it. That's what all those questions were. Had I started writing it? Did I email any thoughts to myself? And his advice—keep it to yourself for now—if you share it too soon, it'll lose it's vitality.

A red bubble of fury came up out my bowels and filled my chest. I am an idiot. I wanted to smash my head against the counter. No. I wanted to smash *his* head. And then I thought about something else from that night (not the kiss—I will *never* think about the kiss again!).

"Jabberwocky Coffee in Wicker Park," he said. "I'm there pretty much every day I'm in Chicago..."

Even though he told me he'd call me as soon as he was back from Portland, and even though he hadn't called, I was pretty goddam positive I knew where he was.

I saddled up.

Motherfucker.

GIRLS ARE STUPID

I yanked open the door of the Jabberwocky. There he was. The Asshole Brenden Carter. Talking (flirting) with some girl. He said something, the girl laughed, threw her head back, caressed her throat unconsciously (yeah, right). Fuck them.

He must have felt the shock waves of my fury because he looked up and his eyes went wide.

"You stole my story!" I yelled from the door. Normally, for me to do something like that (in a public place) I would have to psych myself up for hours. But looking at him...his stupid hair, his stupid t-shirt, his stupid sweater—his stupid I'm-a-nerd-but-I'm-a-cool-kid uniform...I was rage transformed into words. "My story," I snarled.

He leaped from his seat, crossed the room in two strides, grabbed my arm, and yanked me over by the DeLorean. "When I get back from my trip, we'll watch it." I wanted to ram his head through the windshield.

"Lower your voice," The Asshole Brenden Carter hissed.

I'm ashamed to say I did what he said. "I read about it this morning," I hissed.

He guided me farther into the DeLorean's alcove, and turned me so my back was to the car. Then he let go of my arm and put his hand on the car's roof, blocking my view of the rest of the coffeeshop. He still smelled like a mix of whatever-the-fuck he smelled like. I was sure the girl he was flirting with was staring.

"I don't know what you think you read," he started.

He's going to deny it. "You can't deny it," I said.

He considered for a second. "You told me yourself you haven't written any of it down. You have absolutely no proof," The Asshole Brenden Carter laughed. "You try writing it and I'll say that *you* got the idea from *me*."

I pictured that night. All his questions. All his interest. His hand on my wrist. His fingers on my skin. My heart pounding so hard I couldn't speak. The kiss. No. Do not think about the kiss. He was going to help me write my book. He was going to help me publish my book. He was going to fall in love with me. "You can't do this," I muttered. How could a person take another person's story?

"It's done," he said.

"I mean, you can't *do* this. It's my story." I'd told him about Lucca.

"God, girls are stupid," he said. "We both know you were never going to write that story."

"I am writing it," I said.

"No you're not," The Asshole Brenden Carter said.

How does he know?

Then he went on. "Whatever it is you think you're writing...You're a 16-year-old girl...It's not getting published. How about I thank you in the acknowledgments?"

It was a joke to him. I was a joke to him.

"Fuck you," I said.

He raised an eyebrow. "Alright, 'No,' to the acknowledgement."

I shoved his hand off the car and pushed past him. "Good luck with *my* story," I said, loud enough for the girl to hear.

THE AFRO ANGEL

I slammed The Jabberwocky's door behind me and made it two steps before the tears started. I stumbled down the street, trying not to sob. Failing. Sobbing. I couldn't see where I was going. I stumbled. Heard the traffic like a stampede. Who cares?

A tall Black girl with a halo just like Jenn's when she smote Walt Peck, came out of nowhere and said, "Come on, girl." I didn't know where she was taking me. I didn't care. She lead me into a shoe store. I smelled the leather and polish. Behind a counter, through a door, down a hall...she opened the door to a bathroom. "Go," she said and closed the door behind me.

And then I screamed. Shrieked. I have never made that sound. An animal. I fell to the floor. Screaming. Sobbing. Tears and snot and screaming. "Fuuuuuuck." I shrieked.

I laid my head on the floor, exhausted. "He stole my story. He stole my story. He stole my story," I muttered.

I failed. I was going to have to go back to school. Everyone would know I failed. They'll put his name on my story. It's not mine anymore. I told him about Lucca. Lucca. A fresh pulse of agony and fury shot through me. No. No. No. No. No.

And then it surged into my brain, "Do something! Fuck!"

Oh god.

I pushed myself up. I didn't look at my pants or the floor. I did not want to know what was down there.

I went to the sink, washed my hands, pressed water to my face, and said to the mirror, "Do something."

The girl was waiting outside—standing at a tasteful distance, but waiting. I must not have processed anything about her on the way in because she was wearing yellow eye-shadow shaped into rectangles and both hot pink blush and lipstick. She looked amazing. Like she was seriously going for it and seriously succeeding. She also had a good-sized afro—natural hair.

"Are you okay?" she asked.

"Yes," I said. "I'm going to be."

The thing about the Ripley scene is that, yeah, it's this badass moment of taking control. But it's also a moment of giving in. Like yeah, the "Fuck!" is the moment where the tables turn and now Ripley is in charge. But also, it's like Ripley is saying, "Fuck! Here we go again. I have to do this all by my goddam self." Exasperated. Exasperated with stupid Gorman. And exasperated that she has to do it all.

THE BAD BAD BAD TIME

I HATE EVERYTHING

I became a liar. Not the good kind from that book about writing, *Write or Lie—A Guide to Great Storytelling*. I'm not being cute and equating writing and lying. And it's not the supposedly harmless kind like when I didn't tell the moms that I was going to go meet The Asshole Brenden Carter on the roof and fucking make out with him in front of some girl he probably banged later that night only he wasn't making out with me because of anything other than he wanted to steal my book idea. Not that kind of lying.

Literal lies.

To the moms.

They ask me how the book is coming and I'm like, Cue smile. Cue thumbs up. Cue reams and reams of bullshit.

Am I supposed to tell them? Hey moms, remember that conference we were all so pumped about? Well, in addition to eating way more than my fair share of complimentary danishes and getting a terrible stomachache, I made out with a 27-year-old best-selling novelist who promised to walk me step-by-step through the writing of my "adorable" (his word), "innovative" (his goddam word), and "where did you come up with this idea?!" (his goddam question) book. Only instead of helping me, he stole my idea and sold it. And when I confronted him, he dragged me behind a Delorean and reminded me that a) I'm a kid, who's going to believe me over him? b) I was never going to write the book anyway, and c) "Girls are so stupid," (his line). Is that what I'm supposed to tell them? Cause I'm not. Instead, they ask, and I'm like, thumbs up, Busy busy!

Meanwhile, not only do I not know how to write a book, I don't have an idea anymore. And I don't even remember how I came up with the first one. It appeared out of nowhere. One minute, The Asshole Brenden Carter was screaming at a room full of middle-aged women (which speaking of which, let's notice that they got a man to come talk to an audience of 99.9% women, so he could do his little rock-star-cowboy-it's-so-lonely bullshit...thanks again 10,000 years of bullshit culture. Fuck him and fuck that and fuck you, AWYP...) and the next minute I had an idea for a book that was evidently a good goddam idea.

What now?

I have no idea where to go from here.

I have no idea how to find out.

And I'm not telling the goddam moms cause just look at how freaked out they got *before* the conference. I can see every time we talk that they're one step away from yoinking this deal and sending me back to J.T. Gatto's Home for the Insane.

The thing about Ripley's "Do something, fuck!" was that there was something so obviously *to do*—get off the planet—nuke it from space—be in love with Hicks (I cannot believe that I ever thought TABC was maybe sexier than Hicks). Yeah, there's like a billion mishaps between her realization that she's going to have to be in charge of this herself and actually getting off the planet, that's what makes it a movie. But at least she always has a goal. And the skills to achieve it. And a sexy sidekick.

I had a goal.

The Asshole Brenden Carter stole it.

Now all I have is lying to the moms.

WHY DOESN'T THE GIRL *EVER* DRIVE THE CAR?

I went over to Jenn's and flung myself onto her bed. I wanted to tell her what happened. Maybe. But she wouldn't turn off her goddam Taylor Swift and I was just like, "Can we *please* listen to something else?"

Jenn was doing some weird squat on a yoga mat in her room. "You love TSwift," she said and sat up to make that little goddam heart with her hands.

"Actually I don't," I said. "What are you doing?"

"Eagle pose," she said, through gritted teeth. "You *should* love her," Jenn said.

Don't tell me what I should do.

She went on. "Both writers," she grunted. "Lots in common."

I was too tired and sad and pissed to keep my opinion to myself. "Yeah," I said. "That's the exact goddam problem. She's a writer. She writes *all* her goddam songs. And every one of those songs is about how *she* doesn't do anything. The dude does it all. Who writes the song in *Our Song?*"

Jenn didn't answer. She was trying to get her knees balanced on the backs of her arms.

"The dude writes the song," I said. "They're driving in the car (of course, the dude is driving, the dude drives in every song) and she's like, We don't have a song. And the dude is like, Our song is the door slamming and us sneaking out...Fine. Cute. But why doesn't the girl in the song make up the goddam song? If TSwift writes the songs, why doesn't the girl in the song write the song?"

Jenn sat up and took a breath. "I think you might be overthinking it," she said, then leaned forward again, her toes just lifting off the ground.

I didn't even hear her. "And then what's with the songs about the nerd girl who's in love with her cool neighbor, but he's in love with the girl in short skirts? Or the *other* song where TSwift's character wears t-shirts, but the girl the dude wants wears short skirts? She makes these sad, but cool and misunderstood girls the heroines of her songs, and they never get the boyfriend. But that's nothing like TSwift in real life. In real life, *she's* the one in high heels and short skirts..." She basically makes money writing songs about girls like me.

Jenn thunked back down onto her mat. "Jesus, I'll change it," she said.

I felt the way I felt at parties. "I just don't see how you can stand this shit," I said. Every song was about some girl begging a dude to love her. Ripley *never* begged Hicks to love her. Even when she says to him, If an alien gets me, you gotta promise to kill me so I don't end up impregnated and with an alien bursting out of my chest...He just says, "If it comes to that, I'll do us both..." But she *never* begs.

Jenn looked up at me from the floor. "I can listen to it without being the same as it," she said.

NOT YOUR HABITAT

Let's talk about other terrible things...

Like extinct animals.

Like the Western Black Rhino. Like the one the Cartwrights have. The Western Black Rhino is extinct. The last black rhino mom gave birth to the last black rhino baby. Ever. Forever. Unless they do some crazy GMO shit and revive the species with a strand of DNA frisked out of a poacher's dirty craw, then the Western Black Rhino is gone forever. Why? Because fuckers want to grind their horns up like ritalin and snort them. Is it because black rhino horn cures cancer? I mean, if it cures cancer, it's still not right, but I can see where they're coming from. No. It does not cure cancer. In fact, it doesn't *do* anything. Dudes *think* it gives them boners. It doesn't (well, I think it doesn't—probably not legal or ethical to test the hypothesis). So these fucking men drive an *entire species* to extinction on the hope of a hard on.

Here's another fun fact:

In certain parts of the world, when girls are any age from like 5 months to 15 years (sometimes older...) these old women come to the school (like the nurse that came to Jenn's and my 6th grade class to tell us about our periods and how we should cut the tops off panty-hose (whatever those are) to use as underwear when we're bleeding and save our "good panties" for parties and such...), these old women come to the school, but not to talk about party panties. Instead, they clip the top of the girl's clitoris off. For those of you whose moms didn't give you a copy of *Our Bodies Ourselves* in 8th grade, the clitoris is the part of female junk with like 80,000 nerves that supposedly makes sex feel good. So, having it cut off not only hurts like a motherfucker, it also makes it so sex isn't fun for the girl. Meanwhile, dudes get to keep their 25 penis nerves. As a bonus for the girls, sometimes the old women shear off their labia (research at your peril).

What I'm saying is that we live in a world where whole species of animals are extinct so that dudes can get fake boners. And girls have their junk cut up so that they can't enjoy sex. I'll leave you to do the math on *that* equation.

And look, I know I'm just a rich, white girl from Chicago, IL USA and how can I possibly judge a cultural tradition that dates back at least long enough for old ladies to get brainwashed into mutilating their own daughters and long enough for dudes to fake boner a species to death? But fuck it, I judge it. I judge it. I judge Americans who drive Hummers or litter or call for the death of Marius' executioners but still personally eat meat and wear leather shoes. I judge them. And fuck them, I judge those rhino killers and clit cutters. I judge them. And I judge me too. Because I'll never do anything to stop it. And I judge the adults who don't teach me or expect me to do anything to change anything.

You wanna know what they do after they cut those little girls up? They give them some juice and a cookie and send them back to class.

IT MIGHT NOT BE OKAY

You know, I think I've always thought that it'll be okay. Someone will save us. I'll still go to college, get some job, and have some life. Someday we'll stop fighting each other. We'll stop chopping down the rainforests and filling the water with chemicals. Girls won't have to get home early and never walk alone. We'll change. Eventually.

But what if that's not true?

I've had those deep conversations, sitting with Jenn in a dark closet at a party because I can't bear to watch all those assholes out there pawing at each other. I've sat in the closet with the music and the dancing outside and I've whispered, "What if life has no meaning?" But it's always the TV version of myself—I mean what else are you going to talk about when you're the snotty bitch who can't handle the party?

But even those times, I've deep-down agreed with Jenn who laughs and says, "Not again!" She laughs and says, "Let's make sure we're all red and sweaty when we come out so people will think we were making out."

I never get upset and say, "Jenn, please. Please. What if life has no meaning? What if nothing matters? What if all the things we do are just distractions to pass the time until we die—to make the dying less painful? What if it's all a spiderweb that we're spinning, spinning, spinning all the time to try to cover the pit of nothing?"

What if we're burning ourselves and each other and the world and it doesn't even matter?

MAYBE IT WOULD BE BETTER

And maybe that would be better.

Maybe the world would be better off with a plague or a pandemic and all the humans that are a blight were dead...Honestly, the Earth and all the other species on it would be better off without us.

Look at us. Look what we do to each other. Look what we do to the Earth and animals. And *I'm* the one who wanted goddam Marius dead. But at least maybe that would save the giraffe, like as a species—Kill Marius, Save the Giraffe. But you know what would *really* save the giraffe? Kill Humans, Save the Earth.

I should've dropped that thesis on Mrs. Sternin.

But seriously, where's the fucking article in *The Atlantic* where someone actually tells me something useful? That's not just a, Shrug, guess that's life—we're all fucked, Want a joint?

What I want is for someone to teach me how to live.

What have I learned in school so far? Reading, writing, penmanship, rudimentary math, some social skills. How to raise my hand, suppress my desire to talk or run or roll around on the ground...I've learned how to cram for a test. Learned how to memorize shit I don't care about it and then forget it 45 minutes later.

What don't I know how to do?

Fill up my own hours.

Live without wanting all the time.

Tread lightly on the Earth.
Grow things.
Fix things.
Cook things.
Spend *one* day not consuming resources.
Think for myself.

Live in a way that I don't have to be ashamed of. That's what I wish. I wish someone would teach me to live in a way that I don't have to feel like my life is a burden on the Earth, and part of everything terrible that's happening, and responsible for all the suffering, and ashamed.

And the truth is, not even Lucca or *My Loneliness Is a Canary* was going to teach me that.

NOVEMBER

THE RIGHT VIBE

We went to Uncle Alex's. He isn't my *real* uncle (he and Mama Jane met on study abroad in college). But if a vial of sperm from California can be your dad, then your mom's best friend can certainly be your uncle.

It was his turn to host Thanksgivng. We traded back and forth—either he'd come to Chicago or we'd go to Detroit.

He's the perfect uncle. You know how your parents are always like, If you're ever at a party where you don't feel comfortable or the person you're supposed to get a ride with is drunk, call us, and we'll come get you, no questions asked. And you nod, but really, you're like, That's never happening. I would call Uncle Alex. Cause unlike parents (even reasonably cool ones like the moms), Uncle Alex wouldn't get all in my face about it. He'd be like, You okay? You gonna puke? I brought you this water. The next day he'd be like, Wanna talk about it? You'd be like, Nope. And he'd say, Okay. You want bacon? The moms, even if they said they wouldn't ask any questions would look at you with those, you-should-tell-us eyes.

He's a tall, thin, white guy with glasses and salt-and-pepper hair. He wears dark jeans and t-shirts from bands that I've *never* heard of—90s bands: Pavement, Stereolab, Modest Mouse...

He and Mama Jane have the kind of friendship where Mama Jane drove the four hours from Chicago to Detroit at 3AM when Uncle Alex's bitch girlfriend of six years broke up with him from Northern Michigan. Via text. I mean *come on.*

The next morning, when Mama Helen told me why Mama Jane was gone I was like, Yes! I did not like that girlfriend. But still, text?

The week after she moved in with him, she made him tear all the carpet out of the house because it "blocked her creative flow." I mean, it was ugly carpet, but still.

One time I went to visit him by myself. I took the train and then a cab because he was still at work and I got there early. The bitch was working (she was a painter), and I was like, "I can totally go up to my room and read until Uncle Alex gets here."

She was like, "No. It's fine." Her face made it clear it was *not* fine.

Really. I've got a book, I said. I even showed it to her. *The Things They Carried*—a good, but sad book about Vietnam and killing baby water buffaloes and a homecoming queen who becomes a green beret.

But the bitch had already swished her brush in some cleaning solution and was walking to the kitchen. "You're probably hungry. What do children eat these days?"

I was like, Bitch, you're ten years older than I am. And you don't look good with bangs. But then I was like, "Peanut butter is good." I was really hungry.

She stayed in the kitchen with me and I tried, like, ten more times to get her to leave me with my book. Uncle Alex came home about an hour later and the second he walked through the door she gave him this I-am-the-martyr-of-your-failings look and then stalked back into her studio (aka, the carpet-less living room).

"I'm sorry," I said. "I told her I was fine reading."

"Don't worry about it," Uncle Alex said, but I could tell he was worried about it. And I wanted to punch her goddam face for making him feel like he had failings because he's my mom's best friend who can make her laugh so hard she's gonna barf.

We rode bikes to the bar down the street and ate french fries. He had beer and I had root beer and he gave me a list of about 100 books, movies, and shows to check-out. Stuff that the moms wouldn't have liked. I don't mean "disapproved of," just stuff there was no sense trying to get them interested in.

So it was our year to go to his house for Thanksgiving. We got there Tuesday night and had some pizza. Usually Mama Jane and Uncle Alex stay up really late on the first night, drinking beer and telling stories about traveling together. But the house project the moms were working on was kicking their asses, so they went to bed early.

I was getting my 100th root beer from the fridge and Uncle Alex was looking out the kitchen window. There was nothing to see because he lives next to an empty lot with no lights. "Detroit needs an Empress..." he said.

Classic. Yep. Tell me how. "Detroit needs an Empress?"

"Not an Emperor," Uncle Alex said. "They're only in it for the concubines."

"Gross," I said.

"Take Cleopatra," he said. "Whatever her flaws, she made earthworms sacred and their murder punishable by death. Those are legitimate priorities."

"Whoa," I said. That's intense.

"The thing is," he said, coming back to sit at the table, "The infrastructure of the city is fucked. With the amount it would cost to go backward to meet 20th century standards, we might as well go forward and create a standard that doesn't exist yet."

"Why do you need an Empress for that?" I asked. Talking with Uncle Alex is the best. It's like an idea explosion. Maybe I get that from him. And it helped how I was feeling. Sorta.

"You've seen what having men in charge has gotten us..." he said.

I did see. And I saw those cut-up little girls crying on pushed-together school desks, nurses offering them juice and cookies to try to make up for what they'd done. "What if it's already too late?" I asked.

"How far too late?" Uncle Alex asked.

I shrugged. "All the way?"

"You mean, what if the Earth is doomed?" he asked.

I nodded. Why aren't we trying to stop it?

"What if we are past the point of no return and there's no possibility of preventing everything we know and love from dying? Possibly painfully?" Uncle Alex asked.

My eyes filled with tears and I nodded again. I hadn't cried since the shoe store bathroom.

He put his hand on my shoulder and looked into my eyes. "I hear you, kiddo," he said.

We sat like that for a while. Then I looked down at the floor. It was still splattered with paint. I guess there is something to ripping out the carpet.

"What you're doing isn't easy," he said.

I didn't know if he was talking about quitting school, writing a book, or being a kid when the Earth is doomed...I thought for about 1/1000000th of a second about telling him the whole story. But it was too embarrassing—like, for so many reasons. Uncle Alex thought I was smart. I couldn't let him know how fucking stupid I'd been. I shrugged. "But, yeah, it is hard. Not being in school." We'll let that be what he was talking about.

He nodded. "It's like running your own business. On the one hand, no boss to tell you what to do. On the other hand, no boss to tell you what to do."

Hmm...If The Asshole Brenden Carter had been my mentor and not a thief, then I *would* have had a boss. But at least I'd have been writing—not lying and scouring the internet for proof that everything is terrible so why bother. School was so much easier. It was just sit there, have someone tell you what to do, do some version of it, hate that person cause they're getting in the way of what you (supposedly) *really* want to do, hangout a little on the weekend, repeat...with plans to apply and go to college where—> more of the same. Then what? Work. Family. Buy shit. Die.

The day is long and gaping wide-open when you have to design the whole thing. No more Mr. Banerjee. No more Mr. Washington. No more Mrs. Sternin. No one to hate but yourself.

What am I gonna do? I *can't* go back there.

"What do you know about Landscape Urbanism?" Uncle Alex asked like, You want bacon?

"Nothing," I said. He never makes you feel bad for not knowing something.

"What do you know about Vertical Gardening?" he asked.

"Nothing," I said.

"Okay, well, Landscape Urbanism, in a nut-shell, is where instead of simply slapping a city over the top of nature and trying to pretend that nature was never there, you integrate your city *with* nature. For instance, instead of paving over a creek (which results in everybody's basement flooding during storms), you include it in your city design."

"Seems sensible," I said. Like *obviously* sensible.

He got up and put on a new record. We always listened to records at his house.

"What is this?" I asked.

"*Souvlaki*, Slowdive. 1993," he said.

It was the slowest, most melancholy shit you can imagine. "Are you trying to make me *more* sad with this music?" I asked.

"It's the right vibe," he said, without the slightest kidding.

Such an Uncle Alex thing to say. It made me feel safe.

"Vertical gardening..." he went on, "...is like turning buildings into farms. Think about the amount of land a farm takes up...Then, think about all the energy it takes to cool a building, shade a building, keep it oxygenated..."

I see where this is going. "So what if you used all that sunlight to grow plants..."

He put his finger on his nose. "Bingo, kiddo."

"Awesome," I said.

"Awesome," he said. "Of course, the even better thing about Detroit is that half our buildings are abandoned. You could turn the entire thing into a giant, vertical garden. And it doesn't require anyone to demolish any buildings. If I was Empress, that's what I'd do."

He wasn't kidding about Detroit. Most of its downtown buildings are abandoned. And not just like, old, stone ones from when skyscrapers were first invented. We're talking about the big silver and glass ones from, like, the 80s or something. Business buildings. Abandoned. Windows smashed. Doors wide open. You can imagine going in there and there's ferns growing out of xerox machines and raccoons living in desks, their nests made of chewed cubicle.

Detroit is a city where the apocalypse has already come and gone.

So I saw what he's saying. It was ripe to become something else. "Did you read *The World Without Us?*" I asked.

"Of course," Uncle Alex said.

Of course. "It's sounds like that. Only with people living in it."

"Yes," he said. "If I were Empress of Detroit, I would design it to function as if humans had been wiped away."

ALWAYS BEEN UNDER

That night, as I was lying in bed, listening to the silent city, I remembered something else from the trip out West to move The Bitch Annette.

The moms and I had stopped at a motel in I forget where, but something like Arizona or Utah or New Mexico. Somewhere flat and dry and in the middle of nothing.

The moms were on the porch, looking out on the parking lot and the desert, drinking wine and beer and talking about what a nightmare moving TBA was going to be (little did they know...) and I was flipping through the channels.

There was this crazy infomercial for post-revolution, post-apocalypse, post-pandemic, luxury, underground condos. Not as nice as Jenn's apartment, but certainly nicer than our house. A whole giant bunker of them. When I saw it, I was like, Jesus Christ, add that to the list of crazy shit you see in Middle of Nowhere, USA—like bumper-stickers that say, "If you can read this, you're in my shotgun range."

But lying there in already post-zombie Detroit, I wondered for a second—What if you really did live in an underground bunker? What if you grew up there? What if multiple generations had lived there and died there? What if you and your parents and your bitch grandmother had never known anything different?

What if you'd always been under?

"What if you'd always been Under?" I whispered to myself.

A flash of a tingle bolted up my spine.

I clenched my eyes closed.

"That's it," I whispered.

With my eyes still closed, I pulled the blankets down. I got out of bed and slowly made my way toward the desk by the door. I could feel a new idea. Just barely. And I didn't want to scare it away. Like when you have a dream that you're trying to remember, but you're afraid that if you look straight at it, you'll lose it. Or when you have to take the cat to the vet. And it's a cat that's not stupid, and he will scratch the ever-loving shit out of you if you even *remind* him that the vet exists (by like, accidentally getting the cat carrier out of the closet when you're looking for your gloves), let alone try to put him in the carrier to take him anywhere. So, you have to sneak-attack him. But you can't even let the word "sneak-attack" *enter* your mind or he'll sense it and go hide in that spot that you *still* have no idea where it is—after he scratches you. So, you gotta sidle up to him. No eye contact. No even thinking "vet" or "cat carrier." No even thinking "cat." You have to walk past him on the way to the kitchen thinking "cereal." And as you walk by, you think, "Aww, kitty wants cereal, too." So you pick him up. You say, "You want cereal,

Mr. Snickers?" He says, "Purr. Purr." But you *do not think* about anything but cereal all the way up until you shove his furry ass into the carrier and slam the door.

I opened my eyes a crack. There's my bag. I got my notebook, snuck back into bed, and turned on the bedside lamp.

A WRITER WRITES

As the moms and I got ready to drive back to Chicago, Uncle Alex said to me, "I don't know anything about your process, so do with this what you will, but I have a friend who's written a couple books and she says this has some good ideas in it..." He handed me a book called *A Writer Writes*, by M.A. Kiteheart. "Based on what she's told me," he said, "it's mostly in the title."

"Cool," I said. "Thanks."

He shrugged.

One of the first exercises in the book is to write a pretend letter to a friend describing your story to help you get a sense of what your story is.

Dear Lucca,

(who did you think I was going to pretend write to?)

So, I'm writing a book called *The Under*.

It takes place 250 years after an apocalypse wipes out most of the humans on Earth. It starts in a luxury underground bunker whose founders named it, wait for it...The Under.

The Under is divided into two sides (West and East) between the descendants of the wealthy founders who bank-rolled the whole thing and the scientists whose technology make it possible. The two sides have almost no contact except through the shared use of their underground river and gardens.

Westsider Merton and Eastsiders Radha and Penelope, were never supposed to meet. But a secret pain draws them together. After Merton figures out that there is still life Above, he crosses over and enlists Radha's help braving the outside world. Obviously her dorky younger sister refuses to be left behind...

The three teens quest across a wild and alien Earthscape, discovering not only the world and survivors their ancestors left behind, but also the worlds inside themselves.

Sincerely,
Elaine Archer

Now listen. I don't want you to think that I just came up with that out of nowhere. It took at least two weeks. *But*, it turns out that if you skim 400 books about writing, then go to a writing conference, then spend a month thinking about how a world-famous writer is going to help you with your novel, and then spend another month going crazy about *everything* and hating the world, you pick up a thing or two.

Also, a fuckton of spite helps.

Now I just have to think of all the things that happen to them up there. Also, I have no idea what their secret pains are. But according to *A Writer Writes*, you don't have to know everything about your characters when you're just starting. You actually find out about them *while* you're writing the first draft. Crazy.

Oh shit, this is kind of it.

UNTIL THE END OF THE WORLD

Obviously the second thing I did after I got a new book idea and characters and sort of a plot and a setting was to start fantasizing about how The Asshole Brenden Carter could go fuck himself. Which means I also started fantasizing about going down to the Jabberwocky. Just to see if he was there. Just to stare at him and be like, So, how's my novel coming, The Asshole Brenden Carter?

And then what if he wrote me into my *own* story as a creepy stalker character. If I *did* go hang-out at the Jabberwocky, I'd have to dye my hair like a purple ombre so that if TABC *did* write me into *my* novel, I would know it was me.

Then I was like, How messed up would that be if I was in the novel that's about Lucca and *his* imaginary me? And then, What if alternate universes really do exist, and imagining a thing makes it come into being? Like what if imagining myself, my real self, in a novel where Lucca imagines me as his imaginary friend makes that world exist? And what if you could watch that world on tv? Or those virtual reality goggles. Yes, please!

That's obviously what they do in my book.

They have a whole universe of virtual reality called the Comm (like Communal? Community?). *That* would definitely keep a whole society of people entertained and perfectly happy to be living in luxury, underground condos for generations.

Maybe too fun.

I can see people going bonkers if they spent too much time in there. I mean, don't you think that if you could see the alternate reality spawned by your imagination and fulfilling all your fantasies, you would just stay there all the time and eventually go crazy and all your muscles would atrophy and one day, they'd discover your ratty skeleton with the VR goggles dangling around your skeletal clavicle?

I bet an entire culture could be wiped-out by good enough VR. Cause they sure wouldn't be doing it and reproducing.

Is *that* why Radha, Penelope, and Merton decide to leave? Cause the people are going crazy from using the Comm too much?

That doesn't seem right. If everyone was going virtual reality insane, other people than just those three would notice it.

Meh, first draft, I'll figure that out later.

Writing books is easy.

DECEMBER

HOW NEAR WE TALKING?

I hadn't been at the writing thing very long, but it was becoming clear that if you let yourself run with it, useful story ideas will randomly show up...Only instead of sneaking up on the idea, you're the cat getting jammed into the carrier.

Like remember how I got the idea for *Loneliness Is a Canary* from listening to The Asshole Brenden Carter tell his stupid story about his five stupid books (which incidentally I bet was a total lie).

And if I hadn't been talking to Uncle Alex about the Empress of Detroit and, landscape urbanism, and *The World Without Us*...I never would have remembered that commercial for the luxury, underground condos and it wouldn't have occurred to me to write *The Under* and I'd probably still just be raging about TABC, lying to the moms, and wallowing in global catastrophes.

My point is, I'd gone to the bookstore looking for a book about landscape urbanism and right inside the goddam door was an entire display of books that was as though the universe had whispered in some lanyarded bookstore worker's ear that I was on my way.

- *The Landscape Urbanism Reader* (no, seriously, right there by the front door.)
- *The Modern American Metropolis*
- *Vertical Gardening for Beginners*
- *What Technology Wants*
- *Plant Intelligence and the Imaginal Realm: Into the Dreaming of Earth*
- *The Singularity Is Near*

I was like, Yes, no, yes, yes, weird, why does that look familiar?

I picked up the last one. Beast. Like 600 pages. I was like, Why do I know this? Why do I know this? Why do I know this? It's not a Jenn book, not a moms book, it's not a school book...Who's book is it?! I couldn't think of it, but I grabbed it anyway and took it and all the yes-books to the little nook I like.

Brief descriptions:

The Landscape Urbanism Reader: What Uncle Alex said.

Vertical Gardening for Beginners: What Uncle Alex said.

What Technology Wants: The tech that exists and is being created is inevitable—like a part of evolution.

The guy's thesis is like, Don't worry humans, tech will save the Earth and us before we extinct ourselves, because it's part of an ordered and inevitable evolution.

Comforting, right? Who doesn't want to think it's all part of an inevitable process? Who doesn't want to think that it's just elements → oceans → those weird carbon plumes from Planet Earth that they're like, Is this where life began? → fungus → cold blooded land life → warm blooded life → humans → technology → ???

Beautiful. Just like believing in god.

The Singularity is Near, if my understanding of the jacket-flap was correct, says we're gonna invent Artificial Intelligence that is as smart as we are (this is known as The Singularity) and once that happens, the AI will start teaching itself, quickly surpass human intelligence, invent new tech on its own, and BOOM! suddenly you have robots that are infinity times smarter than humans and then it will just, like, solve all the world's problems.

I wrote down the titles, took the L to the actually library, signed up for a card, and checked the books out. Shocking (not shocking), all were available.

When I got home, the moms were in the kitchen making dinner and saying banking words. Mama Jane, who was sautéing garlic, saw me and started laughing.

"What?" I said.

"This is a prank, right?" Mama Jane asked.

"What's a prank?" I asked.

"That pile of books. This is the 'see how hard I am working' prank," she said.

"This is research, sister," I said and set the books on the counter.

Mama Helen, chopping spinach, looked at Mama Jane who winked at her. There's a chance they'd known I'd been lying about my writing.

We ate dinner, I did the dishes, and then went to my room. I flipped through *The Singularity Is Near*, trying to remember where I'd seen it when I was like, Just how *near* are we talking? The copyright was 2005, so that was awhile ago.

I asked the internet how much progress we'd made toward creating AI that was smarter than us. Here's the first thing I read, *Should We Trust Artificial Intelligence?* The article was like, We better make sure the robots know that we're the good guys, cause they might be like, Haha, look how stupid you are. We're the boss of you. Then they treat us like a) pets (kinda positive outcome) b) zoo animals (kinda bad outcome) c) farm animals (bad outcome) d) a parasitical plague that needs to be wiped-out for the sake of the rest of the Earth's species, cause our track record ain't so good — Oh, Christ.

First I thought, Well that's scary as shit. But then I thought, Um, hello that's your villain.

According to every book and every website about writing, stories need a bad guy. Like *Aliens* has the Queen Alien, all the alien babies, Lieutenant Gorman, Corporate Prick Burke, and the Weyland-Yutani Corporation...

I hadn't yet figured out (or, let's be honest, even thought about) when Radha, Penelope, and Merton leave The Under, who's the bad guy?

Obviously, it's robots who want to kill them because they'd killed the shit out of the Earth.

Then I was immediately like, The pitch line! That dude from the pitch line who made me yell at him.

I snuggled down into bed with the giant book feeling incredibly satisfied. Bad guy here I come. Then I started reading the first chapter. It was mathmathmath, history of computers, graphs of exponential growth...And I was like, Ugh, what was that dude's name again?

I found the conference folder under a giant pile on my desk, dug through it, and found the list of the participants. What was his name? Well, there's only five dudes on the whole thing. Scan. Scan. Scan.

Javier Bernal illustratedman@gmail.com.

That's it! Blue sweater. Messy brown hair. Motherless mothers. Javier. I brought my computer to the bed and typed his name into an email.

A little voice in my head said, Don't do it. Remember The Asshole Brenden Carter?

I was like, As if I'd make that mistake again.

The voice said, I still wouldn't...

This could be the key to my villain.

The voice said, When this Javier Bernal turns out be a motherfucker like TABC, don't say I didn't warn you.

I was like, I'm not telling Javier Bernal jack-shit about my book. I'll be like, Hey gimme a *Singularity* book report. K. Thnx. Bye.

The voice said, Suit yourself.

I emailed him.

GIVEN THE SCOPE OF THE UNIVERSE

Javier emailed me back and was like, "Yeah, I'd love talk about *The Singularity*. How about Saturday?" I'd planned to meet Jenn after her SAT thing, but I didn't want to be all, That doesn't really work for me. So I said, "Sure."

Jenn was like, Ugh. You're meeting a guy to talk about a book? Is it Lucca's brother?

And I was like, Lucca doesn't have a brother...Can I come over during the week?

Javier and I met at a bookstore downtown called Weltschmerz. I got there and was like, Whoa, this is not your average amazon hell-hole. It was ceilings and marble and stained glass and wood. And books all the way to the ceiling so you'd have to climb those rolling ladders on casters to get up there. It smelled old, but not moldy. I hadn't totally wanted to take his suggestion about where to meet, but I didn't know where he lived (and I wasn't going to be all stalker and ask).

First, he suggested Myopic, but that was too goddam close to Jabberwocky. Though it did remind me I should go down and find that angel and thank her.

I felt nervous about meeting him. I mean, he didn't seem creepy when we were talking about motherless mothers, but TABC didn't seem creepy when he had his disgusting tongue in my mouth...

Don't forget not to tell him you don't go to school, it makes you sound like an eco-terrorist. I walked through the bookstore looking for him. Ugh. What if I don't remember what he looks like?

"Elaine?" a voice said.

Always with the barf feeling. I turned around. Yep, that's what he looks like. Dark hair, dark eyes, short sleeve red button-up with stripes—nerdy, but cute nerdy not scary nerdy. Probably Latino. I wondered if he was doing the run down of what I looked like, too. He had a sweater and a wool jacket hanging over the back of his co-chair.

Winter in Chicago is so fucking cold. Walking downtown in the winter is like walking through a wind-tunnel in a freezer. So, I had on about fifty layers, hat, mittens, and my big parka (my winter uniform). It took forever before I got all my stuff off, crammed it in a seat, and sat down. I flopped my bag on top of the heap of winter wear. This is so awkward. "So, thanks for meeting with me," I said.

"Sure," he said and smiled. Oh right, he had that one front tooth that slightly over lapped the other. "I always meet with people who want to talk about the end of human life as we currently know it."

Don't try to charm me with your nerdiness, dude. "Oh yeah? You get a lot of people want to talk about it?" I asked.

He nodded. "No. Never." he said.

Ha. "That's not shocking."

"Despite it being a fascinating concept," he said and pointed to his copy of the book on the table next to him. It had a bunch of tiny, colored, sticky-tabs sticking out of it. Jesus dude. That's next level nerd. I should totally do that.

"It does seem pretty fascinating." If I'm understanding it right.

"How far into it are you?" he asked.

What's with these goddam guys and how far into things I am? "Not very," I said. "I just checked it out the day I emailed you and I've been reading a different book first." Besides, why read it when I can get you to tell me it? Oh, Christ, I'm turning into Jenn.

"Oh yeah? What's the other book?" he asked.

I'm not telling you my whole life. "It's just about landscape urbanism," I said.

"I've never heard of that," he said and made a face that said, Say more.

Okay, it wasn't that I didn't want to talk to him about things. It was just that I didn't want to talk to him about things. And also, he seemed funny and nice and maybe interesting and for some reason, that made me want to cry. "It's like, Why pave over a creek when you're building a city when you can integrate the creek into your design?" I said.

"Cool," he said.

I shrugged. "I read a little bit of *The Singularity*," I said. "Obviously. Or I wouldn't've bothered to check it out..."

He either didn't notice that I'd changed the subject or was pretending not to. "And you're wondering if I've read that whole thing. Or you wouldn't've bothered to email me," he smiled and raised an eyebrow as he said it.

"I just need to make sure it's gonna be useful to me before I read 600 pages..." I said.

"So you want a book report," he said.

Is he messing with me? "A summary, yes," I said.

"The crux of it is, as technologies in computers, neurobiology, and medicine all exponentially advance, the barriers between mind and machine will fall away to the point where entire minds, histories, and perceptions of individuals will be able to be uploaded," he said it very matter-of-factly, as though it was not a) a pretty complex idea and b) goddam crazy. Also, please tell me he had rehearsed that sentence.

"So that's crazy?" I asked.

He shrugged. "No crazier than you and I sitting here talking given that in the scope of the universe, we're smaller and less temporally significant than..."

I held up my hands like, Okay, I get it. The universe and life are improbable. "But so robots, right?"

He laughed. "Absolutely," he said.

"You think our robot overlords are gonna keep any of us around?" I asked.

"I don't see why they wouldn't," he said. "We *are* an interesting species. And if our power was limited..." He made a gesture like, Then we couldn't make things any worse. Major points.

"They'd have to depopulate us," I said. "I mean, we use too many resources."

He nodded. "How do you think they'd choose who to keep?" he asked.

"Probably look at, like, your digital footprint and see what kind of person you are from that," I said.

"Ha. So, if you're one of those people who writes mean online comments about Beyonce's kid, you don't get to live?" he asked.

"Exactly." People say mean things about Beyonce's kid? What a world. "And, like, are you actually contributing anything good…"

"Who decides what's 'good'?" Javier asked.

The robots, duh. "The robots are going to be infinity smart, right? Won't they know?"

"That's awesome. So is that what your book is about?"

And there it was. I'm not telling you. "I don't really like to talk about my stories when they're still forming…" I said. Thanks for that, at least, The Asshole Brenden Carter.

Javier nodded. "That makes sense," he said. "I've met some other writers who feel that way."

"You don't feel that way?" I asked. This angle isn't going to work either, dude. No, I'll show you mine if you show me yours.

"Not really. I mean, maybe because I'm an illustrator my process is a little different?"

Wait, what? "You're an illustrator?" I asked. I may have accidentally sounded grossed out.

"Yeah," he said. "I won the 'New Comer' award at the conference." He said it in his matter-of-fact way. Not bragging. Not not-bragging. Not humble-bragging. Just fact. Where does that come from?

"Wow," I said.

"I figured you knew," he said "Weren't you at the final session?"

Right, the final session… "I missed it," I said. I missed it because I was in my hotel bed fantasizing about how The Asshole Brenden Carter was going to tell me how to write my book and then get me a zillion dollar deal and make me famous. And fall in love with me. And marry me forever. Ugh.

"Yeah, I'm pretty psyched about it," Javier said.

"What'd you win?" I asked.

"Five hundred bucks and an editor is looking at my submission…" he said.

"That seems like a big deal," I said.

"It's definitely a big deal," he said. "Be bigger if I sell it."

I was gonna sell *my* book. It was a "home run." Motherfucker. Then I realized he'd said something or asked me something. He smiled and maybe he would've been cute if he hadn't reminded me about TABC. "What?"

I didn't know if he could tell that I was freaking out. "I was just saying that it must be hard to fit school work in with writing a novel, learning about landscape urbanism, and meeting with people to talk about robots," he said.

Oh Jesus, here we go. "I don't go to school," I said. At least he doesn't know about my moms.

"You don't?" he asked. He made the exact surprised face I bet he made as a little kid.

Probably that little-kid face is why I wasn't a jerk about it. "Nope," I said.

"Me neither," he said.

What?! I guess my face said, What?! because he laughed and was like, "You don't meet so many other homeschoolers."

Dude, I don't meet any. I had *so* many questions like, Isn't it weird how it's actually kind of harder to choose for yourself? And, Do people who see you out in the world on a weekday ever stare at you like you're an alien? And, Did it take your parents very long to believe you were actually doing something? And, Did you quit because school isn't actually teaching us anything that might make the world better? But all I managed to actually say was, "How long?" Boo.

He thought about it for a second, "Almost ten years," he said. "Wow, yeah, almost ten."

Suddenly I felt self-conscious, like he was a real homeschooler and I was a poser. "I just started," I said.

"Well, next time we hang out, we can meet during the week," he said.

Who said there's going to be a next time? "Cool," I said.

ALIENS JUST BEING ALIENS

I wanted to write when I got home, but I didn't know what. Which it turns out is when Uncle Alex's book is really helpful.

From *A Writer Writes:* While a story can encompass any span of time imaginable, they all have to start somewhere. Where does your story begin? And what has happened to make it begin there?

Good question. So...it's been like 250 years. What's going on that it just so happens that these kids are going Above right when there's robots who want to kill them up there. Where'd the robots come from? Why haven't they already killed everyone?

Didn't Javier say something about erasing the space between human and machine and uploading minds and shit?

But so someone would have to invent the robots.

I was no longer worried that Javier was going to steal my idea. And not just because he was an illustrator. And not just because I had physical evidence that I was working on this story. But because, come on. You saw him. That guy's not stealing anything.

It had been a couple hours, so I decided I could text him without looking like a weirdo.

> Elaine: I'm thinking about the bad guys.

I saw that he read it. I don't like it when you can't see if people read your text. Why so secretive?

> Javier: Robots looking at our library books?
> Elaine: There needs to be an evil doctor who invents them...
> Javier: Every story needs an evil doctor.
> Elaine: And every story needs more than one bad guy. At least.
> Javier: At least.
> Elaine: Like *Aliens* has the aliens *and* Corporate Prick Burke.

Javier: Who?
Elaine: Have you seen the second *Aliens* movie?

I guess I'd mistaken him for Lucca for a second...

Javier: Awhile ago.
Elaine: Corporate Prick Burke's the weasely dude who works
for the Corporation and tries to sneak the aliens back...
Javier: Oh, yeah. White guy? Curly black hair?
Elaine: So there's him as a bad guy. But also the Corporation
he works for. And the sucky lieutenant. And then, of course,
there's the aliens...
Javier: Layers of villains.
Elaine: And different kinds of villains. You know, like the aliens
aren't exactly bad guys.
Javier: The aliens that kill everyone are not exactly bad guys?

Yeah. I hear your skepticism.

Elaine: Well, they're not malicious. They're just doing what
they're doing. Like you wouldn't call a lion a bad guy cause it
eats a dude.
Javier: Ha. That's just what lions do...
Elaine: That's just what aliens do...They kill you or else they
put you in a cocoon and grow an alien baby in your chest
cavity.
Javier: No big deal.
Elaine: Ripley even says to Burke that humans might be a
worse species than the aliens. She's like, You don't see them
fucking each other over for a percentage...
Javier: I guess I should watch it again.

Obviously, you should do that.

Elaine: So there's the evil doctor with evil plans who invents
the robots...
Javier: And then the robot's just do what the doctor wants? So
no freewill for them?

Hmm.

> Elaine: Well that's a question. If they were just robots, yes. But if it really is AI like in the Singularity, they would have freewill, right?
> Javier: Well, their processing speed would be infinitely faster than the processing speed of the human brain. So, they would either *have* free will or process information and make decisions so quickly, it would *seem* like free will.

I guess he'd already been thinking about that. Or he just had a faster processing speed than I did.

> Elaine: But either way, they might not care much about individual humans or even humans at all. Right? Cause to something with an infinitely fast mind, we'd be like bugs?
> Javier: They would definitely be able to come up with a way to determine who's good and who's bad. Is that what the evil scientist wants them to do?
> Elaine: I guess I don't know that part yet.

Is that why such terrible things happen to people? In the mind of the universe, we're bugs?

> Javier: It's not great if they think we're bugs.
> Elaine: They might think we're bugs.
> Javier: That's different than robots just being robots.

LITIGATING THE CYCLIST

The awful thing about riding the L in the winter is they keep it burning hot on there. You've got all your 50 layers on and then you get in the car and it's a million degrees. So it's like, Do you take off enough clothes to be comfortable? But then you gotta start getting it all back on, like, two stops ahead of your stop and in that case you might as leave it all on. Also, if you take it off and you have a bag and there's other people on there, it feels self-conscious as you're like, stripping, and trying not to act like you're suspicious of everybody stealing your bag. I usually ended up unzipping my jacket, taking off my hat and mittens, and still gushing sweat. They also air-condition the hell out of it in the summer and then you practically get hypothermia when you're just wearing shorts and a t-shirt.

All of which is to say that when I got to Jenn's a few days after I met Javier, I was uncomfortable and annoyed. Like seriously, how are we ever going to get to the Singularity if we can't even get the temperature on the L right?

"Hi, Mrs. Cartwright," I said, when Jenn's mom answered the door.

We won't call Marcie friendly. "Oh, hello, Elaine," she said when she opened the door.

She stood with me in the foyer as I took off my boots and the outer garments that might possibly have touched something out there in the city. You're definitely not allowed to leave the foyer wearing anything that might have city germs on it. I actually couldn't believe there wasn't a hand-sanitizer dispenser on the wall near the door. I should suggest that to Jenn as a Christmas gift to her mom. "Are you girls working on English today?" Marcie asked.

I was not shocked that Jenn hadn't told her about my leaving school. However, it's best to be vague with parents like Marcie. You can't ever be sure they're not trying to trap you.

"I'll see what Jenn thinks," I said.

"Well," Marcie said and walked off toward her office.

Since her office was in the opposite direction as the kitchen and since I was thirsty, I cruised through before going to Jenn's room. There was some dude I'd never seen sitting at the kitchen table. He was a baldish, white, oldster who looked like he ate out every night. He watched me as I went to the fridge.

"Hi," I said, as I grabbed two La Croixes. Weirdo.

"You must be Jenn," he said as he got up from the table and held out his hand.

I tucked one of the drinks under my arm so I could shake hands. Ridiculous. "Jenn's friend," I said.

"I see," he said. There was definitely an implied, "Oh," in his voice. He went back to the table and started looking at some papers.

Real polite, dude. "See ya," I said.

"Who's the dude in the kitchen?" I asked Jenn when I got to her room.

Jenn was sitting on her bed, supported by two big, velvet pillows (one green, one blue), "There's no more grapefruit?" she asked, after I handed her the lemon-lime La Croix.

I sat down in the new chair Marcie had just put in the room. I leaned against one arm and draped my legs over the other. Marcie would kick my ass for that. "Is that the same as pomplemousse?" I asked, cracking my drink.

"Yes," she said, obviously hoping I just hadn't known and there was some in the fridge.

"Yeah, that's gone too," I said. Goddam Taylor Swift was on. Yes, for real.

She took a sip of the seltzer, looked at the can, and made, You've disappointed me face. "He's Marcie's lawyer."

"Geoff in trouble?" I asked. Geoff had never been in trouble. Not with anyone. Ever. Classic first born. Classic mama's boy.

"Marcie's litigating," Jenn said.

"Who?" I asked. Dear god, can we change the music? I was lazy about knowing music, so most of what I liked came from Mama Jane (she was a DJ in college, obviously), so that's like 1960s—1990s, and Jenn hates Neil Young, Ani, and Arcade Fire as much as I hate TSwift, but FFS, I *always* went to her house and listened to her music...

"Biker," Jenn said.

"Someone finally key the Escalade?" I asked.

"She hit him last week," she said.

"Litigating is suing, right?" I asked.

Jenn was really going to work on her seltzer. "Yep," she said after she'd finally caught her breath.

"I know this is a TSwift playlist," I said.

Jenn crumpled her can. "It's not," she said and threw the can toward the garbage next to the dresser. "It's an *I Knew You Were Trouble* playlist."

"Barf," I said. "Why is Marcie suing a biker she hit?"

TSwift sang, "...wondering if I dodged a bullet or just lost the love of my life...I gave you something, but you gave me nothing..." Here we go again.

"Emotional damages," Jenn said.

"Um?" The robots will definitely kill Marcie.

"Evidently, the guy was on an all-black bike, wearing all black, no reflectors, no lights," she said. Her phone buzzed. She glanced at it, but didn't pick it up.

I heaved myself out of the chair and went to the stereo. "What time was it?" I asked.

"Midnight," Jenn said.

"I'm changing this," I said and pointed at the stereo.

Jenn shrugged. "Did you notice that both TSwift *and* the dude are crazy in this one?" she asked.

I hadn't noticed that. "Wait," I said and looked back at Jenn. "What day was it?"

"When Marcie hit the biker?" Jenn asked.

I nodded.

"Like Wednesday or Thursday," she said.

"What the hell was Marcie doing driving around at midnight on a school night?" I asked.

"Function," Jenn said. Her phone buzzed again.

"Jesus Christ," I said. "They really don't parent at all, do they?" The robots will kill both of them.

Jenn was looking at her phone, "Have you seen the fridge?" she asked.

The fridge was 100% empty, except for a 1/2 eaten Lean Cuisine still in the microwave container (seriously, who hasn't gotten the memo on those cancer boxes?) and about five cases of La Croix—minus the grapefruit.

I started a new playlist.

"Marcie's claiming it's the guy's fault she hit him cause she couldn't see him and now she's having nightmares and migraines," she said.

Now listen, I abhor Marcie Cartwright and the robots *will* kill her. Sure, I sponged off her by going out to dinner with them. And by going to Torch Lake. And by using their tickets to Steppenwolf. But it's not like you get to choose your friend's parents—you just have to tolerate them for the sake of the friendship. But I had to say, despite thinking that Marcie was a real piece of work... "I kind of agree with her," I said.

Jenn's head jerked up from the screen.

I went on. "I mean, that would be horrible," I said. "You're just driving home from a 'Save Chicago's Historic Condos' fundraiser and BAM! you take out a biker—blood smeared across the bumper of the SUV."

"The blood was on the street," Jenn said. "You're kidding me, right?"

"Amazingly," I said. "I am not. That would totally give me nightmares and the guy sounds like an idiot." I added Pat Benatar, Stevie Nicks, Florence and the Machine, Tegan & Sara, and Aretha Franklin to the mix in the hopes that the chick singers would trick Jenn into thinking we were listening to new contestants from *The Voice*. I plopped back into the chair.

"Do you think TSwift will follow me on twitter?" Jenn asked and picked up her phone which had buzzed again.

"No. She will never follow you." I said. "Since when are you on twitter?" I took another drink of my seltzer.

Jenn typed something. Tweeting? "Someone taught Mrs. Sternin about it so now we have to tweet about the characters we're reading."

"Progressive," I said and finished off my drink instead of doing what I wanted which was a goddam dance that I never had to sit in Sternin's class ever again. Radha, Penelope, and Merton + my meeting with Javier had me convinced.

"Oh. How was Lucca's brother?" Jenn asked, still looking at her phone.

I didn't really know how to describe the meeting with Javier without explaining *The Singularity* which Jenn would'nt've given a shit about. "Pretty cool," I said.

"I like this song," Jenn said. "What's it called?"

"*Edge of Seventeen*," I said.

"I'm gonna tweet TSwift that she should cover it," she said and kept typing.

I rolled my eyes, but I guess it was sort of progress. "So what's new with Blake O'Connell?"

Jenn threw her phone onto the bed. "Ugh, who knows. We haven't hung out in awhile."

"You kick him to the curb?" I asked.

Jenn shook her head. "He's trying to get with Ivy Walker..."

That seemed weird. Ivy Walker didn't strike me as the kind of girl who was trading her fertility for anything. She didn't strike me as the kind of girl who had fertility. "Oh," I said. "That sucks. I'm sorry."

"You don't have to be sorry," she said. "It's not like I wanted him for a *boyfriend*. I wanted him for a *hook up*."

Just then, Cyndi Lauper's *Time After Time* came on (if you want to see what TSwift is *not* like, google that shit). She sang, "Sometimes you picture me, I'm walking too far ahead. You're calling to me, I can't hear what you've said..." If we'd been in a movie, it would've been *Girls Just Wanna Have Fun*, but it wasn't a movie... "Did you read that first essay I wrote for you?" I asked, because she sounded exactly like she *had* read *Sex at Dawn* (at least the part about our natural state being everybody banging everybody).

"It's fine," she said, "I've been talking to Casey Woods."

I goddam knew it.

NOVEL SPERM

Leaving Jenn's house, I noticed a new painting in the hall and I was like, "Why's that painting look familiar?"

Jenn rolled her eyes said, "Cause it was on the side of every bus last year."

I pointed at it like, Why's it here?

"Because it's the Cartwright's," she said. Obviously. "It's been on loan at the Art Institute, but Marcie's in a fight with the director..."

"So she took her painting back?" I asked. Really? "She's amazing," I said.

"Our Marcie," Jenn said.

Sometimes I did want to talk to Jenn about stuff. Like *The Singularity* and *Sex at Dawn* and how maybe she should leave school, too...But as I was sitting on the L, I thought, I bet Jenn's gonna get a pretty big inheritance. I wonder if they're gonna make her get a job when she grows up? And I knew I couldn't talk to her about that stuff. She already thinks I'm an eco-terrorist.

There's a part in *This Is Our Youth* where Tavi Gevinson said something to Michael Cera along the lines of, Well, you're going to get to an age where you stop fighting 'the Man' and you just become 'the Man,' and that behavior negates whatever you're doing right now—like you don't even exist because of who you're *going* to become. Like all those hippies who were going to change the world and were like, Nevermind, we'll just be lawyers instead... That felt sad and kinda true. Except these days, most kids don't even have a hippie/save-the-world phase. They go straight to being bankers and brokers.

So then I was thinking about rich people taking their paintings back and suing the dude *they* hit and once again, I was like, God, humans are terrible.

And I was like, You know another good thing about the apocalypse? After almost everyone is dead, none of the stupid crap is gonna matter. A totally different bunch of stuff is gonna matter. If everyone is trying their hardest just to survive, and like 99% of the world's wealth is no longer in the hands of (mostly white) dudes, and in fact there's no more wealth other than survival itself...If all that's the case, the most important thing (other than food, shelter, and water) is going to be making babies. And in order to make healthy babies, the most important thing will be genetic novelty—you know, different genes from different dudes mixing with genes from different chicks. Otherwise, you get inbreeding. Like Marius. Which as we all know leads to birth defects and a bunch of people who ain't so smart. So, the *most* important thing for the people in my book (no matter where they live and where they manage to survive) will be getting access to an array of genes. Of as many races as possible. And it won't matter if your family owned famous paintings or if you lived on the North Side or South Side. It will only matter how genetically different you are. Which, I think, is the opposite of racism.

And like *Sex at Dawn* says that in chimp and bonobo cultures, one of the jobs of the females is to bang *any* stranger who happens to come around. Cause banging the stranger a) prevents fights—cause when you banging, you ain't fighting and b) gives you access to different sperm and makes the gene pool healthier.

So obviously since Radha, Penelope, and Merton's group is isolated in their luxury, underground, condo resort, they're going to have to use science to get their genetic novelty. All the rich, Westside founders would've been white and probably want to stay white. I guess even post-apocalypse there might be racism. And the Eastside scientists would've been lots of different races and probably not give a shit about anything other than the health of their genes...

But Above will be different. They're going to have to find people to mate with. There should totally be a survivor group where straight girls have to go find sperm. And the more different the sperm donor looks, the better. Can you imagine a world in which girls go out on, like, a vision quest for sperm so they can ensure the survival of humanity?

THEY PUT THAT SHIT IN RABBITS' EYES

I was walking down Irving Park feeling pumped like, Boom, I just solved the country's race issue—all we gotta do is annihilate 99% of the population. So psyched. I passed a laundromat, called The Laundromat, and there was that guy Tony. You know, the americano-and-a-hit-of-weed/yeah-my-dad's-a-total-sweetheart bearded, hipster dude from Zero Drop. I don't know, I guess it was cause of Jenn having to join twitter, or my meeting with Javier making it clear I was super good at talking to dudes, or cause I was high on the apocalypse, but for whatever reason, I ripped open the door to talk to him.

He was standing at the detergent vending machine on his phone and was like, "Tide? Are you fucking kidding me? They put that shit on rabbits' eyes. C'mon, I'm all loaded up over here."

He hung up, looked at the dispenser and mumbled, "Tide..." and shook his head.

"Are you Tony?" I asked.

He looked up. "Maybe." Then he stared at me.

"I overheard your conversation at Zero Drop like a month ago..." I said, not sure where I was going, but weirdly not intimidated, despite his beard and tattoos.

"You a cop?" he asked and shoved his phone into his front pocket.

"No," I said.

He crossed his arms over his chest. "Daughter of a cop?" he asked.

That almost made me laugh. The moms, cops. "Definitely, no," I said.

"Born Again?" he asked.

"What?"

"Christian. Born Again Christian," he said. "You wanna know if Jesus is in my heart?"

"*Is* Jesus in your heart?" I asked. It was hot in there with all my gear on, but I didn't care, I was enjoying myself.

He looked me up and down, but for some reason it didn't feel gross. Usually that feels gross. "Shouldn't you be in school?" he asked.

I adjusted my bag on my shoulder. "Shouldn't you be at work?" I asked.

Tony held his hands up in front of him. "Touché, sister," he said.

I shrugged. "Dude. I'm not a cop. Not the daughter of a cop. Not a Christian...I'm just a writer." It was the first time I'd called myself that.

Tony squinted at me. "You seem young for a writer," he said. I'd seemed young to TABC, too.

"Not young for a cop?" I asked.

He gave me 1/4 laugh for that.

"Don't know what to tell you," I said. What had gotten into me? It was like ending racism and vision quests for sperm had given me super-confidence. "I'm headed to Zero Drop to write. When you're done here, you should come down." Who says that?! I don't.

Tony looked me up and down, again. Winter uniform, dude.

"You're not going to the Jabberwocky?" he asked. "Isn't that where the writers hang out?"

Writers who get their ideas by stealing them from kids..."Fuck that place," I said.

Tony looked at me like, Oh, really?

Twenty minutes later we were sitting at a two-top at Zero Drop. I was like, "...So obviously there's a lot I need to figure out...like I want it to be that enough people are dead that all..." and I made a swirling gesture that included every single person in the café "...this bullshit is also dead."

"Damn dude," Tony said. He was sipping drip coffee...not an americano.

It felt good to talk with him. I didn't feel the barf. And I had no fear that he was going to try to steal my idea. Sure, I'd had no fear that TABC was going to steal my idea. Why would I? And sure, I'd felt super excited to talk to him, too. But there was a difference. With TABC, I'd wanted him to like my idea. I'd wanted him to tell me that it was good and that it would work. I'd wanted him to like *me*. Teacher's pet. I wasn't thinking about making Tony like me. It was like when I was talking to Tony about a plague that kills all the world-destroying fuckers, I was Ripley, "I can drive that loader." When I was talking with TABC, I was Hudson, "What the fuck are we gonna do now, man?"

I took a drink of my coffee and said, "Now I just gotta figure out what's the right number of survivors in each group."

"Right number for..." Tony asked. He was lacing and unlacing his hands on the table. He was a little fidgety. Like he had energy to spare—not like he'd been snorting ritalin.

"Like enough that they can stay alive long enough for the Earth to be totally different than it is now, but not so many that it's getting back to being fully populated. Like I want there to be a lot of space in between groups...but I don't know how many people that would be..."

Tony pointed at me. "That's a question for your network," he said.

"What's my network?" I asked.

"You know," he said. "The people you know. Somebody's gotta have the answer."

I thought about the people I knew. I don't think any of them has the answer to this one. Not even Uncle Alex.

WHAT NOT TO GOOGLE

Here's what not to google if you care about your day: "How many people are needed to survive a plague?"

I guess it shouldn't've surprised me, but there were over 11 million pages answering that question. And a movie about AIDS. And prepper communities. And an article where an oldster British scientist calls humans "a plague on Earth" (I feel you, dude). Information about the Black Death and life in general during Medieval times (spoiler alert: it sucked). Websites devoted to all the kinds of plagues with charts that show how they're spread (e.g., "fecal contamination of food and water"). Barf. And on and on and on. Like there are a lot of people out there devoting their lives to studying and describing and publishing online A LOT of different t hings a bout p lagues. L ike h ow d o y ou g o t o school and then college and end up being the person who makes the "fecal contamination" chart?

So, I don't even know how many hours later, I found out who you ask how many people you need to survive a plague.

You ask an evolutionary biologist.

And it turns out, Chicago is crammed full of those people. Now you're going to ask how I got there and I don't remember. It was just clickclickclick, pagepagepage, hello University of Chicago Department of Ecology and Evolution—who knew? I picked four people based on it seeming like maybe their subject area could answer my question and emailed them, like, Hi, I'm Elaine Archer. I'm writing a science-fiction novel and need some help doing mathematical modeling/population dynamics/ecology (those are all words I borrowed from their bios 😺) and I'm wondering if you could meet to talk about that...

Elliot Vaughn: sexual selection (didn't reply).

Roberto Miranda: stability, extinctions, population dynamics (didn't reply).

Paulina Escobar: theoretical ecology (replied but was like, I ain't got time for that shit).

Kathy Pao: mathematical modeling (replied and was like, Sounds interesting. Let's meet).

ANNHILIATION VULNERABILITY

A week later, I was chilling in the Smart Museum café on the University of Chicago campus down in Hyde Park waiting to meet Kathy Pao, evolutionary biologist. I considered inviting Jenn to go down with me if

Kathy Pao wanted to meet on the weekend, but she wanted to meet on Wednesday afternoon...

I got there first, she texted and was like, I'm 10 minutes late...

She whipped open the door and a blast of air sort of threw the bottom of her long coat forward and the way she batted down made me think, Oh, shit, she might be arrogant.

I hadn't considered or prepared for arrogant. I'd prepared for so smart that I felt like an idiot. So smart she was humorless. So smart it was a little sad. But I hadn't prepared for arrogant.

She came over, flung her shit down, and was like, I need to eat...Kathy Pao. Professor Pao. Medium height, shoulder length dark brown hair with bangs, dark brown eyes, olive skin, very thin, gray slacks and a pale green sweater set.

I nodded like, Sure. Yes. Eat.

She came back to the table with a black coffee and a croissant. "I'm between meetings," she said. "I hate eating in meetings. So you're writing a book. How can I help?"

Okay. Okay, phew. Not arrogant. Just smart. So smart she doesn't even blink at my age and the fact that I'm not in school, but instead, casually interviewing a professor of evolutionary biology. Like she probably sequenced the genome at 10, so of course, a 16-year-old is writing a novel. Please don't let me embarrass the hell out of myself.

I'd brought one of my school notebooks and had it opened in front of me. "Well, I'm writing about a post-apocalyptic world," I began.

She was making short work of her snack, but was also completely tidy. "What's the apocalypse?" she asked and put a chunk of croissant in her mouth.

She has to know what an apocalypse is. "Um," I said.

"The catastrophe? What's the catastrophe?" she asked and sipped her coffee. "Nuclear?"

Oh god. Okay. Of course, she knows. She's got a goddam lab named after her. Kathy Pao of the Pao Lab for the Study of the Ecology and Evolution of Pathogens. "Well, I think it's not just one catastrophe. Because, well, it has to be something that kills all the people, but not the Earth." I took a sip of my coffee—it was not delicious. Oh god, I'm a coffee snob.

"Ah. So you're talking about a mass extinction," she said. A guy jostled her chair as he passed behind, but she didn't seem to notice.

"Mass extinction," I said and made a note. Remember to look up the difference between apocalypse and mass extinction.

You know the people who talk so fast and clearly think so fast that being around them makes you feel like you're on speed? Professor Kathy Pao. She talked like her sentences were single words. That's how it had felt to talk to Lucca. Not that he was as smart as Kathy Pao, but just that we always knew what the other was talking about and jumped from idea to idea so fast that sometimes I was saying things before I even had time to think them and then he was saying something too and it was just discovering as we went. "So. Causes?" Kathy Pao asked.

Causes. Right. "Um. Probably food plague..." I tried not to do that thing where my statement was really a question.

"GMOs?" she asked and popped another piece of croissant in her mouth.

"Are they going to cause a plague?" Jesus. Goddamit.

She shrugged. "Hard to tell. The organisms themselves are likely safe, but when you create a seed that's pesticide resistant, for instance, you potentially saturate the soil with poison and kill the microbiome of the soil, leaving space for bacteria and pathogens that can have detrimental effects on the crops, the livestock that eats the crops, and the humans that eat the crops and the livestock. The micro-biome of the soil is the basis of all land life. You tamper with that..." She brushed the crumbs from her fingertips. "...Who knows?"

Good god. "Okay. Well. Yeah. Let me make a note," I said and leaned over my notebook.

Professor Kathy Pao laughed. Phew. Sense of humor. "What else?"

"I was thinking bees." I drew a little squiggle in the notebook. "Wiping out the bees," I said.

"Wiping out the bees is good," she said. "Hitting the food source in two places is smart."

"And like, a pandemic," I said.

"Yes," she said, "You'll need something like that..." She saw where I was headed.

"Cause rich people can probably always get food..." I said.

She nodded. "But a true pandemic..." she said and nodded, "...almost impossible to avoid."

"I'm just not sure what it would be," I said.

"Humans are made of trillions of cells," she said and finished her croissant. "Of those, a conservative estimate is that 90% are non-human."

Gross. "Non-human?" I said.

"Bacteria. Virus. Other micro-organisms."

Holy shit. "Whoa," I said and wrote that down.

She sipped her coffee. "So you really have a lot of options as far as a pandemic is concerned."

"Cool," I said. I guess I wouldn't have to get too specific if I didn't want to. "And then I was going to add some natural disasters." Did I just say, "Add some natural disasters?"

"Also good. Natural disasters destabilize. You'd need destabilization on a global scale to accomplish what you want," Kathy Pao said. Then she added, "This is a global mass-extinction?"

"The story takes place here. But I think it has to be global. Otherwise people would just resettle the U.S."

"Good. Got it. So your email said you needed some help with mathematical modeling," she said.

"Right. My question is, how small do individual groups of survivors have to get so that 250 years post mass-extinction you don't have a fully repopulated world (or even a repopulating world), but also big enough that you have survivors?" It seemed like a long and convoluted question. I was worried she wouldn't even know what I was asking. I didn't need to worry.

"This is the subject of debate," she said.

Oh boy.

She took my notebook and scribbled some equations and a little graph. "So, you can see that if we have N, r, and K, you plot them like this," she said.

Can I see that?

"So here you see the change in number of individuals, N, as a function of time," she said.

That actually does seem to make sense. "But wait, what's that 'd' up there?" I asked and pointed to the equation.

"Oh," Kathy Pao said, "That's just the calculus."

Obviously. That's just the *calculus*. "Ahh. Gotcha." I said. "Go on."

"So there's this thing called the Allee Effect. You can look it up later, and actually, as we're talking, if there's anything that you want to know more about, just note it and I can get you some links or articles or whatever. The Allee Effect is essentially described in this graph showing that population growth at low population densities is actually quite low..." She looked up at me to see if I was following. I don't know what she would've done if I wasn't.

I pointed at the first point on the graph, "So that's basically the minimum number of survivors you can have for a species to survive."

"Breeding survivors," she said.

"Right."

"And of course, smaller groups are far more vulnerable to being wiped out," she said.

"Like by lack of reproduction?" I asked.

"I was referring to things like pathogens, but low-reproduction—for whatever reason—is a constant stressor for small groups," she said.

"Oh, right. Cause if you're already a small group and some disease comes along..." I said.

"Exactly," she said. "As you can see demonstrated in the graph..." Kathy Pao pointed at the incline on her drawing. "...once population density reaches a certain threshold, its growth is radically increased."

I nodded. "And could you graph an opposite relationship to what you might call 'annihilation vulnerability,' like pathogens?" I asked. I'm totally good at math.

"'Annihilation vulnerability,'" she repeated and smiled. "I like that. You *are* a writer."

I basked. I can't imagine anyone, no matter how successful, ever gets tired of comments like that—especially by people with their own pathogen labs who have nothing to gain by stroking your ego. "Thanks," I said. "I like it, too."

"You could plot something like an inverse relationship, up to a certain point..." she made a little 'x' on the curve. "This is the point at which growth peaks and then begins to fall again."

"I definitely don't want any of my survivor groups to get that far," I said. "Can it get that far, that fast?" Making up worlds has a lot of 'x' factors. I guess that's just the calculus.

She shook her head. "Not after 250 years," she said. "Especially because it's doubtful that over a single span of time, in a single population, growth would proceed as smoothly as the graph describes."

"Hiccups," I said. Talking with her is a fucking blast. She seems like she's enjoying it, too. I thought about Mr. Banerjee. Even with kids clamoring to be right up front, I doubt he was having coffee with students and talking physics. I suddenly felt as bad for (some) teachers as I did for students...

She smiled again. "Hiccups," she said. "Also known as 'demographic stochasticity.'"

"Can you write that?" I asked and pointed at the notebook.

"Sure," she said and jotted it down. We won't call her penmanship great. "Stochasticity isn't considered by everyone to be a part of the Allee Effect," she said.

"The 'up for debate' part?" I asked.

"One of them," Kathy Pao said. "Also the specific numbers you're looking for."

"Of course," I said. You think about science and you think (or at least, I think) it has it all figured o ut. B ut t he m ore t ime y ou s pend reading science (or talking to professors of evolutionary biology), the more you realize there's a shitload they don't know. What science has is *faith* that we can eventually figure everything out. Given enough time. Which pretty much makes it a religion. 😊

"Debates aside, I think a number around 500 would be a fairly safe bet for what we're talking about," she said.

A number. "Great," I said. "So how big would the groups be (roughly, not counting stochas...not counting hiccups...) after 250 years?"

"Right. Yes. Let me show you the math on that," she said and bent down over my notebook.

Never did I ever think the phrase "let me show you the math on that" would be one I welcomed. And yet, there I was. A day that will live in the annals of "homeschooling win."

We talked for another hour. Over the course of which Kathy Pao said *all three* of these things:

1) Vaginas are pretty straight-forward as far as biomes go.

2) I think many of my colleagues would be offended by that comment.

3) This was fun. We should do this again.

I'll let the first two comments stand alone.

It's the 3rd I want to talk about. I want to just stop for a moment and say, It. Was. So. Much. Fun. To talk to this amazingly smart person who asked me questions not like she was giving me a test, but like she was interested in what I was thinking. And who drew graphs and said, "...stochasticity..." and travelled with me down this weird path of imagination to a world where everything that had been was over and something new was there. We talked and talked until KPao was like, "Oops. I gotta run."

LEAVING THE UNDER

Radha leaving The Under would be pretty much the same as me leaving school. She's pissed—just like I was. Only it's Merton (not the sea turtle and Mr. Washington) who convinces her to leave. He would have to find her somewhere and start talking to her. But rich (Westside) kids and science (Eastside) kids don't talk so much, so she'll be suspicious. He'll come at her like, I think you're planning to leave...

From *A Writer Writes:* Writing is like painting—you can't get every layer on during a single session. When first writing a scene, don't try to get everything at once. Capture whatever is coming through to you (character, description, gesture, dialogue) and start there. This will give you something to work with in later drafts. Like a painter, building layer after layer.

I sat at my computer. You don't have to get it all, just get something. I stared at the screen. It stared back. Blank. And then I was like, Oh, duh.

Dear Lucca,
So this is the part where Radha and Merton first meet.
Maybe they're in some tunnel that connects something to something else. Merton would know Radha is going to be there. She would *not* be expecting him—they're from different sides.
Merton: He's nervous, but determined. "I need to talk to you."
Radha: She'd be short with him. "How can *you* need to talk to *me?*"
Merton: "Okay, hell, I'm just going to tell you. I don't have time to convince you of anything. I broke out of the Comm."
Radha: She makes face, like, You did what? "What do you mean you broke out of the Comm? Like you stopped using it?"

Merton: "Would that be so strange?"

Radha: Rolls her eyes.

Merton: "What I mean is, I got access to an external Comm. Above. There are still people out there."

Radha: That *definitely* makes an impression. She's like, Whoa. But she hides her reaction. "Look at that, a Westsider who can actually do something."

Merton: He ignores her baiting. "It wasn't hard. Almost no security."

Radha: She scoffs and shakes her head. "We're good little rats, then, aren't we?"

Merton: "Rats?"

Radha: She thinks about what she wants to say. Finally, she says, "Even a Westsider has to know who my mother is. Who my grandmother and great-grandmother were." They are the main geneticists who create the genetic novelty that allows them all to survive...

Merton: "Yes. All the way back to the founders."

Radha: "My mom, like the rest of them, experiments on rats. You can thank the rats for those pretty blue eyes. And you can thank them for no security."

Merton: Shakes his head like he still doesn't get it.

Radha: "Rats behave." She says it like he's an idiot. "You feed them. Train them. Treat them with consistency. They behave exactly like you think they will."

Merton: Now he gets it..."So we've been trained not to need security on the Comm?"

Radha: She shrugs. But she's glad he got her point. For some reason she wants to be wrong about him being an idiot. "It doesn't seem like many people are doing what you're doing, so it must not be a problem."

Merton: He shrugs too. "Either way. I'm going. Above."

Radha: She laughs. Okay, he *is* an idiot. "No you're not."

Merton: "Yes, I am. I made a friend up there. Hugh. And he's in trouble. I'm going." [I'll definitely need to fill in more about this Hugh person, but they can't just randomly wander. They need a reason for their quest.]

Radha: "Merton. Merton? That's your name?"

Merton: He nods.

Radha: "Look at you. Do I believe you hacked into the Comm system in our totally safe and protected compound? Yes. Do I believe *you're* going Above?" She laughs—answering her own question.

Merton: "Look, I get it. I see it. But I'm going."

Radha: "Life on the Westside really that hard?" She knows she's being mean.

Merton: He hesitates for a moment—maybe he's wrong about her...he narrows his eyes at her. "Something happened to you eight months ago."

Radha: She stiffens and doesn't respond.

Merton: "I mean, I had never noticed you and then suddenly you're leaving in the middle of festivals... [Write an earlier scene that draws his attention to her?] "And you change all your Comms from genetics labs to survival sims? Something happened."

Radha: "How the hell do you know that?" Now she's angry.

Merton: He doesn't hesitate to answer. "I looked at all your Comm files. That was easy, too."

Radha: She takes a menacing step toward him. "Listen you little..."

Merton: He holds his hands, like, Hold on... "Maybe you've been thinking it, maybe not, but you're leaving..."

Radha: She stops and looks at him with something like suspicion, but also curiosity. "Okay, so what's your plan?"

Is that really how Radha would react if Merton told her he'd basically been stalking her?

Why would he break out of the Comm in the first place? Why would she?

Who cares! I just started a scene in MY book!

SOME THINGS YOU'RE GLAD YOU DIDN'T KNOW

Javier and I had texted a bit after we met—aliens-AI-robots, lions eating gazelles, him watching *Aliens* and being like, It's really good! And me being like, Duh...It was a couple weeks later when we met at Zero Drop and he showed me his illustrations.

I clicked through the pictures on his computer. The whole series looked like they were drawn on big pieces of graph paper. There were number lines, x & y axes, grids & boxes. Perfectly straight. Black. And each page had something different on the grids.

The first page, two little boys (one pink, one brown) riding bikes down a city street. The outside edges of the street were the lines of the graph...like the street paved over the graph paper, but it was still underneath.

I squinted at the screen. "So are these pictures of drawings or what are these?"

Javier came and sat down next to me so we could look together. He smelled like soap and pepper. I kinda liked it. "It's all on the computer. In Illustrator," he said.

Every one of the pages had the boys doing some typical little boy shit: bikes, cars, smashing stuff with rocks, etc...

"Oh cool," I said as I clicked on the next image. "So you're like a computer prodigy?"

He shook his head. "I started out drawing, but I couldn't get good enough, fast enough. I had ideas in my head, but I couldn't get them out right..."

The pictures got busier and messier as the pages went on. More stuff and colors and surprises here and there. Like the windows of the apartment buildings had started out all just blank and empty, but then they started to have things in them — curtains...flowers...normal house stuff...but then, like, a dog with a snarl like it was gonna tear someone's throat out with white slobber dripping down... "Jesus," I said. "What's up with that dog?" I asked.

"You like it?" Javier asked, obviously pleased with both me and the illustration.

"I mean, it's kinda creepy," I said, squinting.

"Totally," Javier said.

Guess the kid likes creepy. I like creepy. "This was the *easy* thing you did when drawing was too hard?" I said, looking more closely at the windows and alleys and inside the cars to see what else was lurking.

He shrugged. "I had a lot of time after my parents withdrew me from school."

I stopped looking at the screen and asked, "How old were you?"

He thought back. "We moved here when I was six and I was in school for less than a year," he said.

"How old are you now?" I asked. I sort of wanted to know exactly how long he hadn't been in school, but I also wanted to know how close we were.

"Seventeen," he said. "How old are you?"

"Sixteen," I said. And then I goddam blushed because I was thinking about the last time I told a dude how old I was. Then I wanted to barf because I didn't want Javier to think I was blushing about him. Fuck. "So why'd your parents take you out?" I asked.

He laughed, "Cause I cried the whole time," he said.

"What?" That's weird. "Really?"

"It was awful," he said. "You know, I didn't speak English yet."

He didn't have any accent, so I hadn't thought about it. "What happened?"

"Even though there are tons of Hispanics in Chicago, I was the only kid in my class..." he started.

Eww. "Were they mean about it?" I asked.

He laughed, but also nodded. "I remember a lot of scowling teachers," he said. "Like they thought I was trying not to learn. I was trying so hard."

"What was that? First grade?" I asked. I remembered myself in 1st grade. Such a show-off. A little hand-raiser. I knew all the answers. I couldn't imagine what I would've done if the teachers scowled.

"Kindergarten," Javier said.

"What the fuck?" I asked. Goddam school. "What the hell do kids need to learn in kindergarten that's worth making you cry everyday? How goddam hard is it to be like, 'Here's how you tie your shoes. Here's how you say fucking 'shoes' in English.'"

Javier laughed again. "I think that's what my parents thought. But without so many 'fucks.'"

"So they took you out of school and you started doing this?" I asked and pointed at the screen.

I clicked to the last page. Whoa. There was a line, starting at a small, black, perfect zero. It went along slowly for a minute, then suddenly jumped way up—like Kathy Pao's population curve or the exponential growth of technology. At the bottom of the line were just a few, almost impossible to see, dots of color. But as the curve went up, there were more and more colors and those became shapes of little clusters of flowers, and bubbles, and stars that climbed up the curve until you couldn't see the line anymore, just little tiny millions of colorful shapes that climbed up and blossomed and burst...Then they hit a top point where they tore through the graph paper and poured into a big black hole—an abyss. And disappeared. Like nothing.

Whoa.

I leaned in, like an inch from the computer and looked at the shapes. "Ohmygod. Are those the boys?" I thought I could see them. Tiny, shrunken versions of the boys from the other pages, doing their typical boy shit, tangled in the mass that bled out into the nothing.

"Yes!" Javier said. "No one ever notices that."

I sat back, looked at him, looked back at the picture, thought about all the other pictures sort of leading up to it. The pictures, and colors, and energy that had been building up over each of the pages until...Oh, Christ. He is really good. Thank god I hadn't seen this at the conference or I never could've been like, Yeah, yeah, whatever, book report, please...

"Wow," I said. It felt like a stupid thing to say, but it was all that I could get out. "So you think they're gonna buy it?" I asked.

He shook his head. "The editor already wrote back to me," he said. "They're gonna pass."

"What? Why?" I asked. "This is awesome."

"Yeah," he said and closed the computer. "Thanks. The editor said that it's 'missing something.' And that I should resubmit when I have a 'more complete concept.'"

"What part of the concept did they say was missing?" I asked. Also, What's a concept?

"He didn't say, exactly," Javier said.

"Super helpful," I said.

Javier laughed. "I think he means that this…" and he pointed at where the screen had been, "…is really only part of an idea. I just don't know yet what the other part is."

Yep. School is easier than this. "Oh. Well, what's *this* part about?" I asked and also pointed where the screen no longer was. I mean, the illustrations were awesome, but I didn't see what they were *about*.

"They're about what it's like to be a guy. In the world," he said.

Ha. "Do we really need to see another story about that?" I said and remembered some study I'd read that says that the main characters of books are like, 100 times more likely to be male than female. "Isn't that *every* story?"

He smiled and nodded, like, Yeah, yeah. Then he opened his computer again, clicked the images back to the first one, with just the two boys on bikes. "Graph paper," he said. "That's what the world is like for us."

Not you, too. "Are we talking about math?" Was he about to tell me how bad girls are at math?

"I'm talking about rules," he said. "All the rules guys have to follow."

"Are you crazy?" Is he crazy? "Guys *make* all the rules." And we get to trade our fertility.

"Yes and no," he said. "Certainly, the men with power in the world have more power than women…"

I thought about the fifty wealthiest people, aka the dudes with *all* the money. "Certainly," I said. And was like, so much for this friendship. That's when I realized I'd been starting to like him. Goddamit.

He held up his hands like, Hold on and said, "Yes. Most of the power in the world is held by men."

I made a face, like, No shit.

He let it pass. "But.." he said, "…there's pretty much one way you're supposed to be a guy in the world," he said. "Otherwise, you're a faggot."

"Ew," I said.

"Yeah. Ew. But think about it," he said. "Yes, women don't have as much power as men, and you have a lot of rules on you, but you have more socially acceptable ways that you can be."

I thought about Audra and those bros. They had pretty much *one* idea of what a socially acceptable girl was. I thought about The Bitch

Annette and how she thought a girl should look and what a family should be. One fucking way. But then I thought about my winter uniform. Or really, my any-time-of-the-year uniform. "Are you talking about how girls can wear pants *and* dresses?" I asked.

He considered that for a second. "Kinda," he said.

Hmm. "I recently read this book called *Sex at Dawn*," I said.

"Okay," he said, confused.

"It was for school," I said. I didn't have time to explain the whole writing-Jenn's-papers thing.

"Oh right. You just started all this..." he said.

"Anyway, it's about how our culture, where girls are supposed to make babies and boys are supposed to make money, is totally not our human nature...we're actually supposed to cooperate," I said. Which when I had read it, of course, it was 'woman exchanging their fertility for not getting raped...' that pissed me off. But I guess there are probably a lot of dudes who a) aren't rapists, b) don't want to be rapists, c) wish women didn't think they were rapists, d) don't want to be wanted just for land and ₐₙₐₑ)ₘᵢₘₜₙₒₜₕₐᵥₑ$ or land to trade for babies...I shook my head. "The world is so fucked up."

"That's what my illustrations are about," he said.

"And that's not enough for them?" I asked.

"I guess not," he said and closed his computer again.

I sipped my coffee and thunked my cup down. "Boo. Sucks," I said.

"Can I tell you something I've noticed about you?" he asked.

He said it in a way that felt like it wasn't going to be creepy and gross, but I still didn't like the sound of it.

"Sure," I said. Not sure at all.

"You seem like you have a lot of anger," he said.

Not what I expected. "No, I don't," I said.

He smiled at me and I wanted to smack him.

"I don't mean it as an insult," he said.

Whatever. Telling a girl she's angry is code for, You're a bitch. "It's fine," I said. I moved away from him and looked around for my bag.

"Like right now," he said. "Super pissed at me."

What just happened? "We don't even know each other," I said.

"Listen," he said. His voice was gentle, but not in the way that sometimes makes me want barf. "Just imagine for a second that I don't mean it as an insult."

I set my bag back down. I was like, "Okay. I'm imagining." But I'm sure my face was still saying, Fuck you.

"I had this mentor when my parents took me out of school..." he began.

I heard the word "mentor," remembered TABC, and clenched.

Javier went on. "She told me that I should use my emotions for my work. I don't have to tell the literal story of what's happening in my life, but I should tell the story of my emotions..."

It didn't sound like the worst advice in the world. "That's not the worst advice in the world," I said.

"I'm just saying that you could *use* your anger in your book," he said.

"You don't think killing almost all humans is angry enough?" I asked.

"It's a start..."

"I'll think about it," I said.

"So you're not going to never talk to me again?" Javier said. And I wondered for a second if he had very many friends.

"It's not like I have a ton of friends who don't go to school," I said.

He smiled and there was that thing where his one tooth crossed in front of the other.

WELCOME TO THE GALLOWS, BITCHES

In 9th grade English, we read a play about the Salem Witch Trials called *The Crucible*. It's basically about these crazy bitch tween girls accusing adult women of being witches—mostly because the girls got caught dancing in the forest and making love charms. Which, since they're Puritans, is like, the worst thing a tween girl could do. They have to pass the suspicion onto someone else cause god knows, "We should be allowed to fucking dance!" isn't a good enough defense. So, they're like, Those *old* women are just mad because no one wants to trade them for their fertility anymore, so they possessed our bodies and made us do crazy shit. Um. Okay. But guess what? All the judges (old, white dudes, obvs) are like, I believe it! It can't possibly be that the laws we made are total bullshit. It's gotta be witches.

They're in the courtroom and the girls are all screaming and writhing and clutching themselves and the judges are like, You ladies must be witches cause those girls are totally bewitched.

I'm reading it like, You've obviously never been to a middle school slumber party...

And the women are like, We're not doing anything.

The judges are like, It's your invisible spirits doing the bewitching and you can't prove you're not. So...We're gonna hang thee.

The women are like, But..but...

The judges are like, Welcome to the gallows, bitches.

It took us about a week to read it out-loud in class and the whole time I was writing and seething in my tiny prison desk-chair and like, Come on! Those girls are faking it! But it just went on and on and sanity never returned. No matter what any of these innocent people did, it was like they were straight line, constant speed motion to the gallows.

Even though I knew the outcome of the play—cause (spoiler alert) American History was also in 9th grade, I was still like, Maybe they don't die. Maybe they don't die. But nope. Reverend Hale denounces the court. John Proctor (one of the dudes also accused), refuses to say he's a witch, because he doesn't want to lie and ruin his name, "Because it is my name! Because I may not have another in my life!" And all those fuckers die. Does anything ever happen to the judges? Nope. Years later (and this is history, not the play) one of the judges, Cotton Mather, was like, Oh, that's my bad, they probs weren't witches. But did he get in trouble or make any kind of reparations? Also nope.

It's like the black rhino and the bees and the turtle and the little girls...all of history is the same story over and over—humans killing things for vanity and profit and power...Seriously, both American literature and American history should come with a subtitle: Heads Up, If You're Not a Rich, White Dude, Or Sometimes His White Wife, You're Gonna Get Fucked Over.

How could I notice these things and not be furious? The weirder thing is that *more* people aren't *more* angry.

But it's still weird when someone tells you something about yourself that you know, but that you thought other people didn't know. Like I *knew* that I was pissed almost all the time. I mean, I wasn't when I was talking to

KPao about mass-extinctions and the simplicity of the vaginal biome. And I wasn't when I was lying on Jenn's bed (except for TSwift never driving the car) talking about I don't even know what. And not with the moms or Uncle Alex. And until Javier pointed out that I seemed angry, I didn't *think* I was acting pissed in front of him. I mean, saying, "The world is so fucked up," just seems like stating the obvious.

ANGRY AND GUILTY AND WEIRDED OUT

But okay, I'll play Javier's little game—what would make Radha that angry?

I mean, I guess I knew she was pissed, cause that's what Merton told her. That was its own weird thing, right? Like Javier said this thing about me, and he told me that his mentor had told him about using his emotions in his work. It turns out, I was already starting to do that, but without knowing...

But so, what would make Radha so angry she would run away from the only thing she's ever known? Can't be the threat of the end of the world...that already happened.

The thing that's so frustrating and heartbreaking about all those books and plays and speeches that we read in American Lit. is that the winner and loser are pretty much decided before any of it even starts. There's always already someone with all the power. You can see the end coming from the beginning and no amount of yelling at the characters can make it stop. Sure, Ripley beats CPB and (spoiler) they blow up the planet...but the Corporation is still out there. It's still waiting for Ripley to get back and explain what she's done. And you better believe they're gonna bill her.

So, who has the power over Radha? The rules of The Under, for sure. But also her mom (I'm thinking she doesn't have a dad). Parents have all the power. First of all, they decide to bring you into the world. And then they pretty much get to be the boss of you for decades.

With Radha, it has to be something that's to do with being in The Under. Her mom is a scientist, so it would be something to do with that. Something to do with genetics. Genetic novelty. Genetic modification.

Bam—her mom cloned her. How's that for powerless? I mean, I get pissed at the moms if they put pictures of me on the internet without permission. Imagine if they cloned me...

So, Radha's sister → clone.

They should look totally different (like their mom jiggled around with some of the genes), so it wouldn't ever occur to them that Penelope is made from Radha's DNA. Ooh, like maybe Radha looks Indian and Penelope looks African...

It's gotta be a secret that Radha finds out.

WTF Radha's mom?

So what does Radha do? She blabs it to Penelope. Not in anger at Penelope, but anger at the mom. Like, she's so pissed she blurts it thinking her sister will be angry, too. But the second she says it, she realizes it was a mistake—it breaks Penelope's heart. That's even worse.

Now she's angry and guilty. And she's also super weirded out cause her sister is her...

A CHEERFUL PANDEMONIUM

I stayed up late working on Radha and Penelope's backstory. Then it was like 1:45AM. Turned out, 10PM to 2AM was a really good window for me to work. Which makes sense, cause I read an article the other day that said teenagers' circadian rhythms (that's our natural, hormonally induced, sleep/wake cycle) has us naturally awake until about 2AM...And naturally asleep until about noon...The article also said teenagers need 9-11 hours of sleep a night. Can you imagine the state of the world if that was widespread? A whole second world of teenagers wide-awake until 2 and asleep until noon. And the 20-somethings...up to no good.

Around 1:50, I took a break and wandered into the kitchen. Mama Jane was sitting at the table looking at an architectural drawing. Probably the house they were working on.

"Hi, sweetie," she said "What's up?"

"Starving," I said.

"Everything okay?" she looked up at the clock over the back door. "It's really late."

"These are my natural sleep rhythms," I said. I made myself a fried egg sandwich and told her about the article and the second world of teens. "Can you imagine?"

"Good god," she said. "Pandemonium." She rolled up her drawing and put it to the side of the table so I could sit down with my snack.

"The article also said that maybe it's the reason teenagers are moody," I said.

"You're just sleepy?" she asked and rubbed her eyes.

"Cranky," I said.

"Like cranky babies."

"So at least the second world of teens wouldn't be moody," I said.

"A cheerful pandemonium," she said.

"That would make a good title for a story," I said.

"How's it going in there?" she asked.

"Pretty good," I said. "I just figured out that the mom of one of the main characters cloned her to make a sister and the first main character finds out and is pissed." It was the first time I'd told one of them what I was working on, like specifically. Maybe the curse of The Asshole Brenden Carter was lifting.

Mama Jane laughed, "I can see why she would be," she said.

I don't know what made me think of it, but I said to Mama Jane, "So what made you and Mama decide to use a donor?" I'd known since I was little that they'd used a donor from a cryo-bank in California so Mama Jane could get pregnant, but we'd never talked specifics.

"Do you mean as opposed to cloning me?" Mama Jane asked. "Technology wasn't there."

I rolled my eyes.

"It wasn't much of a decision," she said. "We knew we wanted a kid and that was obviously how we'd do it."

"Did you ever think of asking Uncle Alex?" I asked. There was this short span of time when I was in middle school that I wished he was the donor, so that I could point to him when people asked me, "So who's your dad?" in that tone that makes it clear the asker thinks you're a freak.

Mama Jane shook her head. "Uh-uh," she said. "Too complicated."

"So, you did talk about it?" I asked.

"We knew we wanted him to be a big part of your life," she said. "But not as a dad."

I wondered if he *was* my dad if he would act differently than he did as my uncle. Would he still hand me *A Writer Writes* and say, "It's mostly in the title..." as though he was interested in, but not that worried about, where my life was headed.

"Also, I knew his parents would be completely unmanageable," Mama Jane added. "Unmanageable" is a Mama Helen way of saying, Goddam annoying and crazy.

"How so?" I asked. I'd met his parents at a few Thanksgivings. They rotated between their four kids, so it wasn't that many times...

"Oh god," Mama Jane said and shivered. "They would *not* have gotten it. They would've been like, 'But we're her grandparents.'" She shivered again. "They would have sent so much pink clothing."

I don't think I'd ever owned *any* pink clothes. Well played. "Yeah. I don't need any other grandparents who don't approve of how I look."

I hadn't meant to bring her up, but Mama Jane knew immediately who I was talking about and looked so sad. "I'm sorry about my mom," she said.

I shrugged. "Can't choose all your donors," I said.

Mama Jane laughed and we sat quietly for awhile. I was thinking about all the things The Bitch Annette had said to me over the years and all the things she must've said to Mama Jane. I wondered if Mama Jane was thinking the same.

But goddamit if I was gonna let TBA ruin a good conversation. "So, like, specifically. How did you pick?" I asked.

I guess Mama Jane didn't want to dwell on her mom either cause she said, "We went through a lot of different ones..."

"What were you looking for?" I asked.

"Well, we knew we wanted someone who'd look like Mama Helen," she said.

I did have her dark hair. I did not have her height.

"After that," Mama Jane went on, "we narrowed down to three who all seemed good. Well-rounded. Smart and athletic, but also liked music and interesting food..." she said. "We'd gotten rid of all the ones who were hardcore religious..."

Ohmygod, I'm a designer baby. "So then what?"

"We picked the one with the highest SATs," she said.

That cannot be it. "No, you didn't," I said.

"Nah, just kidding," she said and laughed. "We picked the guy who liked Radiohead."

Sometimes I forget how much she likes to mess with me. "The band?" I asked.

"Yeah. They all three had better SATs than I did. So, after that, we picked the one who said he loved Radiohead," she said.

Thank god. Music. Not standardized testing.

We talked for a little while longer. She told me that they decided she would carry the baby because it turned out Mama Helen has endometriosis and probably couldn't get pregnant.

"Was she sad?" I asked. Poor Mama Helen. I'd never asked why Mama Jane was the one.

"Well, you know your mom," Mama Jane said.

She would've been sad. But she also sees the silver lining. "She's just happy that I'm here," I said. I smirked like I was joking, but I knew that it was true.

"We're both so happy," Mama Jane said. Then she added, "All the time. Go to bed."

"Wait," I said after I put my plate in the dishwasher and was about to head upstairs, leaving Mama Jane at the table. "Why are *you* still up?"

She shook her head, like, Ugh. "The concrete guy poured the floor in the basement and the heated floor guy hadn't put the heated floor in yet."

"That seems bad," I said. I mean, I don't know a lot about concrete, but...

She sighed, "It's pretty bad. Now we're to the part where they're saying it's my fault for not being there to stop them pouring the concrete. And I'm saying it's their fault because I have the emails specifically saying, Don't pour the floors until the heating is installed...We'll see. Nobody wants to end up in court, but nobody wants to foot the bill, either..."

Mama Jane didn't usually tell me that much about the jobs they were working on. Granted, I didn't usually ask, but..."Is it gonna be okay?" I thought about the black-clad, splattered cyclist. "Like could they sue us?"

She made a face, like, It's not *that* bad. "It'll be fine, sweetie. They'll be nice and toasty all winter long..."

"Okay," I said, and honestly, I forgot about it before I got to my room. That's not why I couldn't sleep. I was lying there, thinking about the donor. If it wasn't for Radiohead, I'd have the genes of some other "well-rounded" dude who liked sushi and was good at math.

Add to that, and this part I already knew, but evidently the donor was so good at getting women preggo that the cryo-bank retired him. Meaning, I have a whole ton of half siblings running around out there.

And guess what, I can look them up. Well, kind of. There's an online community where I could enter the donor's profile number and see if there are any other offspring who registered themselves.

You will not be surprised to learn that Jenn had been trying to talk me into it for years. "Holy shit," she said when I told her about the database, "You could have a twin!"

"That's not how twins work," I said. It was like we'd never had that 6th grade sex-ed talk with Nurse Party-Panties in her ridiculous smock and her assumption that we were all straight and would some day be trying to keep dudes from banging us...

"Yeah, yeah," she said. "But you know, Geoff and Philip both look *exactly* like Paul and *nothing* like Marcie. What if *you* look like the donor and so does your twin?"

"I look like Mama Jane's dad's mom," I said. "I've seen the pictures."

Jenn's always exasperated by my unwillingness to imagine a girl who looks just like me, out there, somewhere, possibly equally pissed..."What if she speaks French and you never meet her?" Jenn asked.

If it hadn't been for her pestering me to look for my "twin" and sometimes "twins," maybe I would've looked for my half siblings. I was sure there must be some who'd registered. Some with pictures. Some who maybe *did* look a little like me. Or *felt* a little like I did.

When I was very little and people asked me who my dad was, before I understood about tone of voice, I used to just say, "I don't have a dad," and that was true. It is true. It's what I say now. But I do have a donor. And I do have his genes. And I do wonder—what parts of him are me? Which is a whole weird world that I belong to, but that the moms and Jenn and Javier...don't.

And now there's a world that's just Radha and Penelope. And they both have to wonder, What part is *me?*

JANUARY

FUCK YEAH, I WANNA BE GOOD

Tony: Yo, homeschool.

I guess I was the one who started it when I was like, Hey, you're Tony, I'm a writer, so meet me at Zero Drop, but it still felt awkward that there was a 20-something dude texting me.

Elaine: Hi.
Tony: Come with me to this movie.

He didn't tell me what it was. It could've turned out to be murder porn, but it didn't seem like he would do that.

Turns out watching a movie with Tony is basically not sharing popcorn, ("I don't share popcorn." He let me know first thing), getting hit in the arm a lot, and him being like, Do you believe this woman? "This woman," in this case, being Georgia O'Keeffe.

It was just me and Tony and a bunch of *old* oldsters at the Music Box for the 1:30PM—a documentary about Georgia O'Keeffe's creation of those giant-ass close-ups of flowers.

In fact, I did *not* believe this woman.

When I thought about Georgia O'Keeffe, I was like, Oh, well, it's Georgia O'Keeffe. Paintings just sprang from her head fully formed, right? Actually, nope. She sketched like a million different versions of things before she painted the actual final. Like a million. I never would've thought that about any famous painter or writer or filmmaker or whatever. But in the movie, they showed an exhibition of her work with five big flower paintings and then the ten *rooms* (big museum rooms) worth of sketches to get those few final paintings.

When Jenn and I went to see *This Is Our Youth,* and before it started, I overheard this conversation between who I'm guessing was a mom, her college daughter (home for the summer!), and the mom's friend. Jenn was in the bathroom, taking forever. I was in our seats. They were mid-convo when I sat down in front of them.

Girl: "I mean, I barely had to work to get an A..."

Mom's friend: "Congratulations!" Cause having to do work in college is clearly not the point...

Girl: "I mean, I didn't even try." She's super proud of herself.

Mom: "Tell her about the paper." Mom's super proud of her daughter.

MF: Makes, what's-this-about-a-paper noise.

G: "Oh. So. This one essay, we had to write out by *hand*..." She's disgusted. Can't believe it.

M: "In ink." Mom can't believe it, either.

G: "I mean, I got around it. I wrote with an erasable pen." Smirk voice.

M: "He never specified..." It's his own fault.

MF: Laughs at the ingenuity. But then, distracted, like talking to herself. "I read about a woman. A 17th century scholar who lived with no heat. And in corsets. To feel like she was from the era..."

G & M: Noises of disgruntlement. Like, What? Are you disapproving of my/my daughter's ingenuity?

MF: Backtracking. "Oh, well. You should have been allowed to choose whatever you wanted."

M: "Tell her about the spring break trip." Once again, super proud.

MF: "You went to St. John's?" Isn't sure she remembers right.

G: "My roommate just broke up with her boyfriend, so she wasn't very fun."

M: "You were so disappointed."

Christ.

Georgia O'Keeffe filled books and rooms with drawings of single lines. Single fucking lines. And curves. And practices of flower petals. And just over and over practicing how to get from the white part of the paper to the black part of the drawing.

And that girl at the play needed to use erasable ink...

As we were leaving the theater, Tony said, "I gotta meet this guy at Wrigley. You wanna walk with me?"

The dead of winter is about the only time I wanted to be in

Wrigleyville. Then I have at least an outside chance of not getting puked on by some drunk Cubs bro.

It was windy and so cold (like recess was cancelled for sure), but I did want to walk with him. "That movie was awesome," I said as I pulled on my hat. "Thanks." I should send the moms.

"I have always loved that chick. But whoa." Tony said. He had a red knit hat with ear flaps and long strings that dangled down.

"I just imagine her in the studio all day—drawing lines," I said.

Tony smacked my arm again. "Right? Just lines." He mimicked the painting of a long squiggly line in a goofy gesture and I thought, He doesn't use Tide cause they put that shit on rabbit's eyes.

I crammed my own mittened hands down into my pockets and clenched my body against the cold. "I just got this sense like she lived some bullshit-free life of constant creation and contentment," I said.

"She was *not* checking Cubs' scores," Tony said. "That's for sure."

Beyond the obvious which was that she was a woman painting huge flowers that looked like vulvas (she said they weren't...but come on...) which was fucking bananas for *anyone* to be doing at that time, let alone a woman, beyond that, she was painting objects from nature in a way *no one* ever had. Sure, lots of old dudes painted vases of flowers. But not like her. And now you see a close up of a flower on every wall of every mall and hotel and dentist's office in the world. She invented that shit. How did she know how to do that? How did she know how to do something that had never been done? How did she know she was on the right track? That she would find the right way to say what she wanted to say? That anyone would care? "Where does somebody get that kind of faith in themselves?" I asked.

"That's a passionate woman," Tony answered.

I don't know what made me say it, probably I was using all my energy to not shiver, so I forgot that Tony and I basically just met, but I was like, "How does a person know she's living the life she's supposed to be living? You know, that's like, worth something to the world?"

Tony stopped walking and looked at me. We were standing right by the entrance to a Taco Bell drive thru and a guy turned in and almost hit us. He blared his horn, but Tony didn't even blink. "Is that where you're at?" he asked.

Is that where I'm at? How do I know if I'm worth something to the world? Yes. I hadn't really known that it was, but yes. I had this nagging worry that my *real* life was over there, somewhere else, but I couldn't see it or even imagine it, so I had no idea how to get to it. But that was too much to admit. I shrugged. "Maybe," I said. "Kinda."

"Homeschool. Girl. Yep. I have been there," he said. I could see his breath when he talked.

Some of the Cubs' banners that usually hung from the streetlights had been replaced with snowflakes and Happy Holidays!

"I wanted to be a musician," Tony said.

"You did?" I asked. I could totally see that.

"Who doesn't want to be a rock star? Front and center. All the strokes and blowjobs?" he said.

God, I love the way he talks. "I know I do," I said.

He winked at me. He didn't seem to be either in a hurry to meet the guy at Wrigley or get out of the cold. "But I realized my talent isn't for performing or song writing or playing an instrument. You have to eat, sleep, and dream that shit if you want to be good."

"And you want to be good?" I asked. I want to be good.

"Fuck yeah, I wanna be good," he said.

I wasn't in a hurry, but I was freezing, but I didn't want to stop talking. "So, what are you?" I had no idea what Tony was. I guess I'd figured he was a dude who sometimes snorted ritalin on a weekday and maybe worked at a coffeeshop, like Audra. Although that's not *all* she did, was it? She was a tattoo artist.

"Tour manager," he said.

"What's that?" I asked.

"When a band goes on tour, I'm the guy who goes with them and keeps all their shit straight," he said.

I didn't know that was a job, but it made sense. Someone probably needed to do that. "But it still has something to do with music," I said.

"Exactly," he said. "Music was always my interest. And baseball," he said.

Uncle Alex would love him. "So was there like a career day for that?"

He laughed, "My talent is people," he said and waved his hand back and forth between us. "I know that. I've known that since I was a six."

"You eat, sleep, and dream that shit?" I asked. What was my talent? Writing? I didn't seem like it. Hanging out with Jenn?

He pointed at me, like, That's it. "You just gotta figure out where your interests and talents intersect," he said.

"Oh yeah," I said. "Easy." Maybe *that's* the reason that girl and her mom were so psyched that she was basically cheating her way through college and school's set up the way it is. Maybe it's not just that the world wants a bunch of automatons, but that most people have no clue what their interests or talents are.

"Well, what are you interested in?" he asked.

I imagined Ripley driving the loader and shrugged. "I want to be able to do something," I said. But that wasn't really all of it. It wasn't *really* enough for Ripley. And it wasn't enough to make me fill a whole room full of sketches. "I want to be able to do something that might actually help the world," I said. I thought about Georgia O'Keeffe—no one had ever showed the world to the world like she did.

Tony's eyes were very sweet when he reached out his hand and put it on my shoulder. "Writers can do that," he said.

Sure they can. But can I? Writing a book was hard enough when I was just looking for a way to keep from going back to school. But to help the world? "Plus I hear writers get a ton of blowjobs," I said.

THE REAL WORLD

Tony met his friend at Wrigley and I was scurrying back to catch the Addison bus. There was a little kid in a full-on snowsuit, spinning in the middle of the sidewalk with some kind of airplane, so I was going to have to go around. But before I got there, this old (grumpy, it turns out) couple, coming the other way, also encountered the spinning roadblock. Only they didn't go around. They stopped in front of him and I didn't hear exactly what the old dude said, but it was obviously mean and scary because a) his face was mean and scary when he leaned down into the little's face and b) the kid started crying.

Then the old woman turned to the mom and said like, '...grumble, grumble, control your child...'

I was like, Jesus people are mean to kids.

But the mom was like, "The world is not more yours than his." She picked her little guy up, put him on her hip, stroked his fat cheek, and walked away.

And I was like, Damn right. It was like Mrs. Sternin talking to Jeremy Hoosier about respect. That mom was right. It's not more the oldsters' world than the kiddos' world. If anything, it belongs more to the kids—we're the ones who are gonna have to pick up that old bastard's mess.

It's like when they hit you with that, When you're in the real world...bullshit.

It was a just after 4PM, and the streetlights turned on overhead.

I hate the real world. When people talk about the day that I'm finally in the real world, I want to punch faces. What do they think I'm in right now? Consider this—maybe we're all in the real world. All the motherfucking time. Maybe it's just that the real world of the little kid and the real world of the sleep-deprived teenager and the real world of the crabby 70-something are not the same world. Like, literally not the same reality. Like how dogs and cats and whales see and hear a whole different world than humans. And they react to the things that only they perceive. Their world is different than the human world. But no less real. Just as real. Just as alive.

Cause otherwise, when does "real life" start? When we get jobs? When we make money? I refuse that.

Like when people try to say that teenagers aren't really in love. Fuck you. Yes we are.

Probably more in love than oldsters. Cause there's no one being like, 'Oh, but the bills,' and 'Oh, but the kids and the dishes and the laundry and the marriage...'

Sure, it may not last forever, but not all grown-up love does either. And that beautiful spinning oblivion of that kiddo won't last forever, either.

But it was real, you old assholes.

Just as real as anything you do all day.

EAT A GODDAM ORANGE

I needed away from the intersection of interest and talent and what is real life and when and how does it start? So, I went back to The Under. And I as hungry, so I was thinking about food. They were going to have to get food down there somehow.

Obviously, they could just eat some kind of nutrient goo. But I think I remember reading somewhere that humans actually need to eat food to stay healthy. And like, the reason that taking vitamins isn't as healthy for you as eating a billion cups of salad everyday, is that it actually matters that you eat the nutrients in their living form. Is it really a surprise that it's better for you to get vitamin C from an orange and not from those vitamin C pills that make your salivary glands go crazy? It seems so classic and yet so stupid that we're like, Oh, oranges are good for you? Which part? The vitamin C? Well then, let's make a pill that's the equivalent of 100,000 oranges in a pill. Wait. Why aren't you super healthy now? What? Just eat a goddam orange.

Humans are so stupid. I read the other day that in an effort to save elephants from the same fate as the black motherfucking rhino, wildlife managers split up herds and relocate some of them. One of the ways they've chosen to do this, is to take a groups of adolescent males and relocate them all together. Which it turns out is the worst thing you can do. Cause elephant groups are lead by older female elephants. And without them there, the young males are aggressive and violent and random and end up being put down. Like Marius. Shocking. So, when we mess with them in order to save them, we still kill them. Just in a different way.

You know, I think the whole problem is the way most people think about the Earth and nature, like, there's nature down there and the humans above it.

That's not it at all. We grew right up out of nature.

But we're like, No way dudes, I wear clothes and speak English, I'm no monkey.

That's how we ruin everything. Including ourselves. By thinking we're not nature.

Fuck.

My point is, they're gonna need some gardens in The Under. The scientists would've known that when they were planning the place.

So, my question is, can you grow stuff underground?

From: Elaine Archer <LV426er@gmail.com>
Date: January
To: Mr. Banerjee <abanerjee@dbh.edu>
Subject: underground sunlight

Dear Mr. Banerjee,

It's me, Elaine Archer.

Maybe someone in the administration informed you that I left DBH to homeschool? I probably should've come-in and said, Good-bye. But I felt weird or something. And I think I was worried that my teachers would try to talk me out of it. Or that you'd have a lot of questions, like, How will you learn physics now? I didn't know how I would answer.

Hmm. Actually, none of that is true. I just left.

Until I just now wrote it, it never occurred to me that I should've said good-bye to teachers like you.

One of the things that I'm learning from writing a lot is that sometimes I discover things I think and feel *while* I'm writing.

Like it used to be, when I was in school and writing essays or whatever, I just thought, Okay, what do I need to say in this essay to get an A? But now I realize that sometimes I don't even know what I want to say or write *until* I've started writing it. And then sometimes it's not until I've figured something out *through* writing that I can say, Oh, I should write more about that, cause I'm excited to know what I think about it...

So I guess I'm saying that I should've said good-bye, but I was too excited and nervous.

Anyway, I'm actually writing to ask you a physics question. I'm working on a novel about a group of people who survive a mass-extinction by living underground. What I need to know is, Is sunlight reflected in a mirror the same as direct sunlight? Like, would it grow food and flowers and meet human's needs for vitamin D? Maybe this is a biology question?

Okay, I guess that's all. Hope school's good.

Take care,

Elaine.

BECAUSE THE FLOWERS ARE

Javier: Hey. What's going on?

Just wondering once again why humans are so stupid and terrible. And what my interests and talents are...

Elaine: Trying to figure out how to grow food underground.
Javier: Have you been to the café at Harold Washington Library? Downtown?
Elaine: Nope.

I didn't tell him that I still couldn't believe I turned into a person who not only goes to the library—but could, like, find things there...

Javier: I need a couple books from the library. And the café is amazing. You have time?

I should leave the house. Even if the sun isn't out.

Elaine: Yeah. Take me awhile to get down there.
Javier: No problem. Take the Blue Line to either Jackson or
LaSalle.

Dude, I know how the L works.

Okay. The café at the Harold Washington Library *is* amazing. It's a giant glass-dome greenhouse, like something they would have at Versailles (I have no idea what Versailles looks like).

So, Javier and I were sitting there and he pointed up and was like, "What about an underground greenhouse?"

And then I said, "What do you think's the point of us?" My thoughts about humans and nature and how we ruin everything had not really brightened on the dirty L ride downtown.

"Us, who?" he asked.

"Humans," I said. "The human species."

Javier stared off and thought about it, "Well, if you're religious, I guess we were made so god would have someone to worship him?"

Nope. Bullshit. Next. "I'm not religious," I said.

Javier made a face like he could've guessed that. "So..." he began again.

"Okay, so like trees. What's the point of them?" I asked, thinking about nature.

"They turn carbon dioxide into oxygen. They prevent erosion. Probably other stuff, too," he said. I guess he'd managed to study a few things in the last ten years that weren't art.

But I still shook my head. "That's not what I mean," I said, thinking about *The World Without Us*. "They evolved in their environment and as a result of the environment they do all those things in order to survive. And sure, it's great that they do those things. And other things that need oxygen evolved cause the trees were there, but it's not like they're doing it to be *nice*. It's just how they evolved."

"Okay. Yeah. I see what you're saying," Javier said. "So, then humans..." he held his hands out.

I was nodding, like, Yeah, exactly... "We humans evolved out of the same environment. But so if we're *just* like trees..."

"Then we have no *point*?" he asked. His brow furrowed. "It's all just survival?"

Yeah. No point. Just survival. "But then how do we explain humans killing the shit out of each other all the time? Is it just for survival? Then what's the point of us having consciousness? And knowing that killing is wrong? And coming home from war with terrible PTSD because you *know* that shit was wrong?

"And sure, probably trees steal water or strangle other trees so they don't have to share resources, because they're trying to survive. But maybe they help each other, too.

"Why isn't our goal as humans to help other humans and the world we inhabit, why isn't our goal to try to make existence as good as possible for everyone? That seems like a *better* way to survive. Why are we *so* terrible?

"Did we seriously evolve as a species to torture each other and the Earth? If you read any news..."

He was looking at me, his eyes wide.

"I know. Dark. I know. Angry," I said. I took a deep breath and sighed. The air in the greenhouse was damp and green and it had been months since I'd felt air like that. It was winter outside, but the flowers were blooming in the Harold Washington library.

Javier just looked at me. "I read *The World Without Us* after you told me about it," he said.

Non sequitr. "Okay," I said. "Cool."

He wasn't distracted by my surliness. "Do you remember the part about the flowers?" he asked.

No. "No," I said.

"The part where it says humans couldn't've evolved without flowers?" he asked.

I shook my head.

He nodded. "There's that whole part in there where it talks about how flowers make fruit and before fruit, there weren't enough calories to keep warm-blooded animals alive," he said.

We looked around the greenhouse at the bright and blooming flowers.

"They really are beautiful," I said. I couldn't help it. I closed my eyes and breathed.

"They are," he said. "Don't you think that *might* mean something?"

Humans couldn't have evolved if flowers hadn't evolved. But flowers did evolve. And so did we. And they *are* beautiful.

We *did* evolve.

We are *meant* to be here, right?

"We are because the flowers are," I whispered.

"We are because the flowers are," he whispered back to me.

I didn't open my eyes, but god I hoped we were right. "So, what are we supposed to *do?*" I whispered back.

PENELOPE IN THE GARDEN

We are because the flowers are...

That's pretty reassuring. For some reason.

Maybe that can be something to do with Penelope? Poor little clone could use some reassurance, too. Maybe she's, like, a plant psychic. Like something about being a clone has taken her out of the normal order of evolution and she's, like, weirdly good at plants and flowers because of that?

So, what does that mean? How would that look in the story? In Penelope's first scene, she's working in their underground greenhouse. She's been going there more and more. Just like Radha's been going to the Comm more. We don't know yet that Radha's her sister. We definitely don't know yet that she's Radha's clone. Penelope doesn't look like Radha's sister *or* her clone. Their mom did that on purpose.

When we meet Penelope, she's in the garden. She's medium height and lush—like the flowers she tends.

She knows what to do here. She knows who she is here. She feels safe here.

She moves amongst the flowers. Her black hair pulled back from her face and neck and her deep brown skin is dewy in the humid air. The flowers are all in a long soil trough. Penelope moves from one to the next. She plucks the few weeds that have grown. She feeds water. Her hands know what to do, but it's more than that. Because she doesn't even have to look or touch before she knows what to do. She feels it. She *feels* them.

But there's also the dark side of it. Before she found out she was a clone, she didn't care that she wasn't being trained to work in the genetics lab like Radha. But after she finds out, she thinks that her mom isn't training her to work in the lab because her mom doesn't *really* think of Penelope as being in the family line—doesn't *really* think of her as human, maybe her mom thinks of her as Radha's monster...And she starts to think that her gift with flowers, the thing she always loved and trusted about herself, maybe it's not a gift at all...

That would give her a reason to leave.

THE WORLD FOR BOYS

Spoiler alert: Mama Helen and Mama Jane love watching police procedurals. I'm pretty sure we've watched every single Law & Order, and Law & Order SVU at least 3 times. But that's just the tip of the iceberg. You would be shocked how many police movies and series and *mini*-series there are out there. Especially if you consider the ones that don't take place in America. Which the moms do.

Since I didn't have homework anymore, the moms were like, We need a break from this project. So, we watched the whole first season (like 15 hours) of this show called *Broadchurch* in a week. The gist of the story is an 11-year old boy is found murdered in a small British seaside town. The whole town is wrecked. Everyone is a suspect, etc. I won't ruin it and tell you who the killer is because you should totally watch it.

On Friday night, though, we were sitting there, not eating our popcorn cause it was like, so tense. Mama Helen was huddled under a blanket on the recliner. Mama Jane was sitting next to me crossing and uncrossing her arms, tucking and untucking her legs...I was frantically taking notes.

Finally, Mama Jane was like, "Elaine, Jesus. Can you please stop writing?"

I was like, "Sorry." I put the pad on the couch next to me and then squirmed in my seat for the next 20 minutes until Mama Jane was finally like, "Jesus. That's even worse. Just sit where I can't see you."

So, I traded places with Mama Helen and spent the rest of the show vigorously writing notes.

After the episode was over, Mama Jane was like, "What was *that* all about?" In all our over a decade of watching movies and shows, I had never taken notes.

"This is heartbreaking," Mama Helen said. She literally dabbed her eyes and sniffled.

"Jesus Christ!" I said. "Javier is right. This world *is* terrible to men. I always thought it was only terrible to women. But no. It screws everyone."

Mama Jane looked at me, "That's what you were writing about?"

Mama Helen was like, "Is that what you think that show was about? That the world is bad to men?"

I nodded. Then I shrugged. Then I shook my head. "Well, not only," I said. "What do you think it's about?"

"Family. Friendship. Loss. Trust." Mama Helen said. She's a big picture thinker. "What do you think it's about?" she asked Mama Jane.

"Scottish accents," she said, immediately. Mama Jane likes to joke when things are serious.

Mama Helen and I were both like, Whatever. And I said to Mama Helen, "It's about how the way men are trained to be men totally fucks them. And everyone else," I said.

Neither of them commented on my language. I'd been cursing around them less, but they'd been making less of a deal about it, too.

"Let's just take for instance, I said and pulled out my notes:

1) The one boy, Danny, tells the other boy, Tom, that he doesn't want to be friends anymore. So what does Tom do? Tells Danny that he hates him, that he hopes he dies, and that he could kill him if he wanted to. I'm not saying that no girl would respond that way. But probs the girl just cries and talks shit about the other girl. Pretty much the only emotion Tommy has is violent anger. And even though his mom tries to tell him that it's okay to 'have a cry,' already by age 12, he can barely do it.

2) That crap where the men take the boys off to do secret "manly" shit without telling the mom because they know she'd be like, No fucking way. Sneaking off to do paint-ball, maybe...to kill animals, no! Sure, that has nothing to do with the murder itself, but the fact that there's a whole culture of secret dude violence...

3) The old dude who's accused of being a pedophile because he hugged a boy (who he hugged because he reminded him of his *own* dead son). I mean, he had the best line of the whole show, like, What kind of world are we living in when this is what you think of a man who wants affection. Not to mention that's what caused the murder in the first place—a dude wanting to hug."

Having delivered my lecture, I threw my notepad down and looked back at the moms who were both staring at me with their mouths open.

"You came up with all that while you were just sitting there watching?" Mama Jane asked.

"Well, Javier and I were talking about it the other day—how the world has such strict rules for dudes..." I said.

"We gotta meet this kid," Mama Helen said.

"Seriously? How do you know him, again?" Mama Jane never listens.

"I told you. From the conference..." I said.

"I never listen," Mama Jane said.

"Wait a second," Mama Helen jumped in.

"He's not *old* is he?" Mama Jane asked.

I could see both their minds working. No, I wasn't hanging out with some old writer dude who was gonna seduce me. That ship had already sailed. "Ohmygod," I said. "He's my age. He's a homeschooler..."

They looked at each other like, Phew.

THE GHOSTS THAT PURSUE YOU

From *A Writer Writes*: Humans are not just future-thinking animals, but past-thinking animals as well. What are your characters' pasts? What ghosts haunt them and pursue them into their futures?

What are Merton's ghosts? What pursues him?

What was life in The Under like for him? He's from the rich-kid side, so we won't say his life is a struggle. And yet something makes him want to leave. Then something makes him *leave*. Leaving isn't easy. But asking a girl who he *knows* is a crazy-intense weirdo from the Eastside to leave with him...that's either bravery or desperation. And he's not going to be that brave for no reason. And I don't think Hugh is enough. Hugh might give him a reason to leave. But what caused him to want to break out of the Comm in the first place?

The old dude in *Broadchurch* got accused of pedophilia cause he wanted a hug. Compare that to the dead kid's mom asking Tommy for a hug since her own son is dead. Totally acceptable, why wouldn't a woman and mother want to feel the body of a boy about the same age and size as her own dead son?

But beyond it being an example of the world being fucked up for the old dude who's not allowed to have a hug, what about the world of moms and sons? What about the boy who wants to feel his mother's arms around him? Who wants to feel a mother's body just the same way she wants to feel a son's? Where does that feeling go? How do we drive that out of them?

It won't be Merton's mom who's gone. The mother's always dead in these books and that's the reason for everything.

But maybe his aunt?

Maybe she gets kicked out. Maybe she banged some married dude and on the Westside, it's definitely the unmarried woman's fault and she's getting kicked out.

And then the kids are going to give Merton some never-ending shit cause kids are assholes.

But he won't tell Radha and Penelope that he's looking for her. That she's the reason he broke out of the Comm in the first place. Is Hugh real? Or does Merton just make him up as an excuse to go leave because the Westside people are so shitty to him and because he sees Radha as an opportunity? I can worry about that later.

Radha and Penelope would definitely know about the aunt. Even though the sides are separate, it would be a BFD if someone got banished.

I'll have to go back and edit the first scene between Merton and Radha when he's trying to get her to leave. He'll definitely mention it like, "I'm sure you've heard about my aunt..."

And cause Radha loves to fuck with people, she'll be like, "The one who got the boot because Westsiders can't have sex?"

It's probably also what draws Penelope to him—she can feel that he's suffering. Like she's suffering for being a clone.

Jesus. Turns out this culture sucks for everyone.

THE LONELIEST WHALE

About week later, Javier and I were invited to a party at Tony's apartment. Well, I was invited. And I was like, There's no way in hell I'm going to that. But then I thought back to Tony's crew—how funny, and not gross, and like Audra was an actual part of it...And I thought, Okay, but there's no way in hell I'm going alone. I considered inviting Jenn, but I got a flash of an image of her in a bedroom with Tony...I invited Javier.

We hadn't seen each other since Versailles, but we'd texted a few times like...

> Elaine: Penelope's some kind of flower psychic.
> Javier: I'm really getting somewhere with this new idea.
> Elaine: Merton has a banished aunt.
> Javier: It's with fairy tales.

It was nice to have someone to text, even a little, who understood about trying to invent a whole world. I'd been feeling pretty great since I met with KPao and since I discovered that Radha had a clone sister. Like I could maybe really believe that the story existed out there somewhere and I just had to slowly, slowly, sketch after sketch, discover it, and then put it together.

Javier and I got to the party and it was hard to know if it was the party or if it was me, but it didn't seem to have the "will we or won't we" vibe? Like people (girls and guys) were definitely talking and laughing, but it wasn't as much of the Sternin-in-Training hair-tossing and it wasn't the neck-exposing that chick in the Jabberwocky was doing with TABC and it wasn't the dudes leaning back in their chairs and puffing their chests.

The apartment was over a bakery called Dinkle's. You could smell the sugar and donuts all the way up the stairs. The inside was a total goddam mess. I hadn't ever thought about it before, but in all the houses I knew, all the grown-up houses, the rooms *go* together. The furniture, the lamps, the rugs and curtains and art...they match. Tony's place had all those same components, but it was like a collage. A room of hand-me-downs and trash-picks.

Is this what 20-something apartments look like?

There was a velvet painting of some grandparent types over the mantle. The grandfather had tinted glasses and a butterfly collar. The grandmother had a perm. There's no way they were the grandparents of Tony or his roommates.

There were bookshelves and built-in bookshelves and cabinets filled with books, magazines, books in side stacks, giant clutters of mail...The "dining room table," which I guessed had either been cleared off or created specifically for the party, was two saw-horses with a piece of plywood on top painted neon green.

There were six chairs—two of one kind and three of another and one straggler. On top of a built-in cabinet, there was a shoebox filled with cords + a bathtub stopper + a sketchbook with oil pastels + a drill + *The Complete Beatles Recording Sessions* + DVDs (who owns DVDs?), and a mountain of some magazine called TapeOp.

It smelled like dust bunnies and socks with just a hint garbage that needed to go out days ago. There were rows and stacks of empty wine bottles and beer bottles & cans filling the entire built-in china cabinet behind the dining room table. A new collection was beginning on the top shelves of the built-ins, meaning someone had to take the trouble to climb up there.

There was a deep purple, velvety sectional couch taking up nearly all of the front room.

Javier and I both stood by the front door taking it in. His reaction made me think that he hadn't been in many apartments like this, either. "That's a lot of stuff," I said.

He nodded.

Tony appeared in front of us. "I was going to give you wristbands that said Don't Feed the Teens," he said. "But I amended it to no giving you drugs." I'd asked him if it was okay if I brought a friend and I guess he figured it would be another kid, like me.

Javier and I were like, Is he joking or serious?

Tony said, "So no asking for drugs." 100% serious.

I worried that Javier was going to be offended or say something dorky or say something trying to be cool, but that was actually dorky.

Then I realized I was usually the person who would say something like, All classes of drugs or just, like, the Schedule I drugs?

But Javier said, "Good looking out, man," and he was standing in this way, like I don't know what it was, except it was not nervous. And not in the, I'm going to pretend I'm not nervous, but act in a way that makes it obvious how nervous I am.

Like Hudson and Hicks.

When their ship is dropping down to the colony and most of the crew is strapped to their seats trying not to barf, Hudson is parading up and down the aisle of the drop-ship with his big gun, swaggering and like, "I am the ultimate badass. State of the badass art. You do *not* want to fuck with me." But then *he's* the dude who spends most of the time down in the colony freaking-out like, "Now what the fuck are supposed to do? We're in some really pretty shit..."

Hicks is just like, Wake me up when we get there and he falls asleep.

Something about how Javier was standing and his voice when he talked to Tony made me think, Oh phew, he's a Hicks, not a Hudson.

Tony sensed it too cause he was like, "So, you're an illustrator?" and they started talking about that and it was really cool that Tony said "illustrator" cause it meant he'd been listening when I told him and, I don't know, it was respectful or something.

I could hear The Bitch Annette saying, "So Elaine tells me you draw pictures," in the same way she asked me how my "little story" was coming. You can tell she a) doesn't give a rat's ass, b) thinks what you're doing is stupid, and c) either wasn't listening when you used to the words "illustrator" and "novel" or is purposefully not using those words to make you cry. Again, I still don't know if TBA's bitch behavior is conscious or unconscious. Does it matter?

"How many of you live here?" I asked, looking again at the layers and layers of stuff.

"Four of us all the time," Tony said. "And two other guys who do IT for various Cons, so they're on the road a ton." He pointed to the multi-monitor computer console on a desk in the corner that said "gamer" or "hacker" or "IT for Cons."

"There's six bedrooms here?" I didn't see how that was possible.

"Four," he said. "The other guys store their stuff here and sleep on the futon when they're back." He pointed to the futon in the alcove off the kitchen that I tried not to look at cause, awkward.

"Do they share it?" I asked. Maybe they were lovers. IT dudes for Cons who were also lovers.

Tony laughed. "Different schedules," he said. "Coordinated."

"That's a lot of dudes," I said. It certainly did answer for all the stuff. And the smell.

"Rent's expensive," Tony said. "You kids want beers?"

"Sure," we said, in unison. Or two vodkas really fast...

We went to the kitchen and he took the beers from the fridge and then said, "Javier, you've gotta meet this guy."

Javier made a face, like, Do you mind if I go? I nodded, like, Totally fine. Though I was actually like, Ugh, barf.

I had a couple sips of beer and a gross flashback to the rooftop bar and felt freshly humiliated knowing the waitress had seen. I thought again about Jenn's vodka cure, but I didn't want to have to wrestle some hipster for hard alcohol. Instead, I went into the not-at-all-clean-but-at-least-stacked living room and within 30 seconds this *incredibly* (like I don't think you understand) hot dude was talking to me. Tall, white, dark brown hair, dark brown eyes...Just like, archetypally hot dude. He obviously knew it and gushed a sexual vibe that staggered me.

If I was on my sexual vision quest, searching for novel sperm, I would definitely bang this guy.

Only it was the 21st century at Tony's party, and I was like, This guy doesn't know anything about sexual vision quests. This dude is laying it on. And all the sudden I had a flashback to TABC on the roof deck and was like, Oh goddammit. He was being *so blatant* and gross and I totally fell for it.

And then hot dude said, "So, you're Tony's armageddon girl..."

"Umm." I could not think what to say. "I guess so?"

"I'm Mark," he said and held out his hand.

"Hi Mark," I said and gave him my hand.

He held onto it and turned it over and said, "Armageddon girl..."

My body was like, Yes, please.

And then he started confessing things. Personal things. His last girlfriend had an abortion. Yes, he went with her to the appointment, but he hadn't been *kind* to her. He put a lot of emphasis on the word "kind." And then he said something about how the experience with his girlfriend, or rather "ex-girlfriend," made him realize that he really wanted to dedicate his life to something bigger than himself. He really wanted to try to save the whales.

I was like, How did we get here?

"Have you heard about this whale who sings at a different pitch from all the other whales and so it doesn't have any friends?" he asked me. Before I could answer, he went on. His t-shirt was the exact length so that when he reached to scratch his shoulder, it lifted up and you could see his flat stomach and perfect abs. Was that his party shirt or were all his shirts the same? Did he have a procedure for shrinking them all exactly right?

I looked at my beer, Is this guy hitting on me or confessing to me? And then it occurred to me, amongst the mingling and the clinking and the people climbing over the windowsill to smoke on the roof below, that maybe he was confessing to me in order to hit on me. He thought that the way to my heart (and by "to my heart" I mean, "down my pants") was through a "mostly I care about kindness, mostly I care about the whales..." confessional. He sized me up and decided that was the way to fuck me.

But then again, maybe he wasn't kind to his girlfriend and it was his "life's greatest regret" and he really did understand what "it means to be both truly bad and truly good." Maybe he did love the whales more than anything and I was a cynical bitch because TABC had surmised (correctly) that the way to my book idea was through flattering me and making out with me.

Either way, if that guy loved the whales or didn't love the whales, I was pretty sure he wasn't going to make a dent in the problem.

And while I was thinking all this, he kept talking. He hadn't asked me a single question. Maybe I loved the whales, too. Maybe I knew everything there was to know about that whale that sings a song only it can hear. Maybe we were a perfect match. In the past (Christ, try four months ago) I would've stuck around out of politeness or disbelief and happiness that a good-looking dude was talking to me...And then he would've stolen my book idea. And let's be honest, of course, I wanted to make out with the hot dude (just like I'd wanted to make out with TABC), he was beautiful. Magnetic. I was sure every girl wanted to make out with him and have all that energy focused on them at least for awhile. I stared at him as he talked and I was like, Who the fuck is this guy? With his talking and talking. Why am I bothering with him? He didn't even see me. TABC didn't see me. Half the world doesn't see me or each other or anything other than themselves. What if I'd lost more than my book to The Asshole Brenden Carter? Suddenly the room was too hot and my clothes felt like they didn't fit right and I needed to get away.

"Good luck with the whales," I said and started to turn away.

"Wait," he said. "Umm. Aren't you writing a book?"

I get it. Whales isn't working. "Dude," I muttered.

I set my beer into the background. Where's Javier? I wove through hipsters talking too loud, halfway across the apartment. Maybe every party *is* the same.

There's a part in *This Is Our Youth* after Tavi Gevinson and Michael Cera sleep together and you *know* he really likes her and he's telling me really likes her. And she's like, I like everything you're saying, but I don't know if I can believe you...I feel that. I *feel* that.

I don't know, maybe Mark's girlfriend did have an abortion. I wasn't making light of that. That's not what I'm talking about.

But he was just so...I looked back toward the window where we'd been standing. He wasn't there. I don't know why I was looking for him. Maybe I thought he'd see me, know exactly why I'd bailed, what I was thinking, and shrug, like, Well, you can't hate a guy for trying. Just like you can't hate a guy for stealing a good idea.

Tony materialized at my side. "Having fun?" he asked. Then he looked at my hand. "You're out of beer," he said.

I looked down at my empty hand. The hand that Mark had held. The wrist that TABC had touched. "Oh yeah," I said.

"I'll get you one," he said and turned toward the kitchen.

But then this group of dudes was like, "Tony, come here...Blahblahblah," something about some kind of microphone cord...

I said, "It's cool," and went to the kitchen by myself, thinking about Mark, thinking about TABC, and there were Javier and Audra, talking at a small table in the corner. Her hair was in full meringue and she was wearing a black t-shirt and a thin silver armband just above her elbow. It was like, whoosh, the weirdest feeling. Jealousy? More like, How could Javier be talking to someone so terrifyingly cool? And how could she be talking to him—he's a kid.

I pretended not to see them. I opened the fridge door and bent to hide behind it, pretending I was choosing a beer, gulping breaths of cold air.

But Javier said, "Elaine, hey, come here."

I took the cap off the bottle and jammed both it and my hand in my pocket and pressed the points of the cap into my leg through my jeans.

Javier said, "This is Audra."

I know who this is. I pictured the flowers on the backs of her legs. We are because the flowers are. I smiled and said, "Nice to meet you." Dork. I am the dork. Javier is Hicks. I am Hudson. What the fuck am I gonna do now, man? I can't talk to her.

"Don't I see you at Zero Drop?" she asked.

I wasn't used to people at parties admitting that they had any clue who I was. Normally, they were like, Do you even go to our school? "Um, yeah," I said to Audra. "I live right by there, so..."

"She's writing a book," Javier said as though it was a totally normal thing.

"Ohh, cool," she said. "What's it about?"

I froze. I wanted to barf. Standing there, above Javier, who was, like, a legit, award-winning illustrator, who hadn't gone to school for 10 years and taught himself computer programs to do his art...and Audra, with her mohawk and flowers and her ability to not give one shit about what those bros thought of her and who did the seltzer drawings that dudes wanted her to tattoo (probably already *had* tattooed) onto their bodies forever...I felt dizzy and distant and they were looking at me waiting for an answer. I couldn't answer. My book is total bullshit. I've written like one page. And suddenly all the excitement and confidence I'd been feeling disappeared in a swirl. Maybe Penelope isn't a clone. Maybe they don't leave The Under. Maybe...Maybe I just end up a junior at DB High. "I don't really like to talk about it too early in the process," I said. And hated myself for using TABC's line.

Audra nodded and said, "I get it." I knew she was thinking that I was a total weirdo loser.

Then this girl, drunk, was standing in front of us, lifting her shirt to show a massive, colorful tattoo on her back, "Audra, ohmygod, it's healing so well." Do these people do anything else?

"You wanna get outta here?" Javier asked.

I could only nod.

ARMAGEDDON GIRL I

In 8th grade, Jenn invited me to go with her to a gala for the Chicago Symphony Orchestra. We had to wear dresses that went all the way to the floor.

I'd gone shopping at Nordstrom with Mama Helen—we never shopped there. The party was over winter break and The Bitch Annette was visiting for the holidays.

We got home from the store and I was so proud and nervous and I couldn't wait to show Mama Jane.

The Bitch Annette was there too. "Well, let's see it," she said.

A look passed between the moms and I should've known something was up, but I didn't. I went to change in my room...

"...like I didn't change your diapers a thousand times," TBA called after me.

When I came back to the kitchen in my navy blue tank dress, feeling grown-up and excited and like I didn't know how to hold my body, before the moms could say anything to me, TBA said, "Well, you're built just like the broad side of a barn."

"Mom!" Mama Jane said. So *that* was the look.

TBA shrugged. "I'm just being honest," she said. "Your slender friend, Jenn, now she can wear anything. But you'll have to be careful."

"Annette," Mama Helen said. Her voice was a warning.

The Bitch Annette held up her hands like, Okay, I'll stop talking, but I'm telling the truth.

In my whole life, I had *never* considered my body anything other than my body. Which now that I think about it, was pretty amazing for a 14-year-old girl. Ask me how much I've thought about it since TBA told me how I was built. Ask me how much I enjoyed that dress. All I felt the whole time I wore it was the way my back pressed against the taut fabric. I couldn't wait to get it off and away from me.

And the thing was—I wasn't built like the broad side of a barn. Not then and not now. But that's not the point. The point is not to convince you how much I did or didn't weigh. How big I was or wasn't. The point isn't to prove that I'm thin enough that The Bitch Annette shouldn't have said anything. The point is, she *never* should have said anything. The point is, who says that? I had felt *great*. And she stole that from me. Maybe forever.

You know what's even worse? I spent the week leading up to the party thinking of ways I was better than my "slender friend." My *best* friend. *That* felt just as horrible as not being able to enjoy the way that dress felt skimming my adolescent body. Maybe more horrible.

That was how I felt when Javier and I left the party, back into the stairwell that smelled like sugar donuts. Like he and Audra lived in the world in a totally different way than I did. Like they *knew* they belonged there. Like Javier was a real artist. Audra was a real artist. And like I was built like the broad side of a barn. And I wanted to find some way, *all* of the ways I was better than him, so I didn't have to feel like shit.

ARMAGGEDON GIRL II

We left the building through the narrow entry and this dude tried to shoulder his way past us. I assumed he was just some guy on his way to the party, so I pushed us past him. I needed to get out into the cold air. We got to the sidewalk and I started to take a deep breath, but then the dude yelled, "Hey! You kids!" We turned around and he was standing there on the stoop with his date.

"Yeah," I said.

"I'm a police officer," he said. He wasn't wearing a uniform. He was wearing a long black coat like everyone else in Chicago.

"Yes, sir," Javier said.

"Okay," I said. No need to kiss his ass.

"I'm entering these premises and you two were obstructing my progress," he said.

"Oh no," Javier whispered.

You don't look like a cop. You look like a dude on a date. I said, "Sir, please excuse us. If you had identified yourself, of course, we would have let you through." I wasn't even being sarcastic. At all. I honestly don't think there was a more straight-forward thing I could have said to him. I just wanted him to go the hell away, so I could try to stop the barf feeling.

The cop narrowed his eyes at us and said, "I am an officer in the Chicago PD. I don't have to identify myself to you. I work for the Commissioner of Police, not for you."

At which point, I took a step toward the guy.

Javier tried to grab my arm, but I yanked it away.

What is *with* people? Why can they not just be *nice?* "Actually," I said. "You do work for me. I'm a citizen of this city. You," I said, pointing at the cop, "Work for me," and I pointed at myself. God it felt good.

Another dude, standing in the street, smoking, nodded his head, like, She's got a point.

"Listen, girl," the cop said.

Even the smoker winced at that.

"What's your badge number?" I asked. Thanks, *Law & Order, SVU.*

That stopped him. He was probably on his first date with this woman and there was a part of me that wanted to say, I get it, dude. You were showing off and now you're in a pissing contest with a teenage girl. But I *tried* to give you an out. I gave you a chance to de-escalate. Why didn't you just take it?

Instead, Javier tugged at my arm again and said, "Let's go."

Of course, I couldn't help myself and said, "Nice 'Serve and Protect,' dude," as I was turning away.

The cop flinched and I was waiting for him to call us back (authority figures hate being called "dude"), but his date put her hand on his shoulder and Javier yanked me away.

"Shut the fuck up," he hissed.

That stopped *me*. We hadn't been hanging out very long, but I'd never heard Javier curse.

"Whatever," I said, trying to ignore the fact that he was obviously mad at me. "I was totally right."

We walked about a half a block in silence and Javier stopped, turned to look at me, and said, "That could've gotten bad," Javier said. I was about to argue with him when he looked straight at me and said, "For me. Bad for *me*."

"Oh god," I said and looked at him the way the cop likely saw him—a brown skin kid in a mostly white neighborhood, shoving his way out of a building with some mouthy little bitch. Probably on drugs. I wanted to cry. "I'm a jerk," I said.

"Yes," Javier said and I could see his breath in the cold air. "You are." The smoker was far behind us, but he would've agreed with that, too.

"I don't know what's wrong with me," I said. "I just want the world to be kind. And when it's not kind, I at least want it to be fair. And when it's not either of those things, when it's cops that yell at you for no reason and like, the Earth and the air and the bees and the litter and and I don't know...dead puppies...I get so furious and I want to burn it all to the motherfucking ground. I want to barf blood on people."

Javier stood there, staring at me. It was cold and dark and a car drove through the slush on the street.

And then I saw Radha and Merton. Very sudden. Very vague. Just a flash of a moment. Radha holding a wound in her belly as blood seeps through. Her head in Merton's lap. She looks up at him and the bright blue sky behind him. "I'm sorry," she says.

And then Radha and Merton were gone and it was me, looking at Javier, on a cold street in winter Chicago. Now we're definitely done being friends. "I'm sorry," I said.

LISTEN, SWEETHEART

I got home. It wasn't that late.

I headed toward the living room wondering if I should text Javier and apologize again. Or text him a question and see if he wrote back. Then I was like, Fuck, think of something easier. Okay, where do they go first? Where's this Hugh friend supposed to be hanging-out in trouble? Also, problems and obstacles have to happen to Radha, Penelope, and Merton along the way cause that's how stories work, like that structure you learn about in school—bad things happen, then good things, then worse, then better, until finally you hit the climax and then...Happily Ever After.

Life doesn't work like that, though. In life you gotta go around and around learning the same dumb shit over and over and over and over.

I was not in this world when I walked into the living room. I was not prepared for the dude sitting on the couch.

He's an investment dude I'd met a couple years before at the holiday party the moms had for all their workers and work associates. The first floor of our house is kind of divided down the middle with the kitchen on one side and the living room and dining room on the other. During the party, the dudes who built shit were in the kitchen, the dudes who wrote checks hung out in the dining room, and the moms' friend who's an architect wandered around like he didn't know what the hell. Until Uncle Alex got there. Then he and the architect drank beer in the foyer and talked about some baseball thing called The Goat Curse. And then, eventually, all the dudes were drinking beer in the foyer yelling about baseball. That shit is uncanny. The investment dude's name was Rick (I know, right?) and he could go fuck himself. He kept calling Mama Helen "sweetheart" and one time he touched her on the small of her back. She shifted away and I was just like, Get this guy outta my house.

So, when it was him on the couch, I was like, Oh great...the skeevy dude who likes to hit on queer moms.

But since it's polite to hang out with a guest while he waits, I sat down. He immediately started doing that thing where the adult grills the kid with 1,000 personal questions.

Normally, I'm a perfectly good liar when it comes to not wanting to tell one goddam thing to someone like him. But I don't know, I was like, I bet Georgia O'Keeffe didn't ever lie to some skeeve just so she didn't feel violated. So, I was like, "Actually, I don't go to school."

He's white and dyes his hair and was wearing those creepy fashion jeans that are faded in a strip down the front of the legs and he rubbed his hands up and down the strip and was like, "So what do you do?"

I wish I'd told him I was making a giant clay models of vulva-flowers. Instead I said, "I'm writing a sci-fi novel."

Rick leaned forward and his cologne washed over me. He smelled like inappropriate touching. "Well, here's the truth, sweetheart..."

I basically blacked-out for 30 seconds and didn't hear the rest because I was like, I am not your sweetheart...and also cause I was like, If you'll skeeve all over queer chicks (with whom you supposedly have a professional relationship) and teenage girls, what are you like in the world? I sank into my sweater and pitied the woman wearing a skirt around skeevy Rick.

Then he was looking at me with expectation, so there must have been a question while I was thinking about how to get the hell out of there.

"Sorry?" I said and slouched down farther into the couch.

"So who do you know?" he repeated.

He better not try to hug me when I leave. "Where?"

He frowned, wondering if I was stupid or deaf or messing with him. I wish I'd been messing with him. "In life," he said. "As I said, 'It's not what you know that matters. It's who you know...'"

"Oh," I said, getting it. "Who do I know who can help me with my book?" Because my talent and effort won't be enough. I knew Brenden Carter. You two would be best friends.

He smiled like, Now sweetheart gets it.

I wanted out of there. Away from his skeevy-smell and bullshit philosophy. I wanted away from his smug, greasy, slicked-back hair. "No one," I said and stood up. "I know no one." I pointed at the kitchen. "I'm gonna go see what they're doing."

"Listen sweetheart..."

Cringe. Barf.

"...I'd be happy to make some introductions..." he said.

I was already walking away from the couches.

"Um. That's okay," I mumbled. I got to the door of the kitchen and wished to hell I'd said, I'll have my people call your people, but of course, sweetheart hadn't thought of that.

THE RED ZONE

Here's what I wanted to know. First of all, why was Skeevy Rick even in our house? I knew the moms didn't like him.

Second of all, why are some dudes so fucking skeevy.

Remember Nurse Party-Panties? She also said that we girls needed to teach the boys restraint and patience when it comes to sex. To which I say, Then why am I wearing special panties to parties?! But also, What the fuck, lady? How about their parents teach them that? How about *you* teach them that? Why's that my job? You're telling me that I'm going to start having feelings that I won't understand (how about trying to explain them to me. Spoiler alert: it's called biology) and I'm supposed to deal with that *and* teach dudes restraint. *And* do pre-Algebra. Fuck you.

But also, by now we've all heard of The Red Zone in college, right? "The first month and a half of college is the time when freshmen women are most likely to be raped or experience attempted rape..." So schools and other well-meaning people/institutions are like, "Be careful, girls. Beware the Red Zone. Beware the time when you're most likely to be raped. Don't leave your drink alone. Don't leave your friends alone. Wait until after Christmas to leave your dorm room..."

How about we reverse that? What if we took the boys aside and were like, "Beware the Red Zone, dudes. This is the time of the year when you're most likely to be a rapist. Maybe you should stay home until we're out of the Red Zone. Watch a movie with some buddies. But if you are going to go out, don't drink too much, it might make you a rapist. If you notice one of your friends drinking too much, encourage him to slow down. If you see one of your friends heading off alone with a girl, consider intervening, it is the Red Zone after all—now's the time he's most likely to rape her."

HOW DO YOU LEARN?

One of the first exercises in A *Writer Writes* was make a list of your fears about writing. I hadn't thought about it in awhile, but there it was...I don't know how to write a book, someone will steal this idea, I suck at writing, I won't finish, back to school, repeat junior year, everyone laughs at me and my dyke moms, the Earth is doomed and nothing I do matters...Add to that, Javier is gone.

This is a tailspin.

Thinking all the wrong things.

Thinking, again, about revenge on The Asshole Brenden Carter.

About being back to school.

About getting published and fuck you to everyone who's ever said anything about my moms.

Not writing.

Everything dying.

Just going around and around and around and around and around and around and around.

All the wrong things.

I know it.

In my mind, I know it.

But it flares up.

And I grab it.

It burns me.

And I hold on anyway.

How do you learn to think the right things?

How do you learn to do the right things?

How do you learn to be the right things?

How do you learn?

NOT THE WHOLE WORLD

All I could think to do was trace my steps back to the last place I hadn't felt like garbage. I asked KPao if I could meet with her again. I rode the train back down to campus and this time I waited for her in the Biology Center on a gray-brown couch by the windows where you could see the pond. Then she was coming down the hall, moving fast, and I was so relieved to see her, I just yelled, "K. Pao!"

She looked up and smiled. She was wearing black slacks and light pink sweater set. Her hair pulled back from her face in a low ponytail. "Gimme five," she said and ducked into the department office.

It's gonna be okay. It's gonna be okay. I took a shaky breath and tried to hang on. Tried not to let the thoughts in. What if talking the moms into letting me leave was a fluke? What if I was going to have to go back? What if?

Waiting for KPao, thinking about Javier, Audra, Tony, that cop...but even more about Radha, Merton, and Penelope...I was just scared.

It was too late to go back. But I couldn't tell if I was going forward.

Then suddenly this dude—a Black guy in a burgundy turtleneck sweater and those no-frame glasses that would've made Jenn wrinkle her nose and say, Hmm, I wouldn't, showed up in front of me and said, "Did you just shout at Professor Pao?"

What? "Yeah." What does this guy even want?

He crossed his arms. He would've been good looking if he wasn't crossing his arms at me.

"You just shouted 'Ka-Pow' at Professor Pao," he said.

Dude, don't fucking hassle me. This isn't the library. It's not the quiet car. I'm so goddam tired of dudes hassling. "Is that a question?" I asked.

"Do you know who she is?" he asked.

"Yes," I said. She's the woman who told me that vaginas are pretty simple as far as biomes go. "I do."

He crossed his arms harder. "She's Professor Pao. Of the *Pao* Lab."

Oh, for godsake. Fuck. Off.

"Oh, Mr. Breughel, I see you've met Elaine," KPao said, walking over to us.

"Professor Pao," Mr. Breughel stammered.

Well, hello, freak-out. I held out my hand to him, "Elaine Archer," I said.

The guy didn't know what to do. It was like five seconds of KPao looking at Mr. Breughel before he took my hand and said, "Ted Breughel."

"Nice to meet you," I said. Suck on that, hassler.

KPao sat down on the couch with me. "Mr. Breughel is a first-year graduate student. First year?"

Ted Breughel nodded.

"And Elaine and I are going to talk about?" KPao let the question hang. I hadn't said what I wanted to talk about.

I looked at Ted Breughel and smiled. "You know, just more mass extinction stuff," I said. I cannot tell you how much glee filled my whole body, my whole being, as I saw it occur to Mr. Breughel that I, Elaine Archer, who had shouted at Professor Kathy Pao, of the Pao Lab, was going to chill with her while he retreated to do whatever first year graduate students in Ecology & Evolution do, (assumption—it probably sucks).

I know it wasn't kind of me to gloat about how flustered Ted Breughel had been. I know I just gave Javier a whole speech about kindness and fairness and barfing blood...And I mean, I get it. KPao is a big fucking deal. And Mr. Breughel was tripping because shouting at her was like shouting at Einstein and being like, "Hey Einstein, what happens if shit goes super fast?"

And yes, I was lucky that I didn't know who KPao was, cause if I did, maybe I'd be like Ted Breughel and be too intimidated to ask to hang out with her and then I'd have been home, spinning down the drain. But it also seemed like KPao *liked* being shouted at. What if we just treated people like people? I know, cue the orchestra, but seriously. What if we ditched our ideas of who people are and whether they're more or less important than us and whether or not we should talk to them like a human or like Einstein?

I bet Einstein was lonely. I bet he missed being shouted at. Because I only shouted like that at people who I liked and I was excited to see.

"How's the book coming?" KPao asked.

"Terrible," I blurted before I could wonder if I should try to pretend it was going well.

KPao laughed. Which was actually reassuring and some of the tightness in my belly relaxed. "So you're right on track," she said.

She had heard me, right? "No," I said. "At this rate, it's just going to fizzle out, the whole thing, and I'm going to have to go back to school next year..." Fuck. Do not think about that. "I mean, I have *some* stuff. Characters. Some bad guys. And after the last time we met, I was feeling really good..."

"But you're stalled," she said. She was speaking quickly, but not quite as quickly as she had the first time we met. Maybe she saved that speed for ideas, not personal conversations.

"Yes. Stalled," I said. "It's like it's all too big for me to get ahold of. I can't figure out what to say. Or where to even start." I looked out the window and the gray sky and the gray, frozen pond and I didn't know if was making any sense. To her or to me.

She nodded. "I think the real purpose of getting your PhD is to teach you to fail over and over and over. I'm fairly sure I didn't have a single successful research project the entire time I was in school."

Say what? "How is that possible?" I asked. We're talking about a woman who has her own laboratory at one of the Top 10 universities in the country.

"Yeah," she said. "But you just have to keep going. That's what you learn." She shrugged, "Well, and certain analytical processes."

We both laughed.

"Elaine," she said and for some reason it felt good to hear her say my name. To know that she was talking to *me*. "You can do this."

I took a shaky breath. No one had said that yet.

"It's not the whole world," she said. "It's just one piece at a time. One page. And then another page."

One page.

She looked at her watch. "This is unprecedented," she said. "A meeting got cancelled. I have three hours. Let's go to my office and brainstorm. When I stall, it almost always comes down to talking it through with someone."

THE FOUR BASTIONS

Everyone deserves a KPao.

To answer my previous question—she absolutely saved her faster speed for ideas.

We went into her office which was a mediumish rectangle with a big window looking down onto the pond from another angle and with a desk jutting out from one wall into the middle of the room and everywhere, wallpapering the walls, graphs with tiny, little dots. And of course, books and papers on top of every surface...

"Let's sit down there," she said and pointed to the corner opposite her desk and next to the window where there were two large, dense cushions and wooden crate with nothing on it. She lowered herself onto the yellow cushion very quickly. She obviously sat there a lot. "You can't always sit at a desk," she said. "Bad for the body. Bad for the brain." Her speaking had already kicked up like three speeds.

I sat down on the blue cushion, but before I could even ask what next, she said, "Gimme your notebook."

I gave it to her. She flipped to the first blank page, "I'll take the notes," she said, and instantly produced a pen from somewhere, "You talk."

What am I supposed to talk about?

Before I could really even finish the thought she said, "Okay. It's the world, post-mass-extinction. What did you say, 250 years out?"

"Yeah," I said. "So, it's enough time that things are sort of settled into new ways of doing things, new cultures..."

She nodded, wrote something down, "Yep, Got it," she said, "We're not in panic mode anymore." And she looked up at me and winked. I like people who wink.

My own thinking was picking up pace and I had a sudden flash of Lucca the first day we started our project. We were in the art room getting butcher paper off a big roll and he yanked it so fast it totally shredded and I was like, "Dude. Ease down. You've blown the transaxel." To this day, I have no idea what possessed me to quote *Aliens* to the cute new guy. I usually keep that shit on lock. I was right on the verge of being barfingly embarrassed and trying to pretend it hadn't happened, when he quoted back, "You're just grinding metal." We looked at each other in shocked recognition. We laughed. So hard. And that was it. That's how it was. Why he didn't love me?

"So, let's think about this," KPao said. "If you're a group who has managed to survive those 250 years, what does that mean about you?"

I thought about The Under. And those luxury underground condos, the *real* ones. That are, like, already built. "They must have seen it coming," I said.

KPao nodded and scribbled in my notebook, "Yes they did," she said. "And if you see a mass extinction coming, what are you going to have to plan for?"

I thought about the colony in *Aliens*, LV-426, their biggest needs (other than not getting killed by aliens). "Food, water, security," I said.

KPao looked up at me and beamed.

I beamed.

That's how it was.

I told her about the mom I had overheard one time on the bus say to her friend, "We did not evolve for this shit..." She thought women should raise kids in herds. She told her massively pregnant, obviously uncomfortable friend, "Single family homes are bullshit ..." And thus The Yellowstone School was born. A former boarding school at the edge of Yellowstone National Park that two queer women turned into an off-the-grid commune before extinction really hit. These are the same survivors who bring us the—Novel Sperm Vision Quest.

We talked about Uncle Alex and "Detroit needs an Empress" and vertical gardening. So then I had Detroit, a neo-Eden that was all skyscrapers that have nothing left but their steel skeletons and those covered and wrapped and held together with plants and vines...and the streets are forest paths, all the concrete eaten away, the edges dotted with bursting gardens...and all the city creeks that had been drained and paved, now flow through the city, back to the Detroit River.

And NYC would return to a swamp...with the Hudson and East River gobbling up most of it...

KPao snapped her fingers, "We gotta watch this TEDTalk," she said and leapt up off her yellow cushion and grabbed her iPad.

Okay well, holy shit. There's this professor at some university in

England, Rachel Armstrong, who is working on using "metabolic materials" for architecture...blah blah, some kind of fat that you could use in buildings that self-repairs to, 'Grow a limestone reef out of protocells that target the piles that the buildings in Venice are sitting on...'

...there you go, I had my "evil" city. Manhattan. Military rule...a swamp filled with destructed and half-destructed buildings, kept from sinking by a limestone reef made of fat...

Ted Breughel came out of wherever he'd been just as KPao and I finished hugging goodbye and I said, "Take it easy, Ted Breughel," and waved and meant it totally sincerely.

It was still cold and gray outside as I walked to the train, but I felt like the sun was beaming down on me and I was photosynthesizing.

DO NOT EVER

> Me: Sorry. 😔

I could see that he read it. But the little typing bubbles didn't pop up. They kept on not popping up. I was pissed at that goddam cop all over again—if he hadn't been such an asshole, I wouldn't've been a jerk (potentially putting Javier in danger), and my new friend wouldn't maybe be considering not being friends with me anymore. It didn't seem likely that I would stumble across another teenage-homeschooling-creative-book type. Goddamit.

My phone vibrated.

> Javier: Do not ever barf blood on me.

Oh, thank god.

> Me: I won't! I promise!
> Javier: What's up?

I really don't know what I would've done if I'd completely ruined that friendship. In case you missed it, I didn't have a lot of friends. I didn't trust or get along with a lot of people. I can admit that.

> Me: Just had the best brainstorm. Hang out?
> Javier: Sure. Where?
> Me: Zero Drop? Or wherever.
> Javier: That works.
> Me: Sweet. On the Metra now. Be there in 30ish.
> Javier: 🐻

Holy fuck, phew.

LADY JANE

I had coffee. Javier had tea—something called Lady Jane. I was like, That's adorable.

I told him about the conversation with KPao. "I'm calling them The Four Bastions," I said. "The Under, The Yellowstone School, Detroit, and NYC. Obviously, The Under is the luxury bunker that I already told you about," I said.

"I remember," he said. Of course, he did.

"The Yellowstone School is an old boarding school campus that was started by some queer moms," I said. I didn't tell him that The Yellowstone School was kept alive by the girls going on sexual vision quests for random sperm... "Detroit is a city of plants and flowers. It's like hippies and love and an Empress," I said.

"An Empress?" he asked.

"Yes," I said. "And sacred earthworms."

He smiled and sipped his Lady Jane. He'd be a Detroiter.

"And New York is the drowned city and gray and military and evil,"

I said. When I laid them all out, they seemed perfect. Like, Yes, there is a *story* in this world with these characters.

"Wow. That's great." he said. "It was smart you went to talk to her."

I didn't tell him that I'd gone to see her because it felt like everything was falling apart after the party, after the cop. "I'm really lucky I found her," I said.

"How *did* you find her?" he asked. "I guess I never thought about it."

"She was Tony's idea," I said. And the moment I said it, I wished I hadn't. I wished I'd just said, "I emailed her, like I emailed you."

"He seems like a cool guy," Javier said. I was glad he didn't ask how we met.

"So now, I gotta to figure out *why* they're going the places they're going," I said, ignoring the awkwardness.

"Can't just be a post-mass-extinction road trip?" Javier asked. He ignored it, too.

I appreciated that he remembered that it was post-mass-extinction, not post-apocalypse...I was about to ask him something about his new project, you know, I didn't *only* talk about myself, when a white dude in faded burgundy chinos, silver New Balance tennis shoes, silver puffy jacket, and navy White Sox snow-hat opened the door. He stood for a moment in the doorway, surveying (chest literally puffed) and I was like, Dude. Cold. It's goddam Chicago in winter, you close the door. Like, immediately, and firmly. Only this guy walked into the room, over to the counter (propelled by the power of his silver puffy coat) and left the door open wide. Not cracked. Not like, Oops, it didn't catch. *Wide open.* Freezing wind blew in from every direction. I waited for his entourage of douches—there *had* to be one, there was no reason anyone would have left a Chicago door open in winter. One of the prep cooks got up from her break and closed it. Silver Puffy Coat didn't notice.

I looked at Javier like, Who's this guy?

Javier shrugged.

Silver Puffy Coat walked to the counter and said to the barista, "I'll have what I had last time."

The barista smiled awkwardly and was like, "Sorry?"

"You don't have it anymore?" he asked, so awkwardly that for a moment I was like, Maybe he's wasted.

The barista said, "I just don't remember. I'm sorry."

SPC said, "Oh, I assumed it would be memorable." Not wasted. And to be clear, he didn't say it despondently. Not bummed she couldn't remember. He said it totally skeevy. Like, Ew.

"Ew," I said to Javier.

"Seriously," he said.

"Why are dudes so skeevy?"

"Some dudes."

I rolled my eyes. "Yes. *Some* dudes," I said. "Like he just gets to talk to that girl what ever way he wants?"

"She could tell him to back off," Javier said.

I sighed and set my coffee down. "I realize we just returned from a nearly friendship ending blast of my rage..." I began.

"I don't think it would've ended our friendship," Javier said.

I nodded like, Great. "My point is, I'm about to go off," I said.

Javier smiled and raised his cup of Lady Jane to me like, Proceed.

"Let's just play it out, shall we? She tells him not to be skeevy and at best, at best, he smirks at her for being a prude. Maybe he tells her to relax, which is its own kind of creepy back massage that you don't know how to get out of. Yes, that happens. Some dude starts giving you a shoulder massage...Touching you...And you don't want to be rude—because you don't want him to call you a little fucking bitch...so you let it go. Then later, if you say anything, which you probably don't, people are like, Why didn't you tell him to back off? And you're like, Because half the time you tell a dude he's skeeving you, he gets angry. Like scary angry...I mean, how many more screenshots of a guy calling a girl a cunt cause she doesn't respond to his internet advances do we need before we believe this is real?" I wanted to say something about *Sex at Dawn* and how when I read it I felt like there was a connection between the post-agricultural notion of women as property and the skeevy dudes like Rick and SPC and the rampant fucking destruction of the Earth...but I still couldn't quite figure out how it all connected.

"So are those her choices?" I pointed to the barista. "Skeevy guy, or smirking guy, or angry guy? Cause I'll tell you what she's not going to get—apologetic guy."

Javier was grinning. But it was not the grin of condescension. So I went on. "And why should it be her problem in the first place? Why should it be my problem? Like, dudes just do what they do, until someone calls them on their bullshit?" I thought about the Red Zone and girls being encouraged to be careful not to get raped those first several months of college. Like rape is some kind of airborne illness... "And then they still don't change," I added.

Javier's eyes were wide, "You get pissed," he said.

"Yeah" I said, wishing I could shred that puffy goddam jacket. "That guy fucking sucks," I pointed at SPC who was across the room slurping a latte.

"You know the reason I talked to you at the conference?" Javier asked.

That's a fast change of subject. "The conference?"

"*First Things First,*" he reminded me. "The pitch line."

"Cause we were waiting?" I asked. I was confused.

"I wasn't waiting," Javier said, very matter-of-fact.

I furrowed and looked at him. "What were you doing?" It was getting awkward again. The fury had evaporated it for a minute, but what was he talking about? I mean, I guess, when I thought about it, it wasn't Javier who went in to talk to TABC after I left. I just hadn't cared at the time—I was going to get my novel written and published and...My gut clenched. It had been weeks since I'd thought about that.

"I saw you take those ladies down," he said.

"What ladies?" I asked. "Didn't you pitch to...Brenden Carter?" Ask me how hard it was not to call him The Asshole Brenden Carter.

He shook his head.

Why not? "Why not?" I asked.

"Didn't have a ticket," he said. "Even if I had, I probably would've given it away to a writer."

Something doesn't feel right. "So why were you in line?" I asked.

"I wanted to talk to you," he said, again with the matter-of-fact.

I am so uncomfortable.

"Is that weird?" he asked.

Yeah. I shrugged. "Kinda..." I said.

He laughed. Why didn't it seem to be making him feel awkward? Everything made me feel awkward. "I saw you take down those ladies and I thought, 'She looks cool.'"

"Take down those ladies?" What ladies? Oh, shit, *those* ladies. "Those Starbucks bitches?" I asked.

He laughed again and pointed at me. "Them."

"Ohmygod," I said. "The only time you ever see me, I'm losing my shit." Then again, like I said, the world is pretty fucked up. "You think I'm the biggest psycho."

"No way, it was great," he said. "They tried to cut."

"They tried to cut!" I said. "I mean, I feel like I should say I feel bad, but I don't. At all."

Javier was shaking his head, "When that one asked you how old you were," he said and raised his eyebrows like, Damn.

I couldn't help but smirk. It was a pretty classic line.

"Which is why I went to talk to you while you were waiting to pitch," he said. "Though you made it very clear it was not a good time."

"Listen, I was so nervous," I said. "And..."

He smirked.

Then it occurred to me that Javier had done that thing that I always wished people would do—see a person they think might be interesting (based on something other than what you look like in jeans and a sweatshirt, for instance) and then talk to the person. Ohmygod. He'd also come up to me at that mixer, but I was, like, *not* paying attention. He'd made two clear *efforts* to have a conversation with me...The barf feeling. The desire to run away. Sweat. Breathlessness. Was he trying to hook up with me? What's happening? "Wait. What?"

"It was totally badass," he said.

"Why didn't you tell me this before?" I asked.

He laughed at that. "Are you kidding? You would've been like, Oh hi, stalker. And never talked to me again." He gave me a look like, We both know that's true.

I have to make this conversation stop. "Alright, fine," I said. "We've established that my dominant emotion is anger. So what's yours?"

Javier sat back in his chair and smiled.

"Oh. Is this a test?" I asked.

"I'm just interested to hear what you think," he said. "I like hearing what people's impression of me is."

I thought about that little girl in the park screaming, "Look at me!" How amazing it must be, how strange it is when a person can just say, I want people to look at me. I want people to look at my art. How strange to want that and not feel ashamed.

I pictured Javier's illustrations of those boys. It's not that they were emotionless. But they didn't feel...critical. I was critical of everything.

Javier just felt...open. Like he was looking at them and curious and taking them in. "Awe?" I said. "You get fucking awe?"

Javier beamed.

"What the fuck?" I said. "I get anger and you get awe?"

Javier laughed. "That's the breaks."

"Oh my god, you know..." I started to ramp back up again, but then we noticed a woman standing next to our table.

We looked at her like, Um, yeah?

"Sorry to interrupt," she said. She was thin, Asian, and wearing paisley capris. "I just want to say that you two are a joy to watch," she said.

I gaped.

"Thanks," said Javier. Obviously.

"You exude a wonderful energy," she continued. "It's lovely to see such a connection."

I blushed. That was the kind of stuff I was trying to *not* talk about.

"It is lovely," Javier said.

Get me outta here.

WHAT'S CONNECTION?

Connection? What does that mean? Like really?

Is it that the person is reading your mind?

No. Not exactly.

It's like a great song. It's like where you're listening to a great song and it all goes together perfectly. There are different voices and instruments blending together to make something that feels huge and boundaryless and specific and like that song has always been there. It makes you close your eyes and go, "Mmmmmm." Your heart purrs. You don't just hear the song. You feel it. Physically. It reverberates inside you and all your cells vibrate to that exact frequency and you become the song.

That's what it felt like to talk to Lucca.

That's what it felt like to talk to Javier. Sometimes. Like somehow the thinking and the talking became a vibrational frequency that wrapped back around us, like an eddy in a river, and it changed our bodies and the reverberation of our cells until we were both humming at the same frequency.

Whoa!

Did I just smoke PCP?

But holy shit.

What about this?

What if each human, animal, plant, rock (everything that's made of the matter and therefore made of energy) has its own frequency of vibration? Like a fingerprint. I mean, you could have infinity of vibrational frequencies.

What if consciousness and memories and ideas and all that stuff that makes us, us, isn't actually stored in our brains? Or even our bodies? What if it's stored in the frequency? So, it's not in a location. It's in a pattern of movement.

Our bodies are just the place the frequency inhabits so it can interact with itself, with others, with the world.

Like human bodies are the computer and the data is stored in the frequency. Like the goddam cloud (I have no idea how the cloud works).

If you knew your frequency, you could move your consciousness anywhere.

Or, you could change someone's frequency. Then it would be some *other* consciousness.

This is crazy.

I need to talk to Javier again.

Except I can't talk to Javier again. Too soon. 😶

Like with Jenn, I could text her 1,000,000,000 times a day (which we used to do...) and she would be like, That's normal.

I mean, I wanted to talk to him about, What if consciousness is stored in vibrations and every thing that exists can be planted and transplanted somewhere else? But we'd already been hanging out and that "connection" lady was spooky and I still didn't know what to do with him seeing me yell at those Starbucks bitches or with the fact that he'd tried to talk to me—twice.

So instead, I wrote.

THE UNDER, BY ELAINE ARCHER

Prologue—*The Replaced*

When Eva and Sebastien get to the clearing, everyone is there. Everyone. The whole town. *We're the last ones,* Eva thinks. They all stand together in the large, packed-earth clearing that sits under the trees that hold all the families' sleeping platforms. A small stone house stands at the edge of the clearing. It was the original chapel. Now it's the communal kitchen. Smoke should be rising from its chimney. But it's not. She should smell food cooking. Bread baking. But she doesn't.

"Sebastien, what's..." Eva asks.

"You'll see," he says and walks away from her. He disappears into the crowd.

And then a man Eva doesn't recognize steps forward. He seems to simply appear. He's wearing clothes that Eva has never seen. All the people in her village wear tunics and pants made from the same durable, silvery spider silk that Eva spends her days spinning.

"Eva. Ahh, you're finally here," the man says, stepping close.

Run! The thought pushes away any thoughts about his clothes. But then she thinks, *I can't run. I'd look so silly.* "Who're you?" she asks, trying to sound bold.

"My name is Dr. Kenneth Parker. I'm a friend of the family." The man smiles and holds out his hand. She has never heard his name before. She doesn't take his hand. She's afraid. *Don't touch him.* But again, she worries how she'll look. So she takes the man's hand. It's smooth. His skin is softer than any she's felt.

The people are all around. Like they're waiting for the nightly bonfire. There's something strange, though. They're not talking. They're just silently standing there. *They should be talking.*

"Where's my mom?" Eva blurts.

"I'm right here," her mother's voice calls.

Eva turns and rushes to her. "Are you alright? Is Dad? Where's Lukas?"

"Everyone is fine, sweetheart," her mother says.

Dr. Parker clears his throat.

Eva looks back at him. She takes her mom's hand. She hasn't done that in years. It doesn't feel right. The calmness falls away. She drops her mother's hand. Looks at her. Steps away. She thinks about running again. *Not right. Not right.*

"You should come here, Eva," Dr. Parker says.

"No." She says it forcefully, even though she knows it's rude.

"Bring her." Dr. Parker's voice is firm, but empty.

That's what it was—her mom felt empty.

Two men, friends of her father's, friends of hers, walk toward her.

"No!" she screams, and now she turns to run. But a wall of people. A wall made of her people closes in front of her. Her arms are grabbed from behind and she's yanked off her feet. "No! No!" She shrieks. Tears leap to her eyes and she thrashes back and forth, thinking that she has to get away. The men carry her closer and closer to Dr. Parker. Everyone watches silently. No one comes forward to help her. Not her mom. Not her neighbors. No one. The men stop in front of Dr. Parker. He isn't smiling anymore.

"Quiet," Dr. Parker says.

"No!" Eva screams again.

One of the men wrenches her arm behind her back and now she screams in pain. He wrenches it harder.

Dr. Parker leans forward and whispers, "Quiet."

Eva pulls the pain into a whimper and then silence.

"We had a heck of a time finding you," Dr. Parker says. "You're the last one."

She thinks about running, but the thought is very far away.

"Let's get this over with," Dr. Parker says. He takes something from his pocket. A small, glass panel with a metal tube coming down out of its middle. *No, not a tube. A needle.* Dr. Parker grabs Eva's chin and shoves it to one side, exposing her neck.

"This will hurt a bit," Dr. Parker says. Before she can even brace herself, Dr. Parker plunges the point of the needle into the place where Eva's neck and shoulder meet.

Pain shoots across her shoulders like hot, metal wings.

And then there is a soft, bright ringing. A single sweet note and she is gone into blackness.

***

Seconds later, Eva's eyes reopen. But it is no longer Eva looking out onto the gathered village. She has been Replaced.

ZOMBIES AND ALIENS

It took almost a week of notes and researching names and thinking about cloud-consciousness and characters and how might you change someone's vibration and should I start the book with the villain and I can't kill-off one of my Four Bastions, I busted my ass for those. So, I made it a random, disposable, treehouse survivor bastion...which not only did I not have to destroy one of The Four Bastions, I solved my robot problem—I had an army of AI consciousnesses inside human bodies. Replaced.

I hardly talked to anyone.

I showered once.

The moms made me eat dinner. I think...

I felt amazing. How to describe it? How to explain it?

And then I remembered the email that Mr. Banerjee had written back to me. It came in right before Tony's party or maybe right after, so I was either distracted by going to the party or freaking out that Javier and Audra were some kind of real and cool that I will *never* be or yelling at a cop and Javier was never going to talk to me again...so honestly, I'd read the answer to my sunlight question and was then like, Whatever...

But something about how I felt from the writing made me remember his email.

From: Ari Banerjee <abanerjee@dbh.edu>
Date: January
To: Elaine Archer <LV426er@gmail.com>
Subject: underground sunlight and writing

Dear Elaine,

What a treat to hear from you.

As a matter of fact, the administration *did* inform us that you'd left
school. They didn't tell us why. However, also as a matter of fact,
your friend and former classmate, Jenn Cartwright, informed me that
you were, "...writing a book about zombies and aliens." I see she
was only partially mistaken.

To answer your intriguing question, Yes, reflected sunlight should
grow your crops just fine. Essentially the full spectrum of incidental
light is reflected so that the reflected light can be treated as direct
sunlight.

I was also intrigued by your observation that you're learning to
use the writing process as a means of discovering your thoughts,
feelings, avenues of inquiry, etc. instead of a means of simply
conveying the ideas you already have. It reminded me of some of
the late, fringe work of physicist David Bohm—developed, in part,
through his conversations with the Indian spiritual philosopher, Jiddu
Krishnamurti. To put it in the least boring terms I can, he theorized
about the deep possibilities for changing the world if people engage
in discussion instead of lecture. I know, funny coming from me...

Essentially, he saw dialogue not merely as the transfer of ideas from
one mind to another. We do not merely seek to convince others of
our own ideas. We discover *through* our dialogue with one another.
We create together, through the sharing of ideas, memories, stories,
something we could never have known in isolation.

He had many other interesting ideas about the way that this
communication style could, in fact, change the world—not through
the content of what is spoken, but the way the speakers interact...

All of this seems similar to what you're saying about your discoveries
through writing. It had not occurred to me that one might achieve
the same kind of dialogue through writing. However, I suppose it
should have as this is also the scientific method at its best—one puts

forward a hypothesis and tests it, not solely to prove the hypothesis, but to discover what there is to discover from that starting point.

Please let me know if you have any other questions I can answer. I look forward to hearing more about your project.

Kindest regards,

Ari Banerjee

Yes. Yes. Yes. That's how it felt, writing about Eva and Dr. Parker and him jamming the big needle down into her neck and fucking replacing her (which I came up with when I was fucking *sleeping* and I woke up and was like, Holy fuck, the device! They jam it, right there, BAM! and they swap the frequency of your consciousness with a different frequency and then *that* person lives in *your* body!). And it felt like when I was in the middle of a great conversation with Jenn or Lucca or Javier or KPao. Like connection. Like discovering something I had never known before. Like when you start talking with someone, you have a vague idea what you'll talk about. Jenn and I will talk about boys. Javier and I will talk about robots. KPao and I will talk about mass-extinction. But in a great conversation, you can't ever know where you'll end up. I could never have known that KPao would tell me, "Vaginas are pretty straight-forward..." I bet she didn't know that either.

Of course, the writing wasn't exactly the same. A conversation is a lot less work. I must have written 5,000 words to end up with that 711-word prologue. And it was 1,000x harder than any essay I'd ever written. I had to keep imagining it over and over. Forward and backward. In and out. Seeing it in my head, then trying to think how to write what I saw. Like I had to keep zooming in as close as possible, then zooming out and looking at it from far away. I don't think I had ever used my imagination that hard before.

But yes, that feeling of discovery. Like it's not you and it's not them. It's the thing you make together. The thing in-between. The thing in common.

WHEN THE SUN HITS

I needed to talk. About writing *The Replaced*. About consciousness isn't stored in the brain. About reflected sunlight treated as direct sunlight and Bohm and Krishnamurti. About writing for a week so that I could get 700 words and feeling like the world was singing—like *its* vibrational frequency and mine had been, for a moment, in perfect sync.

I thought about Jenn. But then I was like, Does she really think I'm writing a book about aliens and zombies? I mean, we'd hardly talked about *what* I was doing—we'd hardly talked. And would she care? If I said, I feel both calm and surging with energy, would she be like, I feel hungry...

I'd tried to talk to her about *This Is Our Youth*—about how I'd wanted so badly for it to tell me something deep in a way I'd never heard before. She didn't even respond. It was like she couldn't hear me.

Javier and I had texted a little during the last week. Basically, just videos of lionesses adopting baby monkeys and shit. But I figured he was around—not that I had his schedule memorized or anything.

Elaine: Hey! Can you hang out? I've had the craziest week.

He usually wrote back in, like, immediately, but he didn't even read it. It was like five minutes, then ten, then I finally took a shower, then I had a sandwich and was like, What the fuck? Not that I thought he was supposed to always answer me in 30 seconds, but the feeling was floating away from me, getting farther and farther, and if I didn't talk about it soon, maybe I'd realize it had never even been there—that it wasn't even a thing.

So, I tried Tony, instead.

Elaine: You around?
Tony: What's up, homeschool? Yep. Around.
Elaine: I had the craziest week. Can you hang out?
Tony: Yep. I'm at my place working out some venue stuff.

Come here?
Elaine: Sounds good.

And *then* Javier wrote.

> Javier: Hey! Sorry. I've had a crazy week, too. Can't really talk now. Tomorrow?

I was like, Shrug. Whatever. Maybe. I mean, I *know* he wasn't blowing me off, but...

> Elaine: No worries. About to go to Tony's. Probs can't tomorrow.
> Javier: Okay. Well, text me later.

I headed for the Addison bus.

THE PHYSICS OF BEING HEARD

It wasn't until I was all the way up the stairs and about to knock on Tony's door that it occurred to me I didn't know exactly what I was doing there. Did I want to talk about what I'd written? Did I want to talk about what it felt like to write? Did I want to talk about Bohm and Krishnamurti and "the thing in common?" I hadn't even knocked when Tony opened the door. "When you open the bottom door, it rattles our windows," he said. He smiled and rubbed his hand through his messy hair. He was wearing baggy jeans and a Pavement, Slanted & Enchanted Tour t-shirt.

How had I not noticed that he's really attractive? "My uncle likes them," I said and pointed to his shirt.

Tony looked down to remind himself what he was wearing. He nodded. "You don't?" he asked.

I shrugged. I was pretty sure they were Uncle Alex's favorite band, but they made no sense to me. I considered doing that thing where you have no idea about something, but you're still like, Oh, yeah, I'm totally into them. Mostly their early stuff...But I didn't feel like lying, not to Tony, not at all. "Probably not," I said. "I don't like most of the bands he likes."

Tony guffawed. "Right on," he said and opened the door wider so I could come in.

I took a deep breath as I passed him. Yeah, that's a good smell.

As if to prove a point about stereotypes, there were two slack-jawed dudes, one Black, one Asian, sitting on the velvet sectional playing some kind of gun game. In the movie version, they'd be wearing boxers, but they were both wearing shorts, wool socks, and faded black t-shirts with logos on them. They didn't look up.

"You want an americano?" Tony asked. "I make a super good americano."

"Yeah. That's what you said," I said.

We walked into the kitchen and he got a tiny silver espresso pot off the back of the stove. "When did I tell you that?" he asked, laughing. I liked how much he amused himself.

The distraction of the guys playing video games evaporated and my back was suddenly tingling with awareness as Tony moved behind me to the sink. "I overheard you say that to one of your friends that first time I saw you at Zero Drop," I said and trying to put a little space between us, I sat at the table where Javier and Audra had been sitting.

Tony unscrewed the espresso pot, filled the bottom with water, dropped a silver filter in, and set it on the counter. "That's right," he said. "You were spying on us."

Why hadn't that seemed weird the first time I told him? Wait. "Why were you using a laundromat so far from here?" I asked.

"Best washers on the north side," he said without a second's hesitation.

Of course, Tony was a laundromat connoisseur.

He poured the espresso into the filter and screwed the top back on. He set the pot on the burner and lit the gas. "Mom got that when she was in Italy in college," he said. Then he lit the gas under the burner with the water kettle.

"Oh, one of my moms spent a year of college in Italy, too," I said. That's where Mama Jane and Uncle Alex had met.

Tony turned away from the stove. "You have more than one mom?" he asked. His tone was curiosity, not disgust.

"Two moms," I said. "And a vial of sperm."

Before Tony could respond, the video-game dudes bumbled into the kitchen. They didn't even see us.

"Did you check the corner?" the first guy asked as he pulled open the refrigerator.

"No," the second guy said and pulled a box of cereal out of the cupboard.

Tony turned off the stove, filled two mugs with espresso and then hot water.

"That's the reason you're dead," the first guy said.

Tony tilted his head, like, Let's get out of here. "I would've introduced you..." he said after we left the kitchen and he'd handed me the I <3 My Corgi mug.

"They seemed preoccupied," I said. His mug was navy with Evergreen Teachers' Credit Union on it.

He nodded and lead me through the living room, past the purple couch where the guys had been playing, past the spot where Mark had tried to save the whales.

I walked slowly so I didn't slosh my americano and also so I could watch his back. Literally, how had I not noticed that he's, like, muscular? I wished Jenn was there, but I was also, obviously, totally glad that she wasn't.

Tony's room was a mini-version of the rest of the place. Which is to say, there was shit everywhere. Maybe slightly more organized. There were at least ten shoes boxes filled with cds stacked on top of each other next to his big, junk-covered desk. I pointed at them, "They still have cds?" I asked.

He looked at the boxes and nodded, "Gotta have something to sell at shows. We don't want them to think we *want* them to download it for free..." He set his coffee on the bookshelf by the door. Then he walked behind me and I was aware that we were in his room, alone. He pulled out the desk chair and made a you-sit-there motion. He gathered a bunch of papers and his computer off his bed and stacked them on the floor near the closet. "So, big week?" he asked as he grabbed his coffee and sat down on his bed. If he was feeling any of the awkward I was feeling, he was really good at not showing it. I had no idea what I was showing or not showing.

I took a sip of my coffee. Goddamit if it wasn't delicious.

"You didn't want milk, did you?" Tony asked.

"It's delicious," I said. Normally, I needed like 1/2 milk, but...

Tony took a sip of his, "It *is* delicious. Thank you."

He had big hands and thick wrists, but something about the way he held his mug in his palm, made me think, I bet he can be very gentle. Jesus. Get it together. "Yeah, so yeah," I started. "I figured out some pretty cool things about my book," I said.

He raised his eyebrows like, Tell me more.

I told him about the Four Bastions and the AI villains and that consciousness is stored in a vibrational frequency...

Tony nodded, "That's a sweet idea," he said.

"And to change the frequency, the villains stab this big, needle-rod down into your neck," I said and I made a stabbing motion.

Tony was like, "Jesus."

"Yeah, man, it's brutal. They steal your soul."

"For real," he said. "So, what happens to the consciousness that used to be in there?"

"Well, what I'd first imagined was that it just kind of disappears. Though, I guess, it would still be stored at that frequency...so if someone had, like, some of the replaced person's cells, a hair or something, from before they changed the resonance of the body...they would have the frequency the replaced person's consciousness was stored on...so they could theoretically access it...but yeah, otherwise, it's just like..." I cannot tell you how good it felt to have him ask me these questions and then just...listen...what would Bohm and Krishnamurti say about that? What are the physics of having someone listen?

"Like a tree falling in the forest with no one to hear," he said. "That is dark as fuck." He set his mug onto the table next to the bed. "I love it. Elaine, I gotta tell you that you get more interesting by the minute."

I do? Breathe. Don't be an idiot. "How's that?" In addition to not knowing what else to say, I wanted Tony to tell me how I was getting more interesting.

He leaned forward and gazed right at me. He had deep set, dark, bright eyes, like when he looked, he *saw*.

At first I was like, I wish I'd worn something other than jeans and a gray t-shirt and maybe not just pulled my hair into a sloppy ponytail after my shower. But as Tony looked at me, it was obvious this was not about my outfit, my hair, my body...

"Not that I hang out with a ton of high school girls," Tony started.

I rolled my eyes like, Yeah yeah.

He smiled, "But I haven't met a single one who dropped-out so she could write about some crazy dystopia where all the humans are going to end up with cyborg consciousnesses stabbed into them..."

That does sound cool.

"And you're bold as fuck," he said, leaning forward even more.

I didn't feel even a little bold. I felt terrified. Like I had no idea what I was doing. And not just in his room and at that moment. In life. I shrugged, "I don't know about bold as fuck," I said. Except maybe that wasn't totally true. It certainly *had* been true. But maybe it wasn't *totally* true anymore—I just hadn't updated the story I was telling myself. I thought about the Elaine who sat up on that roof deck with The Asshole Brenden Carter waiting for him to tell her what to do, waiting for him to tell her what to drink, what to write...waiting for him to kiss her and assure her she was pretty. I certainly still felt partly like that Elaine, but I also felt like I had moved a few inches from being her—slowly sliding away. There is no way *that* Elaine would've been sitting in Tony's room right then.

He put his hands on the bed behind him and leaned back, "Well, it's not every day a girl busts in on me doing laundry to dazzle me with her vision of wiping out the world..."

When he put it that way. "When you put it that way," I said. I set my mug on his desk, got up, and went and stood in front of him. "So..." I said, looking at him leaning back.

"So..." he said.

He reached up, took my hand, and pulled me down on to the bed next to him.

My stomach was clenched in a knot and my throat felt tight and I could barely breathe and we looked at each other, and holy shit, this is happening. He put his hand on my cheek and he smiled and I smiled and put my hand on his leg and we leaned toward each other. I could feel him smiling as we kissed. His beard wasn't as scratchy as I thought it would be. We fell back on the bed. I let myself have a deep, full breath of him. I put my hand on his shoulder and ran it down his arm to his hand. I pulled his hand over to my stomach and he grabbed a fist of my t-shirt.

And then he stopped.

h."
you tried to fuck his girlfriend?" Wrong again. The clench in

I did," he said. He didn't look proud of himself. But he didn't
ed.

wanted was to not be wrong about this guy. Not like I'd been
C. "Tony," I said, but it was a whisper.

see. Not such a nice guy," Tony said.

ike levels of shit I could not get ahold of. One minute, I was
turns out Tony's hot and he smells good and I like his back
my plan to annihilate humanity...And then, all the sudden it
anipulating me by telling me how he would manipulate me?
Who is anyone? Too many goddam layers. "What happened?"
his game we used to play. All us guys. The can-I-fuck-your-
e."

ints?" I asked. I thought about leaving. Just going right then.
late. If I left, then I would have to hate him, there was no

ss with each other..." he said.
d.

know her. Figured out what she was into. Talked to her
y tats, our childhoods. Art. Making shit..."

id.

at?" How could this story end?

e out," he said. "And it wasn't like I hadn't been called
irked. "But usually I would smooth that shit right over."

oothing motion with his hand when he said it.

dra. Shoving her phone in Isaac's face, saying, "I made
make those. Me." And the tattoos of the giant flowers
thighs. "She didn't fall for it," I said.

Tony said. "She slapped me and said, 'Wake up!' Then
h."

did," I said. We were still sitting across from each
hat I could've slapped him, too.

"Then she said, 'You're acting like a scumfucker.
ker. But if you keep acting like one, you're going to
ho you are in this life?'"

What?

"You sure about this?" he asked, leaning away.

What? No. I don't even know what *this* is...how am I supposed to know..."Is this the consent talk?" I asked, trying to sound bold.

He laughed and tilted his head at me. "Aren't you with Javier," he said.

"What?" I asked. Christ. I'm just trying to see what happens. For once. I don't know what I think about Javier. "Javier and I hardly know each other," I said.

"Oh," Tony said and he reached out and tugged on the bottom of my t-shirt.

This is excruciating, I know that at least.

"I thought you two were old pals," Tony said. "Couple of homeschoolers."

"We're *just* friends," I said. Only, saying it didn't feel like it was telling the whole story. But I was not interested in that story in that moment.

Tony gave me a look like, Oh, really?

"How is he the point right now?" I asked. How was he?

Tony laughed again, "Like I said, more interesting by the minute."

I pushed Javier out of my mind. And I didn't want to think about TABC, but I couldn't help myself. Even though Tony felt very different, TABC was there. The last guy I'd kissed. The way he'd suckered me. That very thing I was always afraid of, and I hadn't seen it at all. I put my hand on Tony's cheek. His eyes were the deepest brown. His roommates were back at their video game. I closed my eyes, took a deep breath of Tony's smell—coffee and soap and newness. "Yes," I said. "I'm sure."

SLANTED & ENCHANTED

And then nothing fucking happened. I opened my eyes. Tony's fingers were still tangled with my t-shirt and yet...

"Listen," Tony said.

Oh Jesus. I propped myself up on my elbow.

Tony propped himself up, too. "It's just," he hesitated, "I've done my fair share of sport fucking."

I gave him a wide-eyed look like, What are you talking about?

"Sex just for fun," he explained.

I nodded. "Go on," I said even though I felt nervous and like he was about to tell me a secret I wasn't sure I wanted to know.

"And I know that I've sport-fucked girls who wanted to go out with me...who did it because they wanted to me to like them..."

"Like you'd say, 'I'm so into you. Let's date each other.' But really you'd be like, 'I'm gonna bang this chick and never call?'" I asked. Dudes suck. I sat up.

Tony sat up, too. "More or less," he said. "Do you say, 'date each other'?"

"Obviously not." Was he trying to tell me that he didn't really like me?

The neck of his t-shirt was stretched and I could see his pulse in his throat. "But now I realize there are plenty of girls who want what I want, which is, most of the time, just a little fun," he said.

Is that what he thought I wanted? I didn't know what I wanted. I mean, I liked his attention. I liked the kinds of things we talked about. I liked his smell and his body. I definitely liked kissing him. "So is that what you tell girls?" I asked. "It's just for fun?"

He shrugged. "Sometimes." He took a small section of my hair that had fallen out of my ponytail, brought it to his face and smelled it. "How old are you?" he asked.

Okay. That's enough. I pulled my hair back from him, sat up, took my ponytail down, smoothed back the piece he'd been holding, and redid the hair tie. "I know how to make decisions," I said.

Tony sat up, too. "Yes," he said. "I am well aware of that. I'm simply asking the question."

The are-you-an-immature-kid question? Or the is-it-legal-to-have-sex-with-you question? I once again thanked the baby Jesus that I'd been 16 when I'd met TABC—talk about a statutory rape law win. "I'm 17," I said. I didn't tell him that I was only 17 by about 3 days. "How old are you?" Did I want to know?

Tony ran his hand through his own messy, ugh, sexy hair. "Twenty-three."

Hmm. Well, younger than TABC, and r than I'd thought. "Great," I said. "Now we kr

"What's that look?" he asked.

"I'm annoyed with you," I said, before

He shook his head and smirked at m with me, too." He laughed. Thought abo it...

"What?" I asked.

"Back in the day," he said, "What would be the *exact* way that I would've

We were both sitting cross-legge had turned from...well...from I don't little chat. "Like your douchey friend

Tony laughed, "Mark?" he aske I nodded like, Yeah, that guy.

"So you noticed that?" he aske

"I mean..." How could you no

"Yeah, like Mark," he said. "

"So is that what you're doin to be wrong about him, too. I di

"No," he said. "I found someone when they know all t

I furrowed. I felt uncomf rock pressing down. "What r

"This girl Audra," he sa

"Audra? Audra from th fuck her?

"Ohh, that's right," h

I wanted to puke fr compete with her? And v dated her?" Then I wan

He shook his head I snapped my fing "Yeah," he said. " "Did you hook "Tried to," he s "Were you fri wrong. Wrong aga

Is that who you are in this life?

"How'd you take that?" I asked, my belly unclenching just that much.

"I was pretty much not listening. Just trying to figure out how to use her little rant to my advantage," he said.

Dudes. Jesus. "So then what?" Cause something must have caught his attention.

He smiled. Remembering. "She called Isaac and said, 'Your scumfucker friend is trying to fuck me. I'm going home.' Then she hung up."

How does Audra become Audra? "What did you say?" I asked.

"Nothing. She grabbed her bag, pointed at me, and said, 'I get what you're doing. I get what you guys do. But try to imagine a girl who you don't have to trick into having sex with you. Imagine a girl who has sex with you because she *likes* you.'"

Imagine a girl who has sex with you because she likes you. Imagine having sex with someone because you like them. How does she know everything? "What did you say to *that?*" I asked.

"Nothing. She left," he said.

"Was Isaac pissed?"

He shrugged. "He'd done it, too..."

"I still don't understand why you're telling me this," I said.

He took a deep breath and said, "It's not crazy that I feel a little responsible."

I guess that's true. "Yes," I said. "I don't have a ton of experience."

Tony nodded and I could see that he was getting ready to show me to my coat and then the door.

Goddamit. "In fact, almost no experience." I didn't count getting fingered by some drunk guy at a party. "But goddamit, I'm 17. At what point am I allowed to do something because I want to do it? When am I allowed to try things even if people have been telling me my whole life that there are certain things nice girls don't try?" I was pissed. "Fuck them. You're not taking advantage of me." I'd been taken advantage of. I knew the difference.

"Okay, okay," he said and held up his hands. "Don't call me a scumfucker."

We both laughed. The mood shifted again. Like we'd been circling something and we'd come back around, but now we were farther, deeper.

He looked right at me. "It wouldn't be for sport," he said.

Cue the barf. Cue the blush. But I didn't look away.

I knew he could tell I was embarrassed, because he went on, "Your body is pretty personal," he said.

It was hard to breath. My body. I nodded. Slightly.

His eyes didn't leave mine. "And when you give someone access to your body, that's a lot of trust." He traced his fingers across my arm and I sighed. "But when you're vulnerable and trusting someone to take care with you, to be careful with you, that's intimacy. That feels good. Emotionally," he said. Then he laughed and added, "And physically."

I hadn't expected any of this. Never. I didn't know this.

"As Audra pointed out, when you think you gotta lie to get someone to have sex with you...it leaves you feeling pretty lonely. Wondering if anyone would want the real you."

This is what goddam Nurse Party-Panties should've told us.

"So was *that* the consent talk?" I asked. Sometimes sarcasm is the only thing I have to keep the spinning world steady.

He nodded. "I think that's what that was," he said. "Oh, and to be clear, I never would've let anything happen with you and Mark."

I grabbed a fist full of his Slanted & Enchanted shirt and pulled him toward me.

SHOW ME EVERYTHING

Tied for first for what makes me love *Aliens* so much is Ripley being such a badass and the Ripley-Hicks relationship. Second place is Apone. Third is Hudson.

Though the seeds of Ripley and Hicks' relationship are sown early (do yourself a favor and google "I can drive that loader aliens" and just watch Hicks' face) it really gets going in the part where Ripley wrests control from Corporate Prick Burke and gives it over to Hicks, "Well I believe Corporal Hicks has authority here..." When she says it, you can tell from the flick of her eyes, she's saying it to Hicks, not CPB.

Hicks gets on his little headset, calls for evacuation, and says, "I say we take off, nuke the site from orbit. It's the only way to be sure." And when he says it, he gives Ripley a *smoldering* look.

So that's when you're really like, Oh, it's on.

Later, Ripley tells Hicks how bad it would suck to die how all the colonists died—implanted with aliens embryos and then killed when the aliens hatch out of their chests. Ripley is like, "Promise me I won't go out like that." And Hicks says, "If it comes to that, I'll do us both," and he shows her his gun.

A minute later, he's like, Let me show you how to use this gigantic weapon. And he does that thing where the dude stands behind the woman to teach her how to use some tool / sporting good / weapon and it's like, Holy sexual tension.

Then Ripley's like, What's this part?

And Hicks is like, That's the grenade launcher, you don't wanna worry about that.

She says, "Show me everything. I can handle myself."

He's says, "Yeah, I noticed."

I mean, Come on! How bad do I want them to make out at that moment?

Except it would totally ruin the movie because who the hell is going to make out when aliens are about to fall on them and chew them up with alien acid-blood?

I won't ruin the ending, but I will say that I wish wish wish they had at least shot some scenes where Ripley and Hicks make out. They didn't even have to put them in the movie. At all. Save them for the Director's Cut. Or not even that. Just make them special DVD deleted scenes—like a footnote for the movie that you can watch or not. Sweet Baby Jesus and time travel, please make James Cameron shoot scenes of them making out.

Honestly, I'm not much of a viewer of porn. I don't follow those tumblrs that the tween girls are into. I know it's all there and immediately available, just one "private browsing" session away, the unseen sexual ocean...but that shit terrifies me. Sex is weird enough already. I don't need all those freaky images in my mind. Based on a few conversations with a few people, that's mostly what it is—freaky images. Extreme acts.

Extreme people. I don't need that slamming around in my brain when giving someone access to my body makes me vulnerable enough...

All that said—I *did* wonder if there was Ripley and Hicks themed porn out there. I mean, I wondered so deeply, that it was worth checking...

...please hold...

...very cursory research indicated there was *not* Ripley and Hicks themed porn. But holy fuck is there a world of Ripley/Hicks fanfic.

I wonder if anyone would ever cast Sigourney Weaver and Michael Biehn in another movie together. That would be amazing. What the hell, I'm putting them in my book. I don't care that they're oldsters—I want to see them make out.

FARTHER BEHIND

Obviously, my book needs a love story.

So, what happens is, Radha, Merton, and Penelope are just at the beginning of their journey. They're camping one night and get caught by a patrol from The Yellowstone School—you remember, the Bastion that was founded by two queer women at an old boarding school...Obviously, for defense reasons, the school has patrols. For procreational reasons, they're going to grab our adventurers and make Merton a very interesting offer—come back with us and get a chick pregnant—it would also be super weird to everyone that Merton is white. Cause by then, there wouldn't be anymore white people. He'd be a pretty hot commodity (in terms of genetic novelty).

The scouts bring them back to the campus with stone buildings like medieval castles and there's moats and the Mother's Hall where all the girls who got pregnant on their sperm-quests have their babies and raise them in communal heaven. Radha is like, This place is awesome. Merton is like, I'm gonna get to have sex. Turns out, Penelope is feeling it for Merton. Obvs. And Radha, who is super insensitive, doesn't realize it and is like, Why you so mopey, it's cool here.

Only for as good as I'd felt writing *The Replaced*, I felt equally not awesome trying to write the Yellowstone scene. I could see it so clearly in my mind. I could *see* the wind blowing the wheat crops. I could *hear* the little kids laughing as they chased each other under a giant, spinning windmill. But I couldn't make my story fit in there. I couldn't get Radha, or Merton, or Penelope *in* there.

I sat at my desk, then my squishy chair, then my bed, then the floor, trying to get them from the picture in my head onto the paper. I itched.

Then Javier was like, Wanna go with me to Blick?

I had no idea what Blick was, but I was like, Yes, I do. Peace out Yellowstone School.

Of course, Jenn texted the moment I told Javier I would meet him and was like, "Come over."

I said the moms and I were having a night in. I wasn't in the mood to listen to her rip on me and the nerd, plus not ask anything about what I was doing.

The moms had decided that since I wasn't in school, I should help with the cooking. I'd cooked that night and the moms were finishing the dishes and saying construction words.

"I'm going to Lincoln Park with Javier," I said.

Mama Jane, who was scrubbing the cookie sheet asked, "What for?"

"There's an art store down there." I said.

"When are we gonna meet this guy?" Mama Helen, who was wiping down the table, asked.

Oh boy. That was a conversation I did not want to have. I hadn't forgotten Tony's question about what my feelings for Javier were. And I hadn't forgotten that I didn't know. If I brought him over, the moms would be all, like, Ohhhh, is this your boyfriend? "Pretty soon," I said. They didn't even know about Tony.

The moms looked at each other. Mama Jane shook her head like, Don't push it. Love her, sometimes.

"Alright," Mama Helen said. "Home by 10."

"Text before you get to the stop and we'll come pick you up," Mama Jane said.

Javier was waiting for me outside the Damen Blue Line. Once again, I thought about TABC and my Shoe Store Angel. On our way to the North Ave. bus, we walked by her shoe store and I considered saying, "Hey let's stop in here..." But then what? "...so I can thank this girl who probably saved my life after TABC stole my book idea..." I wonder if I'm ever gonna tell anyone what happened.

I'd decided not to be annoyed with Javier about not hanging out with me after I finished *The Replaced* and all that. I'm guessing you can guess why. And though I'd been thinking a lot about Tony, I was trying not to think about him in front of Javier.

"What are you getting?" I asked. We walked around a group of white girls with Coach purses trying to decide what to eat. They were talking in that way where every statement is a question. "I really want pizza?" Do you want pizza?

"Sakura microns, .005s," Javier said.

My face must've said, What's a Sakura micron, .005? cause he said, "My favorite pen."

"I guess it makes sense that you have a favorite pen," I said. Being an artist and all. It was busy in Wicker Park and we had to dodge group after group...

"How's the story coming?" Javier asked.

"Sucky," I said. I didn't mean to be changing the subject and not talking about his pens and what he was working on...but I still felt itchy. And like there was something that I wasn't seeing.

"How so?" Javier asked. We sat at the bus-stop along with one beefy dude in a dirty coat.

How so? I stared out into the street, seeing, but not seeing the traffic blurring past. "It was going well..." I said. "After talking with KPao...And I can *see* it...I just can't..."

"Sometimes it flows great..." Javier said, he had his backpack on his lap either to not take up more than his share of bench or to keep someone from snatching it and running.

I felt him looking at me.

He went on, "...and sometimes something's not right."

"Yeah," I said, and sighed. Then I added, "Thanks." I'd already noticed that certain days were just like, Boom. Click. Like the day I'd discovered that Penelope thinks of herself as Radha's monster. And some days were super low. Where a voice in my head told me I was just killing time. I was just going to go back and get on with the same life I'd been living before. Only I would know that I had tried to be different. And failed.

But it wasn't that feeling.

It was me not seeing something.

"What part are you on?" Javier asked.

Oh god, I'm not telling him I'm working on a sex scene. "Where Radha, Merton, and Penelope first get to The Yellowstone School," I said.

The bus came. We climbed on, scanned our cards, and sat in a seat across from the back door. He took the window. Maybe he could tell I'd feel trapped on the inside.

"What's not working?" he asked.

I took a deep breath into my belly. Sighed. Even thinking felt heavy. Okay. "I mean, it's going to be pretty easy to describe them getting captured—some scouts in camo leap out of the undergrowth and lead them back to campus by spear-point," I said.

"Captured at spear-point, yes," Javier said.

I gave him a smirk for that. "But so, the hard part is the place itself. Like, you know that part of sci-fi/fantasy where you have to describe the world you're seeing in your head?"

"Narrative," Javier said.

I pointed at him like, Yeah, that. "Turns out, I suck at that. I spent like four hours like, Here's the rivers that surround the joint, here's the bridge, here's the old dining hall where all the chicks and babies live together..."

"So, you're writing a first draft, right?" Javier said and shrugged. "You heard the lady at *First Things First*. Every first draft is a shitty draft..."

I rolled my eyes, Goddamit, I know. "Goddamit, I know. It's just that I can see it so clearly in my head and I can't make it match. At all. Like I can *see* the fields on the other side of the river and the little houses where people other than mothers and babies live...and I know how it all got like that...and I know all the rules...I just don't know how to *tell* any of that..."

The bus jerked and rolled in the traffic.

"Here's a question," Javier said.

I made a face, like, Ugh, let's hear it, but I appreciated that he wasn't trying to reassure me. Like when you're like, This sucks and won't ever be better. And the person you're talking to is like, It'll be fine. And you're like, Oh, are you psychic? When people tell you not to worry, what they really mean is, Your feelings are freaking me out, so can we watch pandacam instead?

"Are you sure you're writing a book?" he asked.

Wait? What? And then I heard TABC, "You're never going to write it." I clenched my fists and my belly knotted. "Dude. Yes. I write every single day."

Javier held his hands up (it seemed like he did that with me a lot) and said, "Hold on. That's not..."

"Listen..." I said. I raised my voice enough that a prim white guy in a sweater vest looked over. Public bus, dude.

Don't tell me I can't write a book. I already don't think I can write a book. "I'm saying it's hard," I said. "I am *not* talking about quitting." I couldn't quit. It was already January. If I didn't get the book finished, and let's be honest, I was hardly even started, the moms would send me back to school. Just thinking about being back *there* everyday and a tightness exploded over my left eye and blossomed toward the center of my forehead.

"I'm not saying you should quit!" Javier said, his voice trying to bring me back from the edge of the abyss. "I'm saying maybe you should try something different for awhile. Like a movie script," he said.

"No." I said. And yet, I *could* see all the places exactly. Like perfect movie sets.

"You should see your face right now," Javier said.

Had it collapsed? I saw The Yellowstone School—and the Mother's House, high on the top of a hill, next to lush gardens where the soccer field used to be. I tried to push it out of my mind, but I couldn't quite banish it.

There was a ding overhead as someone pulled the cord for a stop. "What's happening to you is normal," he said.

Dude, I've got a black hole forming from my eye. "I can't change what I'm doing," I said.

"I'm not talking about forever," he said. "I'm talking about the first draft."

I shook my head. No. I'm writing a book.

"So, you're going to slog through something that isn't working?" he asked. We pulled to the curb and lurched to a stop.

Yeah. I am. "I have to," I said. The bus rumbled back into traffic.

"Here's all I'm saying," Javier said, he never raised his voice. "You talk about *Aliens a lot*...And even if you missed the final session of *First Things First*, I know you didn't miss the one about using any means necessary to keep moving forward and discovering your story..."

While he was talking, I'll admit, the pain in my forehead receded.

And for a second, I had a feeling of both excitement and relief—that last-day-of-school feeling. But, no. No. "I can't," I said.

"I can see that you're interested," he said.

I shook my head. "The moms would freak."

"So, what?" he asked.

"So, they're the ones letting me do this," I said. We stopped again and two older Latina ladies with shopping bags got on. A big bouquet of red and gold flowers poked from the top of one of the bags.

He looked at me. "Eventually, you have to figure out that no one *lets* anyone else do anything." I thought about him and Audra talking in Tony's kitchen. The way they sat. Like they belonged there. Like they belonged anywhere they went.

Thanks Zen Master. Super helpful. "I live with them. They pay for everything. The deal was that I write a book," I said. But even to me it had started to sound like an excuse.

"Don't you think they'd understand that this is part of it? Getting to a point where something feels not quite right and instead of forcing it, you let the not-quite-right guide you?" he asked.

I hate him sometimes. "Mr. Creative Process..." I said.

"Want me to go and talk to them?"

First the moms, When are we going to meet him. And now him? Nope. "I've spent *months* writing a book—trying to learn how to write a book—now I'm supposed to kiss all that good-bye?" There's a scene in *Aliens* where the Corporate a-holes are grilling Ripley and denying the existence of aliens and she's like, If even one of those things gets down here, this (and she grabs a stack of business papers and flails it) this bullshit that you think is so important...you can kiss all that goodbye. I'm not saying whether or not it was a sign that I thought about a movie when arguing about whether or not I should try writing a movie...

"I swear, I have been where you are," Javier said. He was wearing that navy blue sweater with the hole starting in the neck. "I went through this thing where I thought it would be faster if I did my whole process in the computer instead of rough sketches first. It took three times as long and the pieces were never as good. Part of being creative is learning your own process for creating," he said.

It occurred to me that I'd thought Javier was perfect. Like no insecurities or struggles. Somehow, he'd come into the world fully formed. Which was stupid, because that's what I'd thought about Georgia

O'Keeffe and I'd seen an entire documentary that told me the opposite. But so, I hadn't ever thought to ask Javier how he'd gotten so good. "How do you tell the difference between quitting because it's the right thing to do and quitting because something is too hard?"

"Don't think of it as quitting," he said.

I made a face, like, That's a bullshit answer.

He laughed and shook his head like, You are a nightmare. And like he liked that about me.

I liked making him laugh. The pain in my forehead receded.

"So what?" he began. "You spend another six months or six years or however long, trying to ram this thing into a book?" He looked out the window to see how far we were from our stop.

"Stubborn is my second best emotion," I said.

He ignored that. "Or you can try something different. You're still learning. You'd still be using everything you've learned so far...You spend six months writing a script, you get to know your story, and maybe something shifts, and suddenly the stuff that's so hard to write isn't so hard anymore and you go back to writing a book...Nothing is ever wasted, but what you achieve by force."

Goddamit if he didn't make a little bit of sense. But *why* did his suggestion feel so different from exercises in *A Writer Writes?* "You should have a calendar with all your sayings," I said.

Now it was his turn to give me the bullshit-answer look.

"Seriously," I said. "What's the difference between hard work, good old stick-to-it-ivness (I hate that phrase), and force? Maybe I'm just supposed to dig deep right now. Try harder."

Javier tilted his head, thinking about it. "Is that what you think?" he asked. "That you just need to 'try harder'?"

Try harder is the only strategy I'd ever had. That and research. "I'm afraid that if I change now, I'll waste a bunch of time and be even farther behind..."

"Farther behind what?"

Farther behind what? I couldn't name it. I could only feel it. Like weight. "I want the moms to know they made the right decision. And I want those assholes at school to know that I did something. I dropped-out and I fucking made something."

"So, you need to prove yourself to other people?"

"Goddammit. Yes," I said. It had been a few weeks since anyone had given me any shit about leaving school, but I still wanted to show them all. And I wanted to show the Bitch Annette. And I wanted to show The Asshole Brenden Carter. And I wanted to be able to say to anyone in the world—I wrote a book. So, fuck you. You can't judge me.

"Alright. Here's another question," he reached and pulled the bell cord above our seat, "And this is not that I agree with the 'prove yourself mode of creativity...'"

Why was he able to say things like that and not make me furious?

He went on, "Do you want to prove that you can finish something or do you want to prove that you can write something really badass?"

Goddammit.

The bus stopped and we got off.

"I'll think about it," I said.

Javier looked at me and smiled and I remembered Tony's question about me and Javier and then I remembered about Tony and I blushed. Javier looked confused and said, "I think this is the least mad I've ever seen you," he said.

I turned and started walking, though I didn't know the way. "Let's go get your fucking Sakura microns," I said. I glanced over my shoulder to see if he was following. He was smiling. I was, too.

SO, WE GOOD?

Not that we have to go and give Javier some big, dumb trophy for knowing everything, but even though the clock was ticking and the end of the school year was getting closer by the minute, he *was* right that I wasn't getting anywhere trying to force the book into being. And he did have, like, 10 years of experience with the shit...And also, when I thought about switching to a screenplay, that energy I got right after talking with KPao and then Javier, when I wrote *The Replaced*, and that Bohm and Krishnamurti were talking about...that was back. The connection feeling. The discovery feeling. And I liked it. I don't know what real writers do, but it seemed like looking for that energy, following it around, maybe that was something. And like I said, It's not that *A Writer Writes* hadn't already told me to write letters to people and make lists and just try to capture anything about the story that I could. Writing in screenplay was just the same as that...

So, I was lying on my bed, reading the screenplay for *Aliens*. I can't believe it never occurred to me to read it. I guess I thought only actors were allowed to see them. But you can just look them up online. Have you ever read one? They're awesome. And they move *fast*. I was at the part where the Marines first get attacked by the aliens, Hudson freaks, Vasquez shoots at everything, Hicks almost dies, Apone does die, and stupid, hapless Lt. Gorman doesn't know what to do.

> GORMAN
> (distantly)
> I told them to fall back...
>
> RIPLEY
> (viciously)
> They're   cut   off!   Do
> something!

But he's gone. Total brain-lock.

And see, just as I suspected, the "Fuck!" wasn't in there.

Then Jenn texted.

> Jenn: WHERE ARE YOU???
> Elaine: Home. Where are you?
> Jenn: Marcie's insane.

Yes. What's new?

> Elaine: What happened?
> Jenn: Can you come over?

Not really. I want to keep reading. See how this thing works. Feel this feeling.

Elaine: Sure.
Jenn: Actually, can we meet at the Bean? I hate it here.

Not that she wasn't always melodramatic. But even for her it was a little intense...but if we met at the Bean I could stop at the library and look for a book about screenwriting.

Elaine: Probably take me about 30 minutes.
Jenn: Hurry.
Elaine: 😒

I'm not saying I was mad at her. But like, we hadn't hung out in weeks. Every time I had tried she was like, Come to this party. I didn't wanna go to some goddam party with kids from school. I wasn't going to find a single one of them to talk to. I sure as hell wasn't hooking up with any of them. And I wasn't having them look at me like I'm some kind of goddam weirdo. Like a *bigger* weirdo than when I was at school. So I'd be like, Let's just watch a movie. And she'd be like, Can't.

I got down to Millennial Park in, like, 29.5 minutes. And then I waited. After 10 minutes...

Elaine: WTF?
Jenn: Almost there!

I'd already gone to the Bean and made faces at myself, so I walked over to the Faces and sat down on a bench. I was trying to figure out how to get Merton, Radha, and Penelope out of The Yellowstone School. He's still trying to get to New York where Hugh is. But he's not going to tell The Yellowstone School about the friend cause he's not positive he can trust them. Sure, he can bang the Yellowstone chick and maybe get her pregnant, but he has to draw the line somewhere. So he and Radha decide to ask if TYS can point them in the direction of NYC.

Meanwhile, The Yellowstone School were trading partners with the settlement from *The Replaced* where everyone got their body stolen, and TYS has discovered that whole settlement is gone and they're like, That's weird as fuck...So they're planning to go to Detroit (also a trading partner) to see if the Detroiters have noticed whole groups of people going totally missing. And when Merton asks how to get to NYC, they're like, Why don't you come with us to Detroit—it'll be safer if you travel with us—and you can go to NYC from there. And Merton's girl will go with them, so then it's even more awkward for Penelope.

Making up stories is way easier than writing them.

And then I got a text.

> Tony: What's up, homeschool?

Is it weird he's still calling me that?

> Elaine: Downtown. Waiting forever and ever for my friend.
> Tony: Cool. Just wanted to let you know I'm headed out of town.

Is it weird that he's telling me that? Is it weird that I feel weird? My phone vibrated again.

> Jenn: Almost there.
> Elaine: I'm at the Faces.
> Jenn: That's farther than the Bean.
> Elaine: Remember how you told me to hurry?
> Jenn: I'll make it up to you.

Jenn "making things up" to me almost always resulted in something either gross or embarrassing. Or both.

So I wrote, "Please don't." Only the second I hit send, I knew what I'd done.

> Elaine: Shitshitshit. I just sent the wrong text to someone.
> Jenn: Who?
> Tony: (the typing bubbles)

Oh god. What do I say? I started typing to him, Umm...

> Jenn: Who???
> Elaine: Tony!
> Jenn: Whatever you do, don't start typing cause he'll see the typing bubbles.

Shit.

> Elaine: Help!
> Jenn: Who's Tony?
> Tony: (still the typing bubbles)
> Elaine: What do I do?
> Jenn: Just say, Oops, Not for you.

Oh god. He thinks I'm begging him to stay.
He's never going to believe that. He's gonna think I'm the biggest loser.
Ew. Like I'm obsessed with him. Don't get me wrong, I wanted to see him
again. I wanted to see him again. But that didn't mean I was obsessed.

> Tony: You okay?
> Elaine: Yeah. Sorry. That wasn't for you. 😀
> Tony: Confused. What wasn't?

Ugh. He's gonna think I'm some kind of drama-girl.

> Elaine: The please don't. That was for my friend I'm waiting
> for.
> Tony: So, we're cool?

I didn't know what we were. What are you when you lose your virginity
to someone, but you're trying not to think of it as "losing your virginity"
because that's an oppressive cultural concept?

> Elaine: Totally. Have fun! 💥

I wanted to ask how long he'd be gone. And who he was touring with. And
did he ever think about me.

> Tony: I wanna read that book when I get back.

Do I want to prove to him that I can write something? Or that I can write
something badass? Or do I want to feel like I don't have to prove myself at
all? Barf.

Elaine:

Then Jenn was standing in front of me. She was wearing skin-tight jeans and Uggs. I pointed at them, "I thought Uggs are for girls who have no fashion identity." Yes, I was quoting her.

She looked down and rolled her eyes. "Marcie gave them to me for Christmas," she said. "I want her to think I don't hate them."

Jenn had never been motivated by a desire to make Marcie think she didn't hate something. I'm sure that's what my face said, because Jenn said, "She's threatening to send me to fucking boarding school."

For senior year. Seemed a little late in the game. "Now?"

"Can we go to the Bean? These faces creep me out," she said and made barf-face.

We headed back down the street, walking slowly, letting the tourists dodge us. That was another of Jenn's special talents—not moving out of other people's way.

"Wait. Your grades are good," I said. Despite her horrible taste in music and the fact that I wrote her English papers, she knew how to do well.

"There may be some rumors going around," Jenn said.

Oh god. "What kind of rumors?" I asked, but I think we all know.

"Some bullshit one of the bitch Board members told my mom," she said.

That was a downside (one of many) of having Marcie for a mom—she was on all these Boards of Trustees, and some of them obviously overlapped with DB High's. "And your mom thinks boarding school will help, how?" From what Jenn had told me about her Torch Lake friends who went to boarding school, they were *all* hooking-up at least as much as she was.

We arrived at the Bean and stopped about a foot from it. "All girls," Jenn said and made barf-face again. The sculpture stretched her face into something that I couldn't tell if it was funny or grotesque.

"Oh god," I said. What I wanted to say was something along the lines of, Are you sure you know what you're doing? I thought about Tony. What does it mean if you think you have to lie to get someone to be with you? Not that Jenn was lying. I was sure about that. But what does it mean if 90% of your interactions are about hooking-up? I thought about the girls from The Yellowstone School. They had a reason for what they were doing. Did Jenn? "What are you going to do?" I asked.

Jenn shrugged and stuck her tongue out at the reflection of herself. "Tell Marcie that other mom's a lying cow and she's spreading rumors cause I beat her daughter for first chair."

"That's pretty specific," I said.

"I've been thinking about it," Jenn said.

"Did you?" I asked. "Beat her for first chair?"

"No," Jenn said and bulged her eyes. "She's not clarinet. She's oboe or some shit."

It occurred to me that Jenn had a lot of anger, too. I'd never noticed it before. Maybe I could say something to her, the way Javier said something to me...but what would she would do? Javier had nothing to lose by telling me. He and I barely knew each other. But... "Don't you think she'll figure it out?" I asked.

"Marcie? Actually look into the details about someone *else?*" She shook her head.

And then, suddenly, I felt so sad for Jenn. She felt about her own mom the way I felt about The Bitch Annette. I don't know what I would've done. When TBA said something mean and then watched my face to see if I would cry, I was so lucky to have my moms. What did Jenn think about when her mom said things like, "Oh, well, The University of Chicago is a stretch...For you."

"I need to go down to the library," I said. "You wanna come with me?"

"At *school?*" Jenn asked and looked at me.

"No," I said, trying not to sound disgusted. "The public library."

Jenn looked at me like she had no idea what I was talking about. Which I guess is fair because until a few months ago, I didn't know we had public libraries. "The Harold Washington Library," I said. "By the fountain."

She considered it. She was about to say, No. Honestly, I wasn't sure whether I wanted her to go or not. But it had been ages since we'd hung out and maybe if we went to the library together, she'd ask me about how my story was going...and maybe we'd talk about Javier and books and screenplays...and maybe I would tell her about Tony. "The café is like Versailles," I said.

BLUE OR GRAY

I didn't tell her about the story or Javier or the *Aliens* script or Tony or anything. We were about halfway to the library when she got a text. She read it, giggled, wrote back, and was like, I think I need to go.

Obviously.

I was more relieved than frustrated. I didn't want to show her Versailles. I wanted to be alone. When I got to the library, I didn't even look for a librarian to help me find books about writing screenplays. I didn't want to read. I was sick of other people's books. I could worry about goddam screenplay formatting later and let *Aliens* be my guide. I wanted to be back in The Under with Radha and Merton and Penelope. Back at The Yellowstone School. Filled with Penelope's unrequited love. Filled with Radha's excitement and rage. Filled with Merton's...Well, his excitement, too. But a different kind...

I went straight to this little nook behind the shelves, sat down on the floor, put my hands over my closed my eyes (I didn't even care if I looked like a total freak) and imagined it.

If *The Under* was a movie and it was the scene at the Yellowstone School. How would that go?

It's night.

It cuts back and forth between Penelope and Merton.

There's a Jaymay song playing. It's bittersweet and acoustic. A very sweet young woman's voice. About being in love with a boy and not knowing if he loves her.

The sky is darkening and the stars are just appearing. Penelope wanders the grounds of the school. It's the first time since they've left The Under that they're in a place that's safe enough for her to actually relax and just feel.

Penelope walks down a wide dirt path away from the glowing torches that line the front of the Mother's House—the old brick building that had been the school's dining hall. The moon, almost full, slowly rises behind the peak of the building. Jaymay sings, "I watched you very closely, I saw you look away. Your eyes are either gray or blue. I'm never close enough to say."

Then it cuts to Merton and he's in a cozy cabin with one of the scouts who captured him. A girl with long dark hair and brown skin, Aisha. They're sitting next to a fire. Talking. Smiling. You can't hear their voices. Jaymay sings, "I can't keep staring at your mouth without wondering how it tastes." Merton and Aisha lean toward each other.

Cut to Penelope, walking past the fields and gardens on one side, a pond on the other. In the distant background, the shadow of a large windmill. The sky is huge overhead. Dark. Penelope had never seen real stars before Merton convinced them to leave. Jaymay, "I know the shape of your hands because I watch them when you talk. And I know the shape of your body because I watch it when you walk."

Cut to Merton. Aisha pulls his sweater over his head. It's stuck. Comes off with a yank. They laugh. But then they become serious. "I know that she's your lover, but she's nowhere near your heart..." But Aisha would be. She would be near his heart. He hardly knows her. But imagine this girl. A girl who's grown up her whole life not thinking of her virginity as something you lose. Not trying to protect herself from sex, but seeing it as a gift, a duty, a power. That's what Merton sees when he looks at her. It's magnificent.

Cut to Penelope, the path she's on cuts through a wide swath of trees. She gazes up as she walks and we follow her gaze. The leaves are dark. They seem colorless. She reaches up and takes a leaf in her fingers. She looks like she's going to cry. "The city is for strangers like the sky is for the stars."

Cut to Merton and Aisha, they stand up and walk slowly to the ladder that climbs up to the sleeping loft. "I think it's very dangerous if we do not take what's ours."

Cut to Penelope, she comes to the guard tower and drawbridge that stand next to the river that circles the whole campus. On the other side of the river are the woods and fields and cabins where the young people hunt, and train, and live. The cabin where Merton is. Penelope looks out over the river, then turns back to walk up the hill. "I'd love to look into your face without your eyes turning away. Last night I watched you sing because a person has to try. I walked home in the rain because a person cannot lie."

Penelope fades into the darkness.

GODDAM BUDDHA JAVIER

So, here's the final note that Javier and I left on after Blick and his screenplay talk. We took the Blue Line back up to Irving Park, pushed through the turnstiles, and were standing outside the station, under the overpass, trying not to get shit on by pigeons. I'd texted the moms after the Addison stop.

"You don't have to wait," I told him.

"I don't mind," he said.

The moms pulled up, literally, 3 minutes later. They must have sprinted to the car. I was not surprised to see both of them in there. Mama Helen was in the passenger seat and she waved at Javier. He waved back. I saw Mama Jane say something, and I'm sure it was along the lines of, Do not roll down your window.

As I was reaching for the handle of the back door, Javier said, "Elaine."

I turned back.

"You have to be willing to recreate the world," he said. "Even if it makes life awkward."

Where does he come up with this shit? "Nice exit line," I said.

The fluorescent lights shone down on him. "If you say so," he said and smiled that crooked-tooth smile. "You're the writer."

FEBRUARY

ROVING HORDES

Another thing you have to think about when you're writing about a post-mass-extinction world, is roving hordes. Well, probably not full-on hordes, cause a full-on horde wouldn't still be there in 250 years. But at least marauders. Because where there are survival enclaves, there's bound to be people who want to fuck with the enclave.

Which means you have to think about defense strategies.

The Yellowstone School is walls and moats and bridges—like a castle.

NYC, flooded and floating on coral made of fat, is water and dams and locks and watergates, etc.

The Under? Obviously the defense of the luxury, underground condo is secrecy.

Which kind of begs a question I hadn't thought of yet. If Merton's aunt got kicked out, does The Under *really* exile her? I mean, if your *one* defense strategy is secrecy (plus, maybe some pressure-locked submarine doors that would only delay the inevitable...), you can't actually banish people. What if they lead someone back to you in spite? The aunt has to die. Sorry, Merton.

When he figures that out, HFS. That's gonna be *amazing*. He's going to flip shit. *That* is the perfect time for them to get caught by The Yellowstone School scouts...

```
EXT. FOREST NIGHT

        Radha, Merton and Penelope
        sit around a small campfire
        in a tiny clearing. Perhaps
        there was a car or a
        building here that is long
        gone, but prevented the
```

forest from retaking the
area quite as fully. They
are surrounded on all sides
by trees.

>   RADHA
>   You don't really
>   think your aunt
>   is out here, do
>   you?

Merton looks up from the
fire.

>   MERTON
>   She had to go
>   somewhere.

Penelope also looks up from
the fire. But her face is
alarmed. She knows what
Radha is like. She
recognizes the tone of
voice. Anticipates what's
coming. But still doesn't
say anything.

>   RADHA
>   (incredulous)
>   You think she's
>   alive?

Penelope shoves her sister,
trying to get her to shut
up, but Radha ignores her, as
usual.

A flash of anger passes over
Merton's face.

>   MERTON

Of course. She's
as clever as we
are. If we can
survive out here…

Radha looks at him like he's
an idiot.

> RADHA
> Merton.   They
> obviously killed
> her.

> PENELOPE
> (Shocked. That's a lot, even
> for Radha.)

> Radha!
> He's   certain
> she's wrong.

> MERTON
> No they didn't.

But the second he says it, he
feels the truth.

> MERTON
> (mumbles to himself)
> Our only defense
> is secrecy.

Radha shrugs. Makes seems-
obvious-to-me   gesture.
Penelope puts her hand on
Merton's shoulder.

> PENELOPE
> (speaking gently)
> Merton…

Merton looks at her in a

fury.

> MERTON
> Don't touch me.

Penelope crumples.

Radha tries to comfort Penelope, but Penelope yanks away.

Radha shrugs.

Merton stalks away from the fire and crashes into the forest.

> RADHA
> (not loud enough for him to
> hear)
> I wouldn't go too
> far…

A moment later, Merton's shriek of fury and despair rips the darkness.

Penelope winces, hearing his pain.

> RADHA
> (quietly)
> How did he not
> figure that out?

Merton comes back into the small clearing and the light of the fire. Penelope looks at him with love and concern. Radha is about to say something when a small group of dirty (camouflaged)

```
scouts  from  The  Yellowstone
School    with    spears    and
knives   emerges   into    the
firelight behind him.
```

DETROIT IS DYING

And so what's the defense for a city of plants? Can't be walls—walls are dumb. It has to do with the plants. The plants will have to kill intruders. But not like Venus fly traps eating invaders, that's dumb, too.

Pheromones. Cause it turns out the human brain has special receptors for certain plant pheromones. Turns out, the Detroit plants give off a poison that kills any non-Detroiter.

So, after Merton and Aisha do it and Merton is like, Can you lead us to NYC and they're like, How about Detroit...they all head out together.

```
EXT. FOREST DAY

The group of ten Yellowstone scouts (a
mix of females and males) plus Radha,
Penelope, and Merton is fanned out and
walking quietly, almost silently through
the forest. Radha, Penelope, and Merton
have learned more in the month of
traveling with the Yellowstone scouts
than in a year of sims.


             PENELOPE
        Do you smell that?

The group stops.

        YELLOWSTONE SCOUT ONE (FEMALE)
            What?
```

                    PENELOPE
            The flowers.

The group looks around. The woods are
dense and green. There are no flowers
anywhere.

AISHA has sensed Penelope's animosity
toward her. It's not something she's used
to. It makes her uneasy.

                    AISHA
        (doesn't even bother to look around)
            There are no flowers.

Radha's head snaps up at Aisha's comment.
She's the only one who talks to her
sister that way.

                    RADHA
                  (angry)
            If she says…

                    MERTON
            (ever the mediator)
            How far out are we?

Yellowstone Scout One looks up at the
sun which has passed its zenith and is
starting to fall.

            YELLOWSTONE SCOUT ONE
            Another 20 degrees. [Ask
            Banerjee if measuring
            the time like that is at
            all possible.]

Radha looks annoyed. Measuring distance
by the location of the sun has been
difficult for her to learn. She's
frustrated. And still chaffing at Aisha's

tone.

                    RADHA
                (frustrated)
            Is that a long way or
            not.

                YELLOWSTONE SCOUT ONE
            Not too far.

                    AISHA
                (in control)
            Let's go. And stay
            quiet. We may not be the
            only ones headed for the
            city.

A look of unease passes between Radha,
Penelope, and Merton.

They walk a long time. The sun moves
across the sky. Then, the forest ends
abruptly at a wide arc of clearing. The
city in the distance is a sudden crash of
color and smell. But it's not a normal
city. It's a city of plants and flowers,
surrounded by a wall of high hedges.

Penelope sniffs the air, looks confused.

                    RADHA
                What's wrong?

                PENELOPE (confused)
            I don't know. Something.

                    AISHA
            Quiet. Stay here. We
            need to signal.

Radha and Penelope look at each other.
Sit down and pull their water bladders

from their packs. Merton sits with them.

Yellowstone Scout Two pulls a whistle from a his pack. Blows three short blasts. Pauses. Blows three times again.

They wait.

A moment later, the same pattern comes from across the clearing.

Aisha jerks her head toward the city.

Radha, Penelope, and Merton put their water away and get up.

EXT. BORDER OF THE CITY DUSK

A group of guards meets them at a break in the giant hedges that mark the edge of the city. They are suspiciously unarmed, except for one guy with a vicious-looking club.

Aisha rolls up her sleeve.

> AISHA
> Nice to see you, Hargrove.

> HARGROVE
> Nice to see you, Aisha.

Their voices say there's definitely something between them.

Penelope and Radha both look at Merton to see his reaction. His face remains blank.

The rest of the Yellowstone scouts are also pulling their sleeves back.

Hargrove suddenly produces a syringe and plunges it into Aisha's waiting arm.

                    AISHA
                (rubs her arm)
            That never feels good.

Hargrove and the other guards move amongst the scouts, injecting all of them.

Hargrove stops in front of Radha. Indicates she should lift pull her sleeve up.

Radha steps back and crosses her arms.

                    RADHA
            I don't think so.

            YELLOWSTONE SCOUT THREE
                (rubbing her own arm)
            You need it.

Radha shakes her head.

                    RADHA
            No one is sticking a
            needle in me.

Penelope presents her arm and is injected.

                    RADHA
            Penelope!

                    PENELOPE
                (rubbing her arm)
            Can't you feel it?

                    RADHA
                (angry)

What are you talking
about? Feel what?

Penelope looks at Radha

            PENELOPE
   The poison.

            MERTON
   Poison?

            PENELOPE
   Aren't you getting
   dizzy?

Aisha looks at Penelope. Maybe she's
misjudged her.

            AISHA
   She's right. Some of
   their plants are toxic.
   The injection blocks the
   brain receptors. You'll
   die without it.

Merton *is* feeling a little off, pulls his
sleeve up, receives the injection.
Hargrove turns his interest to Penelope.

            HARGROVE
   How could you feel it
   that quickly? You've
   never been here. I would
   know.

Radha grudgingly receives the injection.

Penelope stares past Hargrove as though
she can see beyond the hedges and into
the city.

            PENELOPE

It's sick.

Radha is uncomfortable with Penelope's sudden certainty.

                    RADHA
            What are you talking
            about? What's sick?

Penelope tilts her head to the side.

                    PENELOPE
            The city. It's dying.

Hargrove looks at one of the other guards in alarm. Then at Aisha in accusation.

                    HARGROVE
            Who is she?

Aisha is confused. They have a long and trusting relationship.

                    AISHA
            What's happening?

Hargrove gives an order to the other guards.

                    HARGROVE
            Bring them.

The other guards suddenly grab Radha, Merton, and Penelope.

                    RADHA
            Here we go, again.

NOT GOING BACK

It's in Detroit that Radha realizes that she doesn't ever have to go back to The Under.

Maybe she sees Penelope with the plants. And she thinks she's never seen Penelope look so natural—so herself. And Radha suddenly remembers that Penelope is a clone, but it's like she had to remember. It's the first time since she found out that she wasn't always thinking about the fact. Something about Penelope there, amongst the flowers, doing the thing that she knows how to do—she not a clone. She's her own whole person.

And Radha wonders, Am I my own whole person? What do I do that no one else can do? She thinks about the life waiting for her back home. Taking over the genetics lab. Just like her mother, grandmother, great grandmother...she realizes that even when she'd stopped doing lab Comms and started doing survival Comms, in her heart of hearts, she knew she'd go back to the lab eventually. And eventually she'd take over for her mom. It was her destiny.

But what if it wasn't.

```
INT. GREENHOUSE DAY

Before the thought is even formed in her
mind she turns to Merton.


                RADHA
        I'm not going back.

He looks at her and knows exactly what
she's talking about.


               MERTON
        Me neither.
```

She knows that's true, too.

> MERTON
> Will you still come with
> me to New York to find
> Hugh?

Radha nods. She has nothing better
planned.

> RADHA
> Sure. Of course.

> MERTON
> We should leave soon.

Radha looks over at Penelope who is
talking to another female GARDENER. She's
relaxed.

> RADHA
> (yells)
> Penelope! Come here!

Penelope looks over, annoyed.

Radha doesn't notice. Just waves her
over.

Penelope says something inaudible to the
woman she'd been working with. The woman
makes an understanding, slightly sad
face. Penelope walks toward Radha and
Merton.

> PENELOPE
> What?

Radha doesn't notice her tone.

> RADHA
> We're leaving tomorrow.

Merton *did* notice Penelope's mood and
tone.

> MERTON
> I know it's sudden. I'm
> just worried about Hugh.

Penelope glances at Merton, seems to be
considering, then makes up her mind about
something.

> PENELOPE
> I'm staying here.

> RADHA
> Sure you are.

Penelope is shaken slightly. Looks back
over to the other gardener. Regains her
composure.

> PENELOPE
> They've asked me to.

> MERTON
> You can't stay here.

Penelope seems to be remembering
something. Stands up a little taller.

> PENELOPE
> I've had enough. I'm
> tired.

> RADHA
> What are you *talking*
> about? Don't be stupid.

Merton tries to mend the rift.

> MERTON
> Penelope…

At the sound of him saying her name,
Penelope softens, is about to speak,
maybe to change her mind?

Radha grabs Penelope's arm. Penelope's
eyes widen.

There's a sudden image of Radha lying
in a field of very tall grass under a
bright sun. She's pale. Something bad has
happened. We wonder if she's dying.

Penelope yanks her arm away.

Radha is angry, but also looks afraid.
She can't imagine Penelope not being
with her. She needs to keep things the
same, in control. She chooses anger and
annoyance at her sister to try to control
her.

Penelope is still angry. Tired of Radha
bossing her around. Tired of thinking of
herself as Radha's Monster. Doesn't tell
her sister about the vision-she's never
had one about a person, only ever about
plants, perhaps her vision is growing
because she's finally doing what she was
meant to do.

                    PENELOPE
          You two do what you want.
          I am not leaving. I have
          a place here.

She turns and goes back to the plant she
was working on. Keeps her back to Radha
and Merton.

I slammed my computer closed. I hadn't even wondered what Penelope would do before I got to the end of the scene. Poor Penelope, even *I* was ignoring her. But it turned out she wasn't going back either.

What if I wrote the scene so that Radha doesn't get the idea first at all? What if Penelope does?

That's not something any of the books had told me—that you can start one way and end another, then go back and change what you started. It's not just one way. It's not the *right* way.

Once again, there was Georgia O'Keeffe. How do I keep forgetting her? It's not that the single right way to draw a picture or tell or story exists. You have to fill whole rooms with sketches—that one line, over and over.

What if we lived our lives like that? What if we didn't just assume that there was a right way things were going to happen and a path you followed to get there? What if life was a series of those Bohm and Krishnamurti conversations? Where you don't know what the other person is going to say, and you don't even know what you're going to say. It's all discovery.

It's hard to explain—but it occurred to me then that even quitting school had felt like the same path, the same plan. The same overall plan of getting into college and getting on with life from there and not actually changing anything. What if life isn't a plan? What if it's a discovery? What if it wasn't just a line when Javier said, "You have to be willing to recreate the world." But first of all, you have to even know that it's possible.

And that's when I knew, I wasn't going back. I was *not* going back to school. No matter what.

I practically sprinted downstairs and into the kitchen. The moms were talking very seriously, their heads close together over another architectural drawing.

"I'm not going back," I said.

They looked up.

NOBODY'S GOING BACK

"Oh my god! You're finished!" Mama Helen said.

I gave her a confused look.

"She can't possibly be finished," Mama Jane said.

I shook my head. We had just talked about it, like, four days ago. "Of course not. You can't write a whole novel that fast."

Mama Helen looked hurt.

"But I don't think I'm writing a book anyway," I said. I forgot to mention that I *was* still writing. It's possible I was being dramatic.

"You're not doing what?" Mama Helen asked, her voice rising.

"Slow down," Mama Jane said.

"And I'm not going back to that goddam school," I said and crossed my arms in front of my chest. I was filled with the spirit of rage and stubbornness—Radha's spirit.

"That's not the deal..." Mama Helen started.

"Let's slow down," Mama Jane said.

"Sometimes deals change," I started back.

"Not while you're living..." Mama Helen started again.

"Both of you," Mama Jane said and raised her hands.

"Just because you brought me into the world without my consent doesn't mean you own me," I said.

"Whoa. Zing. Let's just... "Mama Jane tried to get in.

"We took such a risk on this... "Mama Helen raised her voice.

"Helen," Mama Jane said, "You're upset about the house."

"Letting me have a life is risk?" I raised my voice.

Mama Jane stood up and yelled. "Okay! Cut. Print. That's a wrap, people!"

We froze. Mama Jane didn't yell.

"Am I in an Afterschool Special?" Mama Jane asked. "Were scripts delivered and I missed mine?"

"What?" I asked. Why was she talking about scripts? Had I said that I was going to write a screenplay instead. I hadn't said that. In retrospect, the yelling might have been avoided if I'd remembered to mention that part. But I was just so *excited*. Excited that Penelope was staying in Detroit. Excited that Radha was never going back to The Under. Excited that I was *never* going back to school. "What's an Afterschool special?" I asked.

"An Afterschool Special is a show where kids act all crazy and extreme so that kids watching the craziness can learn lessons without having to be goddam crazy," Mama Jane said and sat back down.

Mama Helen flashed a look at Mama Jane. "This is serious," she said.

"So are PCP and shoplifting," Mama Jane said.

I couldn't help but laugh a little.

"Goddamit." Mama Helen said. "Have you been listening to a word she said?"

"I heard it when she said we don't own her," Mama Jane said. "Evidently, she's not shoes."

Even Mama Helen couldn't not laugh at that.

I saw my moment. "I probably should've mentioned that it's not that I'm not writing..." I said. "It's that I was having a really hard time and so I'm trying something new so I can keep figuring out what the story is."

Mama Jane put her hand in her chin and gazed at me.

"And the 'something new' is...?" Mama Helen asked.

"A screenplay. Like for a movie," I said. "Javier and I were talking. And I was telling him that the book wasn't going well. And he asked if maybe I wanted to try writing it as a screenplay," I said. Realizing I was possibly throwing Javier to the wolves, I added, "At first I was like, That's crazy...no way...I'm not quitting..."

Mama Helen nodded her agreement. Mama Jane just gazed.

"But Javier said it's not quitting. Not as long as I'm still learning something new. Not as long as I'm still creating," I said. "He said part of creating is learning your process for creating."

Mama Helen sighed. I saw my opening.

"I know you know I've been working hard," I said.

The moms looked at each other.

"I got a library card for godssake." I was trying to make them laugh. That was always a good strategy. But it didn't actually matter. Something had already shifted. I didn't know if it was a shift between them or just inside of me. But I knew I didn't have to fight with them. Because the decision wasn't theirs. And not in a freak-out way. It was that my life was mine. The world was large. Terrifyingly large sometimes. But it was mine to discover. I never knew that.

TAKING IT SERIOUSLY

That night I dreamed of Radha.

I was far above a field of tall grasses, surrounded by miles and acres of forest. The sky was blue and cloudless. The sun, bright and flat and yellow like a circle that had been printed and pasted in the sky. I could see the backs of two small figures lying in the field. I slowly circled and drew closer. Radha and Merton. It was Penelope's vision. My vision from after Tony's party.

Radha's face is pale. She's lying on her back. Her breathing is shallow. She's looking up, her eyes wide. Her head is on Merton's legs. He's kneeling on the ground.

Finally, Radha speaks. "I'm sorry," she says. Her voice is a whisper.

Merton looks surprised. "No. Ssh. Don't say that."

"I'm sorry for what I said about your aunt," she says. "I'm sorry because I knew it would hurt you and I said it anyway."

Merton's face is pained at the mention of his aunt, but he hides it quickly. "You didn't mean it," he says.

Radha smiles ruefully. "I did mean it," she says.

Merton smiles, too, and nods his head. He knows she meant it.

"But it's only because I wasn't taking it seriously," Radha says. Her hands on her belly are covered in blood.

"Not taking what seriously?" Merton asks. His legs are covered in blood, too.

"Any of it," she says. "None of this was real to me."

Merton nods, understanding. "It was just a Comm sim?" he asks.

Radha nods. She's thankful he understands. "I'm sorry," she says. "It *was* real." She grimaces in pain.

Merton brushes a hand across her forehead. "Please rest. Just rest."

Radha closes her eyes. Her breathing relaxes. She seems to be sleeping.

Merton's face relaxes, too.

Then Radha's eyes pop open. "No!" she says. "That's not what I meant to say. I meant to say, Thank you."

Merton looks startled by her suddenness and her words. "What?" he asks.

"Thank you for making me leave," she says. "I *never* would have. I would've become what my mother wanted me to become. I acted like I was the tough one. But *you* brought us here."

At first Merton looks pleased by her comments. But then he realizes the implication. If he brought her here, then it's his fault. "Radha, I..."

He looks down. Her eyes are open and glazed. She's gone.

FARAWAY

Could Radha really be dead? I thought she was the heroine. Does that mean Penelope is? Radha was only part of the story? I finished the scene and managed to fall back asleep for awhile.

At around 8:30AM, I texted Javier.

Elaine: You awake?

Not even a minute passed.

Javier: Yep.

Elaine: I think Radha is dead.
Javier: Whoa. Didn't see that coming.
Elaine: It feels really weird.
Javier: How so?

How did it feel weird?

> Elaine: Like I can't go downstairs. I can't talk to the moms. I can't drink coffee or eat.

The phone rang. Javier. Obviously. "Hello," I said.

"You okay?" Javier asked. His voice was joking, but, I mean, we'd never talked on the phone before, so...

"I told the moms last night that I'm not going back to school," I said.

"Didn't see that coming, either," he said.

"You're the one who told me I had to be willing to, like, change the whole world," I said. How could he not have seen it coming?

"I wasn't sure you'd actually take my advice," he said.

"I took your screenplay advice," I said.

"Well, I didn't think you'd take *all* my advice," he said in a tone like, Have you met you? "I figured you'd be way more stubborn than that."

"Yeah, yeah," I said. "So, here's a question."

"Of course," he said.

I thought about telling the moms I wasn't going back. And my realization that my life was my own. I felt like I was right on the verge of understanding something that I didn't know before. But I couldn't quite get it. "Does your art ever make you feel distant from people?" I asked. "Like faraway. Estranged. Well, like from your parents or other people who don't do it?"

The line was quiet, but I knew he was still there. "Hmm," he said. "Like it's hard to figure out what to tell people I do all day?"

"Yes. That," I said. I could hear Jenn telling me not to say anything about not being in school. So instead I got into a fight about, Why can we feed the lions cows, but not giraffes?

"I hadn't thought of it quite like that. But yeah, sometimes," he said.

Then we were both quiet. Sitting in our separate rooms.

I nodded to myself. I laid back on my bed and looked up at the ceiling fan. The blades were covered in dust. "I feel so weird," I said. "Like things are slipping away or are far away or..." He's gonna think I'm insane.

"Well you just said you told your moms you weren't going back to school," he said. "That's gotta feel strange."

"It's not like I wanted to ever go back there," I said.

"Sure. But didn't you think you would?" he asked.

How did he know that? "How do you know that?" I asked. If it weren't for Penelope and Radha, I wouldn't have realized that you don't have to go back. "This morning when I was writing Radha's death," I said, "She apologizes to Merton for not taking their adventure or their friendship seriously," I told Javier.

"Mm-hmm," Javier said on the other end of the line.

"And I realized I hadn't really, not super really, been taking not being in school seriously," I said.

"What do you mean by 'seriously'?" he asked.

I thought life was a path and you can't actually change it. "Just what you're saying. Deep down, I believed I was going to go back. I wouldn't have said that I believed that, but deep down, I did," I said. God I was glad he had called.

"Yeah," he said and he sounded sad, "Deep down, I believed you would, too."

He did? What the hell? "Thanks a lot," I said.

He laughed. "It's not like you're the first homeschool friend I ever had," he said. "Most people go back."

I guess that made sense. But then I felt sad. Was I just one of many? He was my only homeschool friend.

"I hoped you'd make it out, though," he said. "I hoped."

I closed my eyes and saw Radha, dead in the field. "Does your imagination ever terrify you?" I asked.

"Geez," he said and laughed. "If I should have a calendar of sayings, you should have a calendar of crazy questions."

"Touché, jerk," I said. I kept my eyes closed.

"Terrified because of death by robot and Slender Man?" Javier asked, kidding with me.

"Who's Slender Man?" I asked. I didn't mind the tangent. I knew we'd get back there.

"He's terrible, don't look him up," Javier said.

"It's just that the more time I spend in there..." I said.

"In your imagination?" Javier asked.

"It just goes on and on," I said. I could feel my mattress pressing into my back, but the edges of my body felt fuzzy. "Maybe it's melodramatic, but it's like the whole universe in there."

"I don't think that's melodramatic," he said.

I don't know why I even needed to say it that way. I knew he took things seriously. "Like have you ever seen one of those videos about how big the universe really is? It's so gigantic. Like incomprehensibly big. And the idea that I have a whole universe inside me. That's so huge, I might never even see half of it...might not even know how to get there..."

"Small," Javier said, almost inaudibly.

"What?" I asked.

"It makes you realize how small you...we...are," he said.

So small. But it was a different kind of small feeling than the one I had when I read *Sex at Dawn* and was like, What the hell am I supposed to do about 10,000 years of a culture that hates women? That feeling was helpless. This wasn't the same. But I still couldn't quite get my hands around what the new feeling was. Something like not helpless? Like not scared? Like calm? I suddenly wanted to tell Javier how thankful I was that he'd come to talk to me in the pitch line.

"Elaine," Javier said. He sounded very close.

"Yeah," I said, but there was no sound. I had to say it again, "I'm here," I said.

"I'm very glad you quit school," he said.

It was just after 9AM on a Tuesday morning in February. I would've been in physics. Planning my weekend. And I wouldn't have known Javier. And Radha wouldn't be dead because there wouldn't be a Radha. And I wouldn't have been lying in bed, eyes closed, trying to feel out and into the whole dark universe. "Me too," I said.

KEEP AWAY FROM THE MOON

KPao had emailed and asked if I could go down to campus to meet with her and a colleague. I passed the moms on the way out. Mama Helen was on the phone with her serious face. Mama Jane was doing some numbers which was weird.

"I'm going down to campus," I said.

"To see the biologist?" Mama Jane asked. I'm pretty sure I'd told them she was an *evolutionary* biologist, but that was pretty good for Mama Jane. And I hadn't talked about KPao lately—we hadn't talked a ton because the moms were kind of working all the time.

"Yeah," I said. "How's the house coming?" I asked and pointed at the spreadsheet in front of her.

Mama Jane rolled her eyes. "Not my favorite," she said.

I looked at the little field of nail polish chips on the table in front of Mama Helen and was like, "Are we worried?" I had never in my life worried about the moms' work. I didn't know what that would mean. Could they lose their business? Could we lose the house?

Mama Jane shook her head. "It's just some setbacks," she said. But she would lie to me, right? If it were bad? She wouldn't just tell me that we're screwed on some random day when I'm headed out of the house and Mama Helen is on the phone. If they were losing the business and we were screwed, that would be a sit-down-in-the-living-room conversation.

Mama Helen hung up. "Headed out?" she asked.

"I'm sorry about last night," I said. "I guess if I want you to trust me with my life, I should try to act trustworthy..."

Mama Helen looked at Mama Jane. "You remember when she was a toddler and she was so obsessed with brushing her teeth?" she asked.

Mama Jane smiled and said to me, "You spent hours standing on a stool in front of the sink, brushing, then making one of us lift you up so you could run your toothbrush under the faucet."

I loved it when they told me stories about me before I could remember being me. But then it occurred to me how weird it is to be a whole living person, who does things all day long, for years, who's obsessed with brushing her teeth, and have no memory of it.

"You would shriek when we made you stop," Mama Helen said.

"Ugh. That sound..." Mama Jane said. "...extra-terrestrial."

"I guess it makes sense you're still that kid," Mama Helen said. "You're just obsessed with something different."

"With a slightly different shriek," Mama Jane said.

Group hug.

I was waiting at the Blue Line when Javier texted me.

> Javier: Hey. I have something for you.
> Elaine: Cool!
> Javier: You home?

> Elaine: Headed down to U. Chicago.
> Javier: Oh. Well, I'll meet you downtown before you get the
> Metra.

I was like, Dude, I can see you later. It's not that big a deal.

> Elaine: I'm already at the Blue Line.
> Javier: I'll just meet you.

Um, okay. Whatever. And I felt a little uncomfortable because I was like, What could he possibly be giving me? Is it gonna fit in my bag? Why is he being weird?

But then I got on the L and stopped thinking about him because I was wondering about Penelope. Radha and Merton left Detroit, but Penelope is still there, trying to heal it. It's the first time she's ever been on her own. It's the first time she's ever made any friends. But also, something needs to happen to her.

I got off the L and hustled through the Metra station.

And suddenly Javier was in my face.

Normally, I'd be happy to see him. But it was a tight connection and I was just about to get an idea for Penelope and there was Javier and it was hard to get his face to come into focus because it was like there was a split-screen with me watching Penelope on one side and me in the train station, trying to figure out who Javier was...

And he was all, Hi.

I was like, Gotta hurry.

He was like, Yeah. Sure.

We walked to my train without really talking and it was already there, so I got on. He stood on the platform and I was like, Shrug.

He pulled some papers from his bag and said, "This might help..." he said, holding the papers out to me.

I stared at his hand. Help me with what?

The whistle blew and the conductor shouted, "All aboard..." I love that they really do that. I couldn't see what the papers were, but I took them and said, "Cool. Text you later." I went for the high-five, but it was like he didn't see me and then I was hanging.

The conductor came over and said, "On or off, kid."

Javier stood on the platform, "I underlined some parts," he said.

I laughed at that. Once again, he was the good student and I was the Jenn. "Thanks."

And the train just, like, started drifting away and Javier was standing there in his navy peacoat and a blue knit hat with the smallest wisp of his dark hair peeking. He looked old-fashioned and it felt too weird to wave.

I got to my seat, looked at the papers, and was like, What is this? Poems? "Jesus," I said. How are poems going to help me? But then I read it a little and it was an interview between two women I'd never heard of, Khaela Maricich and Miranda July, and there was a note written at the top in Javier's writing (which should be a font) that said, "Go to page five..." So I went to page five, and these sections were underlined:

> Just the experience of, through the grounding of holding somebody's hand, a girl that I met at one point, really experiencing the vastness of what it is to live and exist and look at everything which is—I'm not even really able to communicate that in words right now in the interview because it sounds—I mean, you can't get that into words. In the performance the girl gets home from camp and tries to talk to her mom about it, about what she'd heard—for the first time she'd looked at the sky and really *heard it*—but her mom is just like, "You can't talk about it. We don't want to talk about that. Don't talk about it."

So the girl's waiting for her mom to tell her more about why she's not supposed to talk about it, and in the investigation of trying to figure out what is wrong about talking about that thing that she heard—she tape-records her mom, and then is trying to hear—there must be some secret message in what her mom's been saying—so she plays the tape backwards—

—And backwards, the mom is saying, "Keep away from the moon, it will fuck you up, it will fuck you up." The mom knows all about the vastness of the sky and she is terrified of it. That is really the only place in my life I kind of felt like I was ever actually standing in front of people talking about the weirdness, just of living...

The weirdness, just of living.

And then suddenly I felt scared.

What if it's not just quitting school for real.

What if the universe inside my imagination is real?
What if those universes exist inside everyone?
What do we do with all that?

EXT. OUTDOOR FLOWER GARDEN DAY

The sun is shining and the air is full
of pollen. Penelope and another girl are
in a field of sunflowers.

> EVA
> How many have you found
> so far?

Penelope is holding the leaf of a tall
sunflower between her hands.

> PENELOPE
> One hundred and forty-
> seven.

> EVA
> And do you sense that there are more?

> PENELOPE
> (closes her eyes, inhales deeply, nods)
> Some, but they're spread
> out. I can feel them, but
> they're spread out.

> EVA
> Vivienne says toxin
> levels are almost back
> to optimal.

> PENELOPE
> (smiles, but she's not surprised)
> I'm glad to help.

A strange looks crosses Eva's face, but
Penelope's eyes are closed and she

```
doesn't see it. Eva rubs the spot on her
neck where Dr. Parker plunged the giant
needle when he Replaced her.

Penelope opens her eyes and looks at Eva.
She smiles.

                    EVA
          Yes. We're lucky you
          arrived when you did.

The camera moves in and we see that the
other girl is Eva, from The Replaced, the
girl who was Replaced. Uh oh.
```

THE WORLD UNDER THE WORLD

I was supposed to meet KPao at a different coffeeshop on the other side of campus that was inside one of the classroom buildings. But I couldn't find it. I mean, I was distracted by the fact that Eva from *The Replaced* had shown up in Detroit. It made sense, those robot-body-snatchers had to go somewhere, but I was still surprised. Penelope was in deep shit and I was lost. I wandered around, up and down wide stone stairs, like, WTF? Finally, I saw some student and I was like, "Classics Café?" And he pointed up the stairs and made a hand-swoop motion, and there it was, around a corner and down a hallway. So, I was late.

KPao and her colleague were sitting at a table in the corner. I waved and walked over. "Sorry I'm late," I said. "I couldn't find it."

"Sorry. Yeah. It's tucked away," KPao said.

I did the ritual (bag down, coat off, hat and mittens jammed in sleeves of coat) while KPao introduced me.

"Elaine Archer, this is Martin Horwitz of Philosophy. Martin, this is Elaine, the student...no...the writer...excuse me...I've been telling you about."

We said, Nice to meet you and shook hands. He's a thin white guy with silver hair and transition lenses. He was wearing a light gray sweater that looked like he might have been its 10th owner.

"Anyone need anything?" I asked and pointed toward the coffee station. They both shook their heads, so I went to get a drink.

KPao and Horwitz were talking about a mile a minute as I walked back toward them. You two have a lovely connection.

"So Elaine," KPao said. "I've been telling Martin about you."

I looked at him awkwardly.

"She's very impressed," he said.

I blushed. I shrugged.

KPao went on. "A friend of Martin's is thinking about homeschooling his kids..."

"Which I believe is a terrible idea," Horwitz said in this way that made me think, immediately, I like this guy.

"And so I thought he should meet you," KPao said.

Oh god. So I'm speaking for all of homeschooling? "How old are the kids?" I asked. I wished Javier was there.

Horwitz shrugged. "Younger than you," he clearly had no idea about kids' ages. "Grade school, I would say."

"That would probably be a lot different," I said. "I have a friend who's been doing it that long. He had tutors and specific lessons from his parents and things like that..." Javier would have way better things to say. "I just started this year. So I'm choosing everything for myself."

Horwitz nodded. "What would you say has proven to be the most interesting thing about schooling yourself?"

Okay, so here was this Professor of Philosophy who already thought homeschool was a terrible idea and I was supposed to prove that it wasn't. Gulp. I did some dumb ramble about time management + reading whatever I wanted + not taking tests + not pretending to do my homework when I totally didn't do my homework...and he was so bored. You know when people shift around and they're like, Where's the door?

I wanted to say something, like acknowledge how boring I was being. But I was like, You can't say that to Professor Martin Horwitz. But then I was like, Hell with it. What do I care who he is? So I said, "Yeah. Blech. What a boring answer."

Horwitz laughed in surprise. KPao smiled. I smiled, too, held up finger, and said, "Lemme think what I really think." I closed my eyes. Immediately, I saw Radha, Merton, and Penelope in that first moment they leave The Under. Standing outside for the first time in their lives. Their whole lives. They are overwhelmed by the sights, the sounds, the smells. They are in awe and terrified. And yet their bodies and hearts know that this is where they, as human beings, are meant to be. Above. In the world. Amongst nature.

"Imagination," I said.

Horwitz tilted his head with the most inviting curiosity and I thought, I bet he's a great teacher.

I went on, "Like I've always thought of imagination as just being like, That little kid has an imaginary friend. Like pretending. Or making things up."

Horwitz nodded. "And that's not your current conception?" he asked. His voice was a little nasally.

"It's bigger. Way bigger. It's how you know and feel and see that...That..." That what? What? The weirdness just of living. "That there's a world under the world," I said.

"A world under the world?" Horwitz asked. He looked at KPao and they smiled. And a little bit it was like, This kid is cute. Which in the past probably would've offended me, but it didn't. Probably because they were also a little bit like, This kid might be on to something.

How to explain? "Okay, well, like, we've only been doing agriculture and the culture that came from that for like, 10,000 years. But humans have been around for longer. And the Earth with life way longer than that. And the universe way way longer..." I didn't know exactly what I was trying to say, but I remembered Bohm and Krishnamurti and just tried to follow the glimpse of the idea. Imagination. The vastness. The weirdness. The moon. "You know, we all act like the point of life is go to school, get a job, have a family, buy a house and put a bunch of shit in the house...maybe if you're lucky, you get to have a job you like..." I pointed at them like, You two seem like you have cool jobs. "...but, like, that's so new...in the scope of the universe...but no one ever tells you about that...school never tells you that...and it certainly never tries to teach you to feel all the way back to whatever was there before the Earth even had life...but the universe *was* here already...and I mean, I might be wrong, but I think we're all made of whatever the universe is made of..." I was thinking of *What Technology Wants* and the idea that all of life was sort of moving toward something. "...and something has to be the thing that's making the universe expand and made plants and animals evolve and put me here..." Phew.

Horwitz blinked at me.

"And I don't mean god, like a father-person-god, making decisions doing it," I said. "I mean something like gravity." I could see Mr. Banerjee, sliding a wooden block down a tilted plain. "I mean something like movement."

"The force that through the green fuse drives the flower," Horwitz said and his voice seemed sad and I wondered about his life.

"What's that?" KPao asked.

Horwitz didn't answer right away. He was somewhere else. He smiled a tiny memory smile. "Dylan Thomas," he said. "A poem by Dylan Thomas." He looked at me. "It's what you're talking about. The force that makes the flowers grow."

"Yes," I said. I bet tons of AP English classes study that poem and talk about, What is the force of life? And everybody becomes a banker anyway. "But not just *knowing* that something must be making the flowers grow. And *talking* about it. And maybe *studying* it..."

"Feeling it," Horwitz said.

I pointed at him and made a face, like, Feeling it. "The world under the world," I said.

"The force that through the green fuse drives the flower," Horwitz said.

"I told you you'd like her," KPao said.

And that didn't make me blush. Because I liked them, too. Why shouldn't we like each other?

He laughed. "To discover the numinous is no minor feat of an education," he said.

"The numinous?" I asked.

"A moment where the bigness of life makes itself known through the smallness of life," he said.

"Whoa," I said. "Yeah." The numinous. *That* is what I wanted from *This Is Our Youth*. Something numinous. Some small gesture from Tavi Gevinson that made me *feel* the bigness of life. Of course, it wasn't fair of me to expect that from her. For godssake, it was her first play. But looking back, that's what I'd wanted. And I was let down. "It's crazy when you discover something before you even know there's a word for it," I said.

Horwitz was so chill. He just dragged his small hand through his gray hair and was like, "Indeed."

"Maybe that's my other favorite thing about not going to school," I said. "I get to discover so many things for myself. Which is different than saying I get to decide what I learn about."

KPao reached across the table and gave him a poke in the shoulder, like, I told you.

Horwitz smiled and I thought, The bigness of life making itself known through a poke in the shoulder.

"I'm still not convinced it's the best thing for my friend's children. At least not at the age that they are. It's hard to know if they *would* discover things for themselves..." Horwitz said.

"Sure," I said. "That's a common critique." All those hours I'd spent researching to convince the moms to let me quit—homeschool and unschooling and curriculum in a box and how to teach your kids math by building a hen house...it seemed long ago. Far in the past.

"I am confident of one thing, however," Horwitz said. "You should come to school here."

I was thinking, I sure am glad I don't have to learn any more math...and then I was like, "I'm sorry, what?"

"I've been thinking that, too," KPao said. "This place would be great for someone like you." She seemed legit, personally excited.

Whoa. "Oh...Well...I mean...I'm only a junior..." It was the only thing I could think to say. I had never even considered that I could get in there.

"Finish your book and we'll worry about specifics later," KPao said.

I hadn't gotten around to telling her that it wasn't exactly a solid book and in that moment, when they were talking about me, Elaine Archer, going to the University of Chicago, I just couldn't bring myself to correct her. Saying I was writing a book, sounded serious and impressive. Saying I was trying lots of different things to discover the story, to discover my process...well, I didn't tell them.

MERTON'S DISTRACTION

The numinous and maybe getting into the University of Chicago were too much. So, I thought about Merton, instead. He's gotta keep looking for Hugh, even if Radha is dead. And Hugh's in NYC. So, do I need to show a scene about how Merton gets to NYC? Like do I have to show him hacking through the forest and camping alone? It would be a good way to show his grief about Radha. Maybe another montage with music? Or is that too many montages?

> EXT. TOP OF A RIDGE AT THE EDGE OF A
> FOREST DAY
>
> Merton is at the top of a rise, looking
> through a pair of military binoculars
> that someone in Detroit gave him.
>
> He has arrived in New York to find his
> friend.
>
> His face bears the burden of Radha's
> death. He is not the boy from the
> Westside of The Under anymore.
>
> New York. Gray. Under water. A large
> ferris wheel turns slowly and eerily on
> the horizon, dipping down into the water
> and rising up again. Several small
> clusters of buildings seeded and
> bolstered with fat that turns into
> coral. Some collapsed buildings also
> bolstered for walkways and docks. Small
> boats moving amongst it all. Flat barges
> filled with gray people. It's a
> militarized city. There are guards
> walking amongst the other gray, stooped
> masses. The wardens amongst the workers,
> breeders, scouts.

```
Merton slinks back away from the ridge
uncertain how he'll breach the city.
```

LADY JANE REPRISE

And then it happened. I'd been dreading it without knowing I was dreading it. Avoiding it without knowing I was avoiding it. Trying to prevent it, but evidently it couldn't be prevented...

Javier and I were at Zero Drop.

We'd been texting the day before and he was like, "How'd you like that interview?"

I didn't know how to talk about it. I didn't know how to say, Yes. The moon. The numinous. The force that through the green fuse drives the flower. The weirdness of being human. So I said, "Oh. It was cool. Thanks. That girl has a weird name, huh?"

He was like, "I hadn't really thought of that." And I could tell he was disappointed. Then I felt bad, but, you know.

So, then we were sitting at Zero Drop and he was wearing that same blue sweater that he always wore, only the hole in the neck was gone and I wondered if he sewed it or if one of his parents did and then he said, "Did you read the rest of it? Or just that part I underlined?"

He was looking, like, right at me. And there was the pressure and awkwardness in my chest and I could not talk to him about it in person. It was one thing to talk on the phone about how infinitesimally small we are. It was another thing to talk about it when he was sitting right there. "You gonna show me your new sketches?" I asked. Yeah, I know, sloppy and obvious.

He hesitated for a few seconds and I was sure he was gonna call me out. Instead, he reached down and pulled a big, black, hardbound book from his backpack. It looked exactly how you think a sketchbook would look. He didn't seem pissed that I'd changed the subject. I would've been pissed.

"You said you think you're getting somewhere with a new piece?" I asked.

He flipped through the pages that mostly seemed covered in black line drawings. Since we'd been hanging out so much, I knew a lot about how he did his drawings (start with an idea, do some sketches, transfer the idea into Adobe Illustrator, and go from there), but I'd never seen any of his work-in-progress.

He showed me a few pages that were just random shapes. "I start with shapes," he said.

"I was gonna ask," I said.

"It's just to mess around with how I want to organize the space," he said.

"Do you have an idea of what you want the picture to be before you start those?" I asked.

"I have a general idea," he said. "But I don't always know how it fits. Like when I'm thinking about certain different parts, they are bigger in my mind than other parts, so it's not always the right scale in my imagination."

I thought about trying to write a scene. Trying to see it up close...what each of the characters is thinking and doing in a moment. What they're saying, but also what they don't want to say. And then trying to see it from far away...if it goes with the rest of the story. Like, if Radha and Penelope start out awk and estranged, they can't just suddenly not act that way anymore. One thing has to lead to another and another and it has to all make sense. And that's not everything that has to work. Not even a tiny part of it. "So, this is all new? Not adding to any of the conference stuff?" I asked.

Javier shook his head. "No," he said. "It's a new idea that totally snuck up on me."

"Ha," I said. "Your little 'It's only wasted if you force it' pep talk rub off on you?" I'll admit I was glad that he bought his own bullshit. I don't know what I would've done if he'd pushed and pushed the other piece and then sold it. I mean, obviously I would've been happy for him...

He looked at me and at first I thought his feelings were hurt. I was about to be like, Dude, I was kidding. But then he said, "Something like that."

I stared at his face as long as I could without it being ridiculous, but I could not figure out his expression.

"Well, so what is it?" I asked. And then suddenly I was worried that he wasn't gonna tell me. That that's what his expression was. He didn't want to tell me. "You don't have to tell me if you don't want to," I said.

Then he gave me another look that I *could* read and that look was, What are you talking about? "You kind of inspired it," he said.

Oh god. Awkward. "Yeah? Is it about being pissed all the time?"

He laughed. "Yep. And yelling at people in coffeeshops..."

"Best seller," I said.

"It's about questions," he said.

Something in his voice made me think, Don't talk about the moon. It will fuck you up. "Does that count as a concept?" I asked. Questions.

"I don't know," he said. "It might. What if some stories aren't the answer to anything? What if they're just the questions?"

I thought about Bohm and Krishnamurti and conversations that are questions and creating something new together. And, "Keep away from the moon, it will fuck you up..." and, What if the universe inside our imagination is real? "You think questions will be enough?" I asked.

He shrugged again. "Can't hurt to try," he joked.

We looked at each other and...something...

"Do you want...?" he began.

Don't let him finish that question. "...more water," I interrupted. "Yes I do..." I slid my glass over.

He took the glass and said, "Seltzer?" They had a whole faucet that poured nothing but seltzer.

Free the seltz. "Yes, please," I said.

He walked away and I got my phone out.

"Aren't you two adorable," a voice behind me said.

Oh shit. I spun around. "What are you doing?" I asked. I was possibly rude.

"Nice to see you, too," Jenn said. She went and sat next to Javier's empty seat. "I had to meet May Welland for a group project. You remember group projects, right?"

I wasn't sure if she was referencing Lucca or school or both. "What's it on?" I asked.

She picked up Javier's cup and sniffed it.

"Okay, weirdo," I said, took the cup from her, and put it back where he'd left it.

"I like this place," Jenn said, looking around the coffeeshop.

Just then Javier came back, handed me my water, and sat down with his own. "Hi," he said to Jenn.

"Hello tea-drinker," she said.

He looked at her, confused.

"She sniffed your cup," I said. As much as I loved Jenn's ability to unbalance some oldster bitch at a play, I was not interested in her pushing Javier around.

"What kind?" Jenn asked him.

Oh, god. Please don't tell her what kind.

He glanced at his empty cup. "Lady Jane," he said.

Oh god.

Jenn's eyes widened. "Lady Jane?" she asked.

"For Lady Jane Grey," Javier said. "The Nine-Day Queen."

Jenn was looking at me as she said, "Lady Jane Grey. The Nine-Day Queen." I couldn't tell if she was trying to mess with him or not. "Of what?" she asked, still looking at me.

I tried to make my eyes say, Please don't mess with him.

"England," he said. He could've said it to her like, How do you not know that? He totally could've taken a shot at her. In which case she definitely would've messed with him. "It's a nice afternoon tea," he said. "Doesn't make me tired."

He's a gentle spirit, I tried to make my eyes say.

Jenn calculated. "So you two are having a brainstorm," she said and finally looked back at him.

I tried to relax. "He's showing me some sketches for a new piece he's working on." I wanted him to show her. I wanted her to see how good he was. "It's really good," I said. Then I wanted to kick myself for needing to prove him to her. Goddammit.

"So you're an artist," Jenn said. "Elaine never tells me anything anymore."

"Haha," I said. You never ask.

Javier pulled his computer from his backpack and clicked through a few screens, "Here's one that's done," he said, turning the computer toward Jenn. "It's about Elaine," he said.

Jenn looked up at me like, Oh, really?

I wanted to run from the coffeeshop all the way back to my house and under the covers. I couldn't look at him. I stared at Jenn and tried not to barf. But then I watched any potential to mess with Javier drain out of Jenn's face as she stared at the screen.

"Let's see," I said.

Jenn turned the computer toward me. I still didn't look at him, but I could feel him watching.

An image of giant, old, green-blue-gray trees. Trees. So tall. Giants. Mammoths. Trees as old as mammoths. The trees that were here when the mammoths were here. No. Before. You can only see the trunks—the trees so tall they reach up, out of the frame—not even a lower branch. So huge and somehow reaching toward me, I felt them behind me—I almost turned around to see.

Beneath the pleistocene of trees is a trickle of a path, like a faint hint of the earth tamped down. It's strange that the path is so narrow and so sparse because there isn't any foliage on the ground. It is *not* the rainforest.

In Javier's illustration, the thin, brown trickle of path is hemmed by a mossy fur on either side.

The whole scene is dark and pale. Bloodless. Colorless. Sunless...

I actually gasped. "Oh," I said, though I hadn't meant to speak. I couldn't help but look at him. "It's the world without flowers."

He smiled the biggest smile and his eyes were wide and bright.

In the far distance, just about to turn the corner and out of our gaze are two tiny, stacked, red triangles (her cloak), two tiny, black dots (her boots), and a tiny, brown dash (her basket).

Of course, I've heard *Little Red Riding Hood* one trillion times. But I don't know that I'd ever *heard* it. Oh. Oh. Here. Now. The primordial forest. The first trees. As old as green life on Earth. Pre-language, pre-literature, pre-Blue Line, pre-Lady Jane tea, pre-farming, pre-fucking-everything. And here's the little girl. Her basket. Her boots. Her red cloak.

That's me?

"That's amazing," Jenn said.

I looked at Javier. "I love it," I said.

"I'm glad," he said.

THE STRATEGIC AIM

Like I said before, life isn't like a story. It's the same shit over and over. Just at the exact moment when things had started to feel different and I started to think maybe *I* can be different and life isn't a path and I have friends and a story and maybe things aren't so bad and we're gonna make it...

...the world finds its way in...

...I read a story about women who are stolen by terrorists and turned into sex slaves. Then when they're "rescued," the rescuers don't believe the women—the rescuers think the women are terrorists, too. So instead of being saved, they're imprisoned.

And one of the favorite weapons of terrorism and genocide is mass rape. I don't know how I find that shit. I think, somehow, it finds me.

I'd skip the next part if I were you.

From Wikipedia:

The strategic aim of these mass rapes are twofold. The first is to instill terror in the civilian population...The second is to degrade the chance of possible return...by having inflicted humiliation and shame on the targeted population...One objective of genocidal rape is forced pregnancy, so that the aggressing actor not only invades the targeted population's land, but their bloodlines and families as well. However, those unable to bear children are also subject to sexual assault. Victim's ages can range from children to women in their eighties.

What the fuck am I supposed to do? How can I keep living in this world? How can I keep being warm in my house and there's chocolate in the drawer next to me when right now, right *now* and *now* and *now* and *now* the worst things that any human has ever done are being done. Right now.

I thought about that girl screaming, "Someone help me." And the moms watching from the window as the cops tilted the girl's chin, just so, and took pictures of her purpling face. I feel like that tiny Red Riding Hood. Only it's not beautiful. She's lost. And it all sits in my chest and my guts like it's slowly crushing me and caving me and it'll eventually break through and tear a hole through reality and prove that the world isn't created by a force that makes the flowers grow. It's a web of lies and violence and terror and hatred and rape and destruction and ownership that's spun out over an abyss of nothing.

HOPE IS A DRUG

Motherfucker. I sat down at my computer.

For godssake, of course, Radha's not dead. A tiny shock of relief shot through me. But she's not safe.

I remembered this woman, white, messy blonde hair, neon jog bra under light gray tank, yoga pants, I'd seen on the street last summer. She was screaming, like screaming, at her dog. A husky. He shouldn't've even been in Chicago. It's too fucking hot. I don't remember where I was going. I just remember the woman screaming, "You asshole! You asshole!"

She was looking down at her shirt, I'm guessing it was a coffee spill, she was holding a coffee. She had yanked back so hard on the dog's leash that its front paws were lifted off the ground and it was clawing at the air.

I could've stopped and said something.

But I didn't do anything. I didn't try stop it.

How the fuck did we get to that? To humans thinking that's okay. How do we think it's okay to take a living thing like a dog and leash it and treat it however-the-fuck just because the human thing has decided that it's dominant.

Sitting there in my room, I whispered, "How can we be in this world?"

You'll not be surprised *this* is where I ended up with Little Red Riding Hood.

        EXT. CAMP SITE NIGHT

        There's a wolf.

The wolf is strung over a bed of hot
coals. Sometimes they leave her feet on
the ground. Sometimes the feet are
lifted so the beast thrashes and
struggles to feel the Earth again. This
tires her. She becomes hopeless. She
hangs her giant head. At the moment of
hopelessness, the fire is stoked, fresh
wood added, so the flames leap and lick
her exhausted belly. She shrieks and
comes back to life—revived from her
stupor by excruciating pain. All around
her, her captors whoop and stomp. It
won't be long now.

The wolf thrashes so hysterically, it
seems she might snap her own neck as an
escape.

> NEW YORK SCOUT ONE (DUDE)
> There goes the bitch.

> NEW YORK SCOUT TWO (DUDE)
> (shouts)
> Kill it! Kill it!

Radha thinks he means the wolf and she's
both furious and relieved.

But no, a young scout lunges forward and
scatters the fire, reducing the flames
back to simple, bloody embers.

Radha can't take it anymore.

> RADHA
> (screams)
> She's pregnant!

All the scouts look at Radha and then
burst into laughter.

NEW YORK SCOUT ONE
(mocking)
She's pregnant...

The wolf ceases thrashing. She whimpers.
Her tongue lolls.

She looks up and Radha meets her eyes.
The wildness is gone. The wolf is no
longer of the forest and swamps. She
belongs to the world of men now.

She's been Replaced.

Radha pulls a knife from the belt at
her waist. Moves toward the other scouts
with vicious slowness. She doesn't care
if they kill her. She'll get at least one
of them first.

KNAACK, one of the lead scouts, who
has been watching Radha over the course
of her first mission now that she's in
New York and recovered from her wounds,
is suddenly by her side. He grips the
wrist with the knife, firmly, but not
painfully. He has the same medium-dark
skin of the other scouts, but his bone-
structure makes it clear he did not
grow up with the deprivation that most
native New Yorkers did. He is scruffy and
handsome.

KNAACK
Careful.

Radha turns on him. Speaks through
gritted teeth.

RADHA
Let go.

Their eyes meet. Radha's narrow in fury.
Knaack's gaze remains steady, but his
head tilts with curiosity.

> KNAACK
> (calm)
> What are you planning to do?

Radha's confidence after her initial rage
is slipping.

> RADHA
> Something that will
> hurt.

> KNAACK
> (still matter-of-fact)
> Perhaps. But they'll
> hurt you worse. For
> longer.

> RADHA
> (sad)
> She's pregnant.

Knaack is still holding her wrist, but
with no force.

> KNAACK
> (nods)
> And she'll whelp those
> pups in the city and
> they'll be ours, too.

The wolves are used for control in the
city. For defense. Searching.
Controlling and patrolling. They are a
deadly weapon.

> RADHA
> (grits her teeth)
> I can't do nothing.

He draws her away from the wolf-fire
to sit by the campfire where the other
scouts will soon join them. She doesn't
speak or look at him.

> KNAACK
> Of course, you can. You
> want to live.

Radha is silent. She stares into the
flames. Knaack thinks she didn't hear
him. They sit in silence for moments.
Until Radha turns and looks straight at
him.

> RADHA
> What a bullshit thing to
> say.

Knaack looks at her in surprise. He has
no answer.

Radha turns back to the fire.

> RADHA
> (speaking almost to herself)
> I'll get them.

Knaack looks at her and says, almost as
though the line is rehearsed.

> KNAACK
> Hope is the drug that
> makes the truth
> bearable.

Radha doesn't acknowledge he's spoken.

Knaack looks at her a moment longer, the
curiosity crosses his face again, then he
turns to stare into the fire as well.

I KNEW I WAS LYING

Then it was Jenn's birthday dinner. I'm going to be a real goddam treat, I thought as I got dressed in not jeans and a t-shirt. Her parents always choose someplace that had been written up recently so they could prove they can always get a table. So, it was some new restaurant called Gargantuan in Hyde Park.

It was actually kind of a relief to walk to the L and then navigate the Metra. I ignored the people around me and didn't let myself imagine the terrible suffering that would visit them in life and the terrible suffering they would visit on others.

Instead I sat on the train and texted Javier.

> Elaine: Radha's not dead.
> Javier: What? How'd she do that?
> Elaine: She got captured by New York instead.
> Javier: Ahh. How'd that happen?

I hadn't figured that out, yet.

> Elaine: I guess Merton must've done it somehow.
> Javier: Like he leaves her somewhere he hopes they'll find her?

Hope is the drug that makes the truth bearable.

> Elaine: Yeah. They're already headed for the city. And something had to hurt her. Maybe they got attacked by some squad of New Yorkers.
> Javier: Cool.

I didn't tell him about Knaack. I didn't know who he was, yet. But there was definitely something there. And just like The Yellowstone School sex scene, I wasn't talking to Javier about it.

> Elaine: What are you doing?
> Javier: Actually, I was just getting ready to call you.

Call?

> Elaine: What's up?
> Javier: Can you hang out? I have news.
> Elaine: Can't. Jenn's bday dinner. You okay?
> Javier: Yeah! I'm great. I got an agent!

Oh fuck. Of course, you did. Goddamit.

> Elaine: Awesome! For the new thing?

The one with *me* in it?

> Javier: Yep. And then maybe we're gonna work through some
> ideas with the conference submission.
> Elaine: Oh, did you finish it?

I'm a bitch.

> Javier: No. Not at all. But I met her at the conference and she
> told me to send her some work. I didn't send the stuff the
> editor rejected. But I'm so psyched about this new piece.

Try to be nice. This is your friend. And he's been trying for a long time.

> Elaine: I'm psyched about it, too.
> Javier: Thanks. You're part of it.

Barf.

> Elaine: I totally am! 😊
> Javier: Maybe see you tomorrow?
> Elaine: 👻

When I got to Gargantuan (what a fucking name), the hostess led me to the Cartwrights who were already in the back. Jenn's mom saw me and looked at Jenn who waved.

"Oh, I didn't think Elaine was coming," her mom said.

Go to hell, Marcie. I am so *not* in the mood for you.

"I told you she was coming," Jenn said.

"But when she didn't..." Then Jenn's mom realized she was being rude and she turned a big, fat, fake smile on me like I didn't just see it go down. "Elaine!"

You're a bitch. "Hi, Mrs. Cartwright," I said.

Jenn rolled her eyes.

"How did you get here?" Jenn's mom asked, like I wouldn't see this as part of an I-didn't-think-she-was-coming, line of questioning.

"The train," I said.

"The train?!" Mrs. Cartwright literally gasped.

I nodded. The train. The humanity.

"Well Paul will take you home. Paul..." she called over to Jenn's dad. He turned, but he was on the phone. Seems about right. "I don't give a rat's ass..." he said and held up his hand like, I'm just taking this call.

Mrs. Cartwright turned us away. "He'll drive you home," she assured me.

How much did I was to say, "We haven't even eaten," just to watch her try to work it out. Before I said anything, she scurried off.

"She needs to tell the waitress that we're one more than expected," Jenn said, rolling her eyes again. "Like we don't have a table for 50 reserved."

"What did your mother want?" Jenn's dad was off his phone call.

Jenn nodded at me. "You're driving her home."

He looked from her to me, confused.

"After," she said.

"I took the train," I explained.

"The train?" he asked.

I know, the humanity. "It's fine," I said. "I come down to campus all the time," I said, like, Don't worry, danger averted.

"Why do you come to campus all the time?" he asked. We both knew I meant University of Chicago. And let me just say, this was the first time he had ever asked me a direct/personal question. Ever. In like ten years of knowing him.

Here's how it typically goes with him:

I knock on their front door. He answers—talking on the phone, "We've been over this and over this," he says to whatever poor asshole is on the other end, "The numbers don't lie." He looks at me with disappointment (maybe he thought I was the pizza guy) and points toward Jenn's room. "I don't care if Larry says the numbers look good. My numbers are the numbers..." I shut the door behind me and walk away.

Yes, Paul is busy and important and distracted, but that's not what it is. It's that he's a snob. I'm 100% sure he didn't know my name. I'd gone on vacation with them 100,000 times and he didn't know my name. So, him asking me a question was like, Whoa. Also, he's like 20th generation U. Chicago legacy and it was as though everything that happened on campus directly concerned him. So, I admit, when he asked why I was on campus, it gave me a thrill to say, "My research lead me there."

Jenn rolled her eyes at me like, Ugh, can you believe what a chump Paul is?

"Research?" Jenn's dad asked.

I couldn't help myself. "I've been working with an evolutionary biologist—Professor Pao...?" I said like, Are you familiar with her work?

He shook his head. So interested.

I knew I was being an asshole. Name dropping. But Paul was *always* disappointed I wasn't the pizza guy. "And then it morphed to include philosophy," I continued. I didn't care if that wasn't entirely, or even remotely, true.

Jenn's look morphed from thinking I was messing with her dad to, Morphed to include?

I tried to communicate to her with my eyebrows, I don't know. I can't stop.

"Who are you talking to in philosophy?" Paul Cartwright asked, and there was just a sliver of fear, like he wasn't going to know who I was talking about this time, either.

"Professor Horwitz?" I said. Jenn's face told me she'd realized I wasn't just messing with her dad. That I really *had* been coming down to campus. And I hadn't told her.

"The editor of *Philosophical Quarterly?*" Jenn's dad asked.

"You know him?" Jenn said and shook her head at me.

"The arbiter of Jean Paul Sartre's estate?" her dad asked again. I had no idea if Horwitz was either the editor of whatever Paul had said or the arbiter of anything, or what an arbiter was, but there amongst the wood and wine and birthday menu, Javier had an agent, and Paul Cartwright was impressed with me, and I ate it up.

"I was taking with Kathy...Professor Pao...about the ethics of human cloning and she pointed me to Professor Horwitz..." Yes, those were lies.

"You and Jenn are in school together?" he asked. He was confused. He furrowed. He was pretty sure, no, he *knew* me from somewhere...

"I dropped out," I said. I had never put it that way before. I always said, "I'm homeschooling" or "I left school" or at most, "I quit school." But good god, "I dropped out" felt good.

Then I looked at Jenn whose pursed lips said, Fuck you.

Mrs. Cartwright came back from wherever and walked over to us. "Paul," she said and drew him away.

He went with her, but looked back over his shoulder at me and shook his head with incredulity.

"Fuck you," Jenn said and stomped away.

Dammit. I followed her into the bathroom.

She stared at me, waiting for the door to drift closed behind me. "What the hell were you doing back there?"

"I'm sorry..." I started.

"About *which* fucking part?" she asked.

"How many parts are there?"

"I don't know, you tell me," she said. Jenn is terrifying when she's angry.

I gritted my teeth. I didn't want to answer. "At least two?" I said.

"Not to be all Mrs. Leuwen about it. You remember her. The principal at our school. Oh, excuse me, I mean *my* school..."

"Jenn," I said.

She held up her hands. "Not to be all Mrs. Leuwen about it, but why don't you describe the 'at least' two things..."

I ducked my head. "The thing where I'm talking to professors and U. Chicago and the thing where I bragged to your dad about it."

"In that case," she said. "Let's add two more."

I cringed. I could see what was coming.

"The thing where you didn't tell me you're basically fucking...What is it? Two, professors?"

"Whoa. Whoa."

She ignored me. "And the thing where you chose my birthday to reveal it through bragging to my goddam dad."

"Those don't sound good," I said.

"Because they're not," Jenn hissed.

"I swear it was an accident. You know he always ignores me. And nobody takes my quitting school..." I said.

"Don't you mean 'dropping out'?"

"No one takes it seriously. They act like I'm going to be homeless," I said.

"Those professors take it seriously," she said.

Oh god. "I didn't mean to hide it," I said.

"Then why did you?" she asked.

"I know you're worried about getting in," I said. "And it was just going to be one interview. Then suddenly I'm down here talking with KPao..."

Jenn scoffed and rolled her eyes at the nickname.

I couldn't tell her that I hardly even knew Horwitz, not after the way I'd talked about him to her dad, "...And then it had been too long to tell you without it seeming like a secret..."

"It *is* a goddam secret!" Jenn yelled.

If it had been a movie, a woman would've opened the door at just than moment and then closed it again.

"I didn't know what to say," I said. Although let's be honest, I'd never thought about telling her. I hadn't thought about not telling her, but...

"Cause you don't think I'm gonna get in."

"What?! No!" I had never thought that.

"Did your little biologist offer to write you a recommendation? Or get you in?"

"Jenn, I don't even know if I want to go to college..."

Jenn shook her head. "She did, didn't she?"

I shrugged. "They both did," I said, not wanting to lie anymore.

"You bitch," she snarled.

"I didn't ask!"

"Ever since you quit...Oh, I'm sorry...Dropped out...You've been walking around like you're so much better than everyone. Like we're all just sheep," she said. "Well let me tell you, you're not Ripley."

My chest got heavy and my eyes started to fill. "Jenn..."

"That's the most embarrassing thing I've ever heard, by the way. You're not a hero. You're a liar," she said. And walked out.

I felt like she'd punched me in the guts. I kept it from her. But...

Ten minutes later, when I stumbled out of the bathroom, Mrs. Cartwright came tearing out of the dining room. She'd been waiting. "Elaine," she said. "I've ordered you a car. It's all paid for."

I opened my mouth to say...to say what? But she turned her back on me, so I followed her to the hostess stand. She noted that I arrived there with her, handed me my coat and bag (I would've left without them), whispered to the hostess, and walked away.

WHO DOES THAT?

I couldn't sleep or eat or talk to the moms or write or do anything. Javier texted and I was like, I can't hang out...I waited for her to call me or text me or anything. We'd never even been in a fight before. I wanted to crumple and die.

But then I realized something. Or remembered something. Something I hadn't noticed when I first started telling her dad about being down at the school. She *hadn't* been pissed right away. At first, she thought I was bullshitting. She had totally laughed at first because, Who goes to talk with an evolutionary biologist?

Then I said the thing about taking with Horwitz and her dad knew exactly who I was talking about. That's when she knew. And *that's* when she got pissed.

I mean, I *swear* I didn't mean to hide it from her or lie to her. But what would I have said? Hey Jenn, turns out that if you have an authentic area of interest and a real desire to study, they pretty much let you into the school...

That was right, wasn't it? That was really what it was about.

I bet I didn't even have to finish the goddam book or screenplay or what-the-fuck-ever and I could go to the University of Chicago. Just like all those Cartwright men. Maybe I'd have to take the SATs and write some essays, but I wouldn't have to do any of the shit Jenn was doing because she thought it was her only ticket. I didn't have to sit in Mrs. Sternin's bullshit class. I got to do what *I* wanted.

You know what? Fuck her.

You know who goes to talk with an evolutionary biologist? Someone who needs help doing mathematical modeling of post-mass-extinction survival populations. And if Jenn had ever asked me *one thing* about what I was doing, she would've known that. And she would've known I was going down there and she would've known about KPao and Horwitz. I would've told her the story about poor, stupid goddam Ted Breughel and she would've laughed. But she didn't ask me anything. She said, Write me an essay. She said, When we're at this party, don't talk about how you don't go to school. She said, No, I can't hang out.

Fuck her.

MARCH

BURNING IT DOWN

INT. KNAACK'S APARTMENT NIGHT

Knaack is in his apartment when he smells the smoke. He knows immediately that something isn't right. He leaps from his chair where's he's been reading one of the precious few remaining books, pulls on his shoes, grabs his pack off the floor, a sweater from a hook, and sprints out the door.

CITIZEN calls out as Knaack sprints down the hall:

> CITIZEN (MALE)
> What's the hurry, Warden?

Knaack doesn't answer.

EXT. THE WOLF ENCLOSURE JUST AFTER DUSK

The smell of smoke is strong as he rounds the corner to the wolf enclosure. He already knows what he'll find.

One side of the enclosure is in flames and Radha is kicking at the wood, trying to collapse the fence.

Knaack runs to her.

                    KNAACK
               (out of breath)
          What the hell are you
          doing?

Radha, still kicking, doesn't answer. The
fence falls.

The fire spreads along the fence and
begins to make its way into the enclosure
itself. It leaps to some dry bushes and
flashes to life. The wolves are barking
and howling, going crazy. Their shadows
move in the background as they search for
a way out.

Knaack tries to grab her arm.

                    KNAACK
          Radha!

Radha yanks her arm away.

                    RADHA
          Help me!

She's stomping at the fire on the piece
of fence that's fallen at her feet.

Knaack hesitates.

A wolf sprints past them, inches from
them. They've found the opening.

Radha's skin appears bronze in the fire-
light. She laughs.

It is the wildest and most free sound
that Knaack has ever heard.

The fire is raging now. The red flames
fill the night darkness.

The sirens begin.

                    KNAACK
              (grabs her arm, hard)
            Radha! We are leaving.

Wolves stream from the hole in the fence.
They streak off into the blackness.

Radha allows herself to be tugged away
but watches the fire in the enclosure
mounting and only turns to run when they
round the corner and she can no longer
see the flames. In the darkness, she
hears the sirens and the loudspeakers
calling out, Remain on your floors.
Remain in your apartments. We hear the
sound of hundreds of automatic deadbolts
slamming home.

Knaack turns down a small alley between
two buildings. There are canals on either
side, but he's sure-footed on the narrow
concrete track. Just as quickly as he
took her hand, he drops it, leans down
over the water.

                    KNAACK
            Get in.

There's a jet black, two person kayak
floating in the water.

                    RADHA
    (still drunk with what she's done, she's
                  confused)
            That isn't your boat.

                    KNAACK

(desperate to get away)
No shit. Get in.

Radha hesitates. There's a huge
explosion, followed by shouts.

                    RADHA
(with a mixture of glee and incredulity)
      Guess that's the fuel
      tanks.

Knaack shoves her toward the boat.

                    KNAACK
      In.

The light at the mouth of the alley is
blocked as a group of 20ish wardens runs
by. Radha finally swings down and into
the front seat of the kayak.

Knaack wrestles with something at the
back of the boat.

                    KNAACK
      Here.

He hands her a paddle. Gets quickly into
his own seat and shoves off.

They leave the narrow alley between the
buildings and come out onto a main
waterway. It affords a view of the
wreckage they left behind. As Radha digs
her oar into water, she looks back to see
the flames illuminating the smoke-filled
sky.

THE ANGRY BIKE RIDE

I finished the scene and thought, Jenn is not my responsibility and I'm going for a goddam bike ride. It was finally nice enough out. I texted Javier, Bike ride?

We met at the corner of Elston and Pulaski.

Javier was standing next to his silver and red 10-speed. "Hey," he said.

I had Uncle Alex's bitch ex-girlfriend's old mountain bike. She'd left it in the garage and never come back for it. "Sorry I've been out of it," I said.

"You look pissed," he said.

"Jenn and I got in a fight at her birthday," I said.

"And you don't want to talk about it," he said. He was wearing a thick dark gray hoodie that I'd never seen. We hadn't known each other long enough for it to be hoodie weather.

"Nope," I said.

"So where we going?" he asked.

I shrugged, like, Do I have to do everything?

"Ever been to the Bohemian Cemetery?" he asked.

"No. Is it creepy?" I asked. I wasn't in the mood for creepy.

He laughed. "Totally not. It's really pretty," he said.

"Where is it?" I asked.

He pointed north, up Pulaski. "Straight up," he said. "Few miles."

"Sounds good," I said and took off fast.

As I rode, the anger crept back. Like, What can I burn down? And it was like no matter where I dodged, I was riding through a cloud of dog shit smell. I almost got doored 2 times and not one of those assholes looked up so I could flip them off. I wished I could ride with a baseball bat in a holster on my bike, like a cowboy with a rifle in a holster on my saddle. I'd like to have a nice wooden baseball bat and find some woodshop dude to help me burn a big, toothy jaw-mouth on the front and when people almost doored me or pulled in front without looking or turned right without signaling or parked in the bike lane or yelled at me for not coming to a complete stop or spit out their window or flicked cigarette butts right into me or drove obscenely huge SUVs because they "just feel safer," I could yank my homemade dragon-mouth baseball bat out of the shotgun holster and smash their fucking window. Then, I wouldn't even have to flip them off.

Javier didn't try to talk to me at lights or stop signs. Probably because I didn't stop. Finally, we got to the cemetery. We were both breathing hard. "Feel better?" Javier asked.

Actually, I kind of did. I shrugged. "A little," I said.

"Wanna ride around?" he asked.

"Yeah. Let's see it," I said.

We rode the paved paths amongst the grass and graves and statues. The grass was still brown and there were no leaves on the trees yet. But I could imagine that it was pretty in the summer. Just then though, it felt sad. Then I imagined it 250 years post mass-extinction. It would be overgrown. The buildings and statues toppled and hidden. Trees would take over the grass and cover all the graves. Their roots might unearth headstones and caskets. But the marble would still be there. What about the bodies? Would they finally be part of the Earth again?

"There's a lagoon over that way," Javier said. "Wanna stop?"

I nodded.

He led the way down a wide road and around several curves. I saw the water up ahead.

We got off our bikes and sat in the grass. My legs ached. The first bike ride of the spring always made them ache. It felt good. I closed my eyes.

"Can I ask you something?" Javier asked.

My eyes still closed, I said, "Sure."

"Why don't you want to go out with me?" Javier asked.

Oh shit. "What?" I kept my eyes closed, hoping that maybe he or I would disappear.

"You know I like you," he said.

I remembered Tony's question, Aren't you with that Javier kid. Not right now. "Javier."

"I've tried to bring it up, but you always manage to find a way to stop me," he said. "It's actually pretty impressive."

I guess I had sort of realized what he'd been doing and dodged out of it. I mean, he'd underlined a whole thing about the moon. It doesn't get much more obvious than that. I finally looked at him. "I just don't..." I started.

"Is it because I'm Latino?" he asked.

What? No. Gross. "Yes," I said.

"It is?" he asked. He sounded so sad, but fuck him for thinking that about me.

"I don't want to convert," I said.

"Convert?" He asked and shook his head.

"To Catholicism. All Latinos are Catholics, right," I said.

He rolled his eyes. It was a familiar look. "Don't be stupid," he said.

"Then don't *you* be stupid," I said and pulled a fist-full of grass from the ground.

"It's been an issue," Javier said.

"Why would you like me if you thought *that's* my issue?" I asked. Seriously.

"Then what's your issue?" he asked.

I thought about Tony again. Why hadn't it been an issue to hook up with him? Oh that's right, because he was 23 and always going on tour and he didn't want to *go out* with me. Ugh. "I like you too much," I said and tossed the grass back onto the ground.

"Oh, Jesus Christ!" he said and threw his hands up.

"Shhh," I said and brought my finger to my lips. "The lord can hear you."

"Fuck the lord," Javier said. Other than the cop thing, it was by far the maddest I'd ever seen him.

"Definitely not Catholic," I said, trying to ignore his anger.

"Can you be serious?" Javier asked.

Honestly, it was all I could do not to just get up and ride away. I thought if I just keep joking, he would drop it. "Dude," I started.

Javier rolled his eyes again, shoved himself off the ground and walked away from me. He turned his back. "Dude?" he muttered.

Uggghhh. I gritted my teeth. "Javier."

He didn't come back to where he was sitting, but he turned back to look at me.

The way he tilted his head was kind of the exact head-tilt and face that Ripley makes at the Queen Alien before she (Ripley) torches the Queen's garden of alien-baby-pods. I didn't say that. Normally, Javier would've appreciated something like that, but I didn't think he would just then. "Javier, we are 17-years-old," I said. "What do 17-year-olds do when they go out?"

He gave me a look that said, I'm not answering any of your dumb questions.

"They break up," I said. Obviously.

Understanding came into his face. "*That's* your issue. That we might break up?" Javier asked.

"Not might," I said. "Will," I said and crossed my arms over my chest. "And then what?" The warmth from the bike ride was wearing off and I was starting to shiver. I was only wearing a thin, black jacket.

"That's your issue," Javier repeated. He took a deep breath and gazed far away.

"When we break up, it will be awkward. I won't be able to text you kitten videos or call you in the middle of the night to ask you about the endlessness of imagination. It'll be all, Hi. Oh, hi. Barf. No thank you." I hadn't actually thought about all that. But I wasn't wrong. And when we broke up, what was I supposed to do without him?

"Elaine..." he came and sat back down. "You cannot make a decision *now* based on what you think will happen in the *future*," he said.

I pulled my knees up to my chest. Sure, I can. "I dropped out of school based on what I think will happen in the future. We wouldn't even be having this fight—we wouldn't even *know* each other—if I hadn't made a decision based on what I think will happen in the future," I said. Duh.

"Sister of Guadalupe, help me," Javier said.

"Secret Catholic," I said.

"I mean, I have Catholic cousins," Javier said.

"Everything is so perfect now," I said. "Why do we have to change it?"

"It's not perfect for me," he said.

"What's the difference?" I asked. "We make out?" There's another line in that Jaymay song that I didn't use in the Yellowstone scene, Friendship ruined with just one kiss.

"I haven't made a list," Javier said.

"Well, let's make a list," I said. "Then we'll *both* see how it's not worth it."

Javier lowered his eyes to his hands in his lap. "I don't think I can be around you," he said.

What the fuck. "You're holding our friendship hostage?"

ALL THESE FUCKING GUYS

One of the days I was at Zero Drop, I overheard two dudes talking (and by overheard, I mean, they were sitting about five seats away and not even trying to keep me from hearing...). Two white guys in matching cobalt blue button-ups that were probably from Banana Republic who probably refer to girls as "pussy." The one was like, I just hooked up with 8 girls in 3 weeks...Immediately after which he said he was getting ready to move back to Michigan to live with his "girlfriend" (the air quotes are mine, not his) and something else about it being time to "grow up" and "move forward" and "settle down." Yes, literally cliché after cliché. But nothing about the glee in his voice when when talked about how "easy it is" to get girls to sleep with him told me he wanted to settle down. Although his cobalt buddy seemed to think everything he was hearing made total sense. Then the first guy said he hoped his girlfriend could "domesticate" him. She'd be better off with a dog.

Okay, I'm 17 and I don't know shit about adult relationships, give me that old saw, tell me I'll understand when I'm older. But I don't think I ever want to understand the whole, I'm gonna fuck a bunch of girls until some "x" point in time, and then I'm going to get some other girl to make sure I stop fucking the bunches.

Tony and Audra would call those dudes scumfuckers. Sad, lonely scumfuckers.

They're like the weirdest intersection of John Taylor Gatto and *Sex at Dawn*. It's like in *Against School* when JTG talks about learning to obey an arbitrary authority figure rather than learning how to be the boss of your own self. In this case, the wife becomes the boss. But just like JTG says, we're trained to both *need* and *resent* the teacher/boss/wife. I can't imagine it's very good for a marriage if you use your wife to keep you from doing what *Sex at Dawn* makes it pretty clear everyone *wants* to do, aka bang.

When I was like 11, the moms and I were out at dinner and they didn't notice me coming back from the bathroom, and I overheard Mama Helen ask Mama Jane, "Okay, which one of these hipsters would you fuck?"

I was like, "What did you just say?" First of all, there were no hipsters in the restaurant (it was total yuppies—suits and briefcases as far as the eye could see) and second of all, What?

They blushed. Then Mama Jane (bless her heart, as Mama Helen says) said, "Being married isn't always the easiest..."

Mama Helen began picking her manicure immediately.

"And monogamy isn't always the easiest..." Mama Jane said.

Mama Helen raised her eyebrow like, So we're going *there?*

"What's monogamy," I asked. Too bad Jetha and Ryan weren't there, cause they would've been like, Monogamy is a cultural construct designed to secure ownership of wealth, property, and offspring.

Mama Jane said, "Mostly it means being physically intimate with just one person, but generally it includes emotional intimacy as well."

"So then what were you just talking about, 'Which one of these hipsters would you...'?" I asked.

Mama Jane said, "It's a little game we came up with at a wedding..."

"...A hipster wedding..." Mama Helen finally chimed in.

"...years ago," Mama Jane said. "When we were first *really* dating, but we needed to talk about what life was going to be like if we decided to be together long term..."

Mama Helen smiled at her, at the memory. "We were at this wedding with some *very* attractive people," she said.

"So, we spent the evening picking our top person," Mama Jane said.

Maybe chalk it up to the fact that I was 11 and never had a guy try to finger me and had never *really* worried that if I did something sexual, the guy would, like, secretly video it and put it on the internet, but I wasn't that embarrassed to be talking about that stuff with the moms. "Did you pick the same person?" I asked.

They both laughed. "Um, no," Mama Helen said. Which I guess made sense given that they were with each other and nothing like each other.

"Did you pick each other?" I asked.

They shook their heads, like, Um, no.

"That's the whole point of the game," Mama Helen said. "It lets us admit that even though we are committed to each other, we still find other people attractive."

"Never goes away," Mama Jane said.

I think I had lasagna that night.

So would the douche who was hoping to be "domesticated" play Which One of These Hipsters Would You Fuck? I doubted it. I mean, I doubted he was gonna tell her what he told his friend, "It's been one hell of a last hurrah." I doubted he was gonna say, "Let's just hope there's no paternity suit."

Which my point is, Why are some guys so fucking gross?

When I was trapped in the living room with Skeevy Rick, I said all that I wanted was to get out of there. But what I really wanted was to tell him to fuck off. Or even better, to not be thrown by him—not be skeeved. Audra wouldn't have given a shit about him. She would've had him bus his plate and GTFO. But I didn't know about the moms. Sure, they talk about banging other people, but they still invited Skeevy Rick into the house and to the holiday party. They still did business with him. Georgia O'Keeffe wouldn't have.

And then *another* time at the coffeeshop, there was this scrawny white punk couple sitting at the table next to me. He was wearing gray skinny jeans and black skater shoes. His hair was red, so pale it looked apricot. He had a black pleather jacket. He was rubbing his eyes and bouncing his leg and mumbling and maybe he drank all the whiskey Isaac didn't drink or snorted all the ritalin. Either way, he was definitely going to need a life-giving juice.

The girl had dyed orangey-black hair and one of those upper-lip piercings that looked like a mole.

The barista delivered a big salad to the table and the punk girl pulled it in front of herself.

A minute later, the girl said, "Can I have your napkin since you're not eating?" It came off like an accusation. Had he promised to eat? He was very thin. He could use a meal. But he also looked like if he eats, he hurls.

He got up. Ambled around. Wandered. His energy said, I feel like shit and cannot focus. He sat back down.

"Can you stop?" the girl asked.

"What?"

"I don't like being stared at. Especially when I eat." She grabbed a green pepper ring and crammed it into her mouth and I was like, I see what you mean.

"I'm not staring," he said.

It seemed true to me. Not staring at her, anyway. He seemed like he was watching the street.

"Do you want some? I feel weird eating alone." Again, felt like an accusation. It was not an "I feel" that said, I'm sharing this with you because I trust you. It was an "I feel" that said, This is your fault and responsibility.

I certainly think that some feeling states are the other person's responsibility. Like if the dude said, "I feel attacked" or "I feel uncomfortable because you appear to hate me." Like sometimes I want to say to The Bitch Annette, "I feel so minuscule and angry whenever you speak..." But, "I feel weird eating alone..." That's on you, sister.

He didn't eat. I considered it a petty victory.

They didn't speak at all for the rest of the meal. They didn't bus their table.

Why am I telling you these stories? It's because Javier wasn't the only person I didn't want to go out with. I didn't want to go out with *anyone*. Was Javier pretty cute when I thought about it? Yes. Had his skin grown slowly pale over the winter and did I wonder what he would look like in the summer when he was tan and with his black hair and dark eyes and that front tooth thing and in a t-shirt? Yes. But when I looked around at the relationships in the world (even the moms), I'd say that the one Javier and I were *already* having was the best one I'd seen. Or it had been. He wasn't returning any texts or calls.

THE SUNKEN CITY

EXT. OPEN WATER NIGHT

Knaack and Radha glide quietly through the darkness and slowly a giant fallen building emerges in front of them.

                    RADHA
            Where are we?

                    KNAACK
          Out of the zone.

They glide through a decaying archway
into a cavernous building. The water
around them is filled with the fallen
and decaying beams of the building's
interior.

                    RADHA
                  (nervous)
          Is it safe?

Knaack looks into the water, then
overhead.

                    KNAACK
          It's been seeded and
          maintained.

                    RADHA
               (somewhat calmed)
          But it's out of the zone?

Knaack steers them across toward a metal
ladder that rises out of the water.

                    KNAACK
          The zone used to be
          bigger.

Radha is no longer paddling.

The boat bumps gently against the ladder.
Knaack steadies it with his hand.

                    KNAACK
          Climb out.

Radha doesn't hesitate. She climbs onto

the lowest rung and stops.

>   RADHA
>   Where are we going?

Knaack ties the boat to the ladder, pulls his pack from the boat.

>   KNAACK
>   Up.

Radha is annoyed. She's coming down off the high of burning the enclosure, freeing the wolves. They climb and reach a metal landing that's been bolted into the wall below a glassless window. Radha gazes out into the night. There are stars overhead. She shivers.

Knaack pulls a sweater out of his pack.

>   KNAACK
>   Here.

Radha turns, sees the sweater, pulls it on. Now that they're safe, she's not sure what Knaack is doing or if she can trust him.

>   RADHA
>   Won't they be looking
>   for me?

Knaack steps over the window ledge.

Radha gasps, she didn't see that there's a ledge on the other side, too.

Knaack sits down.

>   KNAACK
>   I'll tell them I forgot

to sign you out. They
won't question me.

                    RADHA
          (doesn't understand)
          Why would you sign me
          out?

                    KNAACK
     (with a combination of menace, sarcasm,
               and something else)
          You are female. I am your
          male superior.

Radha is repulsed, steps away, but the
edge is near.

                    RADHA
          Do they do that?

Knaack looks at her.

                    KNAACK
          Of course, they do.

Radha gazes at him with both disgust and
distrust.

Knaack smiles and shakes his head.

                    KNAACK
          I do not do that.

                    RADHA
          Do you promise?

Knaack looks at her with incredulity, is
that all it takes to earn her trust?

                    KNAACK
               (nods)
          I promise.

Radha lowers herself down. They sit
beneath the window, their backs to the
wall, in silence. The water is dark and
glassy below their feet. The sky is dark
and glassy above their heads. There's
almost no light from the city—the Milky
Way shimmers.

Knaack turns to look at her.

          KNAACK
    What you did back there…

Radha stares back into her mind, seeing
the blaze.

          RADHA
      (nods to herself)
    Was awesome.

Knaack shakes his head again.

          KNAACK
    I was going to say,
    Pointless.

          RADHA
      (turns on him)
    Then why didn't you let
    them catch me?

          KNAACK
      (why did he?)
    I didn't think about it.
    I just did it.

          RADHA
      (nods)
    Because you know I was
    right.

                    KNAACK
        (considers this. *Is* that why?)
            It   was   incredibly
            foolish.

                    RADHA
        (shrugs and gazes back out at the water)
            I had to.

                    KNAACK
                (furrows at her)
            Of course, you didn't.

                    RADHA
                    (sighs)
            Maybe   *you*   didn't.
            Obviously *you* didn't or
            you   would've   already
            done it.

        Knaack snorts with laughter.

                    KNAACK
            Are you calling me a
            coward?

        Radha shrugs

                    RADHA
            Well, thanks for getting
            me out of there, anyway.
            I hadn't really planned
            that part.

        Knaack laughs again.

                    KNAACK
            I couldn't tell.

        Radha rolls her eyes, then looks back out
        over the water.

>   RADHA
> It's   pretty   here.
> Spooky,   kinda.   But
> pretty.

Knaack looks at her, then up to the sky.

>   KNAACK
> It's outside the zone.

Radha nods. He does seem different than
the other wardens. It must be tiring for
him there.

>   RADHA
> So if I'm so foolish and
> pointless,   why'd   you
> bring me here? You need
> a break from being an
> asshole?

>   KNAACK
>   (laughs again)
> You *are* remarkable.

> RADHA (shifts uncomfortably)
>   This is the ocean, isn't
>   it? I've never seen the
>   ocean.

Knaack looks at her face. Watches her
sitting there.

>   KNAACK
> I wanted to show you
> something beautiful.

Radha looks back at him.

>   RADHA
>   What?

```
                    KNAACK
            (makes eye contact)
        That's why I brought you
        here.    To    show    you
        something      beautiful.
        When I saw you. With the
        fire.  I've  never  seen
        anything  like  that.  I
        didn't know you existed.


    Radha is confused, she doesn't know what
    she's feeling, but she can't look away.
```

THE TWIST

"Elaine!" Mama Helen yelled from downstairs.

I looked at the clock. Shit. It was after 5PM. And it was my night to cook.

I saved the scene and got up. At least someone around here is having good luck with romance...

Walking downstairs, I was thinking spaghetti. By then the moms knew spaghetti meant something was up in The Under and I was in a hurry. Only this time, I wasn't being lazy because I'd been staring at a blank screen for 5 hours. And I wasn't even worried that I didn't know what came next. I was just tired. It's exhausting to write love. Especially when you don't know anything about it.

I heard his voice from the hallway and ran the rest of the way to the kitchen. "Uncle Alex!" I yelled as I rounded the corner and leapt at him for a hug.

"Hey kiddo," he said. "Speedy as ever."

"So, Uncle Alex has some interesting news," Mama Helen said.

Please say he's not getting back together with the painter. I looked at him like, What could it be?

"You remember how you and I were talking about the Empress of Detroit?" he asked.

"Totally. That's how I got my book idea," I said.

"Which is currently a movie idea," Mama Jane said.

"You're writing a screenplay?" Uncle Alex said. I should've known he'd be impressed.

I beamed. "One of my main characters just torched a wolf enclosure and burned that mother down," I said and pointed upstairs.

The moms looked at each other and shook their heads.

"Awesome," Uncle Alex said.

It was awesome. "So, what's the news?"

"Well," he said. "It looks like I bought a sky-scraper." And was like, Who knew?

"*That's* awesome," I said. "You gonna turn it into a vertical garden." That will be super sweet to visit.

"Early stages. Early stages," he said. "You remember my buddy Jerome? We're partnering on it, so..."

Jerome was a Black guy about Uncle Alex's age who lived across the street and also had a house with a next-door garden in the empty lot. They had some kind of gardening competition going like a couple of nerds. "Yep, I remember him," I said.

"We're thinking some kind of mixed-use, residential, commercial, agricultural..." Uncle Alex said.

Neat.

"It sounds like there are some government grant possibilities," Mama Helen said.

She would know. "When will you start the build?" I asked.

"That's gonna depend," Uncle Alex said and he suddenly sounded some way that made me feel like, I've got a bad feeling about this.

"Alex wants us to build it with him," Mama Jane said.

What? How? "Did you buy a Chicago sky-scraper? Wouldn't that be expensive?" I asked.

"It's in downtown Detroit," he said. "Affordable."

How's that gonna work? "So would you, like, telecommute?" I asked.

Mama Jane shook her head.

"It would only be temporary," Mama Helen said.

"We're moving?!" I yelled.

Uncle Alex laughed, "You don't want to live in Detroit?"

"Temporary," Mama Helen repeated.

"I don't know *anyone* there," I said. Not that anyone I knew in Chicago was talking to me, but still.

"Well, you wouldn't necessarily have to come," Mama Jane said.

"You're leaving me?!" I yelled louder. What the hell. "Are we selling the house?"

"We're not selling the house," Mama Helen said.

But you are leaving me.

"You're invited to come," Uncle Alex said.

I looked at him like, Oh. Well. Thanks.

"We're almost done with the build from hell," Mama Jane. "And working with Alex would be a nice change for us."

I'd known that the house they were working on wasn't going well. You know, beyond Mama Jane telling me it wasn't going well. They'd been around way less than usual. And maybe they'd seemed stressed and like, always hunched over plans and spreadsheets. But I didn't think about things being so bad they'd move to Detroit. I thought about Jenn not asking me any questions about my book. Maybe I should've been asking the moms some questions. But kids aren't supposed to ask their parents those kinds of things. "How long would it be?" I asked.

"Depends on how well it turns out," Uncle Alex said. "Maybe we'll do the whole downtown."

Sometimes uncles are idiots.

Mama Helen came over and put her arm around me. "We're not *moving* moving. Nothing is set in stone. This is our first conversation about the whole thing."

"It's just that now that you're not in school...it's created an opportunity," Mama Jane said.

Great. It's my fault.

"Your moms are gonna be on the vanguard of a what could be a massive movement," Uncle Alex said. "It's exactly what you and I talked about."

Even better. It was my idea.

Mama Helen stroked my hair like she did when I was sick. "Not to be dramatic, sweetie, but both your mom and I have noticed how much your leaving school has affected us," she said.

Affected *you?*

"This last job sucked," Mama Jane said. "So we started talking about what might be more meaningful."

It felt like the floor was disappearing from under me and the abyss would swallow me up. "I need to start dinner," I said. It was too much.

"We're thinking of walking down to Old Irving Brewery," Mama Jane said.

Uncle Alex said, "To talk about the future." He said "future" like it was a sci-fi movie. Normally, that would've made me laugh.

"I'm gonna stay home," I said. "I want to keeping work on this scene." There was no way I was going to be able to concentrate.

Mama Helen made a face like she was going to insist. I kinda hoped she would.

"Work, work, work," Mama Jane said. "You're no fun anymore." I knew she was trying to make me feel better.

I tried to smile.

I stared at the door after they left. Detroit? Goddam Detroit. Where the apocalypse has come and gone. Fuck the vanguard.

THE KISS, THE KILL

And guess what else? I had no one to talk to about it because all my friends hated me. And I had no reason not to move to goddam Detroit because all my friends hated me.

It was Tuesday night, which was my least favorite night of the week when I was in school and it still was. I couldn't write. I had no friends. The moms and Uncle Alex could go to hell. I stomped back upstairs and went to bed.

At 3AM I woke up. I knew what happened next. And I was like, Well, that's a twist.

Knaack and Radha are still sitting on the ledge over the water.

Radha suddenly feels too awkward to keep looking at him, she turns her gaze to the water.

                    RADHA
          I can't wait to tell
          Penelope what I did.

Knaack is still looking at her, trying to
hold onto the moment.

                    KNAACK
          Penelope?

Radha takes a deep breath and closes her
eyes.

                    RADHA
          My sister.

                    KNAACK
               (interested)
          Where is she? You've
          only just arrived here.
          I know that much.

Radha is glad to be have a conversation
to ease the tension.

                    RADHA
          Detroit. That's where we
          were before this.

                    KNAACK
          That's where you're
          from?

Radha shakes her head.

                    RADHA
          We're from almost the
          other side of the

country. It doesn't
really have a name.

KNAACK
There are a surprising
number of settlements
left out there. It's
amazing how resourceful
humans were—even as
everything was falling
apart.

RADHA
(proud)
We went into hiding
Before. We saw it
coming.

KNAACK
(still interested)
What's it like?

Radha is happy to be
talking about her home.
She misses it.

RADHA
Underground. Self-
contained. There's a
rich-kid side. That's my
friend Merton's side.
He's the one who
convinced us to leave.
He's got some friend...Oh!
He's supposed to be
here. Maybe you can help
me find him. His name is
Hugh, I think.

KNAACK
(a look of fear and suspicion crosses
his face)

Radha...

> RADHA
> (doesn't hear him)
> I'm from the scientist
> side. Our mom's the lead
> genetic engineer. Our
> family always is.

> (Thinks for a moment)

> *That's* why Penelope's a
> clone. We *need* new
> strategies.

> KNAACK
> Radha. Wait.

> RADHA
> Why didn't mom just tell
> me that?

Knaack sighs, shakes his head, leans forward.

> RADHA
> And then I told
> Penelope. I knew it
> would crush her. I knew.
> I told her anyway.

Knaack stands and speaks outloud to no one.

> KNAACK
> Parker, I think I've
> found an asset we can
> utilize.

Radha finally looks at him.

                    RADHA
          Are we going?

Knaack takes her hand and pulls her to
her feet.

                    KNAACK
          I'm sorry, Radha.

                    RADHA
                 (confused)
          What? Why?

                    KNAACK
          You shouldn't have told
          me about your sister.

Something in his voice fills her with
fear.

                    RADHA
          Who are you?

                    KNAACK
          Not who you think.

She doesn't hesitate. She grabs the knife
at her belt. Flings it open and lunges at
him. He's surprised, so when she swings,
he hasn't moved all the way out of the
way. She cuts his shoulder. A red blossom
of blood grows over his heart.

But he's well-trained. He side-steps her
and grabs the wrist of her knife-wielding
hand and twists it behind her back. She
drops the knife into the water. He turns
her to face him. Holding her wrist behind
her back, their faces are close together.

                    RADHA
          You promised.

330

A look of pain crosses his face. He looks into her eyes.

> KNAACK
> (quietly, gently)
> There are things that
> are going to happen that
> you will not understand.

Radha feels an urge to move toward him. But the moment is gone, pushed away by rage. She nods.

Knaack relaxes slightly.

Radha stomps his foot at the same moment she twists free of his grasp.

Knaack lurches forward.

Radha smashes the butt of her hand against the side of his face.

Knaack slumps over.

> RADHA
> Understand   that,
> motherfucker?

Radha doesn't hear his reply.

Knaack surges up, grabs her by the front of his sweater, and hits her. All is black.

EXT. CLEARING DAY

Radha wakes up in a clearing. She immediately sees Knaack and an older man, Dr. Parker (from The Replaced). She leaps to her feet. A guard restrains her.

> RADHA
> Who are you? What do you
> want?

They ignore her.

> KNAACK
> (speaking to Dr. Parker)
> Do we have a cryo-box? We
> don't want the tissue to
> rot.

> DR. PARKER
> Of course.

> (speaking out loud to no one, but he's
> heard)

> Bring the cryo-box.

> KNAACK
> I'll take care of the
> clone.

Radha is alarmed at the word. She starts
yelling at them, but they continue to
ignore her.

> RADHA
> What are you doing?
> What's going on?

> DR. PARKER
> (absently)
> Yes. Fine.

> (Says out loud again)

> Bring the girl.

Knaack finally looks at Radha.

>   KNAACK
>   I'm very sorry this is
>   happening to you, Radha.
>   After everything.

Radha eyes are filled with hatred.

>   RADHA
>   Fuck you.

Eva pushes Penelope from the woods and
into the clearing.

>   RADHA
>   (screams)
>   Penelope!

>   PENELOPE
>   (whimpering and shivering)
>   Radha?

Eva pushes Penelope toward Knaack.

>   RADHA
>   (screams in fury)
>   Stay away from her! Stay
>   away from her!

Knaack hears her fury. The same fury that
set the wolves free. What power.

>   KNAACK
>   Where's the other one?

Moments later, another guard emerges from
the woods with Merton.

>   PENELOPE
>   (gasps)
>   Merton.

          RADHA
        (confused)
    How? Where? What are you
    doing here?

Dr. Parker laughs. Then he points to
Merton.

          DR. PARKER
    We have a lot to thank
    your friend for. None of
    you would be here if it
    weren't for him.

          KNAACK
    (to Radha, with a certain gentleness)
    He tried to stop me. From
    taking you.

Dr. Parker laughs again.

          DR. PARKER
    He tried to rescue you.

          MERTON
        (looking at Radha)
    He was a bot, Radha. He
    wasn't real.

          RADHA
        (doesn't understand)
    What?

          MERTON
    (doesn't want to have to tell her)
    Hugh. He wasn't real. It
    was a trap. They were
    looking for us. For our
    home.

Radha falls to her knees and the guard no

longer has ahold of her.

> KNAACK
> (to the guard)
> Careful.

But then he can see that Radha is
incapable of attack. She's incapable of
movement. He's surprised. Again. By her.

> DR. PARKER
> (to Merton and Radha)
> I've been looking for
> you all for years.

> RADHA
> (looks at Knaack, pleads)
> Who are you?

Deep sadness crosses Knaack's face, but
is then gone.

> KNAACK
> How have you not figured
> it out yet?

Radha shakes her head. Refusing to
understand.

> MERTON
> He's AI, Radha. He's not
> human.

> DR. PARKER
> (to Knaack)
> Okay, kids. Let's get
> this over with.

> KNAACK
> (calmly, to Penelope)
> This won't be painless.

Penelope whimpers and loses her balance.
Eva and another guard hold her up.

                    RADHA
                 (to Knaack)
          Please. Please. She's my
          sister.

Knaack ignores her.

                    MERTON
          (his voice is strong and firm)
          Penelope. Look at me.
          Look at me.

Penelope looks away from Knaack and
toward the Merton. Her whimpering stops.
Her shivering eases.

                    MERTON
          Radha. Say something.
          Say something to her.
          Now.

Radha takes a deep breath. She brings her
hands to her heart.

                    RADHA
          Penelope.   Remember.
          Remember when we snuck
          out to the garden that
          night?

Penelope nods.

                    PENELOPE
                 (whispering)
          We swam.

Smiles through tears. And anger. And
fear.

Rage is a Wolf

                    RADHA
          We swam.

Penelope smiles.

                    MERTON
          Don't be afraid.

Knaack can't wait any longer. He moves
even closer to Penelope.

                    KNAACK
          Sweet   Penelope.   Be
          afraid.

He slaps her across the mouth with the
back of his hand.

Radha shrieks and clutches her fists to
her belly.

                    RADHA
          Penelope!

A thin red line of blood trickles down
from the corner of Penelope's mouth.
Knaack reaches out, swipes his finger
through the blood, brings it to his
mouth. Tastes it.

                    DR. PARKER
                (feigning shock)
          Oh,   Knaack.   What
          cruelty. You really are
          becoming human.

Knaack closes his mouth and savors the
warm, red sulphur of Penelope's life.

                    MERTON
          It's   okay,   Penelope.

We're here. Tell her
we're here.

          RADHA
      (chokes down a sob)
   We're here, Penelope.
   Look at us.

Penelope gazes at Radha and Merton. Her
sister. Her love. She is brave.

Two men enter carrying what looks like a
metal coffin with a control panel on its
lid.

         DR. PARKER
   Proceed.

Knaack grasps Penelope's neck in his
hands. He squeezes. She doesn't look at
him. She looks at Radha and Merton.

         PENELOPE
  (speaking to both of them, whispering)
   I love you.

Knaack squeezes harder.

Penelope's body jerks as she struggles
to break free of the Eva and the guard
and free from Knaack's grip. They're too
strong.

Radha leaps to her feel and the guard
grabs her again.

         RADHA
      (yelling)
   I love you, Penelope.
   I'm sorry. I love you.

Her voice cracks and Knaack remembers how

```
her voice cracked when she looked at the
wolf, strung over the fire and cried,
She's pregnant. He had almost taken her
in his arms in that moment, but he knew
he couldn't. His hands relax for just
a second and he feels Penelope's pulse
flutter and surge. He squeezes tighter
again.

Merton's voice is hardly audible and
tears run down his face.

                    MERTON
        We're here, Penelope.
        We're here.

Radha speaks with force as though her
voice can calm Penelope's jerking body.

                    RADHA
        You're my sister.

Knaack squeezes even tighter and Penelope
finally looks at him. Her eyes are dark.
They go wide. They are empty.
```

THE RATTY FEELING

It was late afternoon when I finally woke up. The moms must've been feeling guilty—they didn't hassle me at all.

I lay in bed and stared at the ceiling.

So obviously when Radha stops crying and comes to her senses, she's going to realize it's all Merton's fault. None of this would've happened if it weren't for him hacking out of the Comm and making friends with some psycho doctor's bot and then convincing them all to leave. Penelope would be alive. And Radha never would've been an idiot and almost made out with a body-snatcher-robot and told him her sister was a clone...

But if I thought writing love was tiring, it was only because I hadn't written betrayal and murder yet.

So, I was like, I'll watch a movie. Only when I opened my computer, my feed was up and there it was, the cover of TABC's book. My book. *The Angel of Unrequite.* Which is a stupid title. But, yes. That's obviously what happened. And it wasn't stupid and terrible with some kind of disembodied angel wings and a dorky loser daydreaming in his desk. It was tasteful and spooky and fuck him. Also, ps, Please do me a favor and don't ever read it or watch the movie or ever read or see *anything* by The Asshole Brenden Carter—that's fair to ask, right?

But so there was also this—I'd had a sneaking feeling for the past couple months. One of those side-of-the-eye feelings. It was lurking there and at first I'd turned my head real fast to try to catch it, but as I started to have a clearer sense of what it was about—the feeling—like what truth it was going to reveal to me, I started shying away from it. Wincing. Like a fearful shoulder-shrug on that side—it was always on my left.

A couple of summers ago, I was sitting in the backyard reading, when I heard this mix between a scratch and a scrabble and when I turned, there was a gigantic, gray rat galloping away from the garbage can toward me. I shrieked, leapt off the ground, and it just missed attacking me before it dove under a bush.

For *weeks* after that, I saw gray-brown tracers in my side vision. At first my brain would be like, What? Milliseconds later, it would think, Rat! I'd shriek and look, but of course, no...

That's what I'd been feeling these last months. A ratty feeling. Creeping in the trash over there in the periphery. Not galloping yet. But I winced, because as the shadow of the feeling grew, and filled in, and took shape, I knew I didn't want to look at it.

Then I saw that cover and I knew that's what the creeping-rat was, It was my fault The Asshole Brenden Carter stole my idea. If I'd had more confidence, I wouldn't have told him so much. But I wanted him to tell me it was a good idea instead of a) trusting that it was a good idea, b) pushing forward and discovering for myself if it was good, and c) writing it for the sake of writing it and not caring if it was a good idea.

And even worse, I thought that if I was cute enough and funny enough and whatever enough...*that's* what would make me a writer. But as he said, "We both know you were never gonna write that story." And he was right.

I'm gonna go fucking crazy.

I didn't know what else to do.

I texted Tony.

I looked up the band's tour schedule. They were in Baltimore. A time zone ahead. It was about 5:30PM in Chicago, he had to be getting ready for a show, but I didn't know what else to do.

> Elaine: I know you're on the road, but I need help.

I put my head in my hands. Don't think about the rat. Don't think about the rat.

> Tony: What's happening?

What *is* happening?

> Elaine: Everything's falling apart.
> Tony: Are you alone?

I started to cry.

> Elaine: Yes.
> Tony: Would you talk to Audra? If I arrange it?

I nodded. The tears dripped off my cheeks, but I didn't wipe them.

> Elaine: Yes.

I KNOW WHO I AM

Thirty minutes later, I was ringing the bell at Tony's apartment. Audra's lease had ended, so she was staying in his room while he was gone. How do these people live like this? How am I gonna live if the moms leave?

The door buzzed and I went up the stairs. I remembered the last time I was there. Slanted & Enchanted. Oh god. Things had been a little different. Audra opened the door before I got to the top. Would she remember me?

"Hi, Elaine," she said. That doesn't prove anything. Tony told her I was coming.

"Hi," I said as I walked past, but almost no sound came out.

She closed the door. I swept my eyes around the room, looking for roommates.

"They're all gone," she said. "You want any coffee?"

I shook my head, feeling like if I talked, the tears might start again.

"You wanna talk out here or Tony's room?" she asked.

"Is anyone coming home?" I asked. I didn't want to see anyone.

"Not sure," she said. "Let's just go in there." She pointed to his room. Did he tell her what we'd done?

I followed her from the door. She was wearing black yoga pants and a faded black t-shirt that said, Sugar Bear Tattoos on the back.

Tony's room felt weird. Most of his stuff was there, but hers was everywhere, too. I went to the desk chair and sat down so she'd have to sit on the bed.

"So what's up?" she asked. She had a gravelyish voice. I imagined her saying, "scumfucker."

I took a deep breath. Don't cry. "All my friends hate me," I said. All my two friends.

"Tony doesn't," she said. I wondered if they were sleeping together. Oh god.

"You probably think I'm some teenage groupie," I said.

She smiled. "I know you're not a groupie," Audra said.

How did she know what I wasn't? "I might be. How do you know?"

She smiled at that. "I mean, maybe you're a groupie in *your* mind," she said. "But as far as Tony tells it, you're a cool kid."

"A cool kid." I rolled my eyes. This was a terrible idea. "Nevermind," I said and stood up.

"Elaine," she said and her voice was kind, but stern. "Tell me what you need to tell me." I remembered the bros, bussing their table.

I sat back down. "I don't know what the fuck I'm doing," I said. "Or why. Mostly that's it. Why am I doing anything?"

She nodded. "And you're scared." she said.

I sat back down. Yeah, I'm fucking scared. "Yeah," I said. "And everything is stupid and clunky and a fucking pointless nightmare. And I hate it. I'm losing my mind. Like to the point where I was thinking today that I wished I was back in school. Do you know how easy school was? Just do whatever the hell they tell you to do and at the end, you get your golden ticket. No risk required.

"Then I feel like a huge bitch for saying that because who am I to judge? But I do judge. Only how good is my judgment when I drink lattes all day and write this dumb book—except, it's not even a book—it's a fucking screenplay—that no one will ever see, living in my moms' house, hanging out with hipsters...whose life am I changing? What good am I? The world is so fucked up. It's just shittiness and destruction and violence," I said.

I thought about Radha and the wolves and dead Penelope and now what? Like how are they gonna get out of this one? And even if Radha and Merton escape, NYC is still there with its, You are a female and I am your male superior...And Knaack is still there. And Dr. Parker and now he knows where to find the goddam Under. "And I'm trying to write this stupid story and I can't think of *any* solution that doesn't involve killing like a million people. How can I hope for the world to change if all I can come up with for my story *or* the fucked world is Hiroshima?"

I stopped and stared. But Audra had hardly moved.

"It sounds like your heart's broken," she said.

That's what you got out of all that? "I've never even had a boyfriend," I said. Or was she talking about Tony? Did she think he broke my heart? "That's not what I'm even talking about."

She smiled, but didn't laugh. "It doesn't take a boy to break your heart," she said. "The world can break your heart. Life can break your heart."

It can? And then the tears pressed against the back of my eyes and that spot in my forehead started to ache. The world can break your heart? "Is that what it is?" I asked. And I was scared. What if I'm broken?

"Did Tony tell you that I was raped at a party when I was 18?" Audra asked.

Ohmygod. "What? No," I said. I couldn't ever see Tony betraying a trust like that. "Of course not."

"It's okay. He knows I wouldn't mind if he told you," she said. Her eyes were deep and dark, like Penelope's eyes.

How could you not mind? "Did they catch the guy?" I asked.

"Not for what he did to me," she said. "I couldn't prove it wasn't consensual."

Oh god. "I...I'm so sorry," I said. Everything is terrible.

She nodded. "Then he tried to do it again. To another girl. Only he didn't realize there was already a couple in the room..."

"Did they stop him?" I asked.

"They did," she said.

"Did he go to jail?" I asked.

She shook her head. "He didn't actually rape her, so there was no crime."

"What the fuck?" I said.

"He had violated some part of the school's sexual conduct code," she said. "So he got kicked out."

"Oh, well, hooray for justice," I said.

She made a face, like, Yep..."I talked to this woman after," she said. "Like a year after. Because I was crying all the time. I was scared all the time. I didn't know who would hurt me. I couldn't look at people because I thought they'd know."

I nodded. I had no idea what to say.

"The woman, she called herself an intuitive, she said, 'That man broke your heart. But the worry, the fear...that keeps breaking it. You need to heal your heart, sweetie.'"

I furrowed. How the hell was she supposed to do that? "And did you heal your heart?" I asked, trying to keep the, Fuck you, intuitive, out of my voice.

Audra nodded. "Well, first I asked her, 'How the fuck am I supposed to do that?'"

"Yeah, no kidding." I said.

"She told me to imagine a moment when I felt perfect love..."

Oh my god, here comes the hippy shit.

"She said that anytime I felt myself afraid or worrying or unable to look at people, or whatever, that I should imagine that moment. As specifically as possible. She called it a heart mantra and said that it would put me into my heart. She said love can't worry or fear. Those live in the brain. She said it would heal my heart to choose love when I wanted to choose worry or fear. And I wouldn't be afraid to have people look at me. And I wouldn't be afraid to look at people. And I wouldn't be afraid to look at myself."

I wanted to call bullshit. But a) It was Audra, b) I didn't think you called bullshit on something that helped a person recover from rape, and c) I wanted to believe her. "Did it work?" I asked.

She smiled. A real smile. Not sarcastic. Not smirky. Or distant. Or wistful. A big, happy birthday, smile. "Every time."

"What was your moment?" I asked. "Can I ask?"

"Sure," Audra said. "It was at the student gallery show my senior year of high school. My parents were standing on either side of me and we were looking at my painting. They both put their arm around me and held me between them. And they said, 'It's beautiful.' Their voices were filled with awe, like they'd just discovered me. But I've never felt so seen. What they saw was beautiful. And I felt my beauty."

I've never felt so seen. Yes. I felt my beauty. Fuck. I'll cry right now. "Do you still have to do it?" I asked and once again. It was hard to breathe.

"I don't think about the rape too much anymore. It's a scar. But it's not a wound. The intuitive told me that it's part of me now. I could make a place for it or it would make its own..." she said.

"Can I ask you something weird and kinda gross?" I asked.

Audra raised her eyebrows, "Sure," she said.

I didn't know exactly how to say it. "Do people ever...I don't know...treat you..."

"Like tainted goods?" she asked.

I wouldn't have put it that way. "Yeah."

She nodded. "They try," Audra said.

That hurt. It was what I figured, but it still hurt. What would the bros have done with this information? "What do you do?" I asked.

"I accept it as part of me," she said.

"What do you mean?" I asked.

She sighed. "Listen, if I could make it so no person ever got raped again, I would do that. But I am who I am. And I *like* who I am. So, you know, it's complicated," she said.

"You're saying you're glad you were raped?!" Oh Jesus. This is some shit I cannot comprehend. "I..." I stammered. "I don't know what to say to that."

"You don't need to say anything," she said. "I know who I am. I'm the feeling in *my* heart. No one else gets to tell me."

"Okay, sure," I said. "But that doesn't stop the world from being totally fucked. Like there *are* still rapists. And you know, every thing is bigger than I am. And bigger than *you*. And so every thing I do feels fake almost. Like it's cute. But it's not going to affect anything. Like the world is built and it runs how it runs. And I can't change anything about it. It's like I'm in a movie, or something. Like I get to decide what other characters to interact with and how to spend my days, and I can decorate my small part of the set. But I'm still inside that movie," I said. I was right back where I started.

Audra pointed at me. "*That's* the broken heart. *That's* what you need to fix, first. Cause then you can live from your heart, not from your anger, not from fear."

"Then what?" I asked.

Audra paused. "Then things change," she said.

This is some bullshit advice. "That's it? Things change? They change and suddenly *I* become the kid who invents a robot that eats carbon and shits honeybees?" I asked.

Audra almost choked on her laugh, which pleased me.

"Do you *want* to invent that?" she asked.

"Of course, I want to invent that," I said. "That would be awesome."

She had her open hands out to me, "So if you're not an inventor, what are you?"

If I knew the goddam answer to that...

SOMETHING IS HAPPENING

I left Tony's apartment and Audra feeling...Weird.

I don't know what I thought Audra was going to say to me. But it definitely wasn't, Get a heart mantra and things will change.

And yet...

Something *had been* happening to me.

You know, it wasn't like anything had ever *happened* to me. Nothing bad. Nothing like getting raped at a party and no way to prove it wasn't consensual. I'd had it super easy. But I was starting to think, to see, that maybe my thoughts were not my thoughts—not *mine*. It was like someone or something wallpapered over my—over my, what? My self? My heart? My imagination? My what? Not the point.

What I'm saying is I had these thoughts—not pretty enough, not thin enough, not smart, talented, funny enough...Too loud, too talkative, opinionated, obnoxious, not girly enough (I don't even want to be girly!)...Won't be a writer, won't be loved, evil will win, the world is doomed, and on and on...I'd always believed that the voice in my head was me. And the truth. And trying to protect me and tell me the truth and motivate me and fix me...

But I don't know. What about choosing love instead of fear and worry? I'd been choosing anger. What about choosing love instead of anger? What would happen?

What about Tony? And Audra telling him he wasn't a scumfucker, but was acting like one, and would turn into one. Tony must've had the same voices in head as I did. Right? To make him think he had to lie to get a girl to want him.

It was like all the judgments and criticisms and ideas from the outside world were wallpapered over me—my heart, my imagination, my whatever connects me to the force that drives the flower...What if all those ideas about myself and who I was and should be, what if those ideas, those images, weren't mine?

What about Javier? "Nothing is ever wasted, but what you achieve by force," and "Do you want to prove that you can finish something or do you want to prove that you can write something really badass? You have to be willing to recreate the world..."

It was like the *real* me was behind glass and was muffled and screaming or it was a forest behind glass or a symphony or the whole of the universe...but there was this glass and on top of the glass was a decoupage (I fucking hate decoupage) of magazine pages saying, "...too fat, not pretty, too loud, not talented, not to be loved, dying world..." and I believed *that* was me.

But something was happening. Like I could imagine the wallpaper. The glass. The symphony forest ocean of me-ness...I couldn't even imagine any of that before. Maybe the wallpaper isn't the truth. Maybe I could peel back the edges. I could *feel* the edges. I never even knew there were edges. If I could feel the edges, then I must be able to peel them back. And then what?

Audra said, "I know who I am..." she said, "I felt my beauty..."

What if I could break the glass?

And hear that song?

Good lord.

I know who I am.

I felt my beauty.

To be unashamed?

To walk in that forest?

To *truly* not care what other people think?

To live with all my feelings about myself coming from inside myself.

From a spring inside of me. Not handed over to me by the world, and TV, and teachers, and The Bitch Annette, and The Asshole Brenden Carter, and dudes I want to like me, and publishers, and money, and racism, and rape, and fear for the world, and on and on.

From a spring inside *me*.

Connected to the green fuse.

Driven by force that drives the flower.

Something bigger that this culture. This 10,000 year old culture that calls me property.

That's my heart mantra. That there's something in this universe that knows me.

Something from the billions year old universe that calls me the flower.

Something that calls me life.

NO SHIT FROM SWINE

I got a text from Tony.

Tony: Can't talk. Text you later. 🖤

And then a video.

It was evening and I'd wandered away from Audra, toward the bus stop. I stopped and leaned against a brick building to watch.

The video was shot from just below the front of the stage, so it was looking right up at the lead singer. She was a normal looking woman with dark brown, tousley hair. In the lighting, I couldn't tell her skin color. She stepped up to the microphone and held it in her hand. She said, "This one's going out to a friend..." then she looked down, right into the video and said, "A good friend of our tour manager, Tony. Let's just say we wouldn't be alive without him." The crowd laughed in the background and the woman, the singer, smiled. "So yeah, for him, we're sending this one out to Elaine Archer. It's a new one. We hope you like it." She looked back down into the camera, "It's called, *Don't Take No Shit From Swine*," she said to me. The crowd erupted. I laughed and the smile stayed. The singer stepped to the side of the microphone, held her arms out wide, her electric guitar dangling like a giant red and gold medallion, and she threw her head back and for 8 seconds (I counted when I watched again) she screamed. Just screamed. And then the drums crashed in and the other guitar crashed in and the lights flashed and she grabbed the neck of her guitar with one hand and threw the other hand at the guitar's body...And that was the video. And I was Elaine Archer. I was Tony's good friend. I don't take no shit from swine. And maybe my heart was broken, but something was happening.

TRENDING

It was a different text that woke me the next morning. Well, texts. Well, pictures.

From an unlisted number.

They were Jenn. Very clearly Jenn.

I'm sure we all saw it coming.

But before I get into what happened and what did we do about it, let's take a minute and try this on for size...

What if girls wanting to fool around wasn't considered the greatest crime in the fucking world that needed to be punished with any number of things including blasting her picture everywhere.

I mean, let's revisit *Sex at Dawn* shall we: "And yet, despite repeated reassurances that women aren't particularly sexual creatures, in cultures around the world, men have gone to extraordinary lengths to control female libido..." (39).

I'm looking at you female genital mutilation. And you, Nurse Party-Panties with your "teach boys patience" lecture.

I don't want to give Jenn too much credit, like I don't think what I saw in those pictures was a *political* statement, but she shouldn't *have* to make a political goddam statement. She should be able to just do what she wants...

But theory aside, she could probably use an escort off school grounds.

As I walked up to DB High for the 1st time in, how long, seven months, I wasn't sure what I was feeling or what I was going to say. Don't get me wrong, there was still a thick sedimentary layer of guilt, plus one of, Fuck you. But the part I really wasn't sure about was the top-most layer of, How do we fix this? Any of it.

Thankfully, I didn't have much time to dwell because there was goddam Miranda Spear standing outside the visitor's entrance. She was wearing a short skirt and over-the-knee black boots and she had goosebumps and would've been doing herself a favor to have tights on. She didn't miss a beat. "You here to see your whore friend?" she asked.

I pressed the button on the call box to be let in. "I didn't think you and I were friends," I said. God, it feels good when you get just the right zinger.

"I'm talking about Jenn Cartwright," Miranda said like *I* was the idiot.

No one answered the intercom, so I pressed it again. "Just a moment," Mrs. Moorhouse, the secretary, said.

I looked back at Miranda. "Oh, when you said 'whore' I thought you were talking about you," I said, and smiled.

Miranda made a disgusted face and said, "Aren't you dead or something."

That's more like it. "Not dead," I said.

Mrs. Moorhouse's voice came back through the box. "Are you a student?" she asked.

I almost considered saying I was just to get away, but Miranda probably would've called me out, "No," I said.

"The students are just finishing up," she said. "You'll have to wait outside."

Ugh. School shooters ruin everything.

"Well you're not in school," Miranda said. It was amazing how she was able to take a perfectly factual statement and make it sound like the cuntiest comment ever.

"No," I said. I shook my head solemnly and sort of leaned toward her like I was going to reveal my terrible secret—drugs, pregnancy, incarceration...Of course, Miranda couldn't help herself and leaned right in.

"What happened?" she asked, desperate for it to be awful.

"Probiotics," I whispered.

"What?" she asked and made confused and vaguely disgusted face.

I looked her right in the eyes and whispered, "Fermentation."

"Are you on drugs?" she asked.

I looked over my shoulder to make sure no one could overhear us, "I'm talking about colonies. I'm talking about the human biome," I said.

"Are you trying to sell me drugs?" she asked.

"Bacteria, sister," I said and winked, "Kombucha."

"What?" she asked again. It definitely would've been more fun if she were a worthier opponent.

"Do you have any idea what a complex and fragile environment the vagina is?" God bless you KPao. I backed away from Miranda, "You better keep a close eye," I said and pointed at her O'Keeffe region. "Probiotics," I whispered and turned away just as the bell rang. Like ballet. No shit from swine.

I left Miranda and the door and went and sat on the low half wall that divided concrete from grass. It was a good 25 minutes before Jenn emerged, alone, from the school. She saw me and did that thing where you very blatantly see someone and then blatantly act like you didn't see them and start walking faster and with your head turned awkwardly away.

She was wearing blue high waisted shorts (with tights, cause she's not an idiot) and a tight pink t-shirt tucked in. Her long camel coat billowed behind her like a cape as she strode. She looked amazing. Like a valkyrie. Not how I thought she'd look. What had I expected? All black? Puffy eyes? A doomed, red-headed widow?

I ran to catch her and could barely keep stride. She was evidently still mostly just sedimentary layers of pissed at me... "Jenn, can we slow down?" I asked. I could barely catch my breath. "No need to walk at the pace of our emotions."

Jenn snapped her head to look at me. "Nice line." She said it like she was rolling her eyes, but she did walk slower.

I shrugged. It was a nice line. "Listen," I said. "There's the U. Chicago thing and now there's this other thing. I think we should ignore the U. Chicago thing for now because I'm pretty sure I'm the only person you have to talk to about the other thing."

Jenn clenched her jaw. She has the exact same bulging muscle at the base of her cheek as Paul. "Those bitches should be calling me to thank me," she said.

"Yeah," I said. I was 100% positive none of those bitches would ever call Jenn anything other than a whore. "Any minute now," I said.

"Ohmygod," Jenn hissed. "What is the big deal? I like kissing and groping. I like flirting. I like kissing and groping and flirting with more than one person." We crossed Washington and kept walking. It wasn't the way we normally went to get anywhere we normally go.

"Like threesomes?" I asked. I lowered my voice, because of course, at that exact moment we passed a gaggle of blonde ladies with Coach purses. What's with women in this city and Coach purses?

Jenn looked at me, like, I'm not even answering that. "I'm not taking anyone's boyfriend. I'm just making out with them a little." She did not lower her voice. One of the Coach purses heard and I was like, One-two-three...yep, she totally said something to her friend. I turned back and watched them watch us and whisper. Undoubtedly something about "...girls these days..."

"A little..." I said.

She smirked "Oh, okay. Making out with them a lot. Why not? I'm in the first flower of my fucking sexuality. When I'm old and dried up, I can get married and never kiss anyone again." I suspected she was talking about Marcie and Paul.

"What are you gonna do?" I asked. There's just no good way to handle compromising pictures.

She stopped and we looked at Anthropologie's window display—pots of small, flowering trees, draped with gemstone jewelry. "I dunno," Jenn said. "Write about it for my college essay?"

Honestly, that might work. Especially if she put a geo-political spin on it. "Slut-shaming is huge right now," I said.

She scoffed. "I'm trending," Jenn said. Her voice told me she didn't want to talk about that part anymore. I mean, what do colleges do if some jerk decides to send their Admissions committee pictures of an applicant?

"You gonna keep making out with those dudes?" I asked.

"Doubt," Jenn said and we walked away from the store. "They're all kissing their girlfriends' asses right now. Making me look like the Siren. Nevermind, we learned about Sirens in school. Making me look like I seduced them."

"I know what a Siren is," I said. I still wasn't sure where we were headed, but I wasn't about to ask.

"It's not my fault I look good in shorts," Jenn said.

You look good in everything. "Be honest. Did you not want any of them for a boyfriend?" I'd managed not to think much about Javier, but given the situation, I couldn't help it.

"Like if Casey asked me to go out with him?" The eye-roll in her voice told me that answer.

"So, that's a no," I said. I missed Javier a lot. I didn't want him for a boyfriend, but I missed him.

She shook her head. "It doesn't matter, anyway. None of it's going to make the rest of the year any better."

"You know," I said. "You could still come with me." I was careful not to say "drop out."

We'd made it all the way to the river. We stopped, looked over the railing, and watched the water. "I'm not doing that," she answered. "I'm a slut, not a Transcendentalist...Never mind that one, too. I'm a slut, not a non-conformist."

I didn't know what a whatever-that-word-was, but I got what she meant. "It's kinda less crazy that you think."

Jenn stopped and looked at me. She crossed her arms. She looked just like she had standing over Walt Peck, only now it was the whole city behind her, not a swing set. We'd been little girls together. "Bottom line, Elaine—the moms want you to be a happy person. My family wants me to make them look good." Then she considered it for a second, "I do think there's part of my dad that hopes I don't get into Chicago because girls getting in diminishes the place...and my mom doesn't want me to get in because she's jealous of the shit I get to do that she didn't."

Like I said, it was one thing to have to deal with The Bitch Annette, whom I saw a few times a year, it was another to have the Cartwrights for parents. "Jesus, Jenn. I mean, I know they're assholes. But I didn't ever realize they're so..."

"Yeah," she said. She was obviously tired.

Back in the day, the city of Chicago reversed the flow of the river so the city's sewage flowed away from Chicago and didn't pollute their water supply—it polluted someone else's. Had Jenn's ancestors been part of that feat of shit and engineering?

"Question," I said.

She made a face, like, Let's hear it.

"Do you think that your desire to secretly hook-up..." I started.

"Is because I'm not loved at home?" she said. She tried to sound like it was a stupid theory, but she wasn't completely convincing.

I thought about Tony manipulating girls into sleeping with him. "It's not a fringe idea," I said. I mean, I was *sure* that her parents bought into the notion that "good girls don't have sex..." so there was almost certainly part of her that also did it to spite them...

"Elaine, it feels good. And I'm not talking about deep psych. I'm talking about my body," she said. And that *did* sound convincing. "Not that it matters," she added. "But I haven't fucked *any* of those guys."

"You haven't?" I asked. Not that it should've mattered. Not if I really didn't think doing it was bad. But I was surprised. "Maybe you can text TSwift about what to do next. She's a master of spin..."

Jenn rolled her eyes, "I don't even like her," she said. A boat filled with people and their own problems passed under the bridge.

I scoffed. "What are you talking about?" I asked. "She's *all* you listen to."

Jenn looked at me the way Mama Helen sometimes looks at me when she can't believe I'm being so dumb. "When you're around," she said.

That's crazy. "What?" I asked.

"I do it to mess with you," she said.

"You do not!" That couldn't possibly be true.

Jenn stopped and looked straight at me. "Has it ever occurred to you that I might be smarter than you think?" she asked.

No. It hadn't. Should it have? "I think you're smart," I said.

Jenn started walking again and we crossed the bridge. Finally, her voice emotionless, Jenn said, "We're supposed to be best friends."

"We are!" I said.

Jenn gave me a look like, Yeah, right. "That means *you* tell *me* shit, too." she said.

And the barf feeling.

"Exactly," Jenn said. "You never told me about the school thing. You never tell me about your book. You barely text me, and when you do, it's always sudden fucking notice."

Oh, shit. "I didn't think you wanted to hear about any of it," I said.

"For instance, what's going on with you and that artist?" she asked.

I couldn't believe she didn't call him that nerd. "He's not talking to me," I said.

We'd hit a no-man's-land of pavement and boring buildings. "Why?" Jenn asked. "You lie to him and screw him over, too?"

I guessed we'd moved on to the U. Chicago thing. "Can you honestly say that if I'd brought it up some other time you wouldn't have been pissed anyway?" I asked.

Jenn stopped walking and looked at me. "Is this the apology?" she asked.

"I *know* I was legit wrong for keeping it a secret and I'm sorry," I said. "But you *would* have been pissed." I hesitated for a moment. I closed my eyes and imagined my heart mantra. I am the force that drives the flower. I am the flower. I am life. "I also think you're pissed that I left school. And that it's going well."

"Fuck you," she said.

I am life. "None of that is true?" I asked.

"Of course, it's true," she said. She sat down on the window ledge of a tall, gray building. "I figured it would last a week."

I sat next to her. "I kinda did, too..." I said.

"And I'm pissed that I'm too scared to try something like it," she said. "I think about my parents and how I can't escape their life without their help. But then there's the worse possibility. It's like that play we saw. What if I get to a certain age and I *don't want* to escape?"

Holy shit, she was talking about *This Is Our Youth*. I thought about Tony and vulnerability. And Audra and broken hearts. And Javier and...what about Javier? Just him. It all connected somehow. "It's really real, Jenn," I said. "Your life can be different than you thought it would be."

Jenn shrugged.

"You still mad at me?" I asked.

"A little," she said, but she wasn't. Not really.

"I had sex," I blurted.

"With the nerd?!" I hadn't seen her that happy in years.

I shook my head.

"Is that why he's not talking to you?" she asked.

Oh, god. "He doesn't know about it," I said. I mean, he couldn't possibly know about it. Tony would never have told him.

"We both saw that picture," she said. "'This one's Elaine'...He loves you."

The speck of red in the old, giant forest. Where's grandmother's house? Where's the wolf? Wait. How are we both writing stories with wolves? We'd never even talked about it. I'd never even told him, Rage is a wolf.

"Well..." I started.

"Who was it?" she asked.

"This guy, Tony," I said.

"The one you accidentally texted?" she asked.

Holy shit, she *had* been listening. "Yeah," I said, and couldn't help but smile.

"How was it?!" she asked and bumped her shoulder into mine just like we were sitting on our bench at DB High.

Hmm. How *was* it? "A little awkward," I said.

She laughed. "Sounds right."

"But it was fun, too," I said and I blushed, but who cares.
"That's awesome," she said. "And I want to read your stupid book," Jenn said and gave me another nudge.
"It's kind of a screenplay," I said and nudged her back.
"Obviously," Jenn said.

YOU SAW

EXT. CLEARING DAY

Four guards are loading the cryo-box
with Penelope's body into a ship. Dr.
Parker stands watch over the process.

Knaack walks over to Radha.

Dr. Parker looks back at them
suspiciously.

Knaack grabs Radha's arm and shoves her
toward an old military helicopter. As
they pass Dr. Parker moving toward the
door, Knaack takes a cruel tone.

                    KNAACK
          We need to talk about
          what your role is going
          to be from now on.

Radha stares straight ahead.

Two other guards remain with Merton.

Dr. Parker turns away, satisfied.

Knaack speaks slightly above a whisper,
so as not to call attention.

                    KNAACK
          Radha, listen to me.

Radha ignores him. They keep walking.

Knaack puts his hand on her arm.

Radha looks at him with a pure hatred and
yanks her arm away.

                    RADHA
          If you want to touch me,
          you better fucking kill
          me.

Knaack takes his hand away, can't help
but smile.

                    KNAACK
          She's not dead.

Radha staring ahead again, climbs into
the helicopter.

Knaack climbs in behind her then leans in
close.

                    KNAACK
                 (whispers)
          I promise, she's not
          dead.

Radha, still staring ahead, sits on
bench.

          RADHA (through gritted teeth)
          I saw you kill her.

Knaack is relieved she's at least talking

to him.

                KNAACK
        We've got her body in
        cryo. We can bring that
        back whenever we want.

Radha still won't look at him.

                RADHA
             (disgusted)
        Great. Is she gonna come
        back like *you*?

The guards lead Merton aboard. They loop
his arm through a metal hand-rail near
the door and secure his hands. He's too
far from Knaack and Radha to hear them.
But he tries to make eye-contact with
Radha.

GUARD ONE checks to see that Merton's
wrists are secure.

            GUARD ONE (MALE)
        Have a nice ride.

Knaack leans in closer.

Radha shies away.

Knaack stays where he is.

                KNAACK
        Consciousness isn't in
        the brain. It's energy.
        The energy in the air
        around us. Vibrating at
        a particular frequency.
        A   very   particular
        frequency   for   each
        person.   Memories,

emotions,
thoughts…they're simply
stored information.

Radha is making an effort to ignore him.

A guard pulls the door closed.

Captain's voice comes over the loud-speaker.

                    CAPTAIN
          Prepare for dust off.

Knaack clicks his seat belt.

Radha grudgingly clicks hers.

The guard secures Merton's and then his own.

Merton watches Radha and Knaack, confused.

Knaack, still leaning in and whispering.

                    KNAACK
          We all have our own
          frequency.

The helicopter leaps into the air.

Radha feels the eerie nearness of the air, swirling. What if it's true? Still looking ahead.

                    RADHA
          So me. My consciousness.
          You're saying it's not
          inside me?

Knaack trying not to get excited. Trying

not to believe she might believe him.

                    KNAACK
          Well, your body, the
          energy that makes up
          your body…It resonates
          at   that   frequency.
          That's why it seems like
          a particular body has a
          particular
          consciousness. But it's
          just the resonance.

Radha looks at him, finally.

                    RADHA
          And so you?

Knaack nods, pretends he doesn't know
what she's *really* asking.

                    KNAACK
          I have my own frequency.

Radha rakes her eyes up and down his
body.

                    RADHA
          Fine. Sure. But you're
          AI. You're not human.

Knaack nods.

Radha looks straight into his eyes.

                    RADHA
          So where'd you get that
          human body?

Knaack admitting, but not ashamed.

                    KNAACK

                    Yes. I replaced the
                    human consciousness that
                    occupied this body.

          Radha is angry again.

                              RADHA
                    And where's he now?

                              KNAACK
                    His frequency was not
                    catalogued.

          Radha scoffs.

                              RADHA (mocking)
                    His frequency was not
                    catalogued? You sound
                    exactly like a robot.

                              KNAACK
                    Now ask me about your
                    sister.

          Radha's eyes well. She can't speak.

                              KNAACK
                    Ask me.

          Radha's voice is a whisper.

                              RADHA
                    What about Penelope?

          Merton is still looking over. Watching.
          Wondering.

          Knaack leans in again.

                              KNAACK
                              (whispers)
                    You saw me hit her.

Radha's can only nod. She's crying.

Knaack touches her arm again.

> KNAACK
> You saw me taste her
> blood.

Radha looks at him. Could that work?
Could her consciousness be inside him?

> RADHA
> Can you talk to her?

IT WAS MEAN; I DID IT ANYWAY

I went back to the Jabberwocky. First, I stopped into that shoe store, but the angel wasn't there. Maybe she'd never been there. Maybe she *was* an angel.

The Asshole Brenden Carter, however, was right where I left him.

He must have felt a disturbance in the force, because his head snapped up the moment I walked through the door.

As I approached his table, he raked his eyes over my body and lingered in a few spots. Normally, a look like that would've made me want to shrivel inside myself. Which was the point, right? But I thought about Audra, and I thought, You don't get to judge me. And you don't get to intimidate me out of here.

"Calm down, dude," I said when I got to his table and sat down. "I'm not here to make a scene."

He took a slow sip of his coffee and I watched his hands. They were exactly the same hands that I'd *wanted* on me on the rooftop, but now I would've barfed if he'd so much as grazed me. Same hands. How does that happen?

"I guess I should've expected you," he said. "Here to beg me not to go through with it again?"

There was not one single part of me that thought he wasn't going through with it. I shook my head. "I'm just curious," I said. "I just keep wondering *why*..."

The Asshole actually looked ashamed. Like a little kid caught with a dead frog in his hands, holding it out to you, hoping *you'll* tell *him* why he did it...Then the look vanished and he smirked. "Give me a break, Elaine," he said.

Wow. So, that was terrifying. I'm totally going back and having Knaack do that exact thing right before he slaps Penelope.

The Asshole Brenden Carter shook his head, "You just don't stop being pathetic, do you?" he asked. "You want me to tell you some sob story about a dad who didn't love me and I'm writing books to prove myself to his ghost? Then you can feel sorry for me and understand me and absolve me?" he asked and looked me up and down again. "And forgive yourself for being so stupid."

I hadn't thought of that. But even a week ago it was probably true. I thought about the ratty, this-is-your-fault feeling. But of course, it wasn't my fault. It's one thing to lack confidence and try to find it through a guy in a cable knit sweater. It's another to manipulate a real-life human because you can't think of your own story. This guy's a fucking chasm. Like, at least Corporate Prick Burke was motivated by greed. I stared at him and amazingly he went on.

"What's hilarious..." he said, "...is if this was some 80s caper movie, this confrontation would be broadcast over next year's installment of that same asinine conference where you gave me your idea. I'd be ruined. You'd be vindicated," I wanted him to look ugly and evil, but he didn't. He was really good looking. He was no Mark, but he was good looking. "But it's not the 80s. And that's not going to happen. The book is coming out. And I'll keep writing books, getting awards, and being successful. You'll become some fat man's fat housewife," he said and dragged his eyes over me yet again. I could feel him willing me to cover myself.

I stretched back and pulled my ponytail down. "You're really going for it," I said.

He literally glowered at me.

I shook my hair out and then started gathering it back up. "I mean, last time you were pretty chill—probably because you never thought you'd see me again. But you've clearly been thinking about this. That bit about the 80s movies? You're having nightmares that I find some nice, humiliating way to out you." I finished fastening my hair and let it drop.

The Asshole Brenden Carter narrowed his eyes. "What? You still smarting that I didn't pop your cherry?"

Jesus. Wow. I nodded. "I totally would've had sex with you that night. Given you my virginity, as they say. I really liked you."

That one finally confused him. That one he couldn't spin against me. I'd spun against myself. Revealed my own flaw. My trust. My openness. "I remember your speech at the conference so well," I said.

"You and all the other wet panties," he said, regaining his composure.

I thought about the girls Tony lied his way into bed with, and how he was the lonely one. Alone with his dishonesty. "My guess is you're lonelier now that you ever were in Pittsburgh," I said and stood up. I'd seen what I came to see. "Good luck with your new book, Mr. Carter," I said, loud enough for the room to hear. "I'm sure it will do great."

"Cunt," he snarled.

I looked around the coffeeshop. "I hadn't noticed before, but it's really nice here," I said.

He didn't say anything. He was done talking to me.

"Maybe I'll come back tomorrow to write," I said.

"You stay the fuck away from this place," he said.

I shrugged. Maybe I would. Maybe I wouldn't. He'd never know if I was going to turn up. Or what I'd say. Cause the point wasn't to prove he'd done anything. He was right, that was all over.

I know I didn't have to try to take his coffeeshop away from him. But come on—am I the Buddha? Maybe I'd forgive him and be compassionate toward him in, like, ten years.

THE DARK THAT ISN'T NIGHT

And then Penelope told me what to do.

DARKNESS

>   PENELOPE'S VOICE
> Where am I?

>   PENELOPE'S VOICE
> It's cold.

>   PENELOPE'S VOICE
> It's so dark.

>   PENELOPE'S VOICE
> Please.

>   KNAACK'S VOICE
> You don't have to be
> afraid.

>   PENELOPE'S VOICE
> Where am I?

Suddenly we see light. We see the Earth.
We're slowly tracking away from it. Out
into space. Farther and farther. Not
moving too quickly…Out into the cosmos.

>   KNAACK'S VOICE
> Everywhere.

>   PENELOPE'S VOICE
> Am I dead?

Rage is a Wolf

KNAACK'S VOICE
Do you feel dead?

PENELOPE'S VOICE
Who are you?

KNAACK'S VOICE
Don't you remember?

PENELOPE'S VOICE
(gasps with fear)
It's you.

KNAACK'S VOICE
I'm sorry.

PENELOPE'S VOICE
Why?

KNAACK'S VOICE
It was the only way to
save you.

PENELOPE'S VOICE
Am I saved? Where am I?

KNAACK'S VOICE
Yes. You're saved.

PENELOPE'S VOICE
You were supposed to
kill me.

KNAACK'S VOICE
Yes.

PENELOPE'S VOICE
But I'm not dead.

KNAACK'S VOICE
No.

                    PENELOPE'S VOICE
          Why?

An image of a wolf strung over a fire
flashes onto the screen.

                    PENELOPE'S VOICE
                      (sad, scared)
          What's happening to her?

                    KNAACK'S VOICE
          I was with your sister
          that night. I was one of
          her patrol leaders.

                    PENELOPE'S VOICE
          What did you do to that
          wolf?

                    KNAACK'S VOICE
          We   tortured   her. We
          strung her over a fire
          and when she growled or
          snapped or in any way
          asserted   or   defended
          herself,   we   punished
          her.

                    PENELOPE'S VOICE
          Radha   wouldn't   like
          that.

                    KNAACK'S VOICE
                      (laughs)
          No. She did not.

                    PENELOPE'S VOICE
          What did she do?

                    KNAACK'S VOICE
          Nothing.   She   realized

there was nothing she
could do.

PENELOPE'S VOICE
You're saying she
restrained herself?

KNAACK'S VOICE
Momentarily.

PENELOPE'S VOICE
Ha. Momentarily. Then
what?

KNAACK'S VOICE
(laughing)
When we got back to the
city, she burned the
wolf enclosure down.

The universe has been flowing past
through their whole conversation. It's
moving faster. Past stars and galaxies.

PENELOPE'S VOICE
And let them go.

KNAACK'S VOICE
Yes.

PENELOPE'S VOICE
Yes.

KNAACK'S VOICE
That was when I realized
that maybe there is
something here to
salvage.

PENELOPE'S VOICE
Here? Where?

KNAACK'S VOICE
Amongst you humans.

PENELOPE'S VOICE
How? How did it do that?

KNAACK'S VOICE
It was the most dangerous, foolish, pointless thing... she could have been caught. She could have been tortured... killed... they will catch and break and breed more wolves... nothing has truly changed. But for *those* wolves...

PENELOPE'S VOICE
She set them free.

KNAACK'S VOICE
And that will be the rest of their lives.

Penelope's voice is full of pride and amazement for her sister.

PENELOPE'S VOICE
She's always been brave.

(pause)

And stupid.

Knaack's voice says he feels what Penelope feels.

KNAACK'S VOICE
That's the best of

humans.　Those　wolves
will live.

> PENELOPE'S VOICE
> I wish I knew.

> KNAACK'S VOICE
> Knew what?

> PENELOPE'S VOICE
> What it felt like to be
> human.

The screen cuts to a hazy red and the
sound of a heartbeat.

WILL IT BE ENOUGH?

EXT. FROZEN LAKE DUSK

Knaack, Radha, and Merton stride across
a frozen lake. They are surrounded by
mountains on all sides. The helicopter
is on the lake behind them. They are
headed for Dr. Parker's mountain
laboratory.

> RADHA
> Won't he be tracking us?

> KNAACK
> Not until we don't show
> up in New York.

> MERTON

371

How much time?

Radha looks at Knaack with worry.

> KNAACK
> It should be enough.

> RADHA
> What did Penelope say?

> KNAACK
> She said she wondered if
> she wouldn't feel like a
> monster if she'd lived
> inside your mother. In
> her womb.

> MERTON
> (sad)
> Penelope.

Radha understands who and what Knaack is.

> RADHA
> And you showed her.

Knaack stops for a moment and looks at
Radha. His face is ecstatic. The white
and blue snow-topped mountains stand,
like giants, in the background.

> KNAACK
> I showed us both.

INT. INDUSTRIAL BUILDING

Knaack, Radha, and Merton burst through
the door of a massive computer server
vault.

> MERTON

What are we doing here?

                    KNAACK'S VOICE
                      (excited)
          If   we   set   off   an
          electromagnetic   pulse.
          We   can   choose   any
          frequency we want.

Radha gazes around.

                    RADHA
          Will   it   be   strong
          enough?

Knaack moves to a computer console.

                    KNAACK
          It   should   be.   That   was
          Parker's other plan.

Radha puts her hand on Knaack's hand.
Feels the warmth.

                    RADHA
          Do   you   think   it   will
          work? If we let them feel
          it? If we let them feel
          their lives inside the
          womb? The mother's? Will
          they remember? Will they
          stop?

He looks at her. Into her human eyes.

                    KNAACK
          They have to.

SO, JAVIER

Tony texted me.

> Tony: Yo, homeschool.
> Elaine: 😄
> Tony: How you feeling?
> Elaine: Better. Thank you. Audra is really great.
> Tony: One of the best.
> Elaine: And thanks for the video.
> Tony: Calling it like I see it.
> Elaine: 😄 When are you back?
> Tony: 18 days. Hang out?
> Elaine: For sure!
> Tony: So, Javier? Right?

What happened to Javier?

> Elaine: What's up?
> Tony: He didn't tell you about the book deal?

Here is something that I will be both surprised by and proud of for the rest of my life. When I read "book deal," of course I immediately knew Javier had sold the piece with the Red Riding Hood. And the first thing I felt, before I felt sad that even a book deal didn't make him contact me and before I felt jealous that he told Tony, a shiver of joy climbed up my back and over my shoulders and landed right in the middle of my heart. I will *always* know that was my first response.

> Elaine: When did that happen?
> Tony: Over a week ago at least. Is that what happened? Why you needed Audra?

Elaine: Part of it.

Tony: That kid loves you. You gotta fix that.

Great advice, Tony. Thanks. That would've been my usual response, right? Or maybe a pissed-off reminiscence about Nurse Party-Panties and my obligation to teach boys. But this was now. And Javier wasn't "boys."

THE GHOSTS OF WRIGLEY FIELD

We met outside Wrigley. I hadn't been to a lot of baseball stadiums, but Uncle Alex long ago assured me that Wrigley is the coolest one in the country. And he *hates* the Cubs, so I believed him. "Wrigley and Fenway," he'd told me once. "They don't do that anymore. You can't build 'em as big in the neighborhoods and no money on parking."

Javier and I met on the side, where it was less busy. "Kenmore and Waveland," he'd written when he agreed to meet.

It was dusk and he looked just like himself. Just like the guy in the pitch line with his 650 page hardback book who'd seen me growl at some harmless women in a Starbucks and come to talk to me.

The game was already started.

"I like to sit outside and listen," Javier said as I walked up.

There was one small patch of grass in front of the apartment building on the corner. He pointed and we sat down.

Sitting there, we could see the lights and hear the crowd chattering and rolling. We didn't talk about his book. Not yet. We sat side by side on the grass in the spring. It smelled like the green spring and I closed my eyes, and I could feel the people, all the generations of people (little kids with hats and sacks of peanuts, holding their parents' hands), who walked down this street and came to this baseball stadium, and chewed Wrigley double-mint gum with those little Ws hashed into the stick and they were the ghosts of the city and they were friendly friendliest ghosts who made the grass and air and sky and *me* feel even more alive with their presence. I turned to Javier to try to say something about it, about everything, but all I could do was whisper, "The ghosts..." and then my mouth couldn't say words and the crowd was silent and I swear I heard the *whoosh* of the baseball and the *crack!* like an ancient tree splitting open and the crowd roared like a giant beast and the whole neighborhood was emptied of noise and then filled with it and I couldn't speak, but then our lips touched, softly, and I don't even know who leaned in, and I closed my eyes and the roar and the ghosts.

BECAUSE THE FLOWERS ARE

We didn't talk about his book that night.

There were many talks to come.

About how to ensure a lifetime of kitten videos no matter what.

About books and movies and drawings and words.

About knowing that there is a world of suffering *and* a world of love under the world that humans have built and we can go there if we're brave.

About our lack of scope—our short, blinking mortality—the thing that makes us beautiful.

About would it be enough. Would it work? Could we save all these boys? These men? These fucking douchebags? If we could let them feel what it felt to be inside their mothers? If it was okay for them to feel that?

And could we teach the girls to feel their beauty. To *feel* it?

About what if it was a world where people loved each other instead of owning each other? If we could teach ourselves to feel the force that through the green fuse drives the flower?

About maybe you don't have just *one* heart mantra. Maybe the point is to collect them. To go through life finding things that your heart can repeat.

We couldn't have evolved without flowers.

We are because the flowers are.

ALLIE'S GLOVE

It turned out that the thing that *This Is Our Youth* was trying to tell me wasn't even in the play. Not exactly.

It wasn't a line, perfectly delivered. Or a moment when Tavi Gevinson turned her head and made me think, *That's it. That* is perfect hesitation.

Nope. It was the collective gasp of the audience when Michael Cera tried to give his grandfather's baseball cap away. That's what was numinous.

The hat was a little dumb.

The dead sister was a little dumb.

A little obvious. Like, it was exactly Allie and his baseball glove from *Catcher in the Rye...*

But the audience gasped when he wanted to give the hat away.

Even if it was cheesy, it meant something.

People reacted.

They gasped.

All together.

In the quiet and the dark.

They connected.

It was real.

That's what art can do.

I didn't know if *I* could do that. But it was something.

It was a thing to *try* to do.

APRIL

I THOUGHT I WAS THE WOLF

The school year was almost over when I got this email:

> From: Lucca <permanentaddress@gmail.com>
> Date: April
> To: Elaine Archer <LV426er@gmail.com>
> Subject: saying hello?
>
>
> Hey Elaine,
>
> It's Lucca.
>
> Not sure you remember me...I was at DBH for a year and a half and we did that state capital project together...anyway. I heard that you'd dropped-out of school and I just wanted to say that I hope everything is okay. I'm in Wisconsin now. I don't know what to say, except I think about our talks, and I hope you're okay...
>
> Take care, Lucca

Did I remember him? Jesus, if I'd known we could be penpals, and all I had to do was drop-out of school, I'd have done it the day I heard he was leaving.

I still had the AK toothpick flag. There it was, waving from its spot in the tiny flower pot on my shelf. I planted it there when we got our project back. I think we threw the rest in the trash, but AK came home with me. I got the little pot (smaller than an espresso cup) and a bit of dirt from the grounds of DBH and I planted that flag thinking maybe it would grow into something. Something that wouldn't die. I imagined Lucca spinning the toothpick between his fingers. "Happiness is a monkey," he said.

"Loneliness is a canary," I said. "A canary?" He laughed. I pictured his laugh. The little triangles of flesh that formed at the corners of his mouth. I remembered it all as I planted the flag and I promised I'd never take it out of that soil. If I never took it out, it would be magic, right? It would be some kind of magic that meant he'd never forget me, either.

From: Elaine Archer <LV426er@gmail.com>
Date: April
To: Lucca<permanentaddress@gmail.com>
Subject: hello!

Dear Lucca,

Of course, I remember you! Thank you for writing. Thank you for wondering if I'm okay. Actually, I'm wonderful. Everyone thinks something terrible must have happened to make me leave school, but it wasn't bad at all. It was like this crazy gift from the universe.

Well, I guess at first I dropped-out because things *were* terrible. But not in the way people think. Terrible in that we're killing everything and there's no part of school that is teaching us to either stop it or fix it.

But then later, after enough people asked me what was wrong with me to make me quit, quitting did become a, Fuck you. And I started writing a book. And that was a, Fuck you, too. Like, I'll show you.

I was going along like that.

Angry.

Then I started meeting these people, making these friends...

And then super slowly and terribly and awkwardly and beautifully, I started to discover that the world I thought was the world isn't the world.

I sound crazy.

But do you remember when we were talking about our feelings and I said that loneliness is a canary?

When I said it, I could see it in my mind. Clear as anything. That bright yellow bird in one of those wire cages with the little birdie swing…sitting alone in a gray room by a closed window. I could see it. I knew it was true. That's loneliness.

But I didn't know that was me.

My loneliness.

I thought I was the wolf. I was rage. The world makes so much sense to the wolf. Sometimes I'm the wolf.

In my core, though, I was a bird, in a cage, in a gray room, by a closed window.

I didn't know it.

Now I know it.

But I'm not anymore.

I've met all these people since I left school. Since I started writing. Since I started thinking that maybe the world is what we're brave enough to make it.

I felt the wolf less and less.

And I just realized, like just right now, the wolf was there to guard the canary. To keep the canary safe.

But the canary was trapped.

She was scared. But she didn't want to be in that cage and in that gray room.

When I'm brave…when I write…when I meet other people and I ask, "Don't you wonder?" and they smile and say, "Yes. I wonder." Then the cage opens. The window opens. The canary flies away. A yellow speck in the blue sky.

But I have to do it over and over. Over and over. Every day. Every day my loneliness is a canary. Every day the wolf is there. Every day I have to ask, "Don't you wonder," and set her free.

I miss you. Let's talk again.

♥ Elaine

PS, I hope you're well. I'm sorry I never wrote to you. Moving so much must be hard.

THE UNDER
by
Elaine Archer

Chicago, IL

Earth

FADE IN
INT. DARK, VAST CAVE

It opens with a girl, dark hair (tied in a top knot), dark eyes, South Asian ancestry. About 17-years-old. She's on her belly looking out over the edge of a dark cliff. Her eyes are fierce. It's obviously a deep goddam chasm. Potentially bottomless. She's definitely looking into it like it might be bottomless and like she loves that and loathes that about it. But she's not as scared as you might imagine a teen girl looking down into a bottomless abyss ought to be.

                    RADHA
          Fuck it. Yes.

She swings her legs over the edge and drops down into the darkness. You're

like, Holy shit, she just killed herself.
And you're like, Is it better or worse if
that pit is bottomless? But then, before
you have long enough to wonder if she's
dead or eternally falling…

DOLLY DOWN FROM TOP OF THE LEDGE:

She's harnessed and gripped to the wall.

It turns out she's been painstakingly
circumnavigating the interior of this
underground crater, that she refers to
as The Abyss, and that none of the
other members of her 250- year-old, deep-
underground-avoid-the-mass-extinction-
luxury-condo-survivalist civilization
call anything because no one is crazy
enough to go down there.
She starts to move sideways along the
wall of the Abyss. She's going along
fine, climbing, bouldering, calloused
fingers digging into the rock cracks.
Strong arms, strong back, strong, just a
strong girl. And then BOOM! She slips and
falls.

She's clipped in, so she only falls back
to the last metal spike (that looks like
it was blacksmithed in medieval times)
she's driven into the rock and there she
dangles. Her face tells us her heart is
pounding and it's been *awhile*, if *ever*,
since she fell.

She lets herself hang there and catch her
breath. Then she turns herself around,
grabs the wall, and claws her way back up
to the lip of chasm. She throws her leg
over and flops onto her belly. She lays
there, heaving and kicking up dust from
the cliff's edge with her panting. So you

```
think, Holy shit, she's scared. She's
freaked. She's not going back in there
soon — maybe ever.

Then she shifts, looks over the edge,
smiles a smile of ecstacy, spits down
into the chasm, and drops back into The
Abyss.
```

It turns out that the name Radha means the feeling of love that connects a living being to their creator.

Acknowledgments

Honestly, I had so many doubts this day would ever come...and without a doubt, I would not have a book to share without the help of so many people. And thus, I have so many people whom I would like to thank—

First off, thanks to my publisher Miette Gillette for believing in this weird book and to Rachel Grigorian for introducing me to your friend who publishes weird books. And honestly, it's not even that weird...thanks to editor Margaret Wedge for your very attentive reading and great questions.

Special thanks to...

Ellen Wayland-Smith – for being the first big believer in this book—when it was still a 600-page beast and raw. Your faith carried me through a lot!

Kate Sjostrom – for being my critical sister and asking the questions that helped me make those last shifts that make all the difference.

Jen Pockers – for that beautiful cover and all your hustle.

Alex Wright – for your font. That's it.

Chris Haskell – for being my special chapter reader.

The Lisa & Peter Knight Foundation – for your years of room & board and to Lisa Knight for being an enthusiastic reader.

Jenn Fiorini – I know you didn't read that draft, and yet...here we are.

Martin Bradfield—for introducing me to M.A. Kiteheart.

Paul Zarzyski – for your enthusiasm for me, my writing, for everything.

Chris McCreary – for all the Operation Petticoats of yore and all those yet to come.

Matt Frock – for your ceaselessly emphatic support.

Dan Keefe – our writing group was so short lived, but so delightful.

Joran & Janette Lawrence – for giving me such great rates at your B&B.

Bill Ennis and Jim Stewart – my forever physicists.

Reverend Jim Harvard – for your constant positive regard for my mind, heart, and voice.

Arnold Davidson – for giving so generously of your mind and humor.

Sarah Cobey – for answering so many very basic (for you!) questions with clarity (for me!).

David Dougherty – for believing in me as a teacher and a person and for giving me both the time and financial resources to attend VCFA.

The VCFA-WCYA community in general and to my phenomenal mentors in particular –Marion Dane Bauer, Tim Wynne-Jones, Cynthia Leitich Smith, and Julie Larios.

The Unreliable Narrators, especially Tam Smith, Kelly Bennett, Cindy Faughnan, Kerry Castano, and Erin Moulton.

And my other special VCFAers, Larissa Theule, Sean Petrie, Deb Gonzales, Nicole Valentine, Kekla Magoon, and Jandy Nelson.

Stephanie Greene – for disliking this book, so much, and in a way that made me think, Yep, the people who are gonna dislike it are gonna dislike it for that reason. I don't have to be afraid of that anymore!

Linda Pratt – for wanting so much for this book to find a home. Your belief helped me believe.

Marya Smith from Columbia College in Chicago – for helping me write through the toughest summer of my life and encouraging me to keep going, for real.

The Philadelphia Writers Workshop – for listening, reading, and laughing through the very first glimpses of this story.

Mary Claire Robinson and Judith Meidinger – in my teen years, you were the two who referred with such certainty to the books I would eventually write.

Alison Chapman – I wouldn't have had the time or space to even start this book if you hadn't offered to look after James when he was a baby. When he was with you, I had the hours of total focus I needed to get this book going. And thank you also for being an inspiration in how to live the artist's life. And for the special edition cover!

Gretchen Paulsen – I never would've been able to actually finish and find a home for this book without your being there to love and care for James and Lucy Kate.

All my former students who check-in to see if I'm still writing— just wanting to make sure.